Crown Jewel

Also by Fern Michaels

TRADING PLACES
LATE BLOOMER
NO PLACE LIKE HOME
THE DELTA LADIES
WILD HONEY

FERN MICHAELS

Crown Jewel

DOUBLEDAY LARGE PRINT HOME LIBRARY EDITION

ATRIA BOOKS

NEW YORK   LONDON   TORONTO   SYDNEY

This Large Print Edition, prepared especially for Doubleday Large Print Home Library, contains the complete, unabridged text of the original Publisher's Edition.

ATRIA BOOKS
1230 Avenue of the Americas
New York, NY 10020

ISBN: 0-7394-4039-X

First Atria Books hardcover edition December 2003

ATRIA BOOKS is a trademark of Simon & Schuster, Inc.

Manufactured in the United States of America

This Large Print Book carries the Seal of Approval of N.A.V.H.

Crown Jewel

Prologue

Hollywood, California
1984

    He was a tall man, immaculately dressed. At any time of the day or evening, he could have passed for a Wall Street banker or a Madison Avenue type. His hair had just the right amount of gray at the temples, his skin was burnished just enough to make him look distinguished. His Savile Row suit added the last touch. At the moment, he looked angry.

    "It's not negotiable, Ricky. Either you agree, or I'm out of here, and you're on your own."

    Hollywood's Platinum Boy stared across the room at his brother. He wasn't so stoned that he didn't feel the chill racing up and down his arms. He did his best to focus, to look contrite, and knew he was failing miserably. This was where the rubber was going to meet the road. Not trusting himself to speak, he reached out for the arm of the leather sofa to sit down. Instead, he fell forward. *Shit!*

Philip Lam, older by two years, felt sadness and disgust when he looked across at his handsome movie star brother. On other occasions, he would have rushed to his brother's aid, but not today. Today, yesterday, and the day before yesterday were what had brought him to this point in time.

The Platinum Boy struggled to speak. "You promised Mom . . ."

"Don't go there, Ricky. You screwed that up, too. You couldn't be bothered with going to see her, so don't bring up 'promises' to me. You've used up all your markers. Either you check into the clinic, or I'll dissolve the partnership. I'm not just talking to hear my own voice this time. You will pack your stuff, and you will get to the clinic on your own. All the arrangements have been made. They're expecting you by ten this evening. One second past ten, and you're down the tubes. You have finally brought me to the end of my rope. I won't be here to pick up the pieces. Make sure you understand that, little brother."

"Roxy's making you do this, isn't she?" Ricky said, finally coming up with something he could use to stall his brother.

"You would be wise not to go there either, Ricky. Roxy has nothing to do with this."

"She has everything to do with it. She settled for you because I didn't want her and her baggage. You got my seconds. She's been trying to get back at me ever since. Eat shit, Philly!" When the expression in his brother's eyes turned even colder, he quickly added, "Wait a minute, wait a minute. I didn't mean that. I just got up, I'm not thinking straight. I swear, Philly, I didn't mean that."

Philip Lam stared at his brother. After another year of drugs and booze, he'd either be dead or living in a ditch somewhere. Makeup could do just so much. Eventually, his brain would go, and he wouldn't be able to memorize a script. Looking pretty, even with nips and tucks, wouldn't cut it.

Ricky Lam, Hollywood's Platinum Boy,

was tall and rugged, with unruly, sandy-colored hair that some hairstylist had high-lighted for the cameras. His eyes were an incredible brown—bedroom eyes, the gossip columnists called them. His teeth were perfect, pearly white, thanks to one of Hollywood's finest dentists. Handsome. Gorgeous. A ladies' man. A man's man.

The truth was, Ricky Lam was all those things. He was also a drug addict and a boozer.

"Yes, you did mean it. Don't add lying on top of everything else. What you said about Roxy is a lie. You stalked her, Ricky. You were so strung out, you probably don't even remember it. Go to the library and look it up. It made the headlines. The headline was, 'Platinum Boy Stalks Makeup Artist!' I refuse to have a brother I'm ashamed of. Make no mistake, I am ashamed of you. Remember what I told you about being at the end of my rope."

"I made you rich, Philly. Really, really rich," Ricky whined.

Philip sighed. He'd been down this road so many times he'd lost count. "Get yourself a new business manager and agent, Ricky. Every cent I made off you I damn well earned. If I hadn't invested your money, you would have stuck it all up your nose. Keep doing what you're doing, and it will be gone in two years. Do you even remember how many paternity suits I settled for you? Do you have any idea of how many times I paid out astronomical sums of money to keep your scandals out of the papers? Well, do you?"

"No," Ricky mumbled. Suddenly he felt like shit, like he was something Philly had stepped in. He had to pay attention to what his brother was saying. He wished he could remember what he'd done the night before. It must be Sunday. Yeah, it was Sunday, or he'd be at the studio.

"When I give you your final accounting, you'll know. Now, what's it going to be?"

"How long?" Ricky mumbled again.

"As long as it takes to straighten yourself out. Considering the condition you're in, I wouldn't opt for anything under ninety days. Maybe longer. If they call me tonight and tell me you bailed, I will dissolve our business arrangement the first thing in the morning. Personally, I don't give a damn if you go or not. I don't think you have the guts. You walk the walk, talk the talk, but then you fizzle like a bad Roman candle.

"I left all the information on your desk in the study. There's a one-way plane ticket in a folder. I squared everything with the studio for six months. It was either that, or they were going to cancel your contract. The rest is up to you."

Ricky shook his head to clear it. "Am I supposed to call you? Are you going to be checking on me? What's the drill here? I want to know what I'm getting into."

"I told you. You're on your own. But if you need clarification, no, I am not going to call you, and no, I will not accept calls from you. The main reason is that I won't be here. I'm going to the islands to check on the resorts."

"It's always about you, Philly," Ricky whined again. "It's always *what* you want, *when* you want it, and *if* you want it. You're like some screwed-up ringmaster. Mom must be spinning in her grave at the way you're treating me."

Philip Lam balled his hands into tight fists. He walked over to the chair where his brother was sitting. He unclenched his hands to grasp both arms of the chair and leaned over until he was a hair away from his brother's face. "Look in my eyes and watch my lips, Ricky. I don't give a rat's ass if you are Hollywood's Platinum Boy. I no longer care if you drink your nights away and snort your days into oblivion. I no longer care, do you understand? I'm sick and tired of being called in the middle of the night by the police and by the studio during the day. If and when you come back clean and sober, we will have another talk. That's when I'll decide if I still want to be in business with you. Or if I even want to be your brother. I don't have one iota of confidence that you can cut it, so I'm going to put all the wheels into motion starting tomorrow. If you screw up this time, all you have to do is sign on the dotted line, and our business relationship is over. I will disown you as my brother. You can pump gas for all I care."

"Just like that," Ricky said, rubbing his dripping nose.

"Yeah. Just like that," Philly said quietly.

Philip looked around at the pigsty of a house his brother lived in. "You really should clean this place up. It smells just the way you smell. Like a sewer. Good-bye, Ricky."

Outside, in the early-morning air, Roxy Lam rushed up to her husband. "What did he say? Is he all right? Are you all right, Philip?" she asked, with just the right amount of concern in her voice.

"Yes, I'm fine. I don't know if he's going to go or not. And before you can ask, yes, he tried to pull the same old crap. We'll just have to wait and see how it plays out."

"The best thing I ever did was go to you when your brother started stalking me. It's up to Ricky now. You've gone above and beyond the call of duty. We both need to walk away from this. I have an idea. Let's you and I have breakfast at that greasy spoon we used to go to when we first met. My treat. Reba's in school, and my whole day is wide open." Her voice was pleading, her eyes full of hope.

"That's probably the best offer I'm going to get today. Let's go." His voice was so cold, so controlled, Roxy shivered in the warm sunshine. She just knew it wasn't going to be a pleasant breakfast. She wished that she could just go home.

Ricky Lam watched his brother and his

brother's wife from the window. He started to count. Philly always came back by the time he counted to sixty. When he reached 360 he knew his brother wasn't coming back. For the first time in his life, he felt all-consuming fear.

"I hate your guts, you prick! And I hate your wife, too!" he screamed to the silence surrounding him. Startled at the venom in his voice, he slumped against the wall.

1

Hollywood, California
Fifteen Years Later

Ricky Lam, idol to millions of fans, jammed his hands into his pockets as he strolled the grounds of his palatial Hollywood estate. He looked around, appreciating the beauty of the well-pruned shrubs, the brilliant flowers, and the brick paths that led to a gazebo at the far end of the grounds. All thanks to his acting skills and his brother's wise investment strategies. He picked a delicate, crimson flower, his fingers caressing its silky petals. He shouldn't have picked it. It would die soon. He wished he had left it on the bush. He hurried into the house and stuck it into a glass of water.

The house was state-of-the-art, befitting his star power in the movie industry. At forty-three, he was in top form. With two mini face-lifts under his belt, he could still hold his own with the young studs arriving in Hollywood in droves. He had a tinge of gray at his temples these days, but the studio expertly covered it up. He still had the same dark brown bedroom eyes, the same lean muscular body that had helped make him famous. He was still a hunk.

Variety said he was still the Platinum Boy. They said he had it all. If they only knew. He was probably the loneliest man in all of California. He had one close friend, his stuntman, Ted Lymen. And, of course, Philly. He could never discount Philly. He was where he was today because of his brother. But Philly was not his friend. Philly wasn't even his mentor. Philly was his warden.

His relationship with Philly had never been the same after he'd returned from the exclusive addiction clinic fifteen years earlier. Instead of treating him as a brother, Philly had reduced their relationship to that of business manager and client, sometimes even warden and prisoner. Oh, they still met for dinner once or twice a year, usually at some out-of-the-way restaurant. Conversation was always strained as Philly smoked and drank, and Ricky did neither. They still went to an occasional ball game together, and Philly even came on the set and watched him work when he was in town. But it wasn't the same. It would never be the same again, and they both knew it. It was an accept-it-or-reject-it relationship. Ricky chose to accept it.

No matter what he did, no matter what he said, he hadn't been able to recapture the old relationship. Secretly, he thought Philly was waiting for him to screw up. And, like the stupid ass he was, Ricky wouldn't give him the satisfaction. He never wanted to see that look of disgust in his brother's face again. Never, ever.

In the beginning, when he had first returned from the clinic, Ricky had blamed Roxy because he needed someone to blame. Fifteen years later, he laid the blame right where it belonged, on his own shoulders.

In the dark, late at night, when no one was around, he prayed that Philly would forgive him and throw his arms around his shoulders, and say, "Let's let bygones be bygones." It hadn't happened, and it wasn't going to happen. He knew that now. Fifteen years of being a straight arrow wasn't enough to satisfy Philly.

Ricky flopped down on a custom-crafted chair in the living room, his favorite, and picked up a script. It was untitled. *What kind of scriptwriter doesn't give his work a title?* He was supposed to read it, decide if it was worthy of his talent, then let his agent and the front office know if he was willing to negotiate. He tossed the script back onto the table.

Tomorrow was the final wrap for the movie he was working on, *Seven Hours Till Sundown.* An hour at the most, maybe two, depending on how many takes the director wanted. The wrap party was tonight, though, because once they wound up the film tomorrow, the crew was heading off to Washington, D.C., to start a new film titled *Inside the Beltway.* It was all about a politician's rage on the Beltway. He was glad he had passed on that piece of crap.

Ricky looked at the phone on the table next to him, willing it to ring. Philly was in town for the wrap party and to cart his check off to the bank, at which point he would head back to the islands to manage their two resorts.

Resorts for the rich and famous. All you needed to visit one of them was a bucketful of money and a reservation made two years in advance. It had been Philly's idea to build the resorts, pointing out that Ricky wasn't going to be able to work in Hollywood forever. Leading men had a tendency to get old, and after a while face-lifts left you looking haggard. "You need something to fall back on when that happens, Ricky," Philly had said. "You'll never be happy playing character parts. Get out when you're on top and hobnob with the new elite where you call the shots." It had made sense. As long as he didn't allow himself to get pissed off at his brother's financial prowess, Ricky realized that everything his older brother said made sense.

He looked down at the phone. He supposed he could initiate the call, but to what end? Ricky had never stepped over the boundaries Philly had erected when Ricky had returned from the clinic. Why start now?

He, too, was heading for the islands after the last shoot tomorrow. Thirty days of doing nothing but relaxing in his very own star suite. Philly hated it when he showed up at the resort. Ricky wasn't sure why. The attention he got from the staff? Roxy's strange attitude toward him even though he stayed out of her way?

Ricky continued to stare at the phone. Christ, how he hated tiptoeing around his brother.

He bounded off the chair and loped over to the mantel to pick up two small pictures. His sons. Children he provided for but had never seen. No, that wasn't true, he had seen them once.

It was one of two demands he'd made when he'd signed off on the deals Philly had negotiated with the boys' mothers, young girls he'd had one-night stands with during that wild time in his youth when he was Hollywood's number one hell-raiser. "Try explaining that to your studio and all those young adoring fans," Philly had said.

In exchange for signing a confidentiality agreement, each girl received the princely sum of ten grand a month until her son finished college and the assurance that Ricky would never attempt to interfere in her son's life. One breach on her part and the money stopped cold. Philly had used the word *lawsuit* a lot when he'd talked to the frightened girls. Even to this day, both women honored the agreements. Ricky recalled the excitement he'd felt when he'd laid eyes on his sons for the first time. They'd been three then, little blond-haired boys all dressed up and hating every minute of it. They'd looked at him suspiciously and hung on to their mothers' skirts. He'd just stared at them, committing their faces to memory. It was all he could do.

The boys, born three months apart, were twenty-three now and had never met each other. In fact, neither of them knew he had a half brother. Tyler had lived with his maternal grandparents until he'd left for college because his mother was off singing with a country western band. Max had also lived with his grandparents after his mother married a real estate developer because he didn't get along with her husband. Both boys had finished college and were working. He'd been tempted to call them, invite them to Hollywood, but Philly had made him swear not to seek them out, saying he should let sleeping dogs lie. "And don't try to do it on the sly, either, Ricky, because you'll be recognized, and I'm not pulling any more of your chestnuts out of the fire." That had been the end of that, which didn't say much for him as a father. It was always Philly's way or the highway.

He wondered what his sons would think of him as a person if they knew he was their father. Anonymously, he'd bought the boys their first cars, paid for their college educations and all medical and dental bills. They had both gone to exclusive summer camps and attended the best private schools in their areas. At least that's what Philly told him. Most of what Philly had told him about Tyler was a lie, according to the private detective he'd hired to report on his sons. A report he'd never showed Philly. Tyler had been booted out of the prestigious summer camps, usually three days after arrival. Incorrigible, the counselors said. He'd been suspended eight times while in high school and how he'd graduated was still a mystery. What was even more of a mystery was how he'd gotten into college and managed to graduate in the lowest percentile in the class. But he had graduated. Add up all the arrest charges for speeding while under the influence, loss of driving privileges, and his bad-ass attitude, car wrecks, drug experimentation, and he could have posed for a portrait of his father in his early twenties. A chip off the old block.

Max, on the other hand, could have posed as the poster boy for good behavior.

Ricky stared down at the two golden-haired boys. Three years old. That was how long it had taken to settle everything. His second demand before he'd signed off on the deal was a picture of each boy before he walked away from the six-hundred-dollar-an-hour lawyer's office. The pictures arrived two weeks later in the mail. He set both pictures back on the mantel.

Right now, Ricky thought his life really sucked. The phone still hadn't rung. "Screw it!" he said as he stomped his way back to the master suite of rooms where he hid out most of the time. Big Hollywood star a homebody. It was so damn funny he wanted to cry.

Ricky looked down at the phone he knew resembled something in the White House War Room. It was hooked up to the

alarm system, the security gates, the inter-
com, and the doorbell. It had nineteen buttons he could press if he felt like it. He still
didn't know how to work the damn thing.
The doorbell was the funniest thing of all.
No one could access his property without
going past the part-time security guard,
who had to open the security gates. How
was someone supposed to ring his doorbell if they couldn't get to the door?

The phone rang. Ricky sucked in his
breath before he picked it up. His greeting
sounded cautious. It paid to be cautious
with Philly. "Hello."

It was Ted Lymen, his stuntman. "Yo,
Ricky, just calling to ask if you changed
your mind about going to the wrap party.
You wanna go, I'll stop by and pick you up.
I just got a call saying they canceled the
stunt for tomorrow. We're in a holding pat-
tern until they get a part for the race car.
Probably the day after tomorrow. So, do
you want to go or not?"

Cancellation meant he didn't have to get
up at four-thirty to be at the studio for
makeup at five. Did he want to go? Did he
want to stand around making nice so Philly

wouldn't chew his ass out? "Yeah, sure," was his response. "What time?"

"Eight. Let's do the town afterward. Let's take in the Ozone Club and do a little partying. We both deserve a night out, Ricky. This flick kicked both our asses big-time."

"Sure." What the hell, it would beat sitting around with Philly praying to God he didn't say the wrong thing or make a mistake. "Philly's in town, you know."

"Yeah. Yeah, I heard. So you make nice for ten minutes, and we split. I wish to hell you'd get over that inferiority thing you have with your brother. He's what he is because of you, and don't you ever forget it. Without your money, he'd be working in some cubicle managing other people's money. Go easy on yourself, okay?"

"Okay, I will. I'll see you at eight."

As he hung up Ricky wondered if everyone thought he was a wuss where his brother was concerned.

The minute the gates to Ricky's estate closed behind Ted's Jaguar, the phone inside the mansion rang. The caller left a message. "The part for the car just arrived. The shoot's back on. Be at the studio by five-thirty tomorrow morning." The same message was left at Ted Lymen's home.

The wrap party was like every other one Ricky had attended. Food, liquor, flowers, the women teary-eyed, the guys looking macho as they tried not to worry about whether there was another movie down the road. They all promised to stay in touch knowing full well they wouldn't, unless somehow, some way, they needed a favor and they had your personal unlisted telephone number. In Hollywood, like almost everywhere else, it wasn't what you knew, it was who you knew.

"How are you, Philly?" Ricky said, slapping his brother lightly on the back in a friendly gesture.

"Good. Real good. You're looking fit, little brother. I hear you're coming down to the islands."

"I'm in the thinking stages," Ricky lied. He'd picked up his airline tickets yesterday. "Enjoy yourself," Ricky said, preparing to walk away.

"Didn't you forget something, Ricky?"

Ricky turned and faced his brother. "No, I didn't forget. I just wanted to make you *ask* for it." He reached inside his jacket pocket and withdrew an envelope that he literally slapped into his brother's hand. Seeing the sudden look of embarrassment on Philly's face was worth all the angst he'd gone through that day. This time he did walk away.

"Damn, that felt good," he said to Ted.

"How in hell can handing over fifteen million bucks to your brother make you feel good?"

"I made him ask for it, and I stared him down at the same time. I never did that before. Don't ask me why I had to do it today of all days because I don't know."

"Oh."

"Yeah, oh. You said something about partying . . ."

"I did, didn't I?"

Philip Lam watched his brother walk away. He felt a sudden urge to run after him and give him a big bear hug. He squelched the desire. One soft move on his part, and Ricky would go back to square one. He raised his eyes upward. "I'm doing my best, Mom," he murmured.

Ricky Lam woke, his head pounding. He remembered instantly that he had fallen off the wagon last night to the tune of at least four bottles of champagne. His eyes wild, he looked around to see if anyone was sharing his bed. His sigh of relief when he saw that he was alone was so loud that El-lie, his housekeeper, probably heard it in the kitchen.

He deserved the misery he was feeling. What in the name of God had possessed him to start drinking after fifteen years of sobriety? Philly was the answer. Thank the Lord he didn't have to report to the studio. He'd never make it even if it was just a walkaway part for him. He scrunched his eyes to look at the clock: 6:30. He rolled over with the intention of sleeping all day so the headache banging inside his skull would go away.

The phone rang. No one called him at six-thirty in the morning except Philly, who was also known to call him at five-thirty, four-thirty, midnight, and any damn time he felt like it. The studio also called whenever they felt like it. *Should I answer it or shouldn't I? The hell with it.* The phone kept ringing. The sound was killing his head. He finally picked it up.

"Ricky," Ted said urgently, "the studio

called last night and left a message. The shoot's on. Get your ass in gear, and I'll pick you up in ten minutes."

"Shit!"

"Yeah, shit! Be by the gates, and we'll do a wheelie and get over there in nothing flat."

Ricky made it with a minute to spare. "You're in no condition to drive that race car this morning, Ted. Are you crazy?"

"Probably. However, I don't have a hangover like you do. I ate my breakfast. I also slept four hours. I'm good to go. Did you check your messages?"

"No," Ricky groaned. "Listen, Philly's going to be on the lot. Let's not say anything about last night, okay? I'll go to AA and confess my relapse. I'll go to Makeup before I see him."

Ted nodded. "I was thinking this morning in the shower. I will go with you to the islands if the invitation still stands. I decided to pass on that D.C. flick they're planning."

"Yeah, sure. Glad for the company." At least he would have someone to talk to while he was there.

Thirty minutes later, they showed their security passes to the guards and drove through the gates. Ted headed for the lot where they were scheduled to shoot the car chase scene. They both heard the sound of the siren at the same time. Ted pulled to the side as an ambulance careened past him. Another accident on the lot. Somebody probably broke a finger or sprained an ankle.

When they saw the ambulance skid to a stop on Lot 9, they both hit the ground running.

"What the hell happened?" Ricky shouted to be heard over the chaos.

"Where the hell were you, Lymen?" the director, Donald Sandusky, yelled. "I can tell where you were, Lam, by the looks of you. We waited a goddamn hour for you and had to go without you since time is money around here as you well know. This is the result, and you two can take the blame for it!" He waved his arms to indicate the bedlam.

"What . . . happened?" Ricky croaked.

The director dropped his head to his hands. "Jesus, Ricky, I'm sorry. We had it covered. I swear to God we did. That car was checked five times. Conway, Ted's backup, was driving. I don't know what the hell went wrong."

Ricky looked around at the milling cast, at the crumpled race car. Then he noticed that no one was looking at him. His stomach flip-flopped as the wind kicked up and ruffled his hair. "For God's sake, what are you saying, Sandusky? Why are you apologizing to me? You just got done blaming me and Ted. Make up your mind already." He started walking toward the wrecked car.

Ted Lymen, his face whiter than the tee shirt he was wearing, grabbed at Ricky's arm. "Don't go there, Ricky."

Ricky shook Ted's hand off as he raced to where they were lifting a still form onto a stretcher.

"Oh, Jesus, no!" he screamed. "Not Philly! Oh, God, why?"

Donald Sandusky put his arm around Ricky's shoulder. "He came by the lot. I think he wanted to talk to you. He was standing there watching and the car careened out of control. I think Philip thought it was part of the stunt. He didn't move, Ricky. Hell, may- be he froze. Everyone is crazy right now, so until we can piece to-

gether what happened from rational eye-
witnesses, let's just call it a tragic accident.
I told Philip he might as well leave because
you weren't here, but he said time is
money and insisted on staying. You know
me, I had to relate to that and the budget.
Jesus, Ricky, did your brother ever think
about anything except money? I'm sorry,
this is no time to be talking about money.
My point was, we were prepared to wait
another hour, figuring neither you nor Ted
got the message we left for you last night,
but then with the clock ticking I decided to
go ahead with the stunt. I'm sorry, Ricky, I
wish there was something I could say, but
there isn't."

"I gotta go with . . ."

"No, you don't have to do that. Besides,
the cops want to talk to you. There's nothing you can do now. When did you get the
message?"

"I never did get it. Ted called and picked
me up. What the hell are they blasting the
siren for now? Did anyone call Roxy?"

"No. We thought you would want to take
care of that, being family and all. I wasn't
sure if Roxy came with Philly this trip or
not. As soon as you finish with the cops,

you better tell her before she hears it on the news."

"She came with him. She never lets . . . let Philly out of her sight. At least that's the way it usually is. She's either at the house or the hotel. When they come for just a day or so, they stay at the Beverly Wilshire instead of opening up the house."

Ricky walked away. He needed to sit down. He needed to think. He needed to puke. What he really needed was a *drink*. He knew he'd never, ever touch alcohol again. Tears rolled down his cheeks. He made no move to wipe them away.

It seemed like a long time later when he felt a hand on his shoulder. He turned and looked up to seeTed Lymen towering over him.

"This is all my fault, Ricky. It's not something I can make right either. I don't know what to do, what to say."

"It's no one's fault, Ted, so don't blame yourself. Where is it written that we have to check our messages at night? They could have given us a wake-up call. It's not like they haven't done that before when a shoot was canceled, then rescheduled. It's Philly's fault. Don't you understand, it's his own fault? Why do you think he always managed to show up for the action scenes? He wanted to be part of it. He loved the action stuff.

"Listen, drop me off at Philly's hotel. I don't want Roxy hearing this on the radio or television. She might need me to . . . I don't know . . . just drop me off, okay?"

"Sure. Christ, Ricky, I'm sorry."

"I know, Ted, I know."

He was always awestruck at the hotel where the rich and famous gathered to pay a thousand bucks a night, sometimes more, for a room. Philly loved staying in one of the cottages at the Beverly Wilshire. Usually he booked in advance to make sure he got the same one. Philly had always been a creature of habit.

Ricky walked slowly down the path that led to the little villa and knocked on the door. He wished he'd brought his sunglasses. When there was no answer, he knocked louder, then took two steps back to wait.

She was wearing one of the hotel's fleecy white robes, her hair wrapped in a thick white towel. "Philip went to the studio," Roxy said coolly.

"Do you mind if I come in? I have to . . . we need to talk, Roxy. Don't worry, I'm not going to attack you."

"I mind very much if you come in. Tell me whatever you have to say right here, or else call Philip on his cell phone."

Ricky took a deep breath. *How to say it? Lead up to it? Blurt it out? What?* "Philly's dead. He died in a car crash at the studio. The stunt car careened out of control and hit him. They said he died instantly. I came here to tell you because I didn't want you to hear it on the TV or radio."

He couldn't remember the name of the biblical figure who turned into a pillar of salt, but that's how Roxy Lam looked to him at that moment. She didn't so much as twitch or blink. She didn't cry or sob. What she did, after five, excruciatingly long minutes, was back up, step by step, until she was in the room. The door closed quietly. He heard the *snick* of the lock falling into place.

He turned around, aware of men and young boys moving about. The gardening crew was trimming and weeding the premises. He could smell freshly mowed grass. The smell reminded him of his boyhood, when he and Philly used to take turns pushing the old mower with the dull blades. Whoever mowed didn't have to rake up the grass. Then they invented power mowers with bags attached that caught the grass as it was cut. He wondered how many kids were put out of jobs by the new mowers. And then there were riding mowers. His own gardener had one.

Is it Roxy's place to make the arrangements, or mine as the closest blood relative? he wondered. *Should I knock on the door again and offer my help? Why not? All she can do is say no.* He knocked on the door. When there was no answer, he knocked a second and then a third time. While he waited, he noticed the gardeners looking at him strangely. Maybe it was time to leave.

Leave to go where?

Home to his empty house and the picture of the two little boys on the mantel.

Roxy wanted to bury Philly in a cemetery in Los Angeles and to hold a service at the grave site rather than at a chapel. Ricky fought her tooth and nail on that and finally won when he convinced her Philly needed to rest in peace next to their parents in the cemetery that was close to their old home-town, Placentia. The private service was mercifully short. Ricky listened to the words, wondering how the minister knew so much about his brother. Roxy must have told him. If everything he was saying was true, Philly was already a saint with a giant wingspread. The minister didn't say anything about his hard-ass attitude or his do-it-my-way-or-it's-the-highway philoso-phy. Nor did he mention his two nephews, Tyler and Max. He barely touched on Philly's name before going on to say that he was a wonderful father, which was an outright lie. Reba was Roxy's daughter. Roxy, according to Philly, had married at the age of sixteen. The marriage had lasted six months, and Reba was born three months later. Philly had never adopted Reba, and Ricky wasn't sure why. Maybe because he wasn't able to love another man's child. That had to mean Reba had no claim to his brother's estate. In the end, it wouldn't matter. Philly would have pro-vided for his wife and Reba because that's the kind of guy he was. At least, that's the kind of guy Ricky thought he was.

Ricky looked over at Reba, who was standing next to her mother, having flown in from New York the night before. They were both dressed in black from head to toe. He thought Philly would have hated all that black. He'd always said black reminded him of Halloween, witches, and goblins.

Thank God the service was almost over. The little parade of mourners, and there weren't many, filed past the casket, each with a flower in hand. Ricky purposely waited, Ted next to him, until Roxy and Reba were on their way to their car.

"Some guy over there wants to talk to you, Ricky," Ted whispered.

"Who is it?"

Ted shrugged as he laid his white rose on top of the bronze casket. "He said he's your brother's lawyer."

"Tell him this isn't a good time. He should be talking to Roxy, not me. Is he some kind of ghoul? Go on, tell him. I want this one last minute with my brother for myself." Ted trotted off.

Ricky felt the lump in his throat grow larger as he placed his rose on the casket next to Ted's. He placed his hands, palms flat, on the shiny surface. "I did . . . do love you, Philly. Maybe I should have said it more often. Hell, maybe I never said it at all. If I didn't tell you, I'm sorry. What's making this all bearable for me is knowing you're gonna be with Mom and Dad. I'm going to miss you, Philly. I wish I could tell you I'll look after Roxy for you, but we both know that isn't going to happen.

"Wherever you are, I know you're going to be looking out for me. I know it as sure as I'm standing here. You know how you always used to say, 'This is where the rubber meets the road?' This is it for me. I'll come back, and we'll talk again."

Ricky felt rather than saw the stuntman's presence. "He says your brother wanted his will read right after his death. He reserved a conference room at the hotel where your brother was staying. Roxy and her daughter will be there. You have to go, Ricky," Ted said.

"Yes, I guess I do. Are there a lot of reporters outside the gates?"

"Six deep."

Ricky sighed. "All right, let's go."

He walked away, head high, shoulders squared. And he didn't look back.

2

Something should have changed in the four days since he'd come to see Roxy the morning Philly had died, Ricky thought as he made his way to the main entrance of the hotel. The shrubs looked the same, the gardeners were still scurrying about, the flowers were just as brilliant, the sun just as golden.

There was no reason on earth that he needed to be present to hear Philly snub him in death the way he had in life. Did he really need to hear how much money he was leaving Roxy? No, he did not. Nor did he need to know about Philly's other private holdings and investments. He should have simply declined the invitation to attend. The lawyer, Philly's old friend and confidant, could just as easily have sent him a letter.

His father had once said that a dying person's wishes should always be honored. If this was the last thing he could do for Philly, he'd grit his porcelain caps and do it.

The conference room was small, almost stark, which surprised Ricky. A shiny oval table, with a centerpiece of brilliant orange and gold spider mums nestled among feathery greenery, stood in the center. A silver service with coffee cups sat on a sideboard next to a telephone console, fax machine, and copier. In the corner on a small table was a seventeen-inch television set, along with a VCR. He smelled the coffee, so it must be fresh. He helped himself. He needed all the caffeine he could get.

Ricky carried his cup to the table and set it down. He looked around to see if there was a NO SMOKING sign but didn't see one. It was probably understood that you couldn't smoke. Like he cared. He smoked two cigarettes a day, one with his first cup of coffee and one after dinner. On the occasions when he had sex, he smoked three. Philly had chain-smoked, a three-pack-a-day man. His only vice, according to Philly. In all other areas of his life, he was perfect. According to Philly.

Ricky looked down at his watch. Time is money. Philly would be really pissed that the lawyer hadn't arrived yet. Everyone knew lawyers were all about billable hours. He continued drinking his coffee and smoking his cigarette. A perfect smoke ring sailed upward. Ricky tilted his head until he was sitting directly underneath it. His own personal halo. He smiled to himself, wondering if Philly was watching. Probably, since Philly never missed a trick.

The door opened just as Ricky was about to crush out his cigarette. Roxy and her daughter Reba, minus their black hats and black veils. He expected to see red-rimmed eyes and little or no makeup. Especially on Roxy. But she was perfectly made-up and was wearing pounds of jewelry and at least a pint of perfume. Reba didn't need makeup, jewelry, or perfume. She had youth on her side, twenty-three, if he remembered correctly. She looked . . . for want of a better word, angry.

Roxy looked pointedly at the cigarette

Ricky was about to put out. "Show some respect," she said. Ricky looked down at the cigarette before he brought it to his lips and blew a cloud of smoke in her direction. It was a childish, ridiculous thing to do, and he knew it. Roxy brought out the worst in him. Philly smoked three packs a day, so she should have been used to the smell. When he finally stubbed out the cigarette, he looked at his watch. He'd give the fat-cat lawyer another five minutes, and if he wasn't there by then, he'd leave. The lawyer entered three minutes later and took his seat at the oval table.

Timothy Andreadis was Greek, but he could have passed for Italian, Jewish, or maybe even Spanish. He had a hawklike nose, and the bushy hair that stood away from his head like a shrub gone awry was obviously all his own. He gave the impression of being thick, from his bull neck down to his thick legs and exceptionally big feet. He'd been Philly's lawyer forever. He opened his briefcase and rustled papers before he withdrew Philly's will, encased in a shiny blue cover that acted as a protective sleeve.

"Before you do anything, Timothy," Roxy

said, "I want to say I don't think this is necessary. I know *exactly* what's in the will, and I don't think my brother-in-law needs to be present to hear it all. I resent this." Ricky was surprised at how cold the grieving widow's voice sounded.

"For once I agree with you, Roxy," Ricky said, standing up. "You made it sound imperative that I be here, Tim. Why? Roxy was Philly's wife, so if you don't mind, I'll just head on out. I'm going to the islands today."

"Please sit down, Ricky. Your brother wanted you here." While the attorney shuffled his papers, he asked, "Did you wind up the film?"

"Yes. They used the footage of the car crash. Philly's name will appear in the credits. I think he would have liked that. We finished it the day after . . . *the day after.*"

Tim snapped open the blue sleeve containing the will.

"Coffee anyone?" Ricky asked. When there was no response, he poured himself a cup and lit another cigarette. He remained standing, which seemed to annoy

Roxy. Reba looked up at him, the same angry expression on her face.

"This is the last will and testament of Philip John Lam."

"Timothy, would you please cut to the chase," Roxy said. "We know Philly was of sound mind, and we know he made bequests to some of our employees. I'd like to put this behind me so I can go home and *grieve.* We could have done this next week or the week after. I don't see what the big hurry is."

Ricky's stomach tied itself into a knot as he waited for the lawyer's response. Something was going on here. *Damn, Philly, what the hell did you do?* It looked to him like Roxy was wondering the same thing.

"I'm doing exactly what your husband instructed me to do, Roxy. That's what lawyers do. Now let me get to it, and we can all go home."

Ricky leaned against the sideboard, coffee cup in one hand, cigarette in the other. He stared at his sister-in-law as the lawyer's voice droned on, the legalese dripping from his tongue. Roxy was an advertisement for Rodeo Drive. She wore it well. If it was top-of-the-line and expensive, if it sparkled, glistened, or shimmered, Roxy owned it. He thought he could see dollar signs in her eyes. Philly had said the same thing many times.

"And now to the major part of Philip's will." Andreadis rattled the paper in his hands for effect. "I leave my entire estate to my brother Ricky. To my wife I leave the sum of ten thousand dollars. To my stepdaughter Reba, I leave two thousand dollars. To my nephews Tyler and Max, I leave the sum of five hundred thousand dollars each, said sums to be disbursed by their father when and if he deems necessary.

"All partnerships, all holdings held in my brother's and my names revert to Ricky Lam. All insurance, including the key man policy, is to go to my brother, also.

"The house and furnishings in Laurel Canyon are bequeathed to Roxy Nelson, along with the cars and the boat."

The coffee cup in Ricky's hand slipped to the floor. Brown liquid splashed up his pant leg. He could feel the cigarette starting to burn his fingers. Reba bent down to pick up the cup. She handed it to him, looking shocked.

Roxy wasn't a pillar of salt today. Her face was contorted into an ugliness Ricky had never seen before. Deep guttural curses exploded from her lips as her hands jabbed at the air around her. For one wild moment, Ricky thought those hands were going to reach out and strangle the lawyer.

So much for grief.

The attorney leaned back and waited for Roxy's outburst to subside. When she saw him lean back and steeple his fingers, she calmed down, and said quietly, "I assume there is an explanation for this. When did Philip change his will?" She let her gaze sweep to Ricky. "Just how much did you have to do with this?"

"I'm as shocked as you are. Philly never said a word to me," Ricky said, his eyes glazing over.

"You want to know why?" the attorney said, his eyes on Roxy. "Philip said if you were to ask, I was to respond by telling you, you know why. He said if you still persist in questioning me, I was to mention the word *insurance*. In addition, Roxanne, Philip instructed me to say if you even *think* about contesting the will, everything he did bequeath to you will revert to his brother Ricky Lam. He changed his will exactly fourteen months ago. I believe it was when he got some personal bad news to answer your question."

"This is California. There are common property laws. Everything should be split down the middle," Roxy challenged.

"If, Roxanne, *if* it was held jointly. None of Philip's assets had your name on them, just Philip's and Ricky's names. This will is so airtight, a gnat couldn't get through it. In addition, you signed another document, a prenuptial agreement, explaining all this to you. I have a copy here in case you feel the need to refresh your memory."

"Philip said he rescinded the prenup." Ricky thought Roxy's voice sounded cold as well as desperate. He stared at her, almost expecting chunks of ice to fall off her teeth.

"In that case, you should have gotten it in writing, my dear. The prenuptial agreement was never rescinded."

"I don't believe this!" Roxy screamed, turning to Ricky. "I know you had something to do with this you . . . you poor excuse for an actor."

Ricky threw his hands in the air. "I'm outta here. I don't want it. Give it all to her."

"Your brother said you were going to say that," the attorney said quietly.

Ricky turned back. His eyes narrowed. "He did?"

"Yes, he did. He said he would be forever disappointed in you if you ignored his final wishes. He had great faith in you."

Ricky walked back to the table and stood over the lawyer. "How did he know . . . what if he had outlived me? This all sounds like . . . it was . . . a plan of some sort. He shouldn't have thought he was going to die until he was old. Is there something you aren't telling me?"

"Yes. Your brother had, at best, a year to live. He got the diagnosis of pancreatic cancer fourteen months ago. As far as I know, his doctor and I are the only ones who knew about the precarious condition of his health. Perhaps his passing was a blessing in disguise. He didn't suffer."

Ricky wondered if his own expression looked as stunned as the expression he was seeing on his sister-in-law's face. His brother had been terminally ill, and he'd had no clue. Not one. Obviously, Roxy hadn't had a clue either. The hot tears he held in check pricked at his eyes.

"He wanted it this way, Ricky," the attorney said.

"Wait a minute. Philly was married to Roxy for twenty years. I need to know why he turned his back on her like he did. Otherwise, I'll just turn around and give it all to her once it's settled. What's fair is fair. I'm waiting, Timothy." He glanced in Roxy's direction. A look of hope crept across her doll-perfect face.

The attorney uttered a long sigh. Ricky could see that he was troubled. "Philip valued a promise made. He told me how he promised your mother always to look after you. He said you honored the promises you made to him when you returned from the clinic. That was very important to Philip." Timothy turned to address Roxy. "You, Roxanne, broke promises, according to Philip, and on top of that, you tried to cheat him, and in so doing, cheat his brother. He considered that unforgivable. I'll file this will for probate. Do either of you have any questions?"

Ricky had a barrelful, but he wasn't going to ask them now.

"What about the islands? I had a job there. Did he rip that away from me, too?" Roxy demanded harshly.

"Yes." The will crackled again when the attorney slipped it back into its sleeve. He slid it into his briefcase, then closed and locked it.

Ricky left the conference room in a daze. While he waited for a cab, Timothy Andreadis joined him. All Ricky could do was stare at him. "I'm waiting for a cab. A friend dropped me off after the funeral."

"Would you like to go somewhere for some coffee, Ricky? You look like you're in shock. Accept it. It was what Philip wanted."

"But Tim, to cut Roxy out like that, I just don't understand it."

"They hated each other. Can you understand *that?*"

"No, no, I can't understand that. I always thought they had the perfect marriage. There wasn't anything Philly wouldn't do for Roxy. At least that's how I perceived it. He took real good care of Reba even though he never adopted her."

"That might have been the case once. Philip didn't believe in divorce, as you know. He had many different insurance policies. There was one fifty-thousand-dollar policy with Roxy as beneficiary. All the others had you listed as the beneficiary. About fifteen years ago, right around the time you came back from the clinic, Philip wanted to go over all his holdings. The estate planner in the office is the one who found out what Roxy had done. She'd forged Philip's name on the different policies and put her own name in as beneficiary. As far as I know, he never told her that he knew. He went over everything with a fine-tooth comb and he took her name off everything. He did it legally and had her sign all the papers. I don't know if she knew what she was signing. But she *did* sign them. If you need something more by way of explanation, Philip said his wife betrayed him. The same way she betrayed you. He said you would understand. He came to believe, but only later on, that you never stalked her as she claimed. She's the one who should have been an actress.

"Philip said the one thing you never did was lie to him. He did say you had faults, but lying wasn't one of them. On top of all that, he felt like he had betrayed you. He had a hard time with that. That's all I can tell you, Ricky."

Ricky shook his head. "Let's skip the coffee. I need to go home and think about all this."

"You might want to take this with you," the attorney said, reaching inside his jacket pocket. He withdrew a copy of the will and handed it to Ricky. "If you need me, call," the lawyer said as he tipped the valet and climbed into his Mercedes. "By the way, Ricky, it was a lovely service."

He was alone again, waiting for the valet to commandeer him a cab. He could feel his thoughts ricocheting all over the place. He yanked at his tie before he ripped it off and stuffed it into his pocket. He saw the cab rolling up to the entrance at the same time he saw two teenage girls debating if they should ask him for his autograph. He smiled. They surged forward, pen and paper in hand. He was scrawling his signature when he felt eyes boring into him. Roxy and Reba. Roxy's eyes were full of tears. Reba wore the same angry expression she'd worn in the conference room.

An hour later he was home. He shed his clothes as he walked through his empty house. Within minutes he pulled on his swimming trunks and headed for the pool. The water was cool, clean, and clear. When he surfaced, he shook his head to clear the water from his eyes. He climbed out and wrapped a pool towel, a Ralph Lauren special, around his shoulders.

His sunglasses and a pitcher of ice tea, some cinnamon buns, and a box of tissues sat on a table next to his favorite chair. His housekeeper's attempt to assuage his grief.

As he stretched out in the lounge chair he couldn't help but wonder if his eyes were burning from the chlorine in the pool or because of Philly. Whatever it was, it didn't matter. He could cry now because he was alone. Now he could grieve.

When he couldn't cry anymore, he closed his eyes, hoping for sleep. The past four days he'd prayed for sleep, had even contemplated taking sleeping tablets, but he hadn't taken them because they were a *drug*. He'd promised Philly never to take drugs again. So he'd tossed and turned, walked the grounds, and drunk hot milk. He must have dozed off and on during those days because otherwise he wouldn't have been able to function.

It was four o'clock when he woke. At some point, his housekeeper must have opened the sun umbrella so that he wouldn't get burned. A second yellow Ralph Lauren towel was spread out over his legs. He had to remember to thank Ellie.

Ricky removed his sunglasses. That was when he noticed the bottle of aspirin and the fresh pitcher of ice tea. His reading glasses rested on the envelope. He knew it contained Philly's will. It must have fallen out of his jacket. When Ellie cleaned up behind him, she would have seen it and brought it out to the pool, along with his reading glasses.

Today isn't the day to read this. Maybe there will never be a day.

Life is a bitch!

"Ricky, what brings you here?" Timothy asked two weeks later. He closed the folder on his desk before he got up to walk around and clasp Ricky's hand. "Jesus, you look awful. Aren't you sleeping?"

"No, I'm not. I know it's only been two

weeks, but I'm ready to make some decisions, and in order to do that, I need your help. This isn't going to be a conflict of interest or anything like that, is it?"

"That depends."

Ricky looked around at the office, surprised to see all the family pictures. It was a restful room, with many different plants some secretary must take care of. A small fish tank with colorful tropical fish sat in a corner, directly in Timothy's line of vision. He'd read somewhere that watching fish swim to and fro was supposed to be relaxing. He made a mental note to get some. "How many children do you have, Tim?"

"Six."

"Six kids!"

"Yes. Four boys and two girls. Not a twin in the bunch. We have three dogs, two cats, and a parrot. The house rocks."

"I'll bet it does. Six kids!"

"Philly was godfather to all of them."

Ricky dug the heels of his shoes into the soft carpeting. "I didn't know that. I guess there's a lot about Philly I didn't know. Why didn't I know that he and Roxy hated each other? More important, why didn't I know he was sick?"

"He didn't want you to know, Ricky. Your brother was obsessed with your well-being. He didn't want you to fail. He didn't want you to break the promise you made to him to stay on the straight and narrow. Do you know he had private dicks on you twenty-four/seven? I think he viewed it as a safety net of sorts. One false move, and he would have swooped down on you like the father bird he was."

Ricky could feel his head start to pound. "Then those dicks must have been asleep at the switch the night before he died because I fell off the wagon. All I've done is think about that night, and, no, I haven't taken a drink since. I think I must have had some kind of premonition that something bad was about to happen. That's all I can come up with. By the way, I haven't yet looked at the will. I need to be in a better place than I'm in right now before I do that. But I'll go along with what Philly wanted."

"It's understandable. There's no rush. Now, what is it you need me to do for you?"

"For starters, have the studio void out the old check and issue me a new one. I don't know if Philly had it in his pocket that day or not. He didn't have a briefcase with him. Check it out. Then I want you to break my contract with the studio. Do whatever it takes. I'm retiring. I'd like you to send out the press releases."

Timothy looked at Ricky over the rim of his reading glasses. "Are you sure about this?"

"I'm sure. The second thing I want you to do is get in touch with my sons. Tell them about Philly's bequest. I think I'd like you to go see them personally and explain the situation. I'd like to see them, but I want you to talk to their mothers to make sure they're okay with it. I want it to be the boys' decision in the end. Will you do that?"

"If that's what you want, of course I'll do it." The lawyer cleared his throat. "What are you going to do, Ricky?"

"I'm going to the islands and take over the resorts. I know what you're going to say. I'll learn the business. If I screw up, I'll only have myself to blame. Philly said I was going to have to do it someday. This is my *someday.*"

"Philip hired excellent people who know the business. They'll help you every step of the way. I'll be here for you, too. Don't be afraid to ask for help. If you do screw up, and you will, make sure you tell me. Philip learned the hard way. He made some whoppers, but we made it all come out right in the end."

"Philly made mistakes! That's pretty hard to believe."

"Believe it. Making mistakes is how you learn. Philip never made the same mistake twice. You just *thought* your brother was perfect. He wasn't. He was as human as you and I."

Ricky ran his hands through his hair. "Do we need to talk about Roxy?"

"Only if you want to."

"What do you think would make her happy?"

"The whole ball of wax. She expected to inherit it. In her wildest dreams she never thought it would go to you. She didn't know about your sons either."

"But you said they had a prenuptial agreement."

The lawyer threw his hands up in the air. "They did. While Roxy claims Philip told her he rescinded it, he didn't. Weren't you listening, Ricky? I said your brother wasn't perfect. Philip never told me *everything*. Women like Roxy are three dozen to the dollar here in Hollywood. She said/he said. Look, she isn't going to go on the welfare line. The house alone is worth over a million. Her bank account is robust. She's young, she can work. The will is airtight, the prenup is just as tight. Walk away and don't look back. You're starting a new life, and you don't need to carry baggage with you when you do. That's my advice for the day. So, when are you leaving?"

"In a few days. Ted's going with me. I finally convinced him he was getting too old to continue with those hair-raising stunts he does day in and day out. I guess that's it." Ricky stood up and held out his hand.

"Philip was proud of you, Ricky. I want you to know that. I'm not blowing smoke here. I would never do that to you. A relationship between brothers is a serious thing. I want you to take that knowledge with you. Philip was a complex man. Are you going to go ahead with the Crown Jewel, or are you going to wait?"

"Run that by me again, Tim."

"The Crown Jewel. The third resort Philip had on the drawing board. He bought the land off the Carolina coast years ago. I know he told you about it. You probably forgot. There's a rumor out, possibly it's more than a rumor, that a group of investors are building a huge film studio in the Charleston area a mere forty minutes from the land he purchased."

"I'll be damned. So he really did pull it off. He told me about it three years ago, then he never mentioned it again. I'll have to check it out. Listen, Tim, thanks for everything."

The attorney nodded and pumped Ricky's hand again. "See ya."

"Yeah, see ya, Tim."

3

Reba Nelson carefully folded the few items of clothing she'd brought with her to California. Her WaterPik and cosmetics were the last thing to go into her bag. She looked over at her mother, who was holding a highball glass in her hand. "Isn't it a little early to be drinking, Mom?"

"Of course it's too early to be drinking. It's only ten o'clock in the morning. The sun won't be over the yardarm for hours. What else am I supposed to do? Two weeks ago I had a life and a job that I really liked. I had a husband who spoke to me on occasion and a somewhat stable future. I was the one who was supposed to get the Crown Jewel up and running. I had plans. Now what do I have? I have zero, that's what I have!" Roxy said tearfully, bitterness ringing in her voice. "Another thing," Roxy said slugging from her glass, "it's all Ricky's fault. I know that bastard brainwashed Philly somehow. If it wasn't for him, I'd never have another worry. What do I have? Nothing!" she screamed at the top of her lungs. "I'll fix him, you just wait and see. There are other ways to skin a cat. If it's the last thing I do, I'll get even with that . . . that . . . movie star."

Reba Nelson had seen and heard it all before. She wished she could feel something for her mother, but she didn't. It was hard during her growing-up years to know she was the result of a six-month marriage with a football jock. It was hard living with her money-scheming mother in one-room apartments. She hadn't been a pretty child, and she wasn't pretty now, at least not by Hollywood standards. Her nose was too big, her cheeks too full, and her chin wasn't defined enough. Her eyes, summer blue, were her best feature, along with the honey blonde hair that was naturally curly, thanks to the father she never knew. She did have a good figure, though, because she worked at it. She no longer pretended to care about her mother or her appearance.

"That's not true, Mom. You have this palatial house. Sell it and buy a smaller place. This is California, so you can probably get three or four million for it. You have *bags* of jewelry. You told me once you had it all appraised, and it came in just under two million dollars. Sell it. Get a job. Sell off the cars and the boat, that's another half million, maybe more. If you invest it all, you can live the rest of your life in comfort. Perhaps not as lavishly as you lived with Philip, but it will still be a nice lifestyle. You told me you'd banked all the money you earned in the islands, so I'm having a hard time feeling sorry for you."

"You are an ungrateful young woman!" Roxy murmured. "All that bad stuff you are so fond of throwing at me, it was all for you. I had to take care of you the best way I could. I'm sorry if I wasn't a better mother. I'm also sorry your real father doesn't want to know you. I can't change those things. I neither want nor expect you to feel sorry for me. I need some time to come to terms with . . . with everything."

Reba sighed. She'd heard all this before,

too. "Mom, look around. Do you really need all this opulence? This bedroom alone could accommodate a family of four. What I don't understand is why you would try to . . . *steal* from your husband. Greed is a terrible thing."

"Aren't we sanctimonious this morning? That greed managed to get you through college and medical school, now didn't it? I earned it, that's why."

"Mom, I could have had grants and scholarships, and I would have found a way to make it on my own. Philip's generosity just made it easier for me. I thank God every day for that generosity. By the way, you can have the two thousand dollars Philip left me."

"You're a fool," Roxy said, teetering out of the room.

Reba wiped at her eyes. "Yeah, Mom, I guess I am," she said under her breath. She'd liked Philip Lam. On the rare times when she came home from school, he always managed to have at least one long talk with her. She'd hungered for more but settled for the long talks. He always paid attention to what she said and how she said it. He also seemed to value her opinion. She'd been profuse in her thanks for all his help. His response had been a wave of the hand and the words, "When God is good to you, you have to give back. You are a worthwhile human being, Reba. Always remember that." A week after that particular talk, she'd been stunned to receive a letter from a well-known brokerage house. It said twenty-five thousand dollars had been deposited in a new account bearing her name. The most she'd ever had in her meager checking account at one time was two hundred dollars. She couldn't comprehend the amount. Following the transaction, she'd received a letter from Philip saying he'd handle her tax forms and the gift tax and not to worry about it. He'd added a postscript that said, let's keep this just between you and me. She knew she wasn't supposed to tell her mother, and she hadn't. She'd never spent a penny of the money either. She had no idea what the account was worth today. But after eight years of earning interest the tidy little sum had probably grown to thirty or thirty-five thousand. She wondered what her mother would say if she knew. *Well, she isn't going to find out from me.*

Philip wanted it kept a secret, and it will forever remain a secret.

During her teen and college years, she often wished that Philip would act more like a father to her. Secretly, she suspected, he didn't know how to show his feelings. He was proud of her, that much she did know. He respected her hard work, her good grades, and her ability to get along on almost nothing. His eyebrows had shot up to his hairline the day she'd told him she worked in the Gap twelve hours a week, hating every minute of those twelve hours, so she could get the discounted clothing. He'd approved.

When she'd told him she was going into plastic surgery, he'd been surprised and disappointed until she'd explained that it was reconstructive plastic surgery. Then he'd beamed and hugged her. "Good choice," was all he'd said.

Reba looked around the lavishly decorated room. It was all done in peachy pink. Even the carpet was peach-colored. The draperies, to break up the color, had silver-and-gold thread running through them. The furniture was antique white trimmed in gold. The walk-in closet was bigger than her whole apartment in New York. The bathroom, designed to look like a grotto, was something she'd only seen in magazines. It wasn't for her. She had better uses for money.

She looked around to make sure she hadn't forgotten anything because she knew she wouldn't be coming back. Satisfied, she picked up her suitcase. "I will miss you, Philip," she whispered. She swiped at the tears in the corners of her eyes, feeling acutely the loss of one man who had come close to being the father she'd always dreamed of.

It was time to move on. Time to figure out a way to get back at Ricky Lam for destroying her dream.

Ricky had sent a car to the airport to pick up his sons and bring them back to his house. The main reason was that he wanted privacy, not some jammed airport, when he finally made contact with the two young men who carried his name. He hadn't earned the right to call himself their father. Not yet. Maybe never. He leaned back in his comfortable chair and closed his eyes.

"Jesus, Philly, I wish you were here. I know I'm going to flub this one. The last time I was this nervous was when you gave me that ultimatum way back when. All of a sudden I'm full of what-ifs." He was mumbling to himself and that wasn't good. *Get a grip,* he cautioned himself.

The doorbell chimed. Ricky woke up with a start. Had he dozed off and dreamed he was talking to Philly? It had happened before. He felt groggy. He hated the dreams where he talked to his brother. Really hated them. A cold chill ricocheted up and down his arms.

The doorbell rang a second time. Obviously, Ellie wasn't going to answer it. He walked to the door and opened it wide. He stared at himself . . . twice. He took the initiative. "I'm your dad, but I don't think I deserve that title, so you can call me Ricky. Which one is which? Come in."

They were as tall as he was, six-two. They both looked like they tipped the scales at his same weight, which was probably 180.

"I'm Tyler," the one on the left said.

"I'm Max," the one on the right said. "We

met in the limo. Imagine our surprise when we realized we're half brothers."

The one named Tyler walked around, his face full of awe. He turned. "That was a pretty shitty thing you did, *Pop*. What's with this command performance? Are we supposed to bow, genuflect, what?"

"How about sitting down? If there's one thing in this life that I hate, it's a wiseass and a smart mouth. You're wrong, you know. It wasn't a shitty thing I did, it was unconscionable. I was only twenty when I fathered you both."

"Is that supposed to impress us?" Max asked. "You want to be a father now, is that it? Where the hell were you when we were in the hospital with broken bones or when we were sick? We compared notes in the car on the ride here."

"Probably shacked up with some bimbo or drying out along the way. I don't have total recall, but if you can be specific about those times, I might be able to give you a passable answer. As to being your father, no, I gave up that right twenty years ago. Did your mothers tell you about me?"

Tyler bit down on his lower lip. "She said my father was a no-good bum, and she hated his guts. You want absolution now? Forget it! She never told me your name because she said she wanted to forget she even knew you. Like I said, what's with this command performance?"

"My mother said you were a lowlife sack of shit," Max said.

Ricky threw his head back and laughed. "Both your mothers are right. Back then I was those things. Even more. That was then, this is now."

"You paid for us all those years, right? Are you the one who paid for my car and college?" Tyler asked.

"Yeah. And now you figure because we're twenty-three, finished with college, you can claim us? What's wrong with this picture?" Max asked.

"What's wrong with the picture is that my brother, your uncle, died a few weeks ago. If he hadn't died, I probably never would have sent my attorney to see you. My financial obligation to you ended when you graduated from college. I will provide for your mothers until the day I die. What else do you want to know?"

"What do you want from us?" Tyler asked, his eyes spewing sparks.

"I don't want anything from either one of you. I hoped I could do something for you both. This may sound a little weird to you, but when my brother, your uncle, died so suddenly, I realized how fragile life really is. You're my flesh and blood, and I wanted to see you. I want to help you in any way I can. I'm sure the attorney mentioned your inheritance from your uncle Philip."

"And that would be . . . what?" Tyler asked coldly. He slapped at his forehead. "I bet you want us to head up your fan club. No thanks. You can screw the inheritance, too."

Ricky ignored the comment. "I was hoping I could do something for you. My brother and I own two resorts in the islands. With his death, I'm taking them over and retiring from the film industry. I thought you might like to come aboard and work for me. Now, if you have nothing but contempt for movie stars and high-profile people, you might not want to work for me. You'll be making four times the salary you're earning in the corporate world, seeing as how you started out on the lowest rung. You get free room and board and plenty of time in the sun. The surfing's great in the winter. The golf and tennis are even better. Your social life will increase by a hundred percent. If you don't piss me off along the way, one day it will all be yours."

Ricky paused for a moment, looking at his sons, who gazed at him warily. "I'm going swimming. If you care to join me, there are suits in the cabana. My housekeeper will serve lunch by the pool. If you want to leave, leave. I made my offer. Take it or leave it."

He was shaking so badly when he entered the cabana, he could barely get his pants off.

He headed for the Olympic-size pool, dived in, and swam its length. He climbed out of the pool when he saw his sons coming out of the cabana.

"What are you getting out of this deal? Assuming we agree to any of this," Max asked.

"Two good employees, I hope. There's no room in my life for smart-asses, disrespect, or jealousy. We're health-conscious around here," Ricky said, picking up a vegetable wrap and biting down.

"You got any beer?" Tyler asked.

"No. I'm an alcoholic, so I don't keep it around unless we're having a party."

"Is there anything else we should know about you?" Max asked.

"I was a drug addict until my brother straightened my ass out. I've been clean for over fifteen years." There was no need to mention his little relapse.

"That's it?" Tyler demanded.

"I like women. I mean I *really* like women. Oh, yeah, I'm *really* rich. I'm walking away from Hollywood while I'm still on top. It's time for me to give back. You fall into that category. Now you know everything there is to know about me. Isn't it your turn to share a few things with me?"

The two young men suddenly looked uncomfortable. "C'mon, you already know it all," Max said.

Ricky reached for a second vegetable wrap and laid it on his plate. Overhead, a small cluster of birds took wing, settling in a ficus tree at the side of the pool. He put on his sunglasses. He homed in on Tyler. "Let's see if I remember it all. You got kicked out of Penn State, got reinstated, then kicked out a second time. You did a year in a community college and finally graduated from Florida State when you found a mentor who could see past your bullshit. That's when you got your act together. You were arrested twice, once for speeding on your motorcycle while under the influence and causing a pedestrian injury, the second time for drinking and driving. You totaled your car, and your mother refused to buy you another one. You lost your license for six months and did two hundred hours of community service."

"You, Max . . ." Ricky shook his head as though it were too much to handle. "Looking at you, I would never take you for a brawler. I guess you both had a lot of aggression in you owing to a lack of a male role model. For all your excellence in academics, you were disciplined twice in high school and once in college for settling disagreements with your fists. I don't think there's any point in going over the list of young women who accused you both of various things, none of which could be proved. You both need to learn to respect women. In fact, I damn well insist on it."

"The apple doesn't fall far from the tree," Tyler said, reaching for one of the vegetable wraps. "What was your excuse?"

Ricky eyed both young men through the dark glasses. "I didn't have an excuse. I was out for a good time. My fame and celebrity came too quick and went to my head. I thought I could do no wrong and that the world owed me everything. You see, I did have a mentor, my brother, but I chose to ignore him. In the beginning. Like I said, I had no excuse. Do either of you want to say anything?"

"At least you're honest," Max said grudgingly. Tyler said nothing.

"It's the only way to go. Tea or coffee?"

"Ice tea," Tyler said.

"Coffee," Max said.

"Nice place," both boys said, looking around.

"Yes, it is nice. You both grew up in nice, normal homes, too, so don't try throwing any guilt in my direction. You will never, ever, be able to put one over on me if that's your intention. Been there, done that. I'll know what you're thinking before you think it yourself. Are we clear on that?"

"Crystal," Tyler said.

"Perfectly," Max said.

"I have some business to take care of. Enjoy your lunch. Swim, do whatever you like. I'll be back by three. I'd like your answer then."

Ricky was almost to the French doors when Tyler called out, a snarl in his voice, "What are we supposed to call you?"

"As I said when you first got here, just use my name. In case you've forgotten it already, it's Ricky." He offered up a jaunty wave as he headed into the house and out the front door to his car. He had no destination in mind. His leaving was simply a means to let his sons talk privately. All things considered, the boys had handled the meeting rather well, he thought. He, on the other hand, was a little short of a basket case.

Sunglasses in place, baseball cap pulled low over his forehead, Ricky drove down the winding roads until he came to the first shopping center he saw. He turned on his blinker and parked outside a Target store. At last he could shake and twitch. What did they think? They looked like okay guys to him. For the most part they had their shit together now. He could tell. Still, he'd read suspicion in Tyler's expression, and he couldn't blame him. He wondered if either one noticed that at one point his chest had puffed out with pride as he stared across the table at both of them. He slouched in his seat as though he were waiting for someone.

Ricky stared out the window at a family with a cart full of bags and a box that said DVD on the side. One of the little kids had an Elmo doll and was tossing it high in the air. One of the older ones caught it and ran off until the father shouted one succinct warning. "Bring it back, *now!*" A dog, a collie by the looks of him, got into the act and leaped out of the car when a toddler climbed in and rolled down the window. Ricky watched as the mother, her ponytail flying, raced after the dog. Huffing and puffing, she carried the animal back to the car, rolled up the window, then proceeded to smack the kid's bottom for rolling it down. Ricky felt like cheering. The dog barked shrilly. The father looked at him, pointed his finger, and the dog shut up instantly. A real authority figure. The kid with the Elmo doll bit off its ear and threw it into the front seat, the stuffing flying in all directions. The mother, who looked like she was at her wit's end, leaned over the backseat and grabbed the kid by the scruff of the neck. The kid, red in the face, howled, demanding his Elmo doll. "You just ruined it, so you can't have it back," the mother said through clenched teeth. The dog tried to paw the mother as he yanked at the ribbon holding her ponytail in place.

The father turned around but didn't say a word as he put the car in gear and drove off, the dog barking as he pawed at the windows.

Ricky slouched lower in his seat, wondering what his sons would decide to do. A few moments later, hearing noise and commotion, he sat up and peered out the window. The family with the DVD player, the kids, and the dog were back. The mother and father hopped out of the car, the engine of the car still running. They looked like they were looking for something. Whatever it was, it must be small. One of the kids inside the car was howling his head off, and the dog was still barking shrilly to be heard over the squalling kid. "We have to find the damn thing, Myron. We aren't leaving this parking lot till we find it. Keep looking," the mother shouted.

"Well, it's gone. I can't find it," the father said. "Maybe he lost it in the store. All right, all right, I'll go inside and look. Can't you shut him up?"

"No, Myron, I can't shut him up. He wants his pacifier."

"Then shut the dog up," the harried father said as he stomped off.

"The dog barks when Davey cries. Davey is crying. I hate you, Myron," the mother bellowed. The father raised his middle finger over the back of his head. The mother started to cry.

Ricky hopped out of the car. "Do you want me to help you look? What color is the pacifier?"

"Blue. Oh, my God, you're Ricky Lam! Myron is never going to believe this!"

"Is this what you're looking for?" Ricky said, holding up a blue pacifier he pulled out of the web of the store shopping cart."

"Yessss. Thank God!" Ricky watched in fascination as the mother spit on the pacifier, then wiped it on the sleeve of her shirt before jamming it into the kid's mouth. The dog stopped barking. The silence thundered in Ricky's ears.

"I don't know how to thank you."

"That's okay. I'm glad your son is happy."

"You can't just buy a new one because it doesn't taste the same. He's got it all broken in. You know, it fits and feels right in his mouth. Sometimes if you buy a new one and boil it for like ten hours, it swells up, but my kid knows the difference. One time he cried for six hours. I wanted to kill him."

"Uh-huh," was all Ricky could think of to say. So this was what he'd missed by not being married and raising kids. He wondered if his two sons had had pacifiers.

"Can you give me your autograph? Myron is never going to believe this."

"Is he from Disney?" one of the kids shouted as he rolled down the window. The dog leaped out a second later and took off across the parking lot.

"Oh shit," the mother said as she ran after the dog. "Watch my kids, okay?"

"What do you do at Disney, mister? We're going when we save up enough money. My dad promised. Mom said we shouldn't hold our breath. The one in Florida, 'cause then we can go to see Granny. It costs a lot to fly in an airplane."

Ricky looked down at the license plate

on the car. He memorized the number. "What's your last name?"

The kid with the pacifier in his mouth took it out, and said, "Davey Sanders, and I live at 1106 South Holt Avenue." He stuck the pacifier back into his mouth just as the mother, carrying the dog, arrived. She dumped the dog into the car, fished a pen out of the console, and said, "Just sign anywhere on the box."

Ricky obliged. "What's your first name?"

"Marlene," one of the kids in the back chirped. "I'm Mikey, this is Sally, and this is Toby. Davey told you who he was. The dog's name is Gus."

"Okay, I got it all," Ricky said. It was lucky he had a good memory.

"Well, I guess I'll see you around," he said, holding out his hand to the mother. She pumped it vigorously.

"Thanks again," the mother said.

"Glad I could help." He climbed back into his car and headed toward home. He waited until he stopped for a traffic light before he hit his speed dial. "This is Ricky Lam. I need to speak to Timothy right now."

A moment later, the attorney came on

the phone. "Tim, I need you to do something for me. Six plane tickets, first-class, with an open date. Cargo for a collie dog. Disney in Florida for two full weeks. Whatever the best hotel is in the park. Free tickets to everything. Champagne, fruit basket, junk for the four kids, rental car, all prepaid at the hotel. Here are the names, Marlene and Myron Sanders. Kids are Mikey, Toby, Sally, Davey, and the dog's name is Gus. The address is 1106 South Holt here in L.A. Put a note in the package when you send it out, and say, 'Don't forget Davey's pacifier.' Sign my name. Can you do it ASAP?"

"I'll have my secretary get right on it. Isn't today the day . . ."

"Yes, I left them at home to talk about it. At least Max looked interested, but you can't go by expressions. You should have told me they looked like me. I wasn't prepared for that. It's uncanny. Tyler—Tyler is too much like I was in my youth. I don't think he's interested in me or my offer."

"How do you think I felt when I saw them for the first time? Neither boy bears any resemblance to Philip, though. I was impressed with both of the kids. Tyler will come around. You and I talked about this the other day; no point in rehashing it all again. I'll take care of the Disney situation. Have a nice visit with your sons, Ricky."

Ricky broke the connection. He burst out laughing when he thought about the Sanders family. His good mood stayed with him as he drove home.

4

The two young men looked at each other, their expressions wary. Tyler took the initiative. "It's a little disconcerting to find out you have a brother you never knew about, especially when he looks just like you look. I'm a meat person," he said, eyeing the vegetable roll-ups. "I could really go for a double cheeseburger right now. These things remind me of a bunch of weeds. This is so damn weird. I don't know what I'm supposed to be feeling, and I'm not sure how to act."

Max nodded. "What do you think of our father? I notice he didn't mention any details about our inheritance. Why do you suppose that is?"

"Because he controls the money. He

calls the shots. I've seen all his movies. He's hot box office. I'm not sure he told us the truth about everything. I saw a profile of him once on A&E. He admitted to being wild in his youth, but he's a poster boy for good behavior now. Actually, for a long time now. I didn't know I had an uncle, did you?" Tyler asked. He fiddled with his napkin, his gaze riveted on his half brother.

"No, I didn't know. I think our father is one of those guys who's a control freak. It's going to be his way or the highway. It's his show, so we accept it going in. I think I'm going to go for it but only for a few months. If it doesn't work, for him or me, I walk, and there's no hard feelings. Four times the money I'm making now sounds real good. What are your feelings, Tyler?"

"Not quite the same as yours. He did provide for us, so we have to give him an A for that," Tyler said grudgingly. "He's right about us having a good life. I screwed up, though. I've never been to the islands, as he calls them. Hell, I've never really been anywhere except Florida, Pennsylvania, and home. My mother isn't crazy about me going with him, but she said the decision is mine. She got married, and she isn't really interested in me. Sometimes she pretends, but I can see through it. I hate her husband. How about you?"

Max nodded. "My grandparents pretty much raised me while my mother did the looking-for-myself game. She's got a lifestyle that doesn't include a grown kid. It didn't include a little kid either. She turned all the money over to my grandparents. As far as I know, she never kept a penny. Yeah, I had a decent life with no complaints. I'm going back home to pack up. I just signed a three-year lease on a condo. I'll have to put my stuff in storage and drive my car to my grandparents and leave it there. I think I'm on the hook for the lease, though."

"Wake up, Bro. Let old Ricky take care of it. That's what corporations do when they move employees. They pay for everything. This is no different. I'm going to take my inheritance and call it a day. The hell with him," Tyler said, his gaze on the shimmering blue water in the pool. "I hear a car. *He* must be home. Nice meeting you, Max." Tyler's hand shot forward. Max grasped it.

Ricky walked out to the terrace. He

stared down at the pool area. His sons were sitting in the same chairs, in the same position he'd left them in. He joined them.

"What's it going to be?"

"I'm in." Max held up his hand. "Tyler's out. I want to try it for a few months. How does three months sound? If it doesn't work for me, no hard feelings. You okay with that?"

Was he? It was the best he was going to get, and he knew it. He nodded, struggling not to show his disappointment where Tyler was concerned.

"Then we'll get dressed and head for the airport. Tell me where to report in, and I'll be there," Max said.

Ricky looked at his sons, and said, "I wish you could stay longer."

"We have jobs," Tyler said succinctly. "My boss doesn't care if you're a movie star or not. I'm speaking strictly for myself, not my half brother Max. A brother I didn't even know I had until this morning." This last was said in a hate-filled voice. It did not go unnoticed by Ricky or Max.

Ricky cleared his throat and turned to Max. "Why don't you take a week to make whatever arrangements you need for this transition. I'll overnight your plane tickets and have someone pick you up at the airport on your arrival on Antigua a week from today. One more thing—if you have baggage, leave it behind. By baggage, I mean girlfriends. Cut them loose unless you're engaged. If either one of you is engaged, then we need to sit down and talk. I don't want a string of young women showing up making claims. Are we clear on that?"

"Yes, *SIR,*" Max said, ripping off a snappy salute. "I just signed a three-year lease on a condo. Can you see yourself taking care of that? I don't want to be on the hook for another thirty-six months at seven hundred bucks a pop."

"No problem," Ricky said.

Tyler watched his half brother and father through narrowed eyes. He'd been hoping for more of a reaction from the man who said he was his father. He wondered if he was making a mistake. Hell, how could accepting a substantial inheritance be a mistake? So, he wouldn't get to know this new brother of his. He didn't have a brother yesterday, and he'd gotten along just fine. Maybe at some point in the future he'd look both of them up again. The bottom line was this guy Ricky was a father in name only. *Where the hell were you when I needed a father at Little League, at the bowling banquet, at the hockey tournaments? Nah, man, you aren't getting off the hook that easy,* he thought.

Ricky looked at Tyler to see if he'd had a change of heart. His son sat staring at the pool with a scowl on his face. *Evidently not,* Ricky thought.

He entered the house and called the car service he always used when he didn't want to drive himself. He looked into the foyer at his own pile of luggage. He'd scheduled and rescheduled his own flight so many times, he'd lost count. Tomorrow, no matter what, he was going to be on a plane to Antigua. He made a mental note to call Ted to tell him about his change of plans. Knowing Ted, the stuntman wouldn't pack until an hour before it was time to leave for the airport.

He watched from the French doors as his two sons crossed the pool area and entered the house. A strange, alien feeling washed over him. Right then, he knew he would have given up everything he held dear in the world if Philly could see his sons. Would they come to like him? Expecting love from either one of them was too much to ever expect. More important, would they respect him? He hoped so, but he wasn't going to bet the rent on it. Childishly, he crossed his fingers that Tyler would have second thoughts about his offer once he returned home and had time to think about everything more clearly.

He didn't feel like a father. What *was* that feeling like? It was too late in his life for him ever to be like Myron Sanders. He felt his own loss.

"The car is here. A week from today you'll be in Antigua." He handed Max his card. "That's my private number. If anything comes up, or if you change your mind, call me. Even if it's the middle of the night." As an afterthought he handed Tyler a card, too.

He shook each boy's hand. Both handshakes were firm and hard. He pocketed the condo information Max handed him and watched from the open doorway until the car was gone from sight. He closed the door and felt incredibly alone. There were at least two hundred people he could call to ease his loneliness, but he wasn't in the mood for any of them. "Ellie!"

"Yes, Mr. Ricky, what is it?"

"I'm going out again. Do me a favor, call Ted for me and ask him to dinner. Tell him it might be a good idea for him to bring his bags and spend the night. It's an early-morning flight, and I don't want to miss it. You're sure now you can handle closing up the house and all?"

"I can handle it, Mr. Ricky. I will see you one week from tomorrow. My bags are packed. You already gave me my ticket."

"Speaking of tickets, call Mr. Andreadis and tell him to send two first-class tickets to my sons. He'll take it from there. A week from today for them." He knew he was being presumptuous about Tyler's changing his mind but there had been something in the young man's eyes when they'd shaken hands that had sparked hope in him.

"Do you want to tell me where you're going in case anyone calls?"

"No one is going to call me. I changed the telephone number the day Philly died. To answer your question, I'm going to the cemetery. I want to say good-bye."

Ellie nodded solemnly.

Ricky hugged her. "I don't tell you often enough how much I appreciate all you do for me. You've been with me twenty-five years. You've never once said a cross word to me. I've never heard you complain either. Those early years couldn't have been easy on you. I was pretty wild back then."

"But look at you now."

Ricky pinched her plump cheek. "Are you *ever* going to tell me what you wanted those hundred autographs for?"

Ellie smiled. "I guess I can tell you now. We raffled them off at my church so we could buy new carpeting. It was our most successful fund-raiser ever. Father Michael was so grateful."

Ricky laughed. "Why didn't you just ask me for a donation?"

"Because I couldn't do that. Autographs are different. Go now before it gets too late and they lock the gates. What would you like for dinner?"

"It doesn't matter. I'm going, I'm going."

He was at the door when the house-keeper said, "Mr. Ricky?"

"Yes."

"Your boys are very handsome. They

look just like you did at their age. I'm looking forward to getting to know them."

"Let's just hope they don't behave the
way I did at that age."

He hated coming to the cemetery. And
yet, he came faithfully, almost religiously.
He'd always come alone, and wondered
why that was. Once, Philly had asked him
to come, and he'd said he had other plans.
Of course it was a lie. When he was a little
kid full of piss and vinegar and found himself in trouble, he'd always run to either his
mother or father to tell them his troubles.
To this day, he did the same thing. There
was a time when he'd worn a path to the
two gravestones embedded in the thick
grass. Now there were three. An empty
plot next to Philly's was his. He shivered at
the thought.

His thoughts whirling, he didn't see her
until he was almost on top of her—Roxy.
He turned to leave, not wishing to intrude
on whatever it was she was doing. He
cringed when he remembered the vicious
fight he'd had with Roxy over Philly's final
resting place. She'd wanted a different
cemetery and an elaborate headstone.

With Timothy Andreadis's help, Ricky had seen that Philip was buried next to their parents, as was his wish.

"I know you're there, Ricky. I can smell your aftershave. I was just leaving."

"Take your time," he muttered as he prepared to walk away.

"Ricky?"

"Yes."

"If you stop by the house, I'll give you my folder on all the ideas I had for the Crown Jewel. Surprisingly, Philip gave me free rein. You might want them if you're planning on going ahead with the resort. Or, I can mail them to you. Yes, that might be best. Mailing them, that is."

"Are you all right, Roxy?"

"No, Ricky, I'm not all right. I'm not sleeping, and I'm drinking too much. You know, it wasn't at all like that lawyer said. There are two sides to every story. I apologize for my behavior. For every action there is a reaction. Good-bye, Ricky."

"If it's a question of money . . ."

"It's not. Your people are really on top of things. I got the paperwork in the mail today regarding my pension fund. I didn't even know I had a pension fund. Philip's comes to me, too. I didn't know about that either. I'll survive."

"If there's anything I can . . ."

"There isn't. Good luck."

Ricky watched his sister-in-law walk away. At least she hadn't screamed and yelled at him. Maybe she was taking tranquilizers, and that was why she was so calm. *If she'd hated her husband, what was she doing there? Spitting on his grave?* He hated seeing the way her shoulders slumped and the beaten look on her face.

He sat down in the same spot where Roxy had been kneeling and hugged his knees to his chest. He should have brought flowers. Roxy hadn't brought any either. He'd always brought flowers before. He must not have been thinking clearly, or else he had been distracted by his sons' visit. The graves looked bare without flowers. His mother had dearly loved daisies. Maybe Ellie could make arrangements with a local florist to deliver flowers for all three graves on a weekly basis.

There was so much he wanted to say, but the words were stuck in his throat. He hadn't thought it was going to be so hard to say good-bye. Who was going to come here when he moved to Antigua? No one, that's who. The graves would be maintained, but no one would come by and sit and say a prayer or a few words. No one would come seeking comfort or solace. The thought saddened him.

Ricky looked around the vast cemetery. The forgotten.

He shaded his eyes in the late-afternoon sunshine. As far as the eye could see, there wasn't another human being in sight. Maybe people didn't go to cemeteries late in the day. The living had to get on with the normal routines of their lives.

He'd come to say good-bye, but he couldn't get the words past his lips. Goodbyes were too final. He stood up and dusted off the seat of his pants. "I'll be back."

Ricky was surprised to see Roxy waiting for him by her car. At least he thought she was waiting for him. He walked toward her. "Is there a problem with your car, Roxy?"

"No. I guess I just wanted one of those last, spit-in-your-eye good-byes. I figure I earned it."

Ricky remained silent because he didn't

know what to say. Suddenly, a wave of compassion washed over him when he saw the tears in her eyes and her slumped shoulders. Just for one second, she reminded him of his mother when she was tired and weary at the end of the day.

He found his tongue, and said, "I'd like to go through my brother's personal effects if you don't mind. I'm leaving in the morning so it would have to be either now or later this evening."

Roxy squared her shoulders as she stared up into Ricky's eyes. "Obviously you have me mixed up with someone who cares about your wants and desires." Her voice was so cold, Ricky flinched. "Permission denied." Before he could digest his sister-in-law's biting retort, she was in the car driving away.

Ricky felt like a tired old dog when he climbed into his own car for the drive home.

5

The heat and humidity slapped at them as they exited the plane. Ricky immediately yanked at his shirt and tie, then rolled up his sleeves. Ted Lymen watched out of the corner of his eye as Ricky's gaze swept the crowds of people meeting the plane or seeing friends and family off. Where was the red carpet he knew Ricky was expecting?

They waited, their shirts wet with sweat, for forty-five minutes. "Okay, let's take a cab," Ricky said, annoyed.

Ted gathered up his gear and followed Ricky to the nearest waiting taxi. If he was pissed, he knew Ricky was doubly pissed. The ride to the resort was made in total silence.

Ricky seethed in silence, refusing even to look out the window at the landscape. His employees at the resort had just failed his first test. Standard procedure was that each guest be picked up at the airport in the resort's Lincoln Continental. No guests, to his knowledge, ever had to provide their own transportation to the resort. Especially, the new owner.

His rage was white-hot when he hopped out of the taxi under the portico. One of the valets was lounging against the wall, smoking a cigarette. Ricky slapped it out of his hand, and said, "You're fired!" Inside, he looked for the concierge, who was busy talking to one of the bellmen. Neither man looked at Ricky; they just continued talking. He waited, his eyes on his Tag watch. Finally, the concierge acknowledged him. "Oh, Mr. Lam. It's nice to see you again. I'm sorry I kept you waiting."

"Not half as sorry as I am. You're fired. That goes for you, too," he said to the bellman.

Within forty-five minutes Ricky had fired half the staff and called a meeting of all personnel. "Somebody damn well better have an answer for me," he thundered, as his fist hit the polished teakwood table.

They all started to babble at once. The one name that was repeated over and over was *Roxy.* "Roxy took care of that. Roxy was in charge of that. Roxy made the rounds. Roxy did this and that and everything else in between." *Roxy, Roxy, Roxy.*

"There was no one to tell us what to do," one of the desk clerks said timidly.

"What the hell is this?" Ricky said, upending a box that was big enough to hold three loaves of bread. When no one responded, he said, "They're complaints! Pick them up and correct whatever is wrong. Now! Consider this, you're all on notice. If you want to keep your jobs, hop to it. Otherwise, leave now!"

Ricky stormed out of the conference room and headed for Roxy's office. He took one step inside and backed out again. He found himself blinking at the wide array of plants, knickknacks from grateful guests, pictures of Roxy with satisfied guests, pictures of Roxy with politicians. There were no pictures of Philly anywhere to be seen. There was, however, a picture of Reba on Roxy's desk.

It was a working office, with a computer, printer, fax, telephone console, and wall-to-wall, antique white filing cabinets. White wicker furniture with colorful cushions matched draperies on the louvered windows that looked out onto the lush landscaping that was ragged at best. Obviously everyone was asleep at the switch. He cursed ripely.

Did my brother run the resort, or did my brother's wife?

Ted Lymen poked his head in the door. "You got them on the run, boss. I think I just saw Brad Pitt out there heading for the golf carts. You might want to welcome him before he heads home and does some verbal damage. I took it upon myself to throw out the dead flowers in the lobby. I called the florist and told them I was you. I gave them ten minutes to get their asses out here. If it's okay with you, I'm going to find the head gardener and kick some ass."

"Go for it. If they look at you crossways, fire them. Hell, I know how to mow lawns."

"Gotcha!"

Ricky sat down in Roxy's chair. It was too small for his tall frame. Directly in his line of vision was a bulletin board with an oversize calendar in the middle. He stared at the different notations. If she had done everything that was penciled in, she must have been one busy lady. What had Philly done?

A quiet knock sounded on Roxy's door. "Come in," he called.

"Mr. Lam, I'm Donna Pascal, Roxy's assistant. Isn't she coming back? She said she would call me, but I haven't heard from her. I know she's in mourning but . . ." She knuckled her wet eyes. "I tried to keep up, but it got away from me. Roxy was the authority figure here, the glue that held it all together. All she had to do was look at someone. She never had to say a word. Now, that's not to say she was mean or anything. She was fair, generous, and she cared about the employees. She never missed anyone's birthday, and she always gave a present. She made a point of going to all the weddings and family funerals, that kind of thing. Oftentimes she worked till midnight and was back at her desk at six when the new shift came on. Is she coming back?"

"I don't know, Donna. So what you're saying is, Roxy ran this resort?"

"And the other one in Aruba. The two of us used to fly there on Tuesdays and Saturdays and work all day. She has good employees there whom she trusts."

Ricky wanted to ask her what Philip had done while Roxy was taking care of business, but he didn't. "Thanks for coming by, Donna. Do the best that you can until I can get a handle on things."

"I'm sorry about your brother, Mr. Lam. I didn't really know him, or see him all that much. Tell Roxy I asked about her, and tell her I miss her."

"I'll do that, Donna."

When the door closed behind Roxy's assistant, Ricky got up and moved to one of the white wicker chairs. He got up an instant later and sat back down at the desk. He opened the drawers. Everything was neat and tidy. It was obvious Roxy had a system that worked. He fished out her planner, opened it, and gawked at what she accomplished in a day.

Superwoman. Ricky ran his fingers through his hair as he tried to fathom all he was seeing and hearing. This couldn't be the same Roxy he knew back in Los Angeles. Did she have two personas? Philly had led him to believe Roxy spent all her time on Rodeo Drive or sitting on a satin cushion. Once, he'd told him that she spent most of her time in the bar or on the beach when they were on the islands. Something was wrong here. He shook his head to clear his thoughts.

He lifted the blotter and was surprised to find a sheaf of papers. He scanned them quickly, then put them aside. They looked like something he might want to read at another time.

The phone was in his hand a moment later. He hoped he didn't live to regret what he was about to do. He waited while the phone rang and rang on the other end of the line. Her voice sounded sleepy or maybe just raspy because she'd been crying.

"Roxy, it's Ricky. How would you like your old job back? Name your salary. Or if you want a slice of the business, we can discuss it. I've only been here at the resort in Antigua a little over an hour, and even I can see things are falling apart. . . . What do I mean? Well, no one met me at the airport. I called ahead to make the arrangements. One of the valets was standing up against the wall smoking a cigarette. I fired him. I've been firing people right and left. There's a box of complaints that weighs about twenty pounds, and I'm probably going to be the one who mows the lawn in the morning. Charter a plane and get here as soon as you can. That's if you want your job back." Ricky waited, knowing Roxy would say yes. What he heard stunned him.

Bitterness rang in Roxy's raspy voice. "Oh, all of a sudden I'm good enough for Lam Enterprises. Thanks but no thanks. Was there anything else, *Mister* Lam?"

Stunned, Ricky held the phone away from his ear. "Would it help if I came back to Los Angeles and got down on my knees and begged you. Roxy, this place is *dirty.*"

"No, it wouldn't help one bit. They have soap and water for the situations you describe. And cleaning solvents. Put an ad in the paper or call an agency. I have to hang up now, Ricky. Don't call me again either."

"Roxy, wait, don't hang up. Whatever you were making, I'll double it."

The hysterical laughter on the other end of the phone sent shivers up Ricky's spine.

"Okay, triple. Whatever it takes, Roxy. Full benefits."

"Your brother paid me a token salary of $25,000 a year, Ricky. No overtime. My life was those resorts, and you ripped it the hell away from me. I know that doesn't say much for me, but it's the way it is. I'm way too old to go out there kicking and scratching. You and your brother owe me more than you can ever pay in a lifetime."

"What in the hell are you saying, Roxy? Running these resorts is at barest minimum a two-hundred-fifty-thousand-dollar-a-year job." He heard the hysterical laughter again but this time he could hear the choked sobs behind it.

"Are you calling me a liar, Ricky? Check the payroll records. Your brother was a son of a bitch. Look, I wasn't always an angel either. I got greedy and I tried to forge those insurance policies. I'm not proud of that either, but I did it, and I'm not going to lie about it."

Later he would think about all his sister-in-law said. "A lifetime contract or a contract that stays in effect for as long as the resorts are in business. Two hundred fifty thousand a year plus benefits."

"Three-fifty and six weeks vacation," Roxy shot back.

"Three hundred and five weeks vacation."

"Not in this lifetime, Bubba. And complete control of the operation. What I say goes. I always listen, and if your way is better than mine, we go with what's best for the resort. Take it or leave it, *Mister* Lam."

Ricky felt dizzy with relief. "Okay, Roxy, you got yourself a deal. Before we hang up, I just want to say I had no idea . . ."

"Yeah, it sounds good now. You took your percentage. Did you *ever* look at the books? Even once? Another thing, Ricky, I want something built into the contract. Three years from now, if everything is rosy and the resorts are making money, I want a slice of the pie. Maybe not a full partnership but a very good percentage. Let's call that a sign-on bonus. Every single employee deserves and needs a raise. They also deserve a bonus at Christmastime. Philly wouldn't agree when I proposed it to him. That will be the first thing I do, Ricky. Tell me now if that's going to be a problem."

"You said full control. That will be your decision. For whatever this is worth, Roxy, I'm glad you're back on board."

Ricky looked down at Roxy's day planner. "This might be a stupid question, but do you mind telling me what my brother did when he was here while you were running the show? He sat around looking important? He was visible but untouchable? Of course . . . he handled the money end of things. I think I get the picture . . . Why do I ask? I'll tell you when I see you tomorrow. We can talk about it more then."

Ricky closed the door to Roxy's office. He walked down to another office, which looked like it handled the billing and the other resort activities. He stopped long enough to wait for someone to notice him. "Send a memo to all employees immediately. Roxy will be back on the job tomorrow. Sign it, Ricky Lam."

The following morning, Ricky was everywhere as he waited for Roxy to arrive. He heard himself referred to as a spook, a hard-ass, a jerky movie star, and a nut job. He laughed to himself as his employees scurried about seeing to the wants and needs of the guests. He didn't fool himself. They weren't doing it for him or even for the guests. They were doing it for Roxy because she was coming back.

He still had a good forty minutes until his sister-in-law arrived. How best to kill the time? A trip to Philip's office certainly couldn't hurt.

At best it was spartan. There was a desk with nothing on it but a phone. The chair behind the desk was a deep burgundy in color and looked like no one had ever sat in it. Philip hadn't broken it in. How could that be? Even if all he did was sit around looking important, there should have been some kind of indentation in the buttery soft leather. There was one other chair, a club chair, covered in the same burgundy leather. It looked unused and brand-new, too. A leafy tree with yellowing leaves sat in the corner. On the narrow credenza behind his desk was a picture of their parents, pictures of this resort and the one in Aruba. There were no photographs or paintings on the wall. Nor was there a carpet. The wood floor was shiny but dusty. The hurricane shutters on the windows were open to let in the light and a view of the gardens. It looked to Ricky like a lonely room. His gym back home had more character, more life.

He sat down in the burgundy chair and opened the drawers, one at a time. Paper clips, pencils, pens, rubber bands. A day planner with blank pages. The wastebasket looked untouched, the bottom as shiny bright as the sides. *What did my brother do in here? Roxy said he sat around looking important. If the door was closed, who would have seen him? How did he pass his days? Maybe he spent more time in Aruba than he did here.* He made a mental note to ask Roxy.

He wiggled on the chair until he found the hip pocket of his khakis and withdrew the list he'd found in Roxy's office yesterday. It was four pages of handwritten sentences simply titled: Remember When . . .

Mom was at home when the kids got
   home from school.
When nobody owned a purebred dog.
When a quarter was a decent
   allowance, and another quarter a
   huge bonus.

When you'd reach into a muddy
gutter for a penny.
When all your male teachers wore
neckties and the female teachers
had their hair done and wore high
heels.
When it was considered a great
privilege to be taken out to dinner
at a real restaurant with your
parents.
When the worst thing you could do at
school was smoke in the
bathrooms, flunk a test, or chew
gum.
When a Chevy was everyone's dream
car . . . to cruise, to peel out, lay
rubber, or watch the submarine
races, and people went steady and
a girl would wear a class ring with
an inch of wrapped yarn so it would
fit her finger.
And no one ever asked where the car
keys were 'cause they were always
in the car, in the ignition, and the
doors were never locked. And you
got in big trouble if you accidentally
locked the doors at home since no
one ever had a key.

Remember lying on your back on the grass with your friends, and saying things like, "That cloud looks like . . ."

Remember jumping waves at the ocean for hours in that cold water. And playing baseball with no adults to help kids with the rules of the game. Back then, baseball was not a psychological group-learning experience—it was a game.

Remember when stuff from the store came without safety caps and hermetic seals 'cause no one had yet tried to poison a perfect stranger.

And with all our progress . . . don't you just wish, just once, you could slip back in time and savor the slower pace . . . and share it with the children of today . . .

Remember when being sent to the principal's office was nothing compared to the fate that awaited a misbehaving student at home.

Basically, we were in fear of our lives, but it wasn't because of drive-by shootings, drugs, gangs, etc. . . .

Our parents and grandparents were a
    much bigger threat! But we all
    survived because their love was
    greater than the threat.
Go back with me for a minute . . .
Before the internet or the Mac.
Before semiautomatics and crack.
Before SEGA or Super Nintendo . . .
    Way back . . .
I'm talkin' about hide-and-seek at
    dusk.
Red light, green light.
Kick the can.
Playing kickball and dodge ball until
    the streetlight came on.
Mother, May I?
Red Rover.
Hula hoops.
Roller skating to music.
Running through the sprinkler.
Catchin' lightning bugs in a jar.
Christmas morning.
Your first day of school.
Bedtime prayers and good-night
    kisses.
Climbing trees.
Getting ice cream off the ice-cream
    truck.

A million mosquito bites and sticky
fingers.
Jumpin' on the bed.
Pillow fights.
Runnin' till you were out of breath.
Laughing so hard that your stomach
hurt.
Being tired from playing.
Your first crush. Remember that?
Kool-Aid was the drink of summer.
Toting your friends on your
handlebars.
Wearing your new shoes on the first
day of school.
Decisions were made by going,
"eeny-meeny-miney-mo."
Mistakes were corrected by simply
exclaiming, "Do it over."
Race issue meant arguing about who
ran the fastest.
Money issues were handled by
whoever was the banker in
Monopoly.
Catching the fireflies could happily
occupy an entire evening.
It wasn't odd to have three "best"
friends.

Being old meant anybody over
   twenty.
Getting a foot of snow was a dream
   come true.
Spinning around, getting dizzy, and
   falling down was a cause for
   giggles.
The worst embarrassment was being
   picked last for a team.
Water balloons were the ultimate
   weapon.
If you can remember most or all of
   these, then you have LIVED!
I double dog dare ya!

A huge grin on his face, Ricky folded up the papers and returned them to his hip pocket. Then he laughed. Out loud. So hard, he doubled over, and still he kept on laughing.

A moment later he was on his feet and out of the room.

He had to come up with a use for his brother's office. A use that made sense.

Sooner or later something would come to him. It was called moving on.

*   *   *

Ricky stood on the periphery and watched the staff's reaction to Roxy's arrival. She looks different, Ricky thought. Everything about Roxy looked new. A new hair color, a brownish red with gold highlights and a new softer hairstyle that went with her island clothing—a flowered shift with generous slits on each side showing off well-tanned legs. Her straw hat, bag, and sandals were what all the guests seemed to be wearing. He also noticed she wore very little makeup. A new Roxy. He decided it was a good thing.

He noticed that the staff did everything but stand on their heads and salute her. She, in turn, waved and smiled. He wasn't surprised when she called a staff meeting within minutes of settling into her old office.

He caught up with her at the end of the meeting. Her eyes were wary as she walked by his side back to her office. Her stride was purposeful as she moved along, smiling and waving to several guests.

Inside the pleasant office with the door closed, Roxy called the dining room to order coffee. "Sit down, Ricky. Why?" Her eyes were still wary. "Why did you invite

me back here?" For the first time, he noticed a slight tremor to her hands.

"Good business move, Roxy. I know
squat about running a resort. I'm willing to
learn, but that's going to take a long time.
Without proper management, these resorts
can go downhill fast. Even I know that. In
just the few weeks that you were gone,
things went to hell. I understand your re-
luctance about training me, for want of a
better word. A contract makes it a formal
business arrangement, which affords you
certain protections. All kinds of 'built-ins,'
as they call them. I don't think I'm ready to
take on a partner at this stage of the game.
We can keep our options open in that regard; three years is a long way off."

Ricky pointed to the calendar on the bulletin board. "You need to explain that to
me, Roxy. If my calculations are right, at
best you got four, maybe five hours sleep a
night. What kind of life was that? Where
was Philly while you were doing all this?"
he asked, waving his arms at their surroundings.

Roxy made a funny noise in her throat.
The coffee arrived, she poured. "It was my
life. This place, the work, it was all I had.

I'm sorry I didn't thank you for offering me my old job back. I haven't been thinking very clearly of late. Like I said, I started drinking, didn't eat, couldn't sleep. Philly promised . . . he led me to believe . . . I can't change anything. I just want you to know I'm grateful. Don't take that to mean you can walk all over me like your brother did."

"What did Philly promise you? What did he lead you to believe?"

"That his share of the resorts would come to me. I worked like a dog, Ricky. And right now I feel like a tired old dog that's been kicked one too many times." Her voice was so bitter, Ricky flinched. "I built this place, oh, not the stone and mortar, but I did all the rest." She gulped at the hot coffee. He knew she burned her tongue, but she kept on gulping.

"Why didn't you get it in writing? I don't understand any of this."

"He was my husband, for God's sake. We had an . . . arrangement. I honored my end of it, he didn't honor his. It was a business marriage. We never had sex in all the years we were married. If you want my honest opinion, I think Philly was gay but wouldn't come out of the closet. It's only my opinion. I can't tell you how many of our famous female guests threw themselves at him. He didn't bite. Nor was he flattered. I didn't know that about him going in. Look, Philly gave me whatever I wanted. I think I have thirty-two charge cards, tons of costly jewelry, the latest fashions, a high-end car. He never once asked me what I bought. He paid the bills and gave me a salary. He said he was rescinding the prenup. You're right, I should have gotten it in writing. It was a lousy trade-off, Ricky. He used me, and I used him. I played fair, with the exception of the forged policies, and he didn't; that's the bottom line."

She had to be lying. This simply wasn't Philly. A headache started to hammer away behind his eyes.

"In his wildest dreams, I don't think Philly ever thought you would ask me to come back here. He had you under his thumb, and don't deny it, Ricky. Sometimes he was insidious. Here's another one of my private thoughts. I think he willed everything to you thinking you'd fail. You may not know this, but he was extremely jeal-

ous of you. I'll bet you don't even know
that he never once watched one of your
movies. To him, you had it all. Running a
place like this twenty-four/seven is a full-
time job. You've never been known to hun-
ker down and give a hundred percent.
Again, that's my opinion," Roxy said coldly.

Ricky felt like he was strangling on her
words. She had to be lying, she just had to.
"Why? Did he hate me? Did he hate you?
Christ Almighty, we're talking about my
brother here, not the damn Devil."

"That's as good a name as any. Now, tell
me what you want me to do. You're the
boss."

Ricky shook his head to clear his
thoughts. "I guess you know I fired a lot of
your staff."

Roxy shrugged. "No one is indispensa-
ble."

"You are."

Roxy smiled. She was still pretty at forty-
three. He knew her age because he'd seen
a copy of her driver's license at the
lawyer's office. Aside from the dark circles
under her eyes, she could still hold her
own.

"First things first. Your crazy hours are

going to stop. An eight-hour day is suffi-
cient. There might be times when you have
to stretch it to nine or ten, but that's it. I
don't want you turning yourself into a pretzel over this, but my son Max is coming
aboard. He's young, he's savvy, and he's
good-looking. A definite asset in this kind
of business. You're going to learn how to
delegate authority. You're in charge, make
no mistake. If he screws up, you fire him.
I'll make sure he understands the buck
stops with you. Give your assistant more
authority. She seems knowledgeable as
well as nice. On top of that, she adores
you. Loyalty is a wonderful thing.

"Max will be here a week from today. I
want you to get to know him. Tell me where
he'll fit. Max is good with money. Andreadis told me he had a chance to go to
the London School of Economics. He declined. Let's see if he can step into Philly's
shoes. Also, Max oozes charm. You'll get
the picture when you meet him.

"One more thing; I want you with me.
Don't read something into that statement
that isn't there. If we're going to build the
Crown Jewel, we're going to do it together.
That means we're going to be doing a lot

of traveling back and forth. Camellia Island in South Carolina is not around the corner. You with me so far?"

"Yes."

"All right then. I'm going to call Andreadis unless you prefer another attorney."

"Actually, I do prefer another attorney. His name is Noel Randal, and his offices are in Los Angeles."

"That's a start. Call him. Tell him what you want. Have him get in touch with Andreadis. As long as you aren't outrageous or try to throw in something we didn't agree on, you won't have a problem with me. Let's get everything out in the open from the git-go so no misunderstandings happen later on. Whatever came before today belongs in the past, and we aren't going there. This is a new beginning for both of us. You still with me? You burned your tongue, didn't you?"

"Yes, and yes."

"Do you have any questions, Roxy?"

"Not right now. I need to sit here and absorb all of this. I'm trying to figure out what I did to deserve this."

"You honored your agreement. Do you

mind telling me something? Why did you fight me about Philly's burial?"

"I don't know, Ricky. I guess I wanted to win one. It was wrong. When you saw me at his grave that day, I finally got up the courage to tell him off. I know that probably sounds sick to you, but I wasn't in a good place. It was a hellish life. This," she said, waving her arms about, "was my haven. It was the only place I could be me. Ricky, how did it go with your sons?"

"Max seems okay with it, but Tyler doesn't. I don't think we're ever going to be a warm and fuzzy family, but I want to give them a chance at a good life. I'm hoping for some respect along the way. We'll probably spend the rest of our lives trying to prove things to one another, and we'll miss the good stuff in between. It is what it is. You must be proud of Reba."

"I am. She's not very proud of me, though. She's a whole other story, so let's not go there right now. Every parent wants to be proud of their child and to have that child proud of them. Reba and I were never close, and I regret that. She was very upset when Philly died and she was disturbed, angry even, at not being mentioned more

significantly in Philly's will. I'm just guess-
ing here, but I think she was expecting a
huge bequest just as I was expecting to inherit Philip's share of the resorts. She was
exceptionally fond of your brother. It bothered me a little," Roxy said, looking away
to stare at nothing.

"I called her before I left and she promised to come for a visit. I know better than
to hold my breath waiting for that to happen. Reba has two personalities. A good
one and a bad one. Mostly I just saw the
bad one. She and I never had any Kodak
moments. I truly, truly regret that. Among
other things, she is not a forgiving person.
You know what, Ricky, I don't want to talk
about Reba anymore because I get too upset with myself for allowing her to get under my skin.

"So, do you think your son Tyler will have
a change of heart?"

Ricky shrugged. "I have this . . . dream,
for want of a better word, that he's going to
be with Max when Max arrives. I see him
showing up with a two-by-four on his
shoulder, as opposed to a chip. I think he
needs to prove something to himself, and if
it takes him jabbing at me to prove what-

ever it is, I'm willing to suffer the blows. This parenthood stuff is all new to me." He shrugged again before he threw his hands in the air.

"I appreciate the opportunity you're giving me, Ricky," Roxy said. "By the way, I didn't mail you all the plans for the Crown Jewel. I have them right here if you want to take a look."

"Sure. By the way, Ted Lymen came with me. I'd give him the job as head gardener if I were you. He knows his stuff. My housekeeper, Ellie, will be here next week. Use her on your staff. You can depend on both of them. Let's have dinner in the dining room this evening. Seven o'clock. Don't be late. This door better be locked no later than six. It's a business dinner, Roxy."

"Okay, I'll be there."

6

Camellia Island, South Carolina
Six Months Later

The damp heat overwhelmed him the minute he stepped onto the tarmac. It was the one thing he'd learned to hate in the month he'd been in South Carolina. Ricky told himself the wicked humidity was only a few months out of the year, and he could live with it. There was no such thing as perfect weather anywhere. The pluses far outweighed the negatives; it stayed green all year, the winters were incredibly mild, and golfers could be on the links basically all twelve months. The tennis buffs and pros had no problem with the weather either. It was only June now; but it was already hot as hell. During July and August, he was told, you could see the fat literally melt out of your body.

He was waiting for his two sons, who were due to arrive at any minute on a small private jet. He saw the plane in the distance and waited patiently, in a cotton shirt sticking to his sweaty torso.

Even though his gaze was on the plane, his thoughts were thousands of miles away on his more immediate problem. They were running wild. *Time to take care of business,* he thought bitterly. *Something I should have done a long time ago.*

Ricky mopped again at his forehead with the sleeve of his shirt, his gaze following his two strapping, handsome sons as they loped across the tarmac to where he was standing. He felt his chest swell with pride. His boys, that's how he thought of them. He still remembered how shocked he'd been when Tyler had arrived with Max six months ago, with a wicked grin on his face. "I'm willing to give it a whirl for three months, *Pop.*" The *Pop* was a slur, and they both knew it. It didn't matter. What mattered was that Tyler was willing to give him a chance.

There had been no warm, fuzzy moments, no kind, caring words. That was okay, too. Time, he'd thought back then, was on his side. He could be patient. Both boys, according to Roxy, were exceptional. They worked hard and took criticism well. Both, she said, at some point in time, could take over the resorts. He felt proud.

Now, they had come to Camellia Island for a look-see. "We just want to see what you guys are up to," was the way Tyler had put it. It was a turnaround visit, with both of them leaving on the late-afternoon flight.

The handshakes were firm and businesslike. Perhaps one day there would be a hug. If it never happened, that would have to be all right, too.

Tyler looked at his father and offered up his mantra, "Time is money!"

"Well, if it isn't the California Sunshine Boys," Roxy said, pulling the open-air Jeep alongside them. She wore sneakers, pedal pushers, and a tank top. Her hair was pulled back into a bun. You didn't dress to the nines when you hung out at a construction site the better part of the day. Still, she looked good. Both young men whistled. "Hop in."

They peppered her with questions, wanting to know everything about the progress on the Crown Jewel. "I think I'll defer to your . . . to Ricky."

"If things go the way they've been going, we should be up and running in three, maybe four months. Definitely no later than Christmas. Everything that could go wrong has already gone wrong, so we're not expecting any more problems. I think we have a pretty good handle on everything if the weather holds. Now, if a hurricane comes along, it could screw everything up. Those damn things are vicious as hell.

"They're working on the drywall in the rooms now. Everything's been plumbed and wired. The tennis courts are done. They'll continue to work on the golf course right up until the day we open. The pools are done except for the surface tile on the deck area. Everything we ordered is in and stored."

"You sure that scrip thing is going to work?" Max asked.

"If it's the only game in town, it has to work," Roxy said. "No money on the island. You just use the scrip you buy when you check in at the resort to make purchases at the shops, or you charge them. By the way, how was your flight?" Roxy wished she could tell them how nervous Ricky had been before they'd left for the airport. Maybe someday she'd be able to. She couldn't step over the invisible line Ricky had drawn between himself and his sons. It was that simple.

"Good flight. No problems," Tyler said, then switched back to the subject of the resort asking, "No cars?"

"Again, it's the only game in town. You can go anywhere you need to go in a golf cart. No pollution, no engines revving up, no accidents. No gas pumps, just good, old-fashioned, clean, fresh air," Ricky said. "People are going to be paying top dollar for the privacy and solitude we are guaranteeing. The press can't get here either, and that's a *really* good thing. The only access to the island is our own ferry and helicopter, and of course we're going to have the helipad. It's almost finished. If our guests want to go to Hilton Head, Charleston, or the new film studio, we'll take them."

A frown appeared between Tyler's brows. "You're pretty cut off here. What if . . ."

"We have all of the 'what-ifs' covered, boys. We have fifty suites and three villas. That's it. Small but exclusive. We have our own security force, our own medical people. We managed to snare a five-star chef. I've got two of the most famous actresses in Hollywood willing to make some commercials for the resort in return for one free stay a year for five years. I'll be making a few commercials myself. Roxy is working on the golf and tennis pros. It's a green light all the way. We've been fielding phone calls right and left from people all around the world. Like I said, Roxy has it covered. We're on a roll, guys."

"For our equestrian guests, we decided to include a stable and some bridle paths," Roxy added. "Your . . . Ricky likes to ride. And, I've been saving the best part till last. Are you ready?"

"Yeah," Tyler and Max said in unison.

"We're building, well, it's almost done, a miniclinic. Very high-tech. State-of-the-art. You know, for people who want to come here to get, say, a face-lift or a major overhaul. We'll have a top-notch staff. I'm hoping my daughter Reba will eventually head it up. We're talking pricey and private here.

I told Donna to leak the word, and calls have been coming in so fast I now have a separate book just to log them in. This might surprise you, but the guys are out-numbering the women two to one. What do you think?" Roxy asked. She looked in the rearview mirror to see the expressions on the boys' faces. They nodded approv-ingly.

"I thought Reba's specialty was going to be children's reconstructive surgery," Max said.

"That's true, but 'eventually' is a long time from now. I called ahead, and the ferry is waiting. We just leave the Jeep here and go across. Take a look, our own private is-land," Roxy said, cutting the engine.

Later, over a chuck-wagon-style lunch for the workers, Tyler looked at his brother, concern showing on his face. "Why do you suppose he hasn't said anything? He looks worried as hell. Roxy seems okay, but . . ."

"It's hard for me to believe all this can come together in four short months." Max pointed to the piles of brick and wood, the different trucks, the heavy machinery, and the enormous heaps of sandy soil that were everywhere. "Maybe he thinks it's none of our business. If you recall, we were the ones who drew the original line in the sand. He hasn't crossed it. It wouldn't hurt you to meet him halfway, Tyler." He yanked at his baseball cap, pulling it down farther to shade his eyes from the blazing sun.

Tyler ignored his half brother's words as he stared at Ricky and Roxy, who were deep in conversation, a set of blueprints spread out on a rough table made from bricks and two-by-fours. "Maybe he doesn't know. I suppose it's a stretch to think that since we know, and we aren't movie types. I wonder why he didn't try to squelch it. It can't be good."

"Sometimes silence is golden. The more you say, the more the ghouls have to feed on. Our old man didn't get where he is by being stupid. My grandparents aren't going to like being fodder for some tabloid. They're decent, kind, retired people who enjoy their privacy. They don't understand shit like this. My mother now, she's gonna love it! Let's agree now that we don't talk, and we don't grant any interviews," Max said.

Tyler nodded. "You know what really gets me? Ricky's film studio bought the rights to the book, and the damn thing hasn't even been written. That sleaze Dicky Tee is going to pen it. Ted said it was payback time for Ricky because he walked away from Hollywood when he was top box office. The studio lost *millions.* Ted also said they're going to do the filming here at that new studio outside Charleston. Scandal in Hollywood is nothing new. No one is going to be shocked if they read about Ricky's past drug and alcohol problems. The people in Hollywood and the industry thrive on it as long as everyone's name is spelled correctly. I think Ricky is concerned, not for himself, but for us, our families, and for his brother's memory. His brother was pretty special to him. That's my opinion for whatever it's worth.

"You know what else is weird. I took a subscription to *Variety* just so I could stay on top of what's going on. I go online in the morning to check the *L.A. Times,* too."

Max grinned. "Guess I'm just as weird as you are because I do the same thing. You know what we're doing, don't you? We're closing ranks around our father. It's not just a cut-and-dried business relationship anymore. It would be nice if those two got together, wouldn't it?" he said, jerking his head in his father and Roxy's direction.

"How'd that all happen?" Tyler sounded so befuddled, his brother burst out laughing.

"My grandmother told me there's nothing more important than family. In my wild youth, I didn't realize how right she was. I know it now, though. Everyone deserves a second chance, Ty. Even our father."

Tyler dug his boot-clad toes into the sand. "This is going to be one kick-ass resort when it's up and running. Do you think *he'll* move on when it's done and start some other project? For Christ's sake, what is he searching for? Don't tell me he isn't searching either. I've never seen a more haunted man in my life. Do you think it's *us?* Are we supposed to tell him we love him and forgive him, or something?"

"Wait for the book, and you'll get all the juicy details," Max said, his gaze still on his father. "If you want a wild guess off the top of my head, I'd say it has to do with his brother's leaving his estate to him and not Roxy. I'm not sure he trusts Roxy one hundred percent. It's not our business, Ty."

"I say we make it our business, Max."

Max looked at his brother over the top of his sunglasses. He blinked. Had he heard Tyler correctly? "That means we step over the line. I don't know if I'm ready to do that. I like what I'm doing. Hell, I even like our old man, and I'm crazy about Roxy. I don't want to get my ass kicked out. You're getting pretty damn brave all of a sudden."

"If we don't protect *our own,* who else is gonna do it? Maybe Ricky doesn't care. Maybe he thinks the publicity will be good for him. Actors are actors forever. It's in the blood. I read that in *Variety* and those slimy tabloids. You wouldn't believe the shit those sleazeballs print in the name of news. Ninety-nine percent of it isn't true. Ted told me that, too."

"They're done discussing business. They're talking about us now," Max said.

Tyler swatted him before he picked up a handful of sand and threw it at Max.

"I think it's working, Ricky," Roxy said as she eyed his sons. "They've been slowly developing a brotherly relationship these past six months. They actually like each other. You should be pleased."

"I am. Philly and I never had that kind of relationship. He was steady and reliable, and I was wild and reckless. Oil and water. I looked up to him, though. And, I was afraid of him. I was always afraid of him."

"Get over it. He's dead," Roxy said, coldly.

Ricky blinked at how brutal her words sounded. It was time. Things were starting to move too fast.

"Roxy, we're pretty much done here for the day. After we drop the guys off at the airport, let's go to dinner. I say we get dressed up and have a real date. What do you say?"

Roxy looked shocked. "You mean a business date or a boy-girl date?"

He was going to say a business date, but the words came out differently. "A boy-girl date. I promise not to trample on your affections. We deserve a night out."

"All right. Yeah, okay." She gave a low, throaty chuckle that sent shivers up his arms and made the hair on the back of his neck stand on end.

Ricky threw back his head and laughed. In spite of herself, Roxy grinned as she playfully poked him in the arm.

Tyler nudged his brother's arm the way Roxy had nudged his father's arm. "I like what I'm seeing there. Come on, I want to see the helipad and the tennis courts. I think we might seriously need to think about putting a suggestion in the Suggestion Box that goes something like this, 'Let's take shifts working this resort. Three months each.' Sometimes those damn islands get to me."

"Good thinking! The only problem is, we don't have a Suggestion Box. And, this is an island, too. I'll work on it," Max said. "There's always FedEx. For some reason people pay attention when they get overnight mail. Like I said, I'll work on it. You know, Bro, I get spooked every time I look at you. It's like looking in a damn mirror, except, I'm better-looking."

Ricky watched as Tyler threw his arm around his brother's shoulder. He felt a lump the size of a lemon settle in his throat. Some good had come of this after all. It didn't matter that he wasn't the recipient of his sons' affection.

"Do you happen to know if either one of them is seeing anyone seriously?"

"They date, but no, nothing serious. They put in some long, hard days, Ricky. There isn't a whole lot of time left over for serious relationships. Donna is smitten with both of them, that's for sure. I think Tyler might have the edge. They might look like you, but they aren't following in your footsteps. That's probably a good thing," Roxy said, a little sharply.

"Damn right that's a good thing."

To Ricky, Roxy looked as cool and refreshing as a Popsicle in her lime green sundress and matching sandals. With her tan she didn't need makeup. Lipstick, some perfume, and he was seeing the result. He wondered what she thought of how he looked.

"I like a lady who's on time. Hop in. I brushed out the sand earlier. Sorry there aren't any limos around. Your hair is going to get messed up unless I drive slowly. You okay with that?"

"Well, sure, Ricky. We aren't going to a five-star restaurant, are we?"

"I don't think there's one within a thousand miles. Take your pick, Longhorns or Papa Lupini's."

"Beef or pasta. Let's do the pasta. We're at that age where we have to eat sensibly. I had meat yesterday. I try to eat it only once a week."

"I didn't know that," Ricky said, his eyes on the stop-and-go traffic. "You know what I hate about this damn island? There's only one road in and one road out." He was referring to Hilton Head, where they both had rented condos. "What kind of vacation is it when you sit in traffic wherever you go?"

"It's the golf. People will put up with anything to play on a good course. Speaking personally, this would get real old, real quick for me. Are you sure this is a good idea, Ricky?"

"The Italian restaurant part or the fact that we're on a bona fide date?"

Roxy worked at the stray hairs escaping the bun in her hair as traffic started to move. "The date part. You hated my guts and I hated yours and here we are working side by side for six months and now suddenly, we're out on a date. Why?"

"Why not? You have to eat, I have to eat. Why can't we do it together? People usually go out to dinner on a date. That hate thing . . . I never hated you. I guess I never really understood what it was all about. Of course most of the time back then I was either stoned or drunk. It seems like a life-time ago. This might also be a good time to ask you why you told Philly I was stalk-ing you. I wasn't, Roxy. In my mind, I was chasing you the way a guy chases a girl. I liked you and wanted to go out with you. That's how I remember it. Are you sure you want to talk about this, Roxy?"

Roxy fiddled with the gold chain around her neck. She looked like she was a million miles away. Her voice was low, almost hushed when she replied. "That wasn't how I saw it back then. I really thought you were stalking me. No matter where I went, you were there. I changed my phone num-ber three times, and you still managed to get it and call me. You would show up everywhere I went. You started to scare me. I really did believe you were stalking me. Two different perspectives here. The sad part is, Philly believed me and not you." Roxy sighed.

"I try to bury stuff I don't want to talk or deal with, hoping it will go away. Of course it doesn't. It just hangs out there until one day you *pop.* You're worried about the book and the movie, aren't you? They're going to drag everything out. Past, present, Philly, me, your parents, the boys' parents, Reba. God, I hate that sniveling little weasel Dicky Tee. I just hate it when someone makes money off someone else's misery in the guise of entertainment."

"I feel the same way. I'm going back to L.A. next week, Roxy. You can hold the fort, can't you?"

"Of course I can hold the fort. Are you going because of the book and movie, or are you going for . . . other reasons?"

"The whole ball of wax. I have to resolve this thing with Philly in my own mind. It haunts me. I need to understand what drove my brother, what secrets he was hiding, and he was hiding something. His strange marriage to you, his whole attitude concerning me. Did he really hate me or did he care about me? What did he do besides invest my money? Nothing seems to compute. For my own peace of mind, I need to know. Where's his stuff, Roxy? I need to see his stuff. Why are you so reluctant for me to see his things?"

"What stuff are you talking about? Do you mean his clothes and personal belongings?"

"No, his stuff. Did he keep his books, his

records at home? I'm talking about all his/my business records. Where did he keep them? Is it possible he kept an office somewhere we don't know about? I want to find those things. I want to be able to *see* my brother's life. In some respects now, he's someone who passed through my life that I never got to really know. I want to *know* my brother. It's that simple."

"Ricky, about fifteen years ago Philip told me his quarters were off-limits to me. I didn't know it at the time, but that's when he must have found out I changed the beneficiary on the insurance policies. The first I heard of it was at the reading of the will. I swear to you, Ricky, I never knew he knew what I had done. Philly had his lawyer, Andreadis, send me a letter at the time, do you believe that, telling me not even to think about entering that room. The really weird thing is I wasn't the least bit curious and I don't know why. I think I started to get a little scared of Philly right around that time. I had all kinds of nightmares about what might be hidden in that room. I never even gave a thought to the fact that he had found out about the insurance policies. He had a Medeco lock put on his office door, and he had the only key. He not only changed the lock, he changed the damn door. It's solid teak. At one time Philip had a bunch of different safe-deposit boxes. I don't know where the keys are, and my name wasn't on them.

"Philly didn't trust anyone. He had good reason not to trust me, but I don't think he trusted even his lawyer. He was very secretive, Ricky. I'm not telling you something you don't already know. I can give you the key to the house, and you can do whatever you want. The will's been through probate, so I guess you can break down the door to his office if you want. He also had a post office box. Don't ask me why."

"Why did you do it, Roxy? Why did you change the name of the beneficiary on those insurance policies?"

"Why? Because even though he provided for me and Reba, I was afraid that it was all going to end when he died. I didn't expect him to die so young. I used to have nightmares of being old and penniless, even a bag lady. I think that's every woman's secret nightmare. It was a stupid thing I did, and I deserved to get caught. Everything I did in regard to your brother was stupid. But he cheated me, too. I didn't know about his . . . *problem*. Philly wasn't interested in sex. As far as I know there wasn't a thing in this world that could turn your brother on. I learned that the first week of our marriage. Finally, I just accepted it. If you ever find out all the things you want to know about your brother, I'd like to know what his problem was. Things like that take a psychological toll on a gal.

"Ricky, if all this comes out in that exposé book, it could hurt Reba. She's going to be an excellent surgeon, and medical schools and hospitals care about people's reputations. That weasel, Dicky Tee, can spin and spin, and we won't recognize the story in the end. You have to consider your sons and their families, too. It will turn into a circus."

"Philly was an expert at covering up and paying off. My thinking at the moment is, take the bull by the horns and beat them to the punch."

"Ricky, are you sure you want to do that? That slimeball, Dicky Tee, has a penchant for writing libelous articles and taking the hit later. People read his garbage and believe it. Be sure before you do something you might regret. Ricky, turn off here," Roxy said, pointing to the restaurant. "Not many people here tonight. Maybe we won't have to stand in line."

"If not, it's going to be a first. Maybe all the Memorial Day visitors are gone. The new batch of tourists hasn't arrived yet. Wait till school lets out."

Roxy groaned as she stepped out of the Jeep.

It was a small family restaurant with red-checkered tablecloths and comfortable seating. The floor was black-and-white tile and as spotless as the aprons on the waiters and waitresses. Tantalizing aromas filled the room. Somewhere in the back, probably in the kitchen, Frank Sinatra was warbling.

A young girl, probably a granddaughter of the owners, placed menus and a basket of crunchy bread on the table. She had plump cheeks, sparkling eyes, and a ready smile. No alcohol was served on the premises. Sweet tea, lemonade, and cold soda were the choices.

"Sweet tea," Roxy said.

"Make that two," Ricky said.

Roxy tore a chunk off the loaf of bread

from the basket and spread a thin layer of butter on it. "You should have taken care of everything before you came here, Ricky. Why didn't you?"

"I wasn't ready. I'm not ready now, either, but I know I have to do it before that slimeball writes his book. If you take away his gusto, what does he have left? Not much. It will all be old hat by the time he gets his book out. I suppose I could be wrong. I'm just doing what I think Philly *wouldn't* do."

Roxy looked at her dinner companion over the rim of her glass. "That's your first mistake. You aren't Philly. Do what Ricky would do. If you make a mistake, it will be your mistake, not Philly's. Do you understand what I'm saying here?"

"Yes, I do understand, and I also understand that you still hate him. In addition, you weren't listening. I said what Philly *wouldn't* do, not what he *would* do."

Roxy looked everywhere but at Ricky. Her voice was almost a whisper when she said, "Okay, I stand corrected. There was a time back there in the beginning when I thought I loved him. When I found out . . . it was just to be a business marriage, I asked for a divorce. He said no. He meant no, too. He made me nervous. I had Reba to think about. I was young, and makeup artists don't make all that much money. I stayed. It was a mistake, but it was my choice. Like I said, I was stupid. You'd better be prepared for whatever it is you *think* you might find if you dig beneath the surface of your brother's life. Let's not talk about this anymore."

"Okay. What do you want to talk about? I'm sick of talking about fabrics, tile, grass seed, and face-lifts. When was the last time you had sex?"

Roxy choked on a mouthful of lettuce. When she finally managed to clear her throat, she said, "I don't think that's any of your business."

"Your face is pink. If you tell me, I'll tell you."

"You obviously have me confused with someone you think cares about when you had sex last. I don't care. It's none of my business. My sex life is none of your business either." She chomped down on a slice of cucumber, her face still pink.

"You're rattled. I finally got a rise out of you. I'll be damned," Ricky gloated.

Roxy speared a wedge of tomato with her fork, but she didn't say anything.

"Do you remember how . . . ?"

Roxy leaned across the table. The devil danced in her eyes. "Honey, I could make your head explode with bells and whistles. I could single-handedly blow your socks off, one at a time. I could reduce you to a mass of quivering pulp that would require a week for you to recuperate. If I wanted to. What do you have going for you?" she asked sweetly.

His neck grew fiery hot. He didn't trust himself to speak because his tongue felt scorched. He reached for his tea and fished out an ice cube, which he popped into his mouth.

"Well?"

He noticed, to his discomfort, the devil was still dancing in her eyes. She was expecting a stunning answer. He worked his tongue around inside his mouth before he gave it to her. "I can double that!" he said, his voice croaking with emotion. Or was it from fear and trepidation?

Roxy made a clucking sound with her tongue before she spoke. "How do I know you can deliver?" Curiosity was added to the sweetness in her voice.

Ricky almost choked on the ice cube. He had to come up with another scintillating comeback. Maybe it didn't have to be verbal. He wiggled his eyebrows and grinned. He felt weak in the knees.

Their dinners arrived. They ate in silence, each looking up occasionally as they tried to judge if the other was serious.

They left the restaurant at 9:30. They arrived at their respective condos at 10:10.

They were in bed at 10:25.

Together.

At 6:15 the following morning, Ricky Lam's socks were on the balcony. There were also a bell and a whistle on the glass top table, thanks to Roxy's nocturnal wanderings.

The mating couple rolled over, looked at one another as they groaned simultaneously.

"Where in the name of all that's holy did you learn to do *that*?" Ricky gasped.

"Just never you mind. Did I win or did I win?" Roxy crowed triumphantly.

"Damn straight you won. We aren't dead, are we?"

Roxy lifted the covers. "Hmmm, you are. I'm not!"

He reached for her.

What seemed like a long time later, Ricky opened one eye, his hand reaching out to the other side of the bed. All he felt was emptiness. Where was Roxy? He almost called her name when he heard low murmurings coming from the living room. Who would Roxy be talking to at this hour of the morning? He strained to hear the conversation and finally got up, crossed the room, and listened at the door. Roxy was on the phone, her back to him. A chill washed down his spine. Even at this distance, she looked tense, like she was doing something on the sneak. He thought he heard her say, "He's going back to Los Angeles to my house to break down the door. I knew I should have taken an ax to it myself."

Ricky shook his head to clear the sleep away. Was last night a dream? What the hell was Roxy talking about? More to the point, who was she talking to? All he had to do was walk out to the room and ask. Just like that. Instead, he headed for the shower, his head buzzing. He would have staked his life on the fact that Roxy was on the level with him and that bygones were bygones. Now, he had something else to worry about.

7

Heads turned when the two tall, virile brothers walked through the Miami airport to make their connecting flight. Both were oblivious to the admiring glances and out-right overtures, their minds on other things. It was easy to see the resemblance be-tween the two. It could have been the dark-colored eyes, the same bedroom eyes of their father. Both had sandy hair, regulation cut on their father's insistence, winning smiles, and a devil-may-care atti-tude that was obvious. The easy cama-raderie between them as well as the fact that both were dressed in khakis and open-necked polos enhanced the resem-blance. It was Max who yanked his brother's arm to lead him into a restaurant where weary travelers were bellied up to the bar. He elbowed his way closer, held up his hand to a cute waitress in cutoff shorts and a tight spandex tee shirt. "Two Buds!" He winked as he handed over a twenty-dollar bill, and said, "Keep the change." The waitress grinned and winked back.

"What?" Tyler grumbled. "You aren't going to say something that's going to make me regret coming on board at the eleventh hour, are you, Max? I see it in your eyes, feel it in my gut. You're up to no good, Bro."

"What? What? What? You sound like a parrot. I think we should cancel our flight to the islands, hop a plane for L.A., and go out to the old man's house to wait for him. Hell, you know there's no time like the present to do things. It's that old, 'time is money' saying he drummed into our heads. I have this really weird feeling our father is going to get his ass in a sling if someone isn't watching over him. I know the code to the gate *and* the code to the alarm system." Max took a long gulp from the Bud bottle, his eyes following the waitress in the tight, spandex tee shirt.

Tyler upended his Bud. "And we're doing this because . . . Oh, I get it. So all *three* of us can get our asses in a sling. Is this off the top of your head, or have you been thinking about it? The only thing that might possibly bother me is if something suddenly happened to that bountiful inheritance or the trust funds old Ricky set up for us. Are you thinking his reputation is going to be destroyed? I didn't know you cared, Max. I never thought I would say this but I'm getting used to this *good life.*"

Max gulped at the frosty beer. "There is that possibility. Strength in numbers, that kind of thing. Yeah, it is off the top of my head. Those are usually my best thoughts. Hey, it can't hurt. Look, the resorts are in good hands. A few days with us away isn't going to make a bit of difference. Don't forget, we're bosses, not employees. What do you say, Ty?"

"What if he doesn't want our help? What if he kicks our respective asses off his property? There's a whole bunch of what-ifs here, Max."

"Then we go home. Nothing lost, nothing gained. He's been pretty damn good to us. By the same token, we've been pretty damn good to him, too. I never wanted to admit it, but the guy grows on you," Max admitted.

"Yeah, he does. Grow on you, I mean. Okay, let's do it! We need to make some calls to square things away. You take care of the calls, Bro, and I'll change our tickets." Tyler took off, his duffel slapping against his back.

A young woman with a deep tan and sun-bleached hair whistled approvingly. Max watched as his brother looked over his shoulder and waved enthusiastically. He burst out laughing until the young woman zeroed in on him, and said, "Oooh, I *love* twins." He made a beeline for the bank of phones.

Two hours later after landing at LAX in the wee hours, Max punched in the code to his father's security gate. They sailed up the long winding road to the mansion.

Tyler climbed out of the car and looked at his brother. "Okay, smart-ass, you said you had the code to the gate, the code to the alarm system, but do you have a key to the house? I'd say that's paramount to this little caper."

Max slapped at his forehead. "Son of a bitch! No, do you?"

"Hey, I'm just along for the ride." Tyler grinned. "I guess we can sleep on the lounge chairs or in the cabana until Pop gets here."

"Pop?"

"Yeah, Pop. Yeah, that's how I think of him these days. I stopped thinking of him as Ricky a long time ago. I never call him Pop out loud, though. How about you?" Tyler asked.

"I wanted to think of him as Dad because I never had one. I can't say the word, though. Pop's good. I think I might be able to get used to that." He poked his brother's arm to show that once in a while he came up with a good one.

"Let's pretend we're as smart as we know we are. Where would you hide the key if you were him? I think I'd probably hide it in one of the cabanas," Tyler said.

"No. Too many people use the cabanas. I'm thinking more like under a flowerpot, over the door, taped under a windowsill, maybe under a mat. Maybe in one of those magnetic boxes that hooks on to something. I have a car key under one of my rear fenders. Then again, maybe that's too obvious. Hell, I don't know," Max grumbled.

Three hours later they found the key taped to the drain in the deep end of the pool. Max surfaced, the key clamped between his teeth. He shook his head wildly to get the water off his face and out of his eyes. "To the victor go the spoils!" he shouted gleefully.

"What spoils?"

"Pop's duds. I say we get cleaned up and grab a nap after you cook something for us. Then we head for town and visit some of Pop's old haunts. We can hatch a plan while we're eating. You did say you knew how to cook, right?" Max said hopefully. "I'm starved. All we had on the plane were pretzels."

"Yeah, eggs and toast. Is this another one of those off-the-top-of-your-head ideas? The house has been closed up for a long time. I don't think there are any eggs or anything else. Maybe there's something in the freezer or canned food in the cupboard. If all that fails, we *could* go to a restaurant."

"Should we call Roxy?" Max asked as he fitted the key from the bottom of the pool into the lock. He quickly punched in the code to disarm the alarm system. He immediately went to the huge Sub-Zero refrigerator. It was loaded with juice, water, soft drinks, and ice tea. The side-by-side freezer held enough frozen food for an army. It was all rock solid but neatly labeled. He shook his head.

"Nah. I think we can handle this. Why tip her off? She might call Pop. Hey, look, here's some canned soup, some tuna, and canned spaghetti. We aren't going to starve, that's for sure. Why do you think we should call Roxy?" Tyler asked.

"Maybe she can point us in the right direction, tell us where Ricky goes in this town to see and be seen . . . if, in fact, he really still does that kind of thing. Our father isn't exactly a party animal these days. I'm thinking before we came into the picture, he wasn't doing that bar-hopping scene. Special events, premieres, that kind of thing. Think about it, Ty, he's *old* now."

"Jesus, you better not let him hear you say that. You know those Hollywood leading men. The word *old* is like a dirty word to them."

Max looked at his watch. "If we aren't

going to call Roxy, then we need to come up with a plan."

"My simple mind tells me we snatch this guy, Dicky Tee, and beat the hell out of him, starting with his fingers so he can never type another word, then go to his teeth so they have to wire his jaw shut," Tyler said. "That's my plan. I know it's a little rough around the edges but with two of us ganging up on him, I'm thinking he'll see things our way. I even know what the jerk looks like because I've seen his picture in the tabloids. Wait till he sees us. You realize, of course, that the movie world doesn't know Ricky has look-alike sons. We're going to blow his jockeys off. He's going to think he has the biggest scoop of the year, Bro.

"If you don't like that scenario, we could snatch him and bring him back here and hold him captive until he agrees to scuttle what he considers to be his future Pulitzer prize. What do you think?"

"It is rough, but right now I can't think of anything better, so let's go with it." Max nodded thoughtfully. "The hottest ticket in town is a place called Whispers. It's Friday night, so I say we go *live*. First, though, we throw out some bait. Whom should we call first?"

"To say what?" Tyler asked.

Max rolled his eyes. "Dicky Tee! I say we call the sleazeball and tell him to go to Whispers because . . . because . . . it will help him with the book all Hollywood knows he's working on. You can disguise your voice, can't you?"

"Me!"

"Yeah, you. This way I can do the talking when he shows up at the hot spot, and you can keep quiet. All you have to do is look threatening."

"Where do you come up with this stuff, Max? All right! All right! I'm thinking that weasel is not in Pop's Rolodex. So how do we find him?

"The phone book, or information, where else? You know, hot tips, that kind of stuff. His number will be there."

Max opened two cans of spaghetti and two cans of tuna, while his brother checked with the information operator. His fist shot in the air when he saw him scribble down a number.

While his brother stirred the spaghetti on the stove, Tyler dialed the number the operator had given him. "Dicky Tee, please. Oh, you're Dicky Tee. Is it true you pay for tips? How much? Well, this is a pretty hot tip. Three hundred at the very least. I want to see the color of your money before I spill my guts. Yeah, I'm legit. I heard you're working on a book about that Ricky Lam. Yeah, well, go to Whispers tonight, and you'll get an eyeful. No, I didn't say earful, I said a real eyeful. I'll find you, don't worry about finding me. Just have the bills ready. What time? Time's money, pal," he said, looking at his brother. Max held up ten fingers. "Ten o'clock."

Sweat rolled down Tyler's face when he hung up the phone. "He even sounds like a weasel. I haven't eaten canned spaghetti since I was ten years old. Couldn't you doctor up the tuna with something?"

Max looked pained. "You were supposed to do the cooking. All I know how to do is open the cans. I don't want to learn either, so eat it and shut up. Ten o'clock, huh?"

"Yep. We should be able to take care of business in two hours and be back here a little after midnight if everything goes according to plan. Pop's going to be on the red-eye, so he'll be here when we wake up. I don't have a good feeling about this, Max. Too many things can go wrong in a place like that. The guy himself, the crowds, the bouncers. Cops show up. Think free-for-all! Worst-case scenario, the old man finds out, and our asses are grass. You following me here, Bro?"

"Stop raining on my parade, Tyler. We can ace this and do Pop a big favor and he will never need to know. We'll be the Golden Boys."

"Okay, Bro, let's hit the sack. When we get up, we'll need to find some hot threads for tonight. Our father is a fashion plate, so his sons need to look just as good. We're all the same size, which is good for us. We'll be stylin', Bro."

"Jesus, Pop must own stock in Armani," Tyler said at eight o'clock as he perused his father's wardrobe. Trust me when I tell you, these ain't off the rack. These are *custom.*"

Forty minutes later they stood before a long pier glass and looked at each other. "We look just like him," Max said, his expression full of awe.

"It's damn spooky," Tyler said, his voice sounding jittery. "More so because there are two of us. What do you think that slimeball is going to do?"

"I don't have a clue, Bro. We're winging this. You know what I'm thinking? I'm thinking there are going to be other tabloid reporters lurking around at the club. I think I read somewhere that they stalk those young actresses and actors, hoping for some low-down dirt. Those tabloids actually assign their people to specific actors and follow them night and day. All they need is a few good exclusive shots, and they can retire."

"You read that, huh? If you tell me you read the *Enquirer,* and you have an inquiring mind, I'm going to belt you."

"Sometimes guests leave those things lying around. I read the headlines. Okay, let's get this show on the road. You can drive, Bro. Hey, how are you fixed for money?"

"I have a couple of hundred. How about you?"

"I think I have four hundred. We might have to grease a few palms to get into that place. Pink is definitely your color, Bro,"

Max said, pointing to the shirt Tyler was wearing. He fingered his own pale yellow one.

"We look good enough to make the cover of *People*." Tyler picked an invisible thread from his brother's sleeve. "Remember, we stick together."

It was like any other noisy, crowded club in the country. Designated as the hottest club in town, Whispers was favored by the in crowd on a nightly basis. It was a place to be seen, not necessarily heard, with the loud music, the patrons shouting to each other above the roar of the music, while colored lasers highlighted the gyrating couples on the dance floor.

The line behind the rope was long with disgruntled young people waiting to get into the club or just waiting to catch a glimpse of their current idol so they could jabber on the phone for hours discussing who was wearing what, who was with whom.

Tyler and Max walked straight to the front of the line. They ignored cries of, "Hey, look, there's Ricky Lam! Does he have a twin? Hey, Ricky!"

The doorman/bouncer, who resembled a human Godzilla, stared at Tyler and Max, his eyebrows shooting up to his hairline. He debated for a minute, trying to decide if he should open the door or not. It was the double likeness that confused him. The hundred-dollar bill Max slipped into his hand convinced him to open the door. "Nice to see you, Mr. Lam. The owners will be pleased to see you, too. I didn't know you had a twin," he said out of the corner of his mouth.

"Not many people do. He spends all his time *behind* the camera," Max said.

The young girls behind the long, braided rope started to chant, "Ricky! Ricky! Ricky!"

Max shouted in his brother's ear, but the words were lost. "Hey, Bro, we passed inspection. We play it cool now. Keep your eyes peeled for that worm."

The floor shook, the music rocked, the lights flashed, as the patrons danced, screamed, and flocked to the bar. Laughter rang almost as loud as the music.

Tyler headed for the bar, an almost impossible feat. He wondered what his father's shoes were going to look like at midnight. He pulled his brother closer and shouted in his ear. "This is not my thing, Max. It never was. You into this?"

"Nah. I'd rather sweat at a gym than go through this. There isn't an inch of space between people. We must be getting old." He felt a tap on his shoulder, turned to look down at a petite redhead with a face full of freckles. "You aren't Ricky Lam, are you?" she screamed.

Max screamed back. "Who wants to know?"

"Me. Gracie Lick. You want a drink? My brother's tending bar."

"Well, sure." He watched in awe as the pint-size girl whistled between her teeth. Her brother looked up. He was just a taller version of Gracie Lick. "Do people confuse you with Grace Slick?"

"No, they don't," Gracie bellowed.

"What are you drinking?" she asked.

"Corona," Tyler said.

Gracie held up three fingers. "Corona!" she bellowed at the top of her lungs. "So, are you or aren't you Ricky Lam?"

The brothers shook their heads. Tyler reached over the top of the people in front of them for the beer. He handed over a hundred-dollar bill. "Keep the change," Tyler said magnanimously. Gracie Lick's eyes popped.

"He's a big spender," Max screamed again. "What do you do, Gracie Lick?"

Gracie reached for his arm, and shouted, "Follow me."

They followed, getting elbows in their faces and necks, kicked in the shins, and cursed, as they blindly followed their new leader behind a set of swinging doors.

"What is this place?" Tyler asked, looking around.

"It's the pantry off the kitchen. It's where everyone goes to smoke a cigarette. The help, not the customers. At least you can hear yourself talk in here. So, who are you if you aren't Ricky Lam?"

The brothers looked at one another. "What's that badge around your neck?" Max asked.

Gracie turned it over. "It says I'm a bona fide reporter for *The Wag*. It pays the bills," she said defensively. "My brother and I go to college, and we have a fifteen-year-old sister we support. The pay's good. Wally can make three hundred bucks working the bar on a good night. Not that it's any of your business. I like to be up-front when I'm on the attack. I do Hollywood gossip, that kind of thing. This is the third time I'm asking you who you are. I already told you who I am. You sure look like Ricky Lam. You *both* look like Ricky Lam."

Max pretended to be outraged. "You expect us to talk to a tabloid! I don't think so. Our father wouldn't like that one bit!"

"Max, shut up!"

"Wait a minute here, wait just a damn minute. Your father! Ricky Lam isn't married. Not that that makes a difference, but he doesn't have kids! Aha, the other side of the blanket."

Tyler reached for his brother's arm, pretending to drag him away. "When are you going to learn to shut that mouth of yours? Now look what you did!"

He turned to the reporter, and said, "Look, what will it take for you to keep quiet? How does five hundred bucks sound?"

Gracie Lick placed her hands on her hips. "Do you think I'm nuts? A scoop like this is worth . . . well, it's worth a lot. My brother's and my tuition and a down payment on some new wheels. Now that's money."

"Do you take checks, credit cards?" Max asked.

"You really think I'm nuts, don't you? The guy drops out of sight after his brother dies, then you two pop up. Hey, that's a story in my book, not to mention the book all Hollywood is waiting for."

"How about this?" Tyler said, his voice sounding desperate. "Hold your story, and tomorrow we give you the money. We'll match whatever that rag you work for will pay you. It's just a few hours. Nine o'clock tomorrow morning. Is it a deal?"

Gracie Lick pondered the proposal. "Nah. I like seeing my name in the paper. It instills fear in people."

"That's what this is all about? You like putting fear into people and turning their lives upside down? What kind of person are you? How can you invade people's lives in the name of entertainment? You have to be sick to do something like that." Max's voice rang with self-righteous anger.

"Yeah," Tyler said.

Gracie Lick backed up a step. "I'm not like that. I don't write stuff like that. I write, 'he said, she said,' who was with whom when they weren't supposed to be. If I don't do it, someone else will. I have bills and obligations. I'm honest, and I don't like it that you think I'm not. So there!"

"I bet you have all your own teeth and they aren't capped and you probably speak seven languages fluently and you have no body fat. You're a ghoul!" Max said.

"I am not a ghoul! Tell me your story, tell me the truth, and I'll write it and not speculate."

"And we would trust you . . . why?"

"Because I'm giving you my journalistic word, that's why."

Max guffawed.

Gracie Lick took offense at his laughter. "Fine. I'll write my own version."

"And that is . . ."

"How you tried to bribe me to suppress what I'm going to write. Whatever else I can pick up along the way."

Max looked across at Tyler. "What do you think, Bro? Do you think we can trust her?"

"No, I don't," Tyler said.

"Come on. Give her a break. When was

the last time you heard a sob story like the one she gave us?"

"Last week," Tyler said. "Look, Miz Lick, let's do this. My brother and I will talk this over and call you. I think that's fair."

"No, it isn't fair. I have you here right now in front of me. If you didn't want to be found out, why would you come to such a high-visibility place? Seems to me you two are up to something. Did something happen to Ricky Lam? You must be illegitimate sons. Hollywood loves reading about stuff like this. Are you two as wild as he was in his youth? I heard he's been busy running his resorts. Can you confirm this? Come on, give me a break here. How old are you? Dicky Tee is out by the bar. Does your being here have anything to do with him?"

"You sure are nosy," Tyler said, playing the hard-ass. "I don't see you giving either one of us a break. Who the hell eats all these chips?" he asked, looking at the boxes and crates of every kind of chip known to man that lined the walls of the pantry. He broke open a bag.

"She's a reporter, Bro. Take it easy. She's just trying to earn a living."

"They're bar munchies. The customers

have to pay for them. What's it gonna be?" Gracie asked, her freckled nose twitching.

Tyler decided to needle her. "Are you a dwarf?"

"No, I'm not a dwarf. I'm just short compared to you. Are you a giant?"

"Nope. I'm just tall compared to you," Tyler shot back. He finished his beer and set the bottle on top of a box of Frito Lay chips. Max did the same thing.

Both brothers moved to the door leading to the kitchen. "We're going out to party. That's why we came here. We'll hook up later and give you our answer."

"Liar!" Gracie Lick shouted.

Tyler clucked his tongue as he followed his brother out of the room. "Now we party, then we deal with Dicky Tee!" Max bellowed in Tyler's ear.

Tyler watched as Max homed in on a girl gyrating on the floor by herself. To his practiced eye, it looked like her clothes were sprayed on. Implants, he decided. Contacts. The only person in the world who had violet eyes was Elizabeth Taylor. Pricey porcelain. A wannabe.

"Wanna dance?" Gracie asked.

Tyler shrugged as he moved out to the

dance floor, which had suddenly started to clear. The music wasn't as loud. He could actually hear people talking. Voices raised in anger. "Oh, shit!" he said, moving closer to the voices, one of which he recognized as Max's.

"She's my woman, buddy, buzz off."

"How was I supposed to know that, *buddy?* She was out here dancing by herself. I asked her to dance, and she said yes. Take it easy. She's all yours."

"What? She isn't good enough for you? What's that mean, 'she's all yours'?" The man who was yelling was as tall as Max, a little heavier, and his eyes were glassy. He had a long-necked bottle of Budweiser in his hand that he was swinging wildly, the beer sloshing out onto the dance floor.

Gracie Lick took that minute to let loose with a shrill whistle. A moment later, Tyler saw a camera sail through the air. Gracie did an air dance and landed with the camera in her hands. Neat trick.

"It means, I made a mistake asking your lovely friend to dance. I'm sorry, okay? Let's leave it at that and not turn this into a pissing contest."

"Let's *not* leave it at that."

The girl with the sprayed-on clothes started to dance to music only she heard.

Max sized up his adversary. He knew he could take him. He was in shape, and he wasn't half-drunk like the guy threatening him. He felt rather than saw Tyler step forward to stand next to him. He heard the hushed whispers, heard his father's name coming from the crowd. *Where is the damn owner? He should be here to break up whatever is about to happen. Where the hell are the damn bouncers?*

Then he was on the floor, the dancing girl on his back with a chokehold around his neck. He rolled, the way they do in commando school, sending the dancing girl sliding across the slick floor. He was back on his feet in the time it took his heart to beat five times. He was red, he was yellow, then blue in the shifting lights overhead. The music started up as four burly bouncers stomped toward him. It was all the shouting crowd needed as they converged en masse on the middle of the dance floor.

Gracie Lick moved to higher ground with the aid of her brother. She stood on the bar and got the best shots of the night. Her brother spotted Dickey Tee at the end of the bar trying to outdo his sister. He leaned over, grabbed his camera, and tossed it across the room. The weasel leaped off the barstool and scurried across the room to get his camera.

"Cops!"

"Channel Five News!" someone else shouted.

As Tyler and Max were herded into the police car, Gracie Lick waved. "See ya," she trilled.

"C'mon, Gracie, you saw it all. Tell these cops that guy started it. He decked me. Gracie! C'mon."

"I never saw you before in my life! They started it," she said to the police officer.

"We get one phone call," Tyler said.

"And whom do you suggest we call?" Max snapped.

"Gracie Lick." Tyler laughed so hard his sides started to hurt.

Tired and irritable, Ricky let himself into his mansion. He knew immediately that someone had been in the house during his absence. He stared down at the dirty dishes in the sink, the ones Tyler hadn't

washed. Then he looked in the trash com-
pactor and saw the empty food cans. He
reached out to touch a smear on one of the
plates. It was fresh, so that had to mean either someone was still in the house or had
just left. He frowned. The alarm was on,
because he'd turned it off when he walked
into the house. A professional burglar who
knew his way around alarm systems. His
stomach tied itself into a knot. He should
call the police. Long years of episodes with
them made him reject the idea almost immediately.

It wasn't light out yet, but he didn't turn
on any of the lights. This was his house,
and he knew it by heart. If need be, he
could find his way around blindfolded. He
slid out of his Nikes before he reached for
the biggest butcher knife in the knife rack.
He made his way through the house
silently, checking each room as he went
along.

When he reached the second floor and
his own room, he blinked at the mess he
was seeing. Someone obviously liked his
wardrobe. "Anyone here?" he shouted before he turned on the television. "I'm
armed!" he shouted again as he pawed

through his clothes. His two favorite suits were gone. Son of a bitch! He looked in the bathroom and smelled his aftershave and cologne. *Some asshole broke into my house, used my bathroom, then stole my clothes.*

He swiveled around when he heard his name mentioned on the television. A frown rose between his brows as he walked closer to view the screen. The reporter was babbling a mile a minute, and Ricky had a hard time following what was being said. A heartbeat later he saw his two sons being pushed into a police car. He groaned when he heard the newsman say, "They're both Ricky Lam look-alikes but claim their names are John Jones and Joe Smith. Neither man carried ID, so we don't know who they really are at this point."

Ricky sat down on the edge of the bed and watched as still pictures flashed on the screen, courtesy of a photographer named Gracie Lick. He groaned again when he saw both his sons haul off and land some wicked punches. He laughed out loud when he saw a girl who looked like her clothes were sprayed on jump on Max's back.

Brawlers.

His sons were brawlers.

What were they doing at Whispers?

Wearing my clothes?

The phone rang. "I just saw it on the news," Roxy said. "Are they okay? Are you okay?"

Ricky thought she sounded like she cared. "Just this minute I got in and turned on the television. I'm thinking they spent the night in jail. I don't know what the hell they're doing here, and I sure as hell don't know how they got into the house, but they did. I'm going to take a shower and go down to the station to bail them out. I'll call you when I know something. They were wearing my two favorite suits," he said, outrage ringing in his voice.

"Get over it," Roxy said, a chuckle in her voice. "They're brawlers like their old man. Makes sense from where I'm sitting." Ricky could hear her laughing as she hung up.

8

Ricky Lam caused a bit of a stir, especially among the female officers and detectives, when he walked into the police station. He knew that some of the old-timers were recalling his hell-raising days. He stopped in his tracks as memories assailed him. How many times had Philly bailed him out in those early days? Probably somewhere around a hundred times, maybe more. Probably another hundred times Philly had picked him up from some club or party where the owner intervened on his behalf before the cops showed up. Good old perfect Philly.

The desk sergeant, one of the old-timers, looked at Ricky and grinned.

"Strange seeing you on that side of the desk. You here to bail out the boys?"

"Yes. What are the charges?"

"Do you want me to name them all, or do you just want me to hit the highlights?"

Ricky listened to the litany of charges. When the desk sergeant wound down, he said, "Neither one was carrying ID, Ricky. They did have a pocketful of money, though. Personally, I like the one about inciting a riot. The drunk and disorderly wasn't bad either. I'm not so sure about the assault and battery one. You were charged with inciting a riot nine times as I recall. We arrested eighteen people last night. None of them have made bail yet. Are they your boys? Didn't know you had kids."

"Yes. Yes, they are. Did they call a lawyer?"

"No. You need a lawyer for bail. Come on, Ricky, you know how it works."

No, he really didn't know how it worked. Philly had always handled that end of things. But he pretended he did. He walked over to a pay phone and dialed Timothy Andreadis's number. He needed to think about getting his own lawyer. Timothy Andreadis belonged to the past.

Ricky looked around. He'd seen the inside of a lot of different police stations over the years. They all looked the same—sickly yellow or puke green walls—and they all smelled the same—burnt coffee, sweat, and that undefinable smell of anxiety. He'd played a rogue cop once. He shuddered at the memory.

A K-9 cop with his partner walked through the door. His partner was four-legged and wore a bulletproof vest like his two-legged partner. He wore his shield proudly around his neck. Before he'd left California, Ricky had donated thousands of dollars to the K-9s for bulletproof vests.

"Harry Baker," the two-legged cop said to Ricky, holding out his hand. "My partner, Cyrus. Shake hands, Cyrus." The giant shepherd held up his right paw. Ricky shook it and didn't feel silly at all. He'd been busted four different times by drug-sniffing K-9s. In his other life.

"I'd like to personally thank you on behalf of the whole squad for the vests you donated to the K-9s. You in some kind of trouble?"

"Not me personally. My boys hit a bit of a rough patch last night at Whispers. I'm here to bail them out."

"Cyrus aced that one last night. He found so much dope I bought him a T-bone for breakfast. Didn't see your boys, though. Good luck and thanks again." Ricky nodded as the beefy cop walked to the back of the station.

Ricky made his way back to the desk sergeant. "Can I see the boys?"

"Sure. Hey, Joe, take Mr. Lam to lockup. He wants to see his kids. Listen, are you bailing out Gracie and her brother, too?"

"Gracie and her brother?"

"Yeah, Gracie. She gets hauled in here on a regular basis. She's a reporter for one of those rags. Nice kid. This is the first time for the brother, though. He tends bar at Whispers. Seems he smashed a camera belonging to Dicky Tee, and Dicky is pressing charges. You know who Dicky Tee is, right?"

"Yeah, I know that weasel. Sure, add them to the list. Explain it to the lawyer when he gets here."

"Follow me, Mr. Lam," the officer said.

"You back in Hollywood for good or just visiting, Mr. Lam?"

"Just visiting."

"Can't stay away from this place, huh? Can I get your autograph? My girlfriend would love it. We're both fans." He pulled a small tattered notebook out of his breast pocket. Ricky scrawled his signature. "Thanks."

"My pleasure."

Hands jammed in his Dockers, Ricky looked through the bars at his sons. He wanted to laugh, but he managed to keep a straight face. They looked pathetic, but they didn't look remorseful. He eyed his two favorite Armani suits, his expression pained. One of the sleeves on the suit Tyler was wearing was ripped off at the shoulder. He could see Max's hairy leg through the slit in his trousers. The pink and yellow shirts were nothing but strips of fabric. He leaned against the wall, and said, "Do you have any idea how much those suits cost?"

"Kind of," Max said.

"Not really," Tyler said.

"Do you want to tell me what happened, or do you want me to guess? What the hell are you two doing here anyway? How'd you get into the house, for starters? Never mind, tell me later."

"Hey, Mr. Lam, I can tell you everything you want to know," a voice chirped from somewhere behind him.

"Don't believe anything she says. She's one of those scummy tabloid reporters," Tyler and Max said in unison. "She's the reason we're in here."

"That's a lie about me being scummy. I have ethics," the voice chirped again. "The reason I'm in here is those two . . . those two . . . jerks said I was their ringleader. Listen, my brother and I need to get out of here. We have classes today. Are you two cruds going to tell them the truth or not?"

"No!" Both Lam brothers shouted at the same time. "You spell that, n-o! No!"

This time the chirping voice snarled. "Assholes! See if I help you again! Wait till you read the story I'm going to write! Hollywood doesn't like *boxers.* They like *jockeys.* I saw yours! Green! No one wears *green* underwear."

"You're wearing my underwear, too?" Ricky hissed.

"And your shoes!" the faceless voice

shrilled. "One of them is barefoot! What do you think of that? I'm writing all that down!"

"Shut up, Gracie! Why can't you be quiet like your brother?" Tyler said, pressing his face against the bars so his voice could be heard down the hallway.

"Don't tell me to shut up, you poor ex-cuse for a movie star's son. I'm hungry! Don't they feed you in here? This is police brutality! I'm going to write about this!"

"Shut up, Gracie. No one cares! I'm per-sonally going to strangle you when we get out of here!" Max bellowed, his voice echoing in Ricky's ears.

"And just what do you think I'll be doing while you're *trying* to strangle me? You two *wusses* don't even know how to fight! I had to help you. Me! I helped you! Did you hear that, Mr. Lam? Did you? Well, did you? He threatened me. I'm going to sue. For big bucks!"

"Let me tell you what you'll be doing, Miss Gracie Lick! You're going to be dy-ing!" Max thundered.

Ricky had had enough. He slammed his hand into the crook of his elbow. "Time-out here!" He walked down the short hallway, to where Gracie Lick was kicking at the bars of her cell. He didn't know if he should laugh or faint. He could see now that she wasn't even five feet tall, and he doubted if she weighed even ninety pounds. She stopped her tirade long enough to look up at him. Ricky held out his hand. "I'm Ricky Lam. I assume you are Gracie Lick."

"Yeah. Yeah, I'm Gracie Lick. This is my brother Wally." She pumped Ricky's hand vigorously. Wally stayed where he was.

"I'd like to personally apologize for the boys' crude behavior. Sometimes they can be *oafs.* I'll see to it that they apologize when we straighten this all out. In addition, my attorney will bail you and your brother out of here. I would also like to invite you and your brother out to my house for breakfast. No one is going to strangle anyone."

"We accept," Gracie said gleefully.

"He said we were *oafs,"* Max said.

"It's a Hollywood word. It means jerks, or in our case, assholes," Tyler said. His voice was so sour-sounding, his brother patted his shoulder sympathetically.

"I'll be back," Ricky said as he made his

way to the door. "Try not to kill each other till we get out of here in one piece."

Two hours later they could have posed for the Keystone Kops as they snapped and snarled at one another, with Gracie Lick's voice the loudest.

Ricky looked at his Porsche with the two bucket seats and, in the *hope* of preventing bloodshed, opted to take Gracie back to Whispers so she could get her car. Tyler, Max, and Gracie's brother piled into a cab.

Gracie stuck her head out the window. "If my car was impounded, your ass is grass!" she shouted, as Ricky blasted forward, her neck snapping backward. "Nice wheels," she said in a normal voice. "I've never been in a Porsche before. So, how come you're being so nice to me? I'll have to pay you back a little at a time for the bail. Don't worry, I always pay my bills. What are you three up to? I know you're up to something. I can *smell* it. I have journalistic instincts. They never fail me. Now, if you give me an *exclusive,* I could make some bucks and pay you back sooner."

Ricky looked over at her. "What's a nice girl like you doing hustling like this?"

"It beats waiting tables. Even though I'm young I don't want to risk getting varicose veins. Wally and I are putting ourselves through college. It's taking us forever. Rent is sky-high here in California. We have a fif-teen-year-old sister we're responsible for. Teenagers require a lot of money, and we have to start thinking about college for her. We have cars and insurance, and we have to eat. We both work, but I'm the one who makes the most. Yes, I'm aggressive, but in this business you have to be."

He didn't want to know, but he asked anyway. "Where are your parents?"

"They're dead," she said flatly.

"I'm sorry," Ricky said.

"No, you're not. That's what people say when they don't know what else to say. You didn't even know them, so how can you be sorry? My dad was driving my mother home from a church bingo game, and while he waited for her, he was drink-ing. The accident was his fault. No car, no insurance. An aunt took us in, and when she got done spending the small life insur-ance policy, she told us to take a hike. Now you can say, 'I'm sorry to hear that.' " She started to cry.

Ricky bit down on his lower lip as he risked a sideways look at her. "There are some tissues in the glove compartment. Sometimes life isn't fair," was all he could think of to say.

"Most of the time it out and out sucks," Gracie hiccuped.

"That, too. Okay, we're here. Do you see your car?" The Porsche slid to the curb.

"It's the Beetle over there," she said, pointing to a beat-up yellow car with rusty bumpers and a dent in the passenger-side door. "Tell me where you live, or do you want me to follow you? Or was that invitation to breakfast just something you said back there at the police station to shut me up?"

"You do talk a lot. Is it a defense mechanism?" Ricky asked curiously.

"Yes." She blew her nose with such gusto her whole body shuddered. "Thanks for the ride. Don't drive fast. My car can't go over forty miles an hour. It's good enough for going around town, and I don't have to worry about someone stealing it. Even when I leave the keys in it, no one takes it."

"Remarkable," Ricky said.

"Yeah, it is. What are you making for breakfast?"

"It's a surprise."

"Oh. That means toast. I was thinking of something a little more substantial. I kind of like the mouthy one named Max," she called over her shoulder on her way to the yellow Beetle. "Remember, don't go over forty."

Five minutes later, a cab rolled to the curb. Ricky watched as his sons stepped from the cab. They looked worse in the bright daylight. They pointed to the rented BMW parked four car lengths behind the Beetle. He waited until Wally settled himself in the Beetle before he pulled away from the curb. Gracie tapped her foggy-sounding horn to show she was following him. In spite of himself, he started to laugh and couldn't stop.

"Wow!" Gracie said when she climbed out of the Beetle. "This is beautiful, Mr. Lam. I can't wait to see the inside of the house. This pool is gorgeous. That cabana is as big as our whole apartment. I can't believe I'm actually here seeing this place. It must be nice to be rich." She sighed.

Ricky watched as Max sidled up next to Gracie. He looked like he was about to say something smart. Obviously, Gracie thought so, too. She turned, and, with one mighty shove, Max went flying into the pool. Tyler skidded to a stop, his eyes registering shock, before she swung around and kicked out. Tyler joined his brother in the deep end of the pool.

"That's for telling those cops I was your ringleader. You don't want to mess with me because I can wipe up the floor with you. That means I can tie you into a pretzel and not even break a sweat. I had to take karate because I'm so small. I have a brown belt."

Her voice sounded so triumphant, Max and Tyler believed her implicitly.

"She's telling you the truth," Wally said, speaking for the first time.

Tyler and Max climbed out of the pool, their eyes wary. They stayed as far away from Gracie as they could. She laughed. "Sometimes, size *doesn't* count." The wicked gleam in her eye was all the boys had to see before they raced into the house.

"Do you mind if I walk through your

house, Mr. Lam? I won't touch anything. My brother can help you make breakfast."

"Sure, make yourself at home," Ricky said.

Gracie moved from room to room until she came to the staircase leading to the second floor. She crept up silently and made her way down the hall in the direction of the voices she could hear. Her face flushed and her ears rang as she listened. Eavesdroppers never heard anything good about themselves. She clenched and unclenched her fists. Hot tears pricked at her eyelids as she bit down on her closed fist, and yet, somehow, a sob escaped. She turned and fled.

Max saw her rounding the corner of the hall that led to the staircase. "Well, shit, Bro, we just blew that one. I think it's safe to say Miss Gracie Lick heard our unflattering résumé of her abilities as well as her character."

Tyler sighed as he pulled on a pair of plaid shorts and a wrinkled tee shirt that said HARD ROCK CAFE. "Okay, let's go apologize. I didn't mean all that stuff we were running our mouths about. I was talking to hear myself because I didn't want to think about facing Pop. Come on, Max, shake it."

"She's a loose cannon," Max grumbled as he slipped his feet into scuffed Birken-stocks.

The table was set in the kitchen, and pots bubbled on the stove. "Wally is making breakfast, or maybe it's brunch. It's food," Ricky said, eyeing his sons, his gaze going from them, then to Gracie, who was sitting at the table with her hands folded.

Sitting *silently*.

"No thank you," Gracie said to her brother, as he was about to ladle the concoction he'd been stirring onto her plate. "I'll wait till you eat, then I think we should leave," she said quietly.

Wally looked at her, seeing something in her eyes the others failed to see. "We can go now, Gracie. I'm not hungry either." He set the pot back on the stove before he moved to his sister's side. "I'm ready if you are."

Gracie stood up and held out her hand. "Thanks for bailing us out. It was nice meeting you, Mr. Lam. Is this the address where I should send the check?" She pointedly ignored Tyler and Max.

Nonplussed, Ricky nodded. He stared at his sons when the door closed behind brother and sister.

"This is just a guess on my part, but I think you have about two minutes to make this come out right. I'd go for it if I were you."

They almost knocked each other out as they tried to get through the open doorway at the same moment. He watched from the window as they caught up with Gracie and Wally near the pool.

"Hey, Gracie, hold up," Max called. Gracie ignored him. Max made the mistake of reaching for her arm and found himself heading back into the water. Gracie stopped long enough to say, "You really are an *oaf.*"

Inside the house, Ricky groaned. No wonder his sons didn't have serious relationships. He walked to the door, heard the Beetle cough and sputter before the engine caught. Gracie slipped it into gear and chugged down the driveway, only to return within minutes to demand that someone open the gates. He turned around to press the remote when he saw his sons race to the back of the car. With the horsepower generated by 360 pounds of body weight they pushed the Beetle to the pool and, with one herculean shove, sent it into the deep end.

"I hate your guts, you rich piece of shit!" Gracie sputtered as she surfaced.

"I'm not real fond of you, either," Max said. "Get out, you're stinking up our pool."

Ricky watched the byplay and knew he was getting old. If this was a mating dance, he wanted no part of it. Young people today confused him.

Wally Lick was pissed. Tyler could see it in his face. Max could see it, too. They both backed up until one of the poolside tables was between them and Wally.

"You aren't worth it. Gracie is right, you're nothing but a rich, walking piece of shit breathing air other people need to live," Wally said venomously as he took his sister by the hand and led her down the driveway. The three Lams watched as Wally lifted up his sister so she could scale the gate. Then he climbed over himself.

"I hope you two are proud of yourselves. Get your asses in here and tell me what's going on. *Now!*" Ricky thundered.

"Don't you want us to go after them and see that they get home okay? We have to pay them for the car." Tyler cringed at the murderous look on his father's face.

"And you have to pay to have said car removed from the pool plus your bail plus my two suits and plus a lot of other things. In the house!" Ricky thundered a second time.

"Talk!" he said.

They jabbered about their plan to confront Dicky Tee, then they apologized. "We thought it would work," Tyler said.

"It's not a bad idea. Go after them. See if you can get them to come back. You get more flies with honey than you do with vinegar. You're old enough to know that. I have an idea I need to think about. Take the Blazer."

Out of his depth, Ricky dialed Roxy's private cell phone. The tenseness in his shoulders eased the moment he heard her voice. Something was happening to him where Roxy was concerned, even though he still wasn't sure about her motives.

"Is everything all right?" she asked.

He told her, then listened to her laughter. "Welcome to fatherhood a little late in the game, Ricky." She went off into another peal of laughter.

"The best part is, I think she has a thing for Max. I think he has one for her, too, he just doesn't know it yet. I think I miss you, Roxy."

"You think?"

"No, I do. Miss you that is." He waited to see what she would say. His heart almost leaped out of his chest when she said, "I keep looking around expecting to see you, but you aren't here. I guess that means I miss you, too."

Yesss! Ricky's fist shot in the air. "Uh-oh, I hear the Blazer. They must be back. I'll call you later."

Ricky sipped at his now-cold coffee and waited while the four sorry young people walked into his kitchen. He took his time looking at them individually for a minute, hoping to unnerve them. "Sit down," he said, his voice ringing with authority. "Don't talk until I tell you to talk."

They sat, their lips clamped together.

"It's a given that we will replace your car, Gracie. In fact, if you are amenable, I'll sign over the title of the Blazer to you. My sons, and yes, they are my sons, will reimburse me for all your expenses as well as their own. In addition to that, I'd like to make you and your brother an offer. You can take it or leave it, the decision will be yours. When I relocated to Antigua, I closed up the house and the grounds and paid off the people who worked for me. I can see now that I need someone to take care of things. I'm offering you the caretaker's cottage beyond the pool. It has three bedrooms, three baths, a living and dining room, and a kitchen, of course. You'll be responsible for keeping up the property, seeing that the electronic fence is kept oiled, the lawn cut and trimmed. And the pool needs to be taken care of. You will have the use of the pool and the tennis courts. I'll pay you both a decent wage, so you can give up your jobs and concentrate on your schooling. A school bus stops down the road, so your sister will not be a problem. In return for this, I want you to write a story as soon as possible so that it hits the wires in order to take the wind out of Dicky Tee's sails. I'd like to see the article in the *L.A. Times* as opposed to your paper, Gracie, but I'll take whatever I can get."

Gracie squared her shoulders. "It

sounds like both a bribe and charity at the same time. Why would you do all that for us? You don't even know us." She looked at Max and Tyler, who had the good grace to look away.

"Everyone needs some help along the way. In this case, supply and demand. I was going to call an agency to hire a couple to maintain the house and grounds anyway. I need to get my story out before Dicky Tee gets his book out. I can handle the studio and the movie deal that is pending on my own. I help you, and you help me. It's a win/win situation from where I'm sitting. If you need more of an incentive, think about this. You'll be home with your sister in the evenings. You won't be working all night and sleeping during the day, and you'll have a steady paycheck. You can carry more credits and finally get your degrees. I'll pay you a month in advance."

"I suppose you want our answer right now," Gracie said.

"The sooner the better," Ricky said.

"My brother and I need to talk about it. We make our decisions together. Excuse us."

Outside in the bright sunshine, Gracie

looked up at her brother. "They're watching us, so make it look like we're disagreeing. My God, Wally, this is the answer to all our problems. We can actually live here and not trip over each other. Annie will have the pool and the tennis courts. We can sit out here and study. I won't have to work for that ugly paper, and you can give up smelling like a distillery. Our only expense will be our food. We won't be eating macaroni and cheese three nights a week. And gas. That Blazer looks pretty good to me. What do you think?"

"Okay. We need to find out what the salary is. What about our lease?"

"Our lease will become Mr. Lam's problem. He seems like a nice man, Wally. Unlike his sons." Her voice rang with bitterness. "I hate their rich-ass attitude."

"Okay, let's do it. Can you get the story in the *L.A. Times?* That's what he seems to want."

"A piece of cake. I know three different people who know six different people who can go the distance to get it in there. I can do it, Wally. Annie is going to be so happy. Maybe we can get her into a good Ivy League college. That would be so great!"

"Here they come," Ricky said.

Gracie did the talking. "We decided to take you up on the offer for our sister's sake. We do have a problem, though. We have six months to go on our apartment lease, and we can't afford to break it. You'd have to be responsible for that. We also need to know what the salary is."

"I'm willing to take care of the lease. How does five thousand a month sound for the two of you? If you want to leave the Blazer in my name, I'll continue to pay the insurance. If I sign it over to you, you pay the insurance. There's a phone in the care-taker's cottage. You pay for your own long-distance calls. Water, electric, and heat are included in the deal. I'll throw in a perk. A ten-day vacation yearly at one of our re-sorts for the three of you. You okay with that?"

"We're okay with it. Keep the Blazer in your name," Gracie said.

"Then we have a deal. Now, when do you want to start working on your article?"

"I can start on it this afternoon. I'd like to go home and change my clothes. I need to get a photographer I know to come out here for some professional shots of the three of you. I also need to call the people I know at the *L.A. Times*. We need to quit our jobs, and one of us has to be home when Annie gets in from the library. I can be back here by three o'clock."

"Let's do it!" Ricky stood up, his hand extended. Gracie didn't look at either Max or Tyler as she headed out the door with her brother.

9

Ricky eyeballed his chastised sons with a jaundiced eye. "I have an appointment with my brother's lawyer and have to leave right now. I want this kitchen cleaned up by the time I get back, and while you're at it, clean up my room and my bathroom. Then I want you to sit on your hands and not get into any more trouble until I get back. Do we understand one another?"

Both young men nodded, their eyes miserable.

"Good. Then you will see me when you see me."

Forty-five minutes later, Ricky was sitting in Tim Andreadis's office. He got right to the point the minute the amenities were over.

"Something has come up, Tim, and I need some advice." He told him in short, curt sentences about Dicky Tee, his son's attempts to waylay the tabloid reporter, and of Gracie Lick and his plan. "Look, I don't give a hoot about what that scumbag writes about me because he's done it before. The studio put him up to this to get even with me. Everyone in the know will see through that. What I care about are Tyler's and Max's grandparents, Roxy's daughter Reba, and defiling Philly's memory.

"Roxy finally gave me permission to go through Philly's room at the house. I was wondering if you have a key to the Medeco lock Roxy said Philly had installed on the door. Where's his stuff, Tim? I'd also like to know why Philly had you write Roxy a letter telling her not to try to enter that room. What the hell is in there? What was my brother hiding?"

The lawyer leaned back in his chair and stared at Ricky, an uncertain look on his face. "I don't know, Ricky. I just did what Philip asked me to do. I do not have a key, nor do I know where he kept his personal effects. I assumed it was that room."

"You don't like Roxy, do you, Tim? Did you ever take the time to get to know her?"

Andreadis pursed his lips. Ricky thought he looked like he'd just bitten into a lemon. "No, I really didn't know her. I only know what Philip told me, and, yes, that colored my opinion of her. I also didn't like the way she acted at the reading of the will. She's a gold digger, Ricky. That type never changes. The daughter now, that's something else. Philip was good to her, but he had mixed feelings where she was concerned. Once he said to me, like mother like daughter. Does that answer your question?"

"I like Roxy. A lot. Maybe more than a lot. She told me some really strange things about her marriage to my brother. Did you know they never, ever, slept together? Did you know it was a marriage in name only? Did you know that single-handedly, she ran those two resorts? What that means is she worked like a damn dog while Philly sat around and looked important. I can prove all this, Tim. Philly's life, from what I understand, defies belief. I don't want that tabloid reporter getting downwind of anything that has to do with Philly. Will you please tell me what the hell was going on?"

"Your brother did not confide his secrets, if he had secrets, to me. All I did was handle his business affairs, of which there were many. Even if he had told me things, I'm bound by confidentiality. What I will say to you is, I don't think it's wise for you to get involved with Roxy, which is what I think you're doing.

"Do you want me to file an injunction to try and stop the publication of the book? I can do that, but then you open up another can of worms. Suddenly, everyone will want to know what it is you're hiding that you don't want to come out in a book. I think your idea to beat the man to the punch and do your own story is a good one. Whatever that story may be. Hollywood is very forgiving, as you must know."

Ricky licked at his dry lips. He was right back where he started. He stood up and looked down at the attorney, who was still sitting. "We hadn't been close for years and years, but I miss him," he said simply. When the lawyer didn't respond, Ricky walked to the door. His hand was on the doorknob when the attorney finally spoke.

His voice full of anguish, he said, "Philip was insanely jealous of you. He never said those words, but I could see it. And, yet, he did his best to take care of you the way he thought you should be taken care of."

Ricky turned to look over his shoulder. He didn't say a word or respond to Andreadis's declaration. He closed the door behind him.

In his car with the window rolled down, Ricky cranked the stereo system to the max and peeled out of the parking lot. He wasn't going to think about what the lawyer said. Not now, maybe not ever.

The three men watched her climb out of the Blazer, their expressions full of awe. She was dressed in a trim pumpkin-colored business suit and high heels. Her briefcase was leather, scratched and scarred, but still chic. Her shoulder bag was Chanel. Little did they, or anyone else, know that everything about Gracie Lick was either secondhand or a knockoff. In what little free time she had, she shopped at secondhand stores where the rich and famous recycled their clothes and accessories. Her thick, red hair was piled high on her head, giving her, along with the heels she wore, added height. She adjusted her designer sunglasses, while she waited for a mangy-looking photographer named Jonas to join her. The little group continued to watch as Gracie waved her hands about, evidently telling him what she wanted photographed.

Gracie Lick was lookin' good. And she knew it.

Ricky opened the door and motioned for Gracie to enter with the photographer. She blatantly ignored Max and Tyler. She reeked of professionalism when she made the introductions. The photographer merely grunted.

"Let's head for the study," Ricky said. He hated discord, he really did. He motioned for everyone to take a seat. He winced when Gracie placed a tape recorder in the middle of the coffee table. Once words were spoken, they couldn't be taken back. He nodded to show it was all right for her to turn it on.

Gracie whipped out a pen and flipped back the cover of a steno pad. She posed her first question and waited.

Max and Tyler, while they knew some of

the story of their father's life, listened with rapt attention. At times their expressions went from shock, to disbelief, to horror, to admiration. The man they thought of as Pop was baring his soul, and they didn't want to miss a word.

At eight o'clock, Ricky held up his hand to halt the interview. "Let's call it a day and pick up tomorrow afternoon. You can work with Max and Tyler in the morning or wait until afternoon. I have some things I have to tend to in the morning. Would you like to go to dinner with us, Gracie?"

Gracie looked over at Ricky, her dark eyes unreadable. She shook her head as she packed her recorder and steno pad into the scarred briefcase.

"Come on, Gracie, you have to eat," Max said, hoping to wipe away the day's negative activities and emotions.

Gracie whirled around, her dark gaze on both brothers. "Let's be clear on this, *Mister* Lam, I wouldn't go to a dogfight with you, much less sit at a table. That goes for you, too," she said, jabbing a finger in Tyler's direction. The sound of the lock on the briefcase *snicking* into place was the only thing to be heard in the otherwise quiet room. She jerked her head in the photographer's direction. "Good night, Mr. Lam."

Max's voice was defensive when he said, "She's like a Jekyll and Hyde. One minute she's a whack job, the next minute she's downright ugly, and, following that, she turns into a professional know-it-all."

Ricky stood up, stretched his arms, and worked his neck to loosen the tight muscles in his shoulders. He stared down at his sons. "You hurt her. Women are very unforgiving when you attack their vulnerabilities. I suggest you find a way to set things right with her. I like Miss Gracie Lick. I also like her brother. Right now I like them more than I like you two. Both of you have had it too good, and don't bother to deny it. Neither one of you could go out there and kick and scratch to make ends meet. That's because neither one of you ever had to do that. Gracie and her brother work together as a team, and they take their responsibilities seriously. They have a sister to take care of, and they've been doing it the only way they know how. I admire both Gracie and her brother. You two, I do not admire."

Both brothers looked uncomfortable. "What do you suggest we do?" Max asked quietly. They had just been reduced to a fat zero in their father's eyes with six little words. *You two, I do not admire.*

"Oh, no, you're on your own, and you get no advice from me. Just remember this, for every action there is a reaction. It's all about accountability. Yours. Now, are we going to dinner or not?"

The dream was a bad one. He was standing on the edge of a cliff with a rope around his waist. He looked over his shoulder at Philly. "Are you sure you have the strength to hang on to it?" he shouted to be heard above the wind and the crashing waves down below.

"Don't you trust me, Ricky? Didn't I promise you and Mom that I would always take care of you?"

"Yes, you did promise, Philly. Are you sorry you made that promise? Are you sorry you're so honorable? Tell me the truth, do you hate me?"

"You hit the magic jackpot, Ricky. Yes, yes, and yes."

"Why? You're going to let go of the rope, aren't you?"

"You don't know that, Ricky. Why did you say that?"

"Because I'm afraid of you. I can't see inside you, Philly, the way you can see inside me. We're brothers, and I don't know who you are. I never knew who you were. I'm taking this rope off now. I'm not coming back here till I find out who you are."

"It doesn't work that way, Ricky. You do what I say when I say it. If you don't, I'll let you flounder for all the world to see. Now, put that rope back around your waist."

"No."

"Yes."

"Take your damn rope and stuff it, Philly. I'm not jumping off a cliff because you tell me to do it."

Ricky woke, sweat pouring down his face, his heart pounding in his chest. He could feel his whole body trembling. *What was that all about?*

It wasn't light out yet, but he could hear the early birds chirping outside his window. It was a sound he loved. The beginning of a new day. He rolled over to look at the clock on the nightstand: 5:20. He might as well get up, shower, shave, have some coffee, and head for Roxy's house. He wasn't going to think about the dream he'd just had.

Thirty minutes later he was pouring his first cup of coffee. He looked up to see both his sons standing in the doorway. He wondered if they, too, had had bad dreams. He asked.

"No, we just heard you moving about. Last night you said you were going to your brother's house this morning. We want to go along. Three heads are better than one."

"All right. Wait a minute, what about Gracie?"

"She's not coming till this afternoon. We'll be back by then, won't we? We can always postpone until tomorrow if we find the mother lode you're looking for—your brother's secret files. There are telephones, you know."

"Still defensive?" Ricky said, staring at his son.

Max shuffled his feet. "Yeah, I guess so. Ty and I are going to head on back to the islands tomorrow morning. Unless you need us to stay on."

"I think I can handle it. If we do the photo ops this afternoon, you're good to go. I don't want either one of you holding back. If you have something to say, I want you to say it. Is that understood?"

"How do we know Gracie won't . . . ? Hell, she can paint us any way she wants just to get even with us."

"You *don't.* You're going to have to rely on Gracie's professionalism. She's not who you think she is. I wish you two would get that through your heads."

"I'll drive," Tyler said. He hated seeing the look of disappointment that was on his father's face. It was obvious that Max felt the same way he did.

An hour later, following his father's directions, Tyler drove up a long, horseshoe-shaped driveway. Father and sons piled out of the car.

"I could count on one hand the number of times I've been here. Three altogether, I think," Ricky said.

"Why is that?" Max queried.

"Philly never invited me. Roxy didn't like me. The three times I did come here I was either drunk or stoned. I wanted to fight with Philly over something. Maybe he thought I would taint this hallowed ground. I think we went to two ball games. We managed dinner once or twice a year. It was very stressful. I think we both tried to avoid direct contact with each other."

"There are no security gates like you have. I guess people didn't line up to get his autograph or think he was important enough to follow him around," Max said. Ricky looked at him sharply but didn't say anything.

It was a beautiful house, a large Tudor on a street with equally magnificent houses. The other houses were well tended, the grass clipped, the flower beds weeded, and the shrubbery pruned. Roxy's grounds looked neglected and bedraggled. Ricky knew someone came once a month to do lawn maintenance, but that was it. He wondered if the neighbors complained. Whom would they complain to? Like he cared.

Ricky fitted the key into the lock on the front door. It turned effortlessly. The alarm system blinked, then the red light glowed steady. Roxy hadn't turned it on. What was the point, she said, if she was on the islands?

Ricky looked around the interior of the house, struggling to remember even some small detail. No memories surfaced. It was a house that didn't look lived in. A house decorated, down to the smallest detail, by some professional decorator using his or her own taste. He didn't like Oriental trappings of any kind, and he also detested lacquer. It wasn't a Roxy house or whatever he perceived to be a Roxy house.

It was all about Philly. *Why doesn't that surprise me?* he thought.

"Look," Tyler said, "the fireplace has never been used. The brick is clean and shiny." Ricky thought about the huge cherry logs he burned in his own fireplace in the winter when the weather cooled or when it was a raw, rainy day. He personally loved fireplaces.

They trooped through the house, all the rooms opening into other rooms, the Oriental decorating theme carrying throughout the house.

"This doesn't look to me like it was ever a happy house. It's cold and kind of sterile-looking," Max said. "For sure there were no dogs or cats. What are we looking for?"

"I don't know." Ricky sat down on a brocade sofa that looked like it had never been sat on. He told his sons about his early-morning dream. "I want to know who he was, why he did the things he did. I want to know why he and I never had a brotherly relationship. Roxy doesn't know. Philly's lawyer, if he knows, will take Philly's secrets to the grave with him. There are secrets. I've always known that. I just don't know what those secrets are."

Tyler frowned. "Exactly what kind of relationship did you have with your brother when you were growing up? Was it normal?"

"Was it normal? Probably not. We were never pals. We had to work. I grumbled and complained but he never did. He called me a pest. Philly was a loner, with few if any friends. I always thought he was our parents' favorite. He told me once I was their favorite. He liked to hang out in the kitchen with Mom. He always set the table. I had to clear it. We had separate bedrooms. His was neat and tidy. Mine was a mess. I had tons of junk. I only made my bed when Mom threatened to ground me. Philly's bed was always made. He saved his money, I spent mine. One time I saw him ironing. Mom showed him how. He was meticulous. I was messy, my clothes always wrinkled. Mom hated to iron. I didn't care.

"Philly always cleaned his plate at mealtime, then said how good everything was. I was picky and finicky, preferring junk food. No, we were not close."

"What about your parents?" Max asked.

Ricky shrugged. "I guess they were like everyone else's parents. They didn't put up with any nonsense from us, especially me. They didn't show affection if that's what you're wondering. We were not a warm and fuzzy kind of family. In my teens I was a rebel, always in trouble and it carried through in my career. A couple of times I tried to make it right, but it didn't work. Back then it was all about me. I'm not making excuses here. Do I have regrets? Bushels of them. You can't undo the past. It's gone."

The boys looked at each other but said nothing.

"Okay, let's get to it. We came here to find out about my brother."

"Don't take this the wrong way, Ricky, but I bet if you turned Gracie loose on this end of things, she could find out everything you want to know," Max said.

Ricky headed for the stairs leading to the second floor. "It just might come to that. I won't have a problem asking for her help. Reporters have sources, access to things normal people don't have.

"Roxy said Philly always kept his study locked. They had separate bedrooms. My brother wasn't a warm, fuzzy person in his personal or professional life. Roxy didn't have a key to the study but gave me permission to break down the door. With the three of us, we should be able to do it. Tyler, go out to the car and get the tire iron."

His sons gaped at him. "Are you sure you want to do this?" Max asked.

"No, I don't want to do it. I have a feeling I'm not going to like what I find. But I'm still going to do it. I should have done it the week after he died, but I was in such shock I was lucky I could function at all. This is a Medeco lock, and it takes a special key that Roxy didn't have. Special locks, special keys, tell me Philly was hiding something."

Tyler returned with the tire iron. His expression was doubtful when he looked at the door. "It's solid," he said, thumping on the shiny, teak door. "I guess we should pry off the molding and the frame and go for the hinges. What do you think, Max?"

"Hell, I'm no carpenter. Let's give it a whirl!" He looked at his father. "Did you consider a locksmith?"

"Roxy told me you have to have the Medeco key number or get a duplicate from the person who made the key. She tried to get a copy but was unsuccessful. I'm just going with what she told me."

Two hours later, sweat dripping down their faces, Max undid the hinges and slammed at the door with his shoulder. It caved inward enough so that they could squeeze through the opening. The Medeco lock continued to hold fast.

Disappointment ringing in his voice, Tyler looked at his father. "It's just an office."

"With locked filing cabinets," Max said. "Put some muscle behind that tire iron and open them, Bro."

The master lock on the mahogany filing cabinet popped open with one twist of the tire iron. "That was almost too easy," Tyler said.

Ricky looked around the twelve-by-fifteen-foot office. It was plain. There were no pictures on the walls, the beige draperies were closed. He opened them. Sunlight flooded the room. He looked down at the beige carpet and was surprised to see little tufts of fiber. That only happened when new carpeting was installed. Philly had lived in that house off and on for almost twenty years. Maybe he had redecorated it fairly recently. Maybe he didn't spend much time in the colorless room. It was almost an exact duplicate of the office in Antigua. Goose bumps dotted Ricky's arms.

There was only one chair behind the desk. One chair was meant to discourage visitors. Or, maybe no visitors ever crossed the threshold. He was surprised not to see a computer. There was no fax, no television set, no VCR, and no answering machine. There was a wastebasket with nothing in it. He opened the desk drawers on the left side of the desk, one at a time. One held paper clips and rubber bands. A second held pencils and pens. One held a calculator, a stapler, and a hole-punching gadget. The middle drawer was completely empty.

The drawers on the right side of the desk held plain white paper and plain white envelopes. An unopened roll of stamps was pushed back into the corner.

A day planner with no entries, compliments of a brokerage house, was in the next drawer. The last drawer held a desk calendar and a paperweight. Everything looked new, just the way the office in the islands looked.

"In the movies, when they hide something, they always tape it under the drawer or behind it," Max volunteered.

Ricky upended each drawer. Nothing. He looked disgusted.

"It always works in the movies," Max said lamely.

"Let's each take a drawer in the file cabinet. Like I said, I don't know what we're looking for, but I guess we'll know it when we see it. On the other hand, maybe there's nothing to find."

"Wait!" Tyler said. "Just because there's no answering machine doesn't mean your brother didn't have voice mail. This must be a private number. I'll work on it, and you and Max do the file cabinets. There might be a message on here."

Ricky was incredulous. "After six months?"

"You never know," Tyler said, lifting the receiver and holding it to his ear. "Somebody has to be paying the bill for this phone because it's still connected. If no one cleared the voice mail, there could still be messages. That happens in the movies, too. They must base stuff like that on some kind of fact."

"I'm sure Roxy is paying the bill. She does come back here from time to time. I'm not sure, but I think Reba does, too. Roxy said it didn't pay to disconnect everything, then have it all reconnected each time she or Reba comes here. All right, you work on the voice mail, and Max and I will do the file cabinet. On second thought, let's just pack it all up and take it home with us. I feel like a sneak going through my brother's things like this. You can work the phone end of it from home, can't you, Tyler?"

"I don't see why not. I'm starting to feel like a detective," he mumbled.

"For someone with a secret life, your brother sure had a lot of files," Max said. "Why don't we just take the drawers? It will make it a lot easier. They'll fit in the trunk of the Beemer."

"Good idea. We only have to make one stop at the grocery store. I'm tired of eating out of cans, and I'm tired of eating out. I'll grill us some steaks tonight."

Gracie Lick shifted gears as she steered the Blazer up the steep, winding roads that led to Ricky Lam's house. Suddenly she saw a dark streak flash in front of her. She slammed on the brakes, jolting Jonas, the photographer, forward. She was out of the car a second later, racing to the side of the road. "Oh, no," she wailed. "C'mon, c'mon, I need some help here!" she shouted to the photographer. A second later, she stripped off her secondhand Armani jacket. A second after that, she yanked and pulled at her silk blouse. "Oh, you poor baby! Look, she's so thin, and she looks starved. These must be her pups. Look, that must be the father. Oh, God, how did this happen? Easy, easy, I won't hurt you," Gracie crooned. "C'mere, baby, come on."

The photographer watched as one of Gracie's shoes slid off and rolled into the ditch the father dog was guarding. He looked down to see three sickly-looking pups. He backed up when the male dog showed his teeth.

Fearless, Gracie stretched out her hand, palm down, so both the male and female could get her scent. The female licked her hand. Tears sprang to Gracie's eyes as she picked up the pups, one by one, and wrapped them in her jacket and blouse. She looked down at her skirt and knew it had to come off. "Quick, open the car door. They have to see we're going to take them *all* with us. Move, move!"

The three pups cradled in her arms, Gracie still managed to pat the mother dog on the head. A second later, she was on her feet, the male and female dog right behind her. They looked at her, then at the open door. She tried to shoo them inside. When they didn't move, she climbed in and scooted over on the seat. Both dogs leaped into the back with her. "Shut the door, Jonas, and drive!" she ordered.

"Yes, ma'am," the photographer said, sliding behind the wheel. He ripped up the road going ninety miles an hour. Gracie shouted out the code to the gate. Jonas punched it in, and the gate slid open. He barreled through, his foot heavy on the gas pedal.

"Okay, this is good," Gracie said. "Now, get out and open the door for me."

Max, alerted to the sound of the Blazer's engine, opened the kitchen door. "What the hell . . ."

Gracie ran inside, the dogs trailing behind her. "Some asshole probably dumped these dogs, and they're starved. Call a vet. Make some food. Don't just stand there, dammit, do it! These pups might die. They're cold and they're hungry. Send your brother to the store to get baby stuff! I thought I told you to move! Now!

"Tyler! Ricky! I think you better come out here!"

Tears rolled down Gracie's cheeks. "Why in hell do I always have to do everything? Can't you follow a simple order? Go!"

Ricky looked at the crying girl, at the pups in her arms, at the two strange dogs in the middle of his kitchen. He knew exactly what to do. "Tyler, call a vet. There's a vet clinic about two miles from here. It's on . . . Piedmont, I think. Tell him to come here right away and be sure to say it's an emergency. Max, go to the drugstore and get baby bottles with nipples, the smallest ones you can find. Get some baby cereal. And some newborn baby formula. Burn rubber, son."

Ricky dropped to his knees. He remembered another time, much like this one, when he'd found a stray dog with pups and taken them home. God, how he'd loved that dog, and the dog had loved him. It had hated Philly, though. He reached out to stroke both animals. "I know, you're hungry. We're going to fix you up all right."

"Throw stuff in a pot and boil it. Meat, vegetables, potatoes. You'll have to mash it up. Their stomachs aren't going to be able to handle anything else. I don't know how long they've been on the run. The pups look to be brand-new," Gracie said. "They won't die, will they?"

"Not if I can help it," Ricky said as he ripped the paper off the steaks he'd just bought. He filled a pot with water and did just what Gracie told him to do. Then he ran to the linen closet in the downstairs bathroom. He returned with monogrammed, sky-blue towels that looked to be as big as tablecloths. He had a bunch of matching washcloths under his arm.

"We can't bathe them, they're too little. But we can clean them up and make sure they're warm. I'll put the towels in the clothes dryer for a few minutes so they'll be nice and warm. Be careful now, we'll do it here on the floor so they can see we aren't hurting their offspring. Put them down slowly, Gracie. Wet these cloths with warm water."

"The vet is on the way!" Tyler said happily. "Five dogs! That's just what this place needs. I never had a dog."

When the pups were cleaned up and wrapped into snug little bundles, Gracie looked at her dirty clothing. For the first time since her arrival, she was aware that she was in her underwear wearing one high-heeled shoe. She was glad she was wearing decent underwear even if it was a cheap store brand.

The mother dog padded over to the little mounds, sniffed and stuck her nose inside the blue towel. She lay down next to the pups, her eyes alert and watchful. The male dog sat on his haunches watching everyone.

"I'm surprised you were able to get them in the truck. But it's obvious they trust you."

"I can keep them, can't I? I won't let them ruin your guesthouse. I promise."

"Of course you can keep them," Ricky said.

Max blew into the kitchen like a wild gust of wind. "I got everything!" he said triumphantly. He did his best not to look at Gracie's underwear. Gracie snatched the bag out of his hand. "Now what?"

"We're waiting for the vet," Ricky said. "I'm cooking what was supposed to be our dinner for the dogs. Once the vet checks the dogs and the pups, you and Tyler are going to give them a bath. Gracie and I are going to feed the pups. Believe it or not, I do know how to do that."

"Vet's here!" Tyler said, pressing the button that would open the gates.

He was young, probably somewhere in his midthirties. His name was Adam Sutter. If there was one thing Adam loved above all else, it was a human's devotion to an animal. They all talked at once. If he was surprised that Gracie Lick was in her underwear, he didn't show it. His job was the dogs.

Forty minutes later he pronounced all five dogs on the road to recovery. "You got to those pups just in time. If they can't suck, you'll have to use an eyedropper. I have some in my bag. It's round-the-clock feeding."

"We can handle it," Ricky said.

"You bet," Tyler said.

"Just tell me what to do," Max said.

"I'd like to see this family in a week. I make house calls."

"Gracie, you know your schedule, you set it up. I'll be leaving in a few days, and Max and Tyler are heading out tomorrow."

Gracie stood up. That's when they all noticed her underwear. Adam Sutter smiled approvingly. "How about if I call you when we all calm down around here. To- morrow sometime," Gracie said sweetly.

"You could give me your phone number. I'd like to call to check on the dogs."

"I just moved here and don't know what it is. I *will* call you, though."

"I can stay on," Max said, not liking the way the vet was looking at Gracie.

Gracie correctly interpreted the look.

She looked up at the vet, and said, "I'm a reporter, Dr. Sutter. Maybe when things calm down, we could discuss my doing a feature article on you for all the pet owners in the area."

"I'd like that a lot. Just call me. I'm available most evenings." He was eyeing her, openly now, and it was clear he was liking what he was seeing. Gracie smiled. Adam smiled.

Max scowled.

Adam waved good-bye when Ricky handed him some bills.

Gracie waved, her bosom heaving with gusto.

Max's middle finger shot in the air. Behind Adam's back, of course. Gracie didn't miss it, though. She just looked smug.

"Ah . . . Gracie, I'm sorry about your clothes. I can lend you some shorts and a tee shirt. They'll be big, but they will *cover* you," Ricky said. "Max, take Gracie upstairs and find her some clothes."

Tyler grimaced. "They're going to end up killing each other, you know that, don't you?"

"My money is on Gracie Lick," Ricky said. "Who are you betting on, Tyler?"

"Gracie. I'm no fool. She's got him wrapped. He just doesn't know it yet." He slapped his thigh and doubled over laughing. In spite of himself, Ricky laughed, too.

They listened, grinning from ear to ear as Gracie's and Max's voices carried down the back stairway.

"What, are you blind, Gracie?" Max said heatedly. The guy's a T&A man. I should know, I'm a guy."

"I bet you think I don't know what that means. Well, I do, smart-ass. Just because you're a tits-and-ass man doesn't mean he is. I found him utterly charming. He saved those dogs. What did you do? You went to the *drugstore*. That doesn't count in my book. Anyone can go to the drugstore. You're an *oaf.* Now, if you're done staring at my tits and my ass, I'd like to get dressed."

"Don't flatter yourself, Gracie. I've seen better tits on a sixty-year-old lady. As for your ass, it looks to me like it's *drooping.*"

Gracie balled up her fist and let it fly. Max toppled backward with the force of the blow.

Down below, Tyler looked at his father. "Okay, she either kissed him, or she bopped him good. I think she bopped him."

Ricky grinned as he hauled out the blender. He fished the meat and vegetables out of the pot and dumped them into the blender. His hand secure on the top, he pulsed the contents until he was satisfied with the consistency. He filled two large plates. He looked down at the dogs, who were waiting patiently. "You get it as soon as it cools."

When Max came back downstairs, there was no doubt about what Gracie had done.

"Wow! I am impressed, Max! I bet by tonight that shiner is going to glow in the dark. I can't believe that itty-bitty little girl hit you. You never told me you were a T&A man, Max." Tyler was talking softly so that his voice wouldn't carry up to the second floor, where he knew Gracie Lick stood listening.

"Shut up, Tyler. I was brought up to respect girls and women, and that means you don't hit them even when they slug you. Let's just forget this. Tell me what you want me to do."

Ricky set the plates down on the floor.

Both dogs watched him until he gave the signal they could eat. Starved, as he knew they were, they didn't gobble. They licked their plates clean and waited. "More?" He filled their dishes half-full this time. Again, they licked the plates clean.

"They shouldn't give you any trouble with the bath. The tubs in the laundry room are oversize, so you can do both of them. Warm water, not hot. Dry them thoroughly, then wrap them in the towels and let them sleep by the pups. We'll carry the pups into the laundry room, so they can keep their eyes on them. That's important to new mother dogs." Authority rang in Ricky's voice. His sons stared at him, accepting his word as gospel.

Gracie Lick entered the kitchen dressed in shorts that hung below her knees and a yellow tee shirt with the words STAR POWER emblazoned on the front and looked at the three men. "Where's my photographer?"

"Out by the pool, where he's been since you got here. I heard a splash a little while ago," Max volunteered. "I hope you aren't paying him by the hour." Gracie ignored his comments as she trotted into the laundry room to check on the pups.

"It's time to feed these guys. I can do it in here, while you guys bathe the mother and father. I don't want these dogs traumatized, so let's try to make this a lovely experience for them. In other words, screw up with these dogs, and I'll kick your respective asses all the way to the gate."

Ricky watched his sons scurrying about for towels and shampoo. He turned away so he wouldn't laugh out loud. He had things to do. He said so to Gracie.

"That's okay. I can talk to them while I'm feeding the pups. Jonas knows what I want in the way of pictures. I appreciate your letting me keep these dogs, Mr. Lam." Honesty rang in her voice when she said, "I would have found a way to keep them if you had said no. I hate people who abuse animals."

"I knew that."

"On your way out, Mr. Lam, will you ask Jonas to come in with his camera. I'd like a few shots of your sons bathing the dogs. Human interest opposed to a shot of them hanging out in some bar or sitting on a Harley. Everyone identifies with dogs."

"Do you think, Gracie, you could go a little easier on Max? I think he really likes you, but you might be intimidating him. You know, just a little."

Gracie reared back in horror. "Are you suggesting I skew the interview, Mr. Lam? You've got the wrong person if you think that."

"No, no, that's not what I meant. I meant on a personal level. That boy-girl thing."

"There is no boy-girl thing. Max is a . . . *clod.*"

"Is a clod one step up or down from an oaf?" Ricky asked, knowing instinctively that his gut decision to hire Gracie to do the story had been right.

"I heard that," Max said. His eyes flashing angrily, his jaw grim as he glared at Gracie.

"Eavesdroppers never hear anything good about themselves. How does it feel, Mr. Velvet Tongue? Don't bother telling me because I don't want to know. Wash those dogs, they smell from being in that ditch. Be sure to put conditioner on them after you shampoo them."

"Conditioner?" Tyler queried.

"Yes, it makes the hair soft so it doesn't tangle."

Ricky looked at his sons. He shrugged.

Gracie filled the three eyedroppers and placed them on a paper towel. She started to feed one of the pups, the mother dog at her side. "See, I'm just helping you out until you're well enough to nurse them. Go ahead, sniff it, taste it if you want." She smiled when the dog did just what she told her to do.

Max, a bottle of conditioner in his hand, thought Gracie's smile the most beautiful smile he'd ever seen. He was about to say something nice when Gracie jerked her head in the direction of the sink. She raised one bare foot to make her point.

Max turned on the water in the laundry tub.

"Oh, you sweet little thing, you took three whole droppers." She watched as the mother dog dropped to her haunches, her gaze on the pups. She appeared satisfied that nothing was going awry.

"What kind of dogs are these?" Tyler asked.

"I think they have some Lab, maybe some shepherd in them. Does it make a difference?" Gracie asked.

"Are you always this obnoxious?" Max

demanded as he soaped the male dog's head. "What the—"

"Smile for the camera!" Gracie said, picking up the second pup. She brought it to her cheek. He felt soft and warm. She wiggled the eyedropper into his mouth and watched while he struggled to take his nourishment. "Rinse those dogs well. Did you bring down a blow-dryer?"

"Blow-dryer?" Max said incredulously.

"They're big dogs. How do you expect them to dry themselves? Do you want them getting sick? Blow-dryers dry hair. The dogs have hair. I rest my case."

"Listen, you . . . *wannabe journalist,* these are your dogs. My brother and I are helping you. We-are-helping-you! Get it! We-do-not-have-to-do-this. Get it! We-are-being-kind-and-generous-with-our-time. Get it!"

"Kiss my ass, you movie star's son. Ex-movie star. Don't talk to me."

"Why would I want to do a stupid thing like that?" Max blustered.

Gracie laid the second pup down and filled the three droppers for the last pup. "Because you're stupid, that's why. I told you not to talk to me."

"He's flirting with you, Gracie. The oaf thinks this is how you go about it," Tyler said as he lifted the male dog out of the tub. "Isn't that right, Max?" It was clear from Tyler's tone that he knew all about the finer art of flirting.

Gracie Lick's face turned a rich shade of pink. She concentrated on the pup in her arms.

Max didn't deny his brother's statement. Instead, he pulled the plug in the sink and waited for the water to gurgle down the drain. He started to fill the tub back up, checking the water to make sure it wasn't too hot or too cold.

In the war of words, it was Max Lam 1, Gracie Lick 210, maybe 910.

10

Ricky Lam walked into his study, where the file drawers from his brother's office now sat on the floor, beckoning him. His stomach worked itself into a knot just thinking about going through them.

Maybe he should call Roxy. He smiled at the thought. He didn't stop to think about it or the time difference. He dialed the number of her rented condo. He wondered what she was doing. He asked when her voice came on the line.

"I'm baking bread. I bought one of those bread-making machines yesterday. I love the way the house smells when bread is baking. I have stew simmering, and I baked a peach pie. I don't like eating alone, though."

"Do you put lots of soft butter on the bread? Philly and I used to fight over who got the end. Mom called it the heel. She'd cut off each end of the loaf so we wouldn't fight, even though it was hard to slice the rest of the loaf without the ends. She used to make strawberry jelly from those little sweet berries. If I close my eyes, I can picture it and remember the taste. Do you make jelly?"

"No. I buy mine."

"Store-bought is good, too." He didn't mean to ask the question, but the words rolled off his lips. "Do you miss me?" It took her so long to answer, he was about to prompt her. The knot in his stomach started to tighten.

"Yes, I do miss you. What are you doing?"

He told her. "I swear to God, I don't know what to do about Max and Gracie. I must be getting old if I can't relate to that mating dance they're doing. It's a new world out there."

"Yes, it is. They'll work it out. Five dogs, huh? You sure lead an interesting life, Ricky Lam."

"Roxy, I haven't looked in the files yet. What do you *think* is in them?"

"Ricky, I haven't a clue. I don't know, maybe secret offshore accounts. Maybe he was an internet freak of some kind. I guess that isn't it because Philly didn't have a computer, at least that I know of. On the other hand, maybe he was just a person who didn't interact well with others and was a loner. What I do know is he was as screwed up as you and I were at one time. You took responsibility early on. I'm just now getting there. When I allow myself to look back at my life, I cringe at some of the things I did. I'm not sure I even want to know about Philly. Does that answer your question?"

"No, not really. You wouldn't happen to know Philly's password for his private voice mail, would you?"

"No."

"Where did he go? What did he do? Did he spend his time sitting in those empty offices playing with the paper clips? What?"

"I don't know, Ricky. He dressed for business every day, though. Suit, tie, white shirt. Sometimes he would loosen the tie, but he never took it off. He never took off the jacket either. Did you go through his things in his bedroom? I never did. When he died, I just closed the door. I would have locked it if I'd had a key, but I didn't. When are you coming back?"

She sounded like she cared. "Day after tomorrow. I'll call you before I leave. Is your bread done?"

"Five more minutes. I'll make some for you when you get back."

The knot in Ricky's stomach loosened up. "I'm going to hold you to that." Her warm chuckle stayed with him long after he had hung up the phone.

Why was it that misfits always seemed to find one another? Did they wear an invisible sign only noticeable to other misfits? Did they smell different? Did they act different? He shrugged, realizing he would probably never know the answer.

He was on his knees now, ready to paw through his brother's life. He looked up when a shadow crossed the doorway.

"Want some help?" Tyler asked. "I figured if I left the two of them alone, they might come to some kind of agreement with each other."

"Sure," Ricky said.

Tyler sat down on the floor and pulled one of the file drawers closer.

An hour later, Ricky looked up. "This is just brokerage statements, insurance policies, tax returns, deeds, bank statements, canceled checks, and receipts. What's in your drawer?"

Tyler looked over at his father. "You've been brutally honest about your old life. Why didn't you tell Max and me that you guys were adopted?"

"We weren't adopted. Where did you get an idea like that?"

"From this file. It says your brother was adopted. If your brother was adopted, there's a good chance you were too since he was older than you. See for yourself."

Ricky reached for the file. He could feel his fast-beating heart slamming around inside his chest. He read through the file twice before he closed it. "I guess this explains what Philly did behind closed doors. All he needed was a phone and a tape recorder to communicate with the outside world. He must have taped his conversations but I don't know why. I never knew, never suspected Philly was adopted. I always wondered why there were no pictures of my mother when she was pregnant with Philly. I have dozens of her patting her stomach before I was born. There was one in front of the hospital, with Mom holding me and my father handing out cigars. I wonder how he found out that he was adopted. That must have been a terrible blow to Philly. If he knew growing up, he sure never told me. I never knew! What else is in that drawer?"

"All kinds of good stuff. Do you want me to leave so you can go through this alone? I don't mind."

"No, stay. I don't have any secrets. What kind of good stuff?"

"His marriage license. Roxy's name isn't on it. It's someone named Lee Ann Oliver. Here's one with Roxy's name on it. I guess his first wife died."

"Philly was never married before he married Roxy. If he was married, I sure as hell didn't know about it. Let me see that license."

"He had three kids, too. These aren't the originals, but they are copies of three birth certificates. He's listed as the father. The mother is listed as Lee Ann Oliver. There are no divorce papers or death certificates.

Three girls. Melanie is twenty-four, Sara is twenty-two, and Emily is twenty. That means . . . you have three nieces, and Max and I have three cousins. They aren't really blood relatives, though. Does that count? Strange that there aren't any pictures here."

"There must be some kind of mistake," Ricky said, staring at the certificates in his hands. "Why did he keep it all so secret?"

"You said you never really *knew* your brother, that you weren't close. I guess he was a very private person. Are you going to be able to let it go at that?"

"No!" The word exploded from Ricky's mouth like a gunshot. "I need to know everything there is to know about my brother. I don't care if he was adopted or not. He was my brother." He continued to stare at the certificates in his hands as he tried to understand and accept what he was seeing.

"Do you think Philip felt the same way about you?" Tyler asked hesitantly.

"No. But it doesn't matter. What else is in that drawer?"

Tyler pawed through stacks of corre-spondence held together with oversize paper clips. "He was obviously trying to get the adoption records unsealed and wasn't having much luck. From everything you said about him, it's strange that he wouldn't have offered a sizable bribe to get the information he wanted. Money usually works in cases like that. Unless . . ."

"Unless what?"

"Unless one or the other of his parents was someone really influential. In which case the records might have been destroyed. Do you think your parents knew who his biological parents were? Do you have any aunts or uncles they might have talked to? Maybe even neighbors or close friends?"

"I have a ninety-seven-year-old uncle who lives in a nursing home, but he doesn't even know what his own name is. He won't be any help. Philly and I both sent money over the years for his care. I'm sure Philly's lawyer is still doing it because I haven't heard otherwise. As for my parents' neighbors, one family still lives in the old neighborhood. I could call them or go and talk to them. I imagine Philly already did that. It would probably be an exercise in futility to go to Placentia, where we grew up."

"Ricky, why don't you turn the whole thing over to Gracie? She'll know where to look and how to go about it. People respond well to pretty, wholesome girls like Gracie. She can be charming and a bully at the same time. Pay her for her time. I'll bet she'll jump at the chance to help you. I'll go downstairs and help Max with the dogs, and I'll send her up."

Ricky nodded.

Tyler hesitated in the doorway. "Maybe asking Gracie to help isn't such a good idea after all. Maybe you should hire an experienced investigator, especially if you want this kept private. Gracie is, after all, a tabloid reporter."

"You're young, Tyler, so maybe you won't understand this. I trust Gracie. She knows all about life and how hard it is. I saw her with those dogs. That girl has heart, and she has a soul. If she gives her word that she'll keep this confidential, that's good enough for me. I'd stake my very life on her professional ethics. That girl will not leak anything to the media. When you're kind and decent to people

they respond in a like manner. That's another way of saying I trust Gracie. So if it's
all the same to you, send her up."

The files of correspondence were inches
thick. It must have been important for
Philly to find out who his parents were. He
tried to put himself in his brother's place. If
the situation were reversed, he knew he
would leave no stone unturned in his
search for his biological parents, which
was exactly what Philly had been doing.

Gracie entered the study. "Mr. Lam, Tyler
said you wanted to see me. Is something
wrong? Please don't tell me you changed
your mind about us living here, or the
dogs."

"No, no, it's nothing like that. I want to
hire you to do something for me. Do you
have any spare time?"

"Right now, I do. When September
comes around, I won't. What is it you want
me to do?"

Gracie sat down, Indian fashion, and listened to Ricky explain the contents of the
file drawers and what he wanted her to find
out. "I'll give you a generous expense account. I'll want accurate record keeping. I'll
give you a set amount to . . . pay for your

information. When and if those payouts hit five or six figures, you clear it with me first. Can you do it? And I expect you to sign a confidentiality agreement."

"That goes with the territory, Mr. Lam. Look, I'm not Woodward and Bernstein. All I can do is try. I do have sources, and I know people who have other sources. Don't get your hopes up is what I'm saying. Is there a deadline on this?"

"No, but I'd like to get to the bottom of this as soon as possible. I have to get back to South Carolina no later than the day after tomorrow. Max and Tyler are leaving tomorrow. If you pull this off, you get a full month at either resort. You want it in writing?"

"No. Your word is good enough for me."

"How are the dogs?"

"They're all sleeping. It will be time to feed the pups again in a few minutes. I think Jonas got some really good pictures. I brought my laptop with me, so I can work on the story this evening. Will it be all right if I stay over at the guesthouse? Tyler said he'd give Jonas a ride back to town. I'll take the dogs with me, so they don't keep you awake tonight. My sister and brother will be up this evening to bring me my files and some clothes. I hope it's okay if they stay."

"That's fine. How's it going with Max?"

"We're being civil to one another."

"Civility is good. It's a start."

"A start for what?" Gracie asked, her eyes narrowing.

Ricky shrugged. "Less angst, less stress. Max is really a nice guy. Women find him incredibly attractive. According to Tyler, they fall all over him." He wondered if what he was saying was true. He shrugged again.

"Well then, I guess I'll leave you to your files."

"After I finish going through them, I can have the boys take them over to the guesthouse for you. Go through them thoroughly. I want you to call me every day with a progress report. You pull this off for me, and I will be forever in your debt."

"That's really not . . ."

Ricky didn't think it was possible for the girl standing in front of him to be embarrassed, but she was. She flushed and wouldn't meet his gaze. This was a girl who wasn't used to people saying nice things to her or, for that matter, doing nice things for her. She had so many defense mechanisms in place, it was going to be hard for Max to break through them.

"I have one more drawer of files to go through, then they'll be yours. I really appreciate this, Gracie."

"I'll do my very best for you, Mr. Lam. I'll investigate this matter fully."

Ricky was about to tell her to call him Ricky, but he realized he would always be Mr. Lam to Gracie. He wondered where this insight was coming from all of a sudden.

Ricky eyed the last file drawer before he got up to pop a Coca-Cola from the minirefrigerator in his office. He carried it back to his desk. He hadn't had a cigarette that morning, so he could smoke one now. Talk about stress. How in hell was he going to tell Roxy her husband was a bigamist? Who was Lee Ann Oliver? According to the certificate in the file drawer, she was his wife. And according to the birth certificates of her and Philly's daughters, she lived in Tanglewood. He closed his eyes as he tried to picture the people at the church and cemetery the day Philly was buried. He would have remembered a woman with three daughters. He mentally did a head count. He could account for everyone graveside. Only three pews in the church had been full, and there hadn't been anyone standing or sitting in the back.

Had Philly and his first wife separated? Did Lee Ann Oliver even know her husband was dead? Did Melanie, Sara, and Emily know their father was dead? Maybe they weren't the kind of people who read the newspaper or the obituaries, preferring to get their news from television.

Then there was the most important question of all. Why didn't Philly leave his estate to Lee Ann Oliver and their daughters? Why did he leave it to him? Well, he was going to have to do something about that immediately.

Puffing furiously on the cigarette, he pulled out the telephone directory. When he found what he was looking for, he slammed it shut and crushed out his cigarette. After draining the Coke bottle, he threw it into the wastebasket. He looked at the last file drawer. He could go through it tomorrow.

He headed for his Porsche, calling over

his shoulder that he would bring home more steaks for dinner. It vaguely registered with him that his two sons were sitting at the table with Gracie, carrying on what seemed to be a normal conversation. God did move in mysterious ways.

He knew where Tanglewood was, and he had Lee Ann Oliver's address committed to memory, thanks to the telephone directory. He was on her street in forty minutes, looking for the house number. He crossed his fingers, the way he had when he was a little kid, hoping that she still lived there with her daughters.

It was a pretty little brick house. Well maintained, too. The driveway held four cars. Three daughters plus a mother made for a family of four. Evidently everyone had her own car. The flower borders and shrubs were pruned and well cared for. The beds had recently been mulched. He sniffed. The lawn had been cut, probably earlier that morning. A sprinkling system whirred in the back. He could see water arcing to his left.

Ricky parked in the center of the driveway, behind a Ford Bronco and a Ford Taurus. He yanked his baseball cap lower, adjusted his sunglasses, and hopped out of the car to make his way to the front door. The main door behind the screen door was open. He could hear Bon Jovi wafting down from the second floor. Something was baking in the oven. Whatever it was, it smelled good. He thought about Roxy then and the bread she'd been baking when he talked to her earlier.

He pressed the doorbell. It played a six-note tune, but he couldn't identify it. He took a step backward to wait.

Lee Ann Oliver was pretty in a whole-some way. He bet that in her youth, she'd been thin because Philly had always looked twice at slender blondes. Now she would be considered pleasingly plump. She was a real blonde, too. She smiled a greeting. Like Gracie Lick, she had a beau-tiful smile. He wondered if the daughters looked like her or Philly.

"Yes." She said it like yes, not as a question.

Ricky cleared his throat. "I'm Ricky Lam. Philip was my brother. I was wondering if I could talk to you."

"Of course. I wondered when you would come by. Come in." She held the door open. He stepped inside and looked around. It was just as nice and comfortable as it looked from the outside.

She was taller than she looked through the screen door. When she'd been young, people had probably referred to her as willowy. "I would have come sooner if I had known. I didn't find out about you until two hours ago. You didn't come to the funeral. Why is that?"

"We weren't invited, Mr. Lam. We did go to the cemetery later in the day when everyone was gone. We all said our good-byes. What can I do for you? I'm sorry. Would you like some coffee or perhaps ice tea. I just made both."

"Coffee if it isn't too much trouble." It was easier to talk over some kind of a drink. At least that's what his mother had always said. His father had said it, too.

Ricky blinked in surprise when he entered the large, old-fashioned kitchen. It was an exact replica of his mother's kitchen. *Cozy* was the word that came to mind. Even the little clay pots of herbs on the windowsill were the same. "Did you . . . did you decorate this kitchen?"

"No. This house was a mess when we

bought it. Philip gutted it and basically started from scratch. He did it all. He had some very definite ideas when it came to this kitchen. I didn't argue with him because I don't really have any decorating sense. I liked the result, and that's all that matters. My girls and I spend a lot of time here in the kitchen. Now, tell me, what brings you here?"

Ricky removed the baseball cap before he stuck his sunglasses into his shirt pocket. "I never knew about you. I thought Philly was married to Roxy. He married her. I saw the marriage certificate. I saw yours, too. That makes my brother—your husband—a bigamist. I'm realizing more and more as the days go on that I never knew my brother, who, by the way, isn't really my brother. He's my adopted brother. I just found that out today, too. Can you explain any of this to me?"

The woman sitting across from him stared into his eyes. She seemed to be struggling with herself as to what she should say. "Philip and I didn't have . . . what you would call a traditional marriage. It was more of a business arrangement. He wanted children. I was willing to give him those children. He wanted a son. The truth was, he was obsessed with having a son. It didn't work out. I was willing to keep trying, but it was such an ordeal for him that . . . well, it was just an ordeal. He needed . . . *incentives*. After Emily was born, our third girl, he blamed me for not delivering a boy. He was never mean or ugly to me, but he was clearly disappointed in my inability to produce a son. It didn't matter to me that I had three girls and no son. Yes, Mr. Lam, we only had sex three times in our marriage. I feel terrible telling you things like this about your brother. Obviously, you didn't know about any of it."

Ricky tried to digest the information. Lee Ann's arrangement with Philly sounded similar to what Roxy had told him about her marriage. "Did Philip live here?"

"No. He made day visits. To check on us. To give me money. That kind of thing. That went on for a few years, then it stopped. A few months after Emily was born, the checks started to arrive in place of Philip. His telephone calls stopped, too. I hadn't seen him in six or seven years before his death. I really can't remember, but I think I only talked to him once in all those years, and that was to tell him the house needed a new roof. A few days later a roofing company arrived, and I had a new roof. I never spoke to him again after that call. The neighbors thought we were separated. I didn't tell them otherwise. It was none of their business anyway. Philip wasn't the least bit interested in the girls. However, he did provide for them. I basically raised them as a single mom."

"Did you know he passed away?"

"Not right away. I heard about it on the news the day of the funeral. I was stunned. My girls cried all day. It's terrible to lose a parent, even when the parent doesn't love you."

"Yes, yes, it is a terrible thing," Ricky said, remembering the death of his own parents. He'd loved them, though, and they had loved him.

"Did Philip provide for you and the girls on his death?"

"The checks stopped after he died. I have a job. We manage. Emily has two more years of college. Things will be better then. I have some savings."

"Oh, no, that's not right. I'm sorry about

all of this. I wish I had known sooner, but
Philly was always such a private person
there was no way I could have known. He
didn't like people prying into his business."

"I learned that very early on. Would you
like some more coffee?"

"No, thank you. This is fine." He looked
into his cup. He couldn't remember if he'd
had any of it or not. He grappled for something to say. "Did you love Philip? Did my
brother ever talk about me to you? It's important for me to know this. I just don't understand any of this. You knew about his
marriage to Roxy. How did you handle
that?"

"No, I did not love your brother. As I told
you, our marriage was a business arrangement. He did speak of you several times
but only in passing. He made comments
when he was working on the kitchen. I
think he was talking more to hear himself
than anything else. He said you were a
movie star. He made the term sound obscene. Life is never easy, Mr. Lam. Yes, I
knew about Roxy, and, no, it didn't bother
me. Please don't judge me. I had three
daughters to worry about, and, like I said,
it was a business arrangement. In my heart

of hearts, I assumed Roxy didn't fare any better than I did. I simply didn't care. Eventually I came to the conclusion that your brother had some mental problems, and I was relieved when he stopped coming by the house. I'm sorry for being so blunt, but it's the truth.

"Would you like to meet my daughters?" she asked.

"Yes, I would."

Lee Ann walked down the hallway to the living room, where she called out to her daughters.

He could see traces of their mother in them, but, overall, all three looked just like Philly.

"This is your uncle Ricky. Didn't I tell you he would come to see us someday?"

They didn't look impressed, and he couldn't blame them. What kind of uncle was he not to show up until six months after their father's death.

"I've got to be going. It was nice meeting you all. I'd like to come again sometime."

"The door is always open," Lee Ann said. Her tone said she knew damn well he would never be back.

"Walk out to the car with me, Lee Ann,"

he said, when Philly's daughters went back upstairs.

Ricky slid into the bucket seat and reached into the glove compartment for his checkbook. He scribbled one off and handed it to Lee Ann, who could only gape at the amount. "My attorney will be in touch with you. You and your daughters will never have to worry about money for the rest of your lives. I'm just sorry it's taken me so long to find you."

"I don't know what to say."

"I *will* be back," Ricky said, starting up the engine of the powerful car.

His thoughts scattered every which way on the drive home. *How could Philly have been so callous in regard to his family? A business arrangement that didn't pan out by producing a son. That was reason enough for Philly not to provide into the future. What a cruel thing to do.*

The man had left a half million dollars each to Max and Tyler and nothing to his own blood children. Was it as simple as his sons' carrying on the Lam name? Or was it bitter gall that he couldn't produce an heir? He wondered if he would ever know. "What a son of a bitch you were, Philly," he muttered.

A thought occurred to him later when he punched in the code to his private gate. Maybe Philly had set him up. Maybe he was giving him a taste of what it was like to trail after someone and clean up his mess. The more he thought about it, the more he liked Roxy's theory that his brother had set him up to fail. *Shit!*

11

The next morning, Gracie stood by the front door, waiting for the dogs to come back in. She saw the limo coming through the gates, and knew that Max and Tyler were getting ready to head for the airport. She let the dogs in and closed the door securely before she walked across the lawn and around the pool. The least she could do was wave good-bye. They walked over to her. Tyler stuck out his hand. She shook it politely. Out of the corner of her eye she could see Ricky standing in the doorway. Her gaze returned to Max, who looked like he was about to stick out his hand. She closed the distance between them, reached for the collar of his shirt, and pulled him forward. She planted her lips on his and all but sucked out his tongue before she released him. Tyler caught his brother, or Max would have fallen.

"There's smoke coming out your ears, Max," Gracie said.

"She ain't kidding, Bro. I can see it from way over here." Tyler guffawed. "Put one foot in front of the other, and you'll get to the car. You can do it, Bro."

Ricky laughed his head off as he prepared to make coffee. Maybe it was just a swirl of early-morning fog circling his son's head. Then again, maybe it was smoke. He knew in his gut that Max was never going to be the same. He remembered the bells and whistles from the night he'd spent with Roxy. He laughed harder, remembering his socks on the balcony.

Satisfied that his bags were packed and he hadn't forgotten anything, Ricky headed for the second floor. He marveled at how quiet it was without his sons in residence. He missed them already. He wondered if he should call them. Would it hurt for him to tell them he missed them? Would they consider it an invasion of their space? Or, God forbid, would they think he was acting like a father? He had *felt* like a father these past few days. It was a nice feeling.

His intention, when he climbed the steps to the second floor, was either to watch television or a video. He really didn't feel like doing either. Maybe he should go through the last file drawer, then carry it to the guesthouse and hand it over to Gracie. It was late, though. He debated with himself. He could still go through it and give it to her before he left for the airport the following day. *Yeah, yeah, that's what I'll do.*

God, how he hated going through Philly's things. He hated learning about his secrets. He thought about his own life, open book that it was. Now. Philly had done his best to keep it secret, though. Like his own? Was that what he'd wanted? To have his life rival that of his bad-boy brother? If so, it was a sick desire.

Go through this junk already and get it over with. Put it behind you. You can't undo the past. It's gone.

Ricky sat down on the floor, pulling the heavy drawer toward him. He took out the first folder in the stack. What the hell . . . This was his mother's stuff, things she'd kept from his school years. His kindergarten drawings, his school pictures, dried flowers, a colored macaroni bracelet, handmade holiday cards. Report cards that clearly indicated he was a little short of hopeless when it came to academics. How did he ever manage to get through school? Things his mother kept. He'd wondered, after her death, what had happened to her things. Once, when he was almost sober, he'd asked Philly, and his brother's response had been that he'd taken care of everything. At least that's how Ricky remembered it.

Philly always took care of everything.

He reached for another file. A copy of his birth certificate, copies of his social security card, copies of his first driver's license. His SAT scores, which were in the crapper, his immunization records. Two copies of everything. More pictures. Stacks and stacks of pictures. Of him. Not Philly. "Jesus, Mom, what did you do here?"

His eyes burning, he continued his search. His yearbooks. All of them. Maybe this was just *his* file. Where was Philly's file? People didn't adopt babies unless they wanted them. Did they? There had to be a file on Philly somewhere. Maybe Philly hadn't liked what was in his and had thrown it away. Maybe these things had just been shoved into a box, and neat-freak Philly had created the files. Philly would do something like that. Everything neat and tidy and in its place.

And then the worst thing of all. Yellowed newspaper clippings of some of his Hollywood escapades Philly hadn't been able to squash. His body burned with shame as he read through the articles. Here it was, his own personal hell. In chronological order no less.

"Ah, Mom, I'm so sorry. I got off the track there. The drugs did things to me. So did the alcohol." His mind wandered backward in time to his first big paycheck. He'd driven to his mother's house, half-drunk, in his brand-new Mercedes convertible, and staggered into the house. He'd written out a check that had a lot of zeros on it, but she wouldn't take it. He'd wanted to buy her a big, grand new house, but she didn't want it. She didn't want the new car either. The truth was, she didn't want anything from him. She never accepted a dime from him. He'd arranged with a local florist to deliver flowers to her every week.

Philly told him years and years later that she threw them in the trash. Ricky had bawled when he'd learned the truth.

Those first years in Hollywood when he'd been drunk or stoned, most of the time, he hadn't gone home for the holidays. Never once. Philly always went home, though. He was the one who got the Christmas tree, decorated it, bought presents. He was the one who decorated the house on the outside with colored lights. Perfect Philly did it all.

Ricky hadn't known any of that until he'd been out of rehab for about a year. Clean and sober, he'd gone home, but his mother was already ill. She'd just stared at him as if he were a stranger. Basically, he had been a stranger at that point in time. The round-the-clock nurses asked him not to return because it upset his mother. His tail between his legs, he'd left and gone back to his own house.

He'd found out at his mother's funeral, from the neighbors, what a good son Philly was. They didn't have to tell him what a degenerate son he was. He could see it in their faces.

He knew in his heart, in his mind, in his

gut, that he could never make that right.
Maybe that was another reason the rehab
had worked.

So much shame.

So much guilt.

So many regrets.

Ricky reached for the last folder. Taped
to the manila folder were two keys and two
pieces of paper. He pulled the tape loose
so he could finger the keys. One looked
like the key to his mother's house, and the
other looked like a key to a safe-deposit
box. One sheet of paper was a copy of the
form a person filled out to rent a safe-
deposit box. Underneath his mother's signature was his own scrawl. He looked at
the date. He'd been nineteen when he
signed the form at the bank. The second
paper was the actual deed to his mother's
house. He'd been seventeen when his
name was added to the deed, the year his
father had died from Parkinson's disease.
He wondered why Philly hadn't found a
way to open the safe-deposit box. Why
hadn't it been part of the probate process?
Maybe no one had known about it. But
Philly had known. Maybe he'd been afraid
to take a chance to try and pass himself off

as Ricky Lam. He'd already been famous at nineteen, when he'd signed the form.

He looked down at the deed. A deed meant a person owned the property. Hadn't Philly sold their mother's house? Ricky thought he had. Then again, maybe Philly hadn't been able to sell it. Philly must have paid the taxes on it all these years.

Ricky looked down at his watch: 9:30. He was on his feet a second later, with the keys from the file cabinet in his pocket. He barreled down the steps and out to his car.

He was going *home.*

An hour later he cut the engine of his car and looked around. It was a quiet street, with streetlights and large shade trees lining the sidewalks. Sidewalks where he used to ride his bike with Jimmy Stevens. They hadn't been allowed to ride in the street back then. He'd played stickball and kick the can in the street after supper, when there was no traffic, but the moment the streetlights came on, he had to be either in his own yard or Jimmy's yard. Jimmy had lived three doors away. He wondered where Jimmy was these days. He made a mental note to find out.

He didn't think it was possible for a

neighborhood to look the same some twenty-five years later, but this one did. Neighborhoods usually recycled themselves at different points in time. Older people retired and moved away, making way for new people with kids to move in. The baby boomers and the yuppies got transferred or moved east for whatever their reasons were. The area as well as the street reminded Ricky of Lee Ann Oliver's house.

Ricky didn't realize he was holding his breath until he slid the key into the lock. It turned effortlessly, and that's when he let loose and howled his grief. For one brief second, he felt disoriented. *What in God's name am I doing here?* His hand shook as he pressed down on the latch. It gave easily.

And then he was inside his old home. The light switch was on the left. He leaned back against the closed door. He squeezed his eyes shut. If he didn't turn on the light, if he didn't open his eyes, if he didn't look at anything, he could simply turn around, go out the door, and lock it. He could pretend he didn't know about

Philly's keeping the house. And just what good would that do him?

His breathing suddenly ragged, vision rose behind his closed eyelids. A memory of another time such as this when he was eight years old. His parents had gone to the church bingo with some neighbors and Philly was baby-sitting him. Philly had been generous that day, allowing him to play outside past the time the streetlights came on. He'd been playing stickball with Jimmy and some of his other friends, when the rock he was kicking around bounced up and ricocheted crazily right into the Donners' front window. The boys scattered like mice with a cat on their tail. Their house had been dark because Philly was upstairs in his room. He'd leaned against the door then, just the way he was leaning against it now, with his eyes closed. When he felt Philly's hand on his shoulder, he'd almost jumped out of his skin. Then he'd started to cry and blubber. Philly's hand had been comforting and gentle, that much he remembered.

Philly hadn't turned on the light but told him to go upstairs and take his bath. That's when the knock sounded on the door. He was at the top of the steps when Philly finally turned on the light and opened the door. He could see Mr. Donner, who was as mad as a man could be. He couldn't believe his ears when he heard his brother say, "Ricky and I were upstairs doing our homework. He's taking his bath right now."

Philly never came into the bathroom, never said a word, and he hadn't told their parents either. It seemed as if Philly thought the accident had never happened. But it had. For days he'd anguished over what he had done, but he had never owned up to it. Not because he was afraid of punishment but because he was afraid if he told the truth, Philly would hate him forever. To the best of his recollection, he'd repaid about seventy-nine cents of the cost of the broken window. Creeping out of his bed after everyone was asleep, he'd run across the street and put his five or ten cents in the Donners' mailbox. He'd never told anyone about that either.

Memories like this were not for the faint of heart.

Ricky fumbled for the switch. The small foyer and the living room were flooded with light. His jaw dropped, and his eyeballs stood at attention when he looked around.

He didn't walk, he ran through the rooms, one after the other when the realization hit him. *Son of a bitch! This was where Philly lived. This was where Philly spent his time. This was where he hid out.* He whipped around the corner in the upstairs hallway to Philly's old room. He gaped in disbelief. The closet bulged with clothes, casual clothes, dress clothes, a tuxedo. The dresser drawers were full of underwear, socks, tee shirts, pajamas, and shorts.

The most interesting thing of all was the built-in desk with a state-of-the-art computer, printer, fax, copy machine, and a telephone with enough buttons to light up a room. The bunk beds were the same, too. No, no, they weren't. The mate to Philly's bed that had been his was now here in Philly's room next to the other bed.

Ricky ran back down the hall to his old room. He turned on the light switch. His room was empty. There wasn't a single thing in the room to indicate a small boy named Ricky Lam had ever inhabited the room. There wasn't even a carpet on the floor. He was standing on squares of plywood. He could see the thin strips of nail-studded lath for the original carpet.

The shutters that used to cover the windows were gone, replaced with pull-down shades.

Trying to absorb what he was seeing, Ricky walked from room to room. Everything looked the same except for the thick layer of dust everywhere. Obviously no one had been in the house since Philly's death. Who paid the bills on the house—the light bill, the water? Six months was a long time for anyone to carry a bill. Eventually, the house would have been sold for nonpayment of taxes. Then he remembered one of Philly's habits. He paid everything ahead, sometimes by years. He never actually received a bill that said pay by such and such a date. Everything carried a credit balance.

Ricky sat down at his mother's kitchen table. He needed to think about all of this. Philly had thought he had a year to live. During that year, would he have gotten rid of this house, his files, all his records? Probably. He thought he still had time to take care of matters. He hadn't expected to die so suddenly or so tragically.

A moment later he was off the chair. He opened the refrigerator. Yes, Philly had lived here. Petrified food in containers. A milk jug with residue on the bottom. Soda pop, beer, wine, canned juice. The vegetable bins were full of blue-green mold that was nothing more than thick powder.

The freezer was loaded with meat, all with freezer burn. The cabinets were loaded with staples, the same things Ricky had in the cabinets at his house. Philly must have cooked for himself. The thought surprised him. Everything about Philly surprised him. *Everything.*

Ricky walked into the laundry room. He almost cried when he opened the door to the dryer and saw Philly's clothes. He slammed it shut. The appliances looked new.

The living room was the same. There was his father's recliner. Philly's reading glasses were on the table, along with a James Michener novel. A pair of worn, scuffed slippers were under the table. A dish of hard candies, individually wrapped, was on the coffee table, along with a pile of newspapers and six month-old issues of *Newsweek* and *Time* magazines.

The mantel over the decorative fireplace was full of pictures. Of Philly, of his mother, two of his father. He walked closer to see if there was one of him. He knew there wouldn't be. He wasn't disappointed.

He went back upstairs, down the hall to his mother's room. He turned on the light. It was exactly the way he remembered it except for the thick layer of dust.

The bathroom was next. It, too, was the same, with the exception of the thick, designer towels with matching bath mats. They were all white and monogrammed, even the mats. The toiletries were pricey name brands.

The medicine cabinet held aspirin, seven prescription bottles, cologne, aftershave, and shaving cream, along with a razor. Two new toothbrushes still in their wrappers were on the bottom shelf, with a new tube of Colgate toothpaste. Philly had planned on coming back here.

He turned off the light. He marched down the hall to Philly's room, where he walked over to the window to look across at what used to be the Windhams' house.

He wondered if they still lived there. If they did, what did they think about Philly's not coming home for six months? Who mowed and tended the lawn? The Windhams had to be old by now. Even good neighbors like the Windhams wouldn't continue to take care of a neighbor's property. Would they? Maybe he should go over and knock on their door. No, the house was dark. Another time. Or, he could simply call them and ask.

Ricky sat down and turned on the computer. Philly had AOL and Quicken. Without a password he wasn't going to get anywhere. He longed for a cigarette. Well, hell, Philly was a three-pack-a-day man. He rummaged in the desk drawers and found an unopened pack of Marlboros. He wondered what would happen if he smoked a six-month-old cigarette, and found that he didn't give a damn. He lit up. He stared at the screen in front of him while he puffed on the cigarette.

He was far from computer literate. What little he knew he'd learned from Roxy. It was a way to keep in daily contact with his two sons without acting like a father.

Roxy said all the records concerning the

resorts, including the one they were building on Camellia Island, were computerized.
Backed up, and then backed up again for
safety reasons. Aside from emails, he
checked the front pages of the *L.A. Times*
and *USA Today* and the weather. That was
the extent of his computer use.

He needed to call Roxy. He dialed her
number, even though it was one o'clock in
the morning in South Carolina. Her voice
sounded sleepy but alert. "Hello."

"Roxy, it's me. Listen, I'm sorry to wake
you. I found the place where Philly lived.
Hid out, whatever. It's our old home. I'm
here now. Don't fall asleep on me, Roxy. I
need your input here. You with me, Roxy?"

"Yes. I'm making coffee. I went to bed at
nine-thirty, so I've had some sleep. Talk to
me."

He did. "Six months, Roxy! All the bills
must have been paid in advance."

"Philip loved direct deposit and having
bills paid directly from the bank. It was less
for him to oversee. There's no reason to
think he wouldn't have carried that over to
his own personal checking account. If my
memory serves me right, he used to keep
fifty thousand dollars in his personal

checking account. I don't know how I know this, Ricky. I'm assuming I either overheard it or he told me himself. Think about it. Basic utilities, lawn maintenance with a firm that had direct billing. It makes sense. You could ask his lawyer. Then again, maybe this was one of those things he kept secret. I don't know what else to tell you."

"Think, Roxy, do you have any idea what his computer password would be?"

"I don't have a clue."

"This whole thing is making me crazy. It's beyond bizarre."

"I told you several times that Philip wasn't the person you thought he was. My personal feeling is he wanted to be you. Without your faults. You can run with that or not."

"You can hold the fort, can't you? I'm going to need a few more days here."

"It's not a problem. They're installing the bathroom fixtures tomorrow. Oh, by the way, I got a confirmation today that John Edward, the famous psychic, will attend our opening. If you can't figure out what's going on, maybe you can consult him on a professional level. I have his phone number if you need it. How do you feel being in your old home?"

"It's spooking me, Roxy. I feel like Philly is here watching me, hating it that I'm here. He went to such great lengths to keep all this a secret, and here I am, seeing everything. I'm going to pack up the computer and take it home with me. Tomorrow I'm going to check out my mother's safe-deposit box, since it has my name on it. I wish you were here, Roxy, I really do."

A low, throaty chuckle came over the wire. "I take it you miss me."

"I do. Something's happening to me where you're concerned. I don't ever remember feeling quite like this before." He smiled when he heard the chuckle again.

"And to think we used to hate each other's guts. Ricky, if you want me to come to California, I can call one of the boys to come here and oversee things."

"No, it's okay. I should be able to clear things up in a few days. If not, I'll just turn it over to Gracie. Two days, that's it, and then I'm heading back to the Crown Jewel. What are you going to do now that I woke you up?"

This time the voice purred a response. "I'm going to sit here and pretend you're sitting across from me. I'm going to tell you all my secret desires, all my innermost secrets, and you're going to tell me yours."

Suddenly he found it difficult to breathe. "And then . . ."

"Then I'm going to . . ."

"Yes? What? Can you make smoke come out of my ears?"

"Oh, honey, I can light a whole bonfire in those ears of yours. Smoke is just smoke. Flames now, that's something else entirely. 'Night, Ricky."

Ricky looked at the pinging phone in his hand after Roxy hung up. He burst out laughing. *Damn, she's good.*

He turned off the computer and disconnected it. Just to be on the safe side, he took the monitor and the printer as well, not knowing if they would be compatible with what he had at his own house.

Outside in the quiet night, he looked around. *Will I ever come back here?* He simply didn't know. The street was deserted, most of the houses dark. A lone lamp glowed at the end of someone's driveway farther down the street. It was cool, and it felt damp.

Ricky backed his car down the driveway, his headlights arcing on the Windhams' mailbox. Only the name wasn't Windham now, it was Nebitz. Well, that took care of calling the Windhams.

God, Philly, what demons were inside your head? Hot tears burned behind his eyelids as he shifted gears and drove off. A high keening sound escaped his lips. In the whole of his life, he'd never felt such sadness.

It was midnight by the time Ricky disconnected his own computer and moved it to one of the guest rooms down the hall. He had Philly's computer hooked up within minutes. He clicked on AOL. For the next hour, he played with every imaginable password he could think of. He went through the calendar, dates, years, names of everyone they both knew. Nothing. His own password was simple, RLMS. Ricky Lam, Movie Star. Just for the hell of it, he typed in RLMSB. Ricky Lam, Movie Star's Brother. He almost fell off his chair when the screen came to life. Son of a bitch! Had he ever told Philly his password? He must have. Then again, maybe Philly was one of those hacking wonders he was always reading about in the papers and hearing about on the news.

For some reason he expected to find hundreds of emails. What he was seeing was probably no more than twenty or so. That made sense. Who would try to contact Philly after his death? He counted them, his finger tracing the emails on the screen. There were twenty-four altogether. Twenty-three of them dated the week of his death. The last email on the list had come through four months after his death.

Ricky read the emails slowly, trying to absorb what he was seeing. They appeared to be responses to queries that Philly had sent out. Queries concerning his biological parents. All twenty-three were regretful. The writers were unable to help simply because it was either too long ago or they were the wrong people.

The last email was different. It was from someone named Martin Mangarella. He said he was Martina Mangarella's son. Ricky read it eight times.

Dear Mr. Lam,

I'm sorry to have to tell you this, but my mother Martina Mangarella passed away last year. When my mother retired from the Oakhurst Orphanage, where she worked all her adult life, she copied and brought home files, which she stored in the basement. She knew it was wrong, but she did it anyway. I asked her once why she did that, and her response was, there might be a fire, and all the records would be destroyed, and then the poor souls would never be able to find their children or their parents. I, personally, do not approve of sealed adoptions. The reason being, I'm adopted. My mother always felt the same way but was powerless to help the people who tried to find loved ones while she was in the orphanage's employ. On her retirement, she said she would never seek out people, but if they managed to find her, she would help them any way she could. You can either call me or send me an email and we can arrange to meet and to discuss payment for the information. Of course if

*you don't find what you're looking for,
there will be no charge.*
Sincerely yours,
Martin Mangarella.

Ricky not only memorized the email, he memorized the phone number at the bottom. "I'll be damned!"

If Philly had lived the year his doctor said he had, he would have been able to read this particular email. Sometimes life just wasn't fair.

At one minute past eight the next morning, Ricky dialed the number from Martin Mangarella's email. He identified himself and explained, in detail, the circumstances for the call.

"Yes, I remember the email from Mr. Lam and my response. I wondered why he didn't respond. I'm sorry about his passing. Are you Ricky Lam, the movie star?"

"Retired movie star, Mr. Mangarella. Yes, Philip was my brother. I'd like to arrange a meeting with you as soon as possible."

"Well, sure, Mr. Lam. I own a hardware store, and I don't open till ten o'clock. If I'm late, my manager can open for me." He rattled off his address and gave directions. "You really are the movie star, huh? I think I've seen most of your movies. I'm what they call a movie buff."

And the price is going up, up, and up, Ricky thought. "I can be there in forty minutes, Mr. Mangarella."

"I'll be waiting, Mr. Lam."

Martin Mangarella was as good as his word. He was sitting on the front steps of a small, brown, shingled house. The neighborhood as well as the house reminded Ricky of his own childhood home and Lee Ann Oliver's house. It was that kind of a neighborhood.

He was a small man with shell-rimmed glasses that almost hid his dark brown eyes. He was dressed in jeans, sneakers, and a yellow tee shirt that had MANGARELLA HARDWARE on the pocket. He stood up to shake hands. His grip was firm and hard. His smile was shy, Ricky thought.

"Everything's in the basement. I have all the boxes up on shelves in case of leaks or whatever. They're pretty moldy and smelly, but I don't think that will matter to you. We should probably discuss the fee now before you start looking. It's not going to take

you very long. My mother labeled everything, and all the boxes are in alphabetical
order."

"How much is the fee, Mr. Mangarella?"

"You see, that's just it. I don't know what
to charge you. What is it worth to you? I
don't want to gouge you because I understand how important this is to you. I'm not
trying to get rich off this. By the same token, I shouldn't be giving this information
to you for free either. I guess you should
just give me a number, and I'll take it."

"How does fifty thousand dollars
sound?"

"That sounds just fine, Mr. Lam. If you'd
said five bucks, I would have said fine to
that, too."

"You know what, Mr. Mangarella, I knew
that. Fifty thousand it is. Now, if the answers I'm looking for aren't in there, you
get five bucks. Deal?"

"Deal. Do you want my help, or do you
want to do it yourself?"

"I'd like to do it myself if you show me
where to look. Can I keep the file?"

"No, you can't keep it, but you can make
copies on my machine. I have a small of-

fice off the kitchen with a copier. Fifteen cents a copy. Is that okay with you?"

"Yes, sir, that's okay."

Martin Mangarella's basement ran the entire length of the house. It appeared dry and well maintained. Heavy-duty shelves lined all four walls and were filled with cardboard boxes. Neat labels were on the end of each box. Martin went immediately to the L section.

"I had no idea so many people adopted," Ricky said, looking at the hundreds and hundreds of boxes.

"My mother cross-filed a lot of them. The last name of the parents giving up the baby, and the last name of the adoptive parents. There are six cartons of L's. There are approximately sixty files to a box, depending on the thickness of each file. Some of the files are really two files clipped together, so be careful when you go through them. Take your pick. I'll be upstairs in the kitchen if you need me. Would you like some coffee?"

"No thanks."

It took Ricky a good five minutes before he could summon the nerve to reach for the first box. He pulled it down and set it on an old enamel table whose edges were chipped and rusty. He was starting to get a headache. His heart pounded furiously inside his chest.

Twenty-five minutes and forty-two files later, Ricky found the file with the names, Bertha and Arthur Lam, written in ink on the side and again on the front. Bertha and Arthur Lam were his parents. Their friends always called them Bee and Artie.

Perspiration beaded on his forehead. He had to wipe the palms of his hands twice on his pants until they felt dry. What was he going to find inside the file? Would he be able to handle it? He tried to imagine Philly standing in this exact spot, staring down at the folder. *What would he have been thinking? How would he have looked? Would his hands have been clammy like mine are? Would he have been sweating? Above all, would he have been excited, or would he have been filled with dread the way I am?*

What if he couldn't handle what he found in the file? What if whatever he found only made things worse? What if there were no names in the file?

Ricky opened the flap and stared down

at the papers inside. There weren't many, six, he counted. Two pages had been typed on an old typewriter, probably an Underwood, with a carbon ribbon. The O on the typewriter punched a hole in the paper, the E hit above the line. Still, it was easy to read, and Mrs. Mangarella, if she was the one who had made the handwritten entries, had excellent penmanship. More than anything, though, it was the white envelope that intrigued him. At one time, it had been sealed, he suspected. It was a short, handwritten note with just a few lines. He felt a knot form in his throat when he read the ink-faded words.

Please, whoever you are, if you're adopting my son Caleb, please tell him how very much I loved him. Tell him I didn't want to give him up but I had no other choice.

Caleb's Mother.

When he finished reading through the file twice, he closed the flap and laid it on the old enamel table. He put the cover back on the box and returned it to the shelf. His body stiff with shock, he made his way up the steps to the kitchen, where his host waited for him. He pulled a five-dollar bill out of his pocket and handed it to Martin. Then he scribbled out a check and laid it on the kitchen counter.

Martin Mangarella counted out the exact amount of change and handed it over with the photocopies.

Ricky's tongue was so thick in his mouth he didn't think he would be able to speak. "Are you going to read that file, Mr. Mangarella?" he finally managed to ask.

"No. Why would I want to do something like that? If there are any secrets in that file, they're safe. That's one thing you will never have to worry about." Ricky believed him implicitly. He didn't know why, he just did.

Ricky drove home in a daze. He forgot all about his intention to go to the bank to inspect the safe-deposit box. All he could think about were the contents of the file on the seat next to him.

12

Back home, Ricky slid the manila folder across the kitchen table. He wondered if Martin Mangarella had charged him for the folder or if it was a freebie. He looked over at the coffeepot because it was better than looking at the manila envelope. The left-over contents of the coffeepot looked way too dark to drink, just as the contents of the envelope were way too scary to read again. Because he needed to do something—anything but think about what he'd just learned about his brother—he rinsed out the pot, added fresh coffee and water. He wasn't even sure if he wanted a cup of coffee. The truth was, he didn't know *what* he wanted.

While the coffee dripped, Ricky called

Roxy's cell phone. "I changed my mind, Roxy. I'd like you to come here if you can manage it. Do you think you can get a flight out anytime soon? If not, charter a flight." Ricky held his breath waiting for her response.

Roxy didn't ask why. "Should I call Tyler or Max?"

"Max has his hands full getting ready for Carnival. Call Tyler. Get back to me with your ETA, and I'll meet you."

Her voice was husky, little more than a whisper. "Is it bad, Ricky?"

"Let's just say it's a mind-bender, okay? We'll talk when you get here."

While the coffee dripped into the pot, Ricky placed a call to his old studio to speak with Donald Sandusky. He spoke quietly and forcefully. "Tell them to cancel the planned movie and book. Go with me, and I'll give them an Academy Award movie. Do it, Sandusky, you won't be sorry."

His second call was to a longtime friend, a well-known screenwriter. He spoke slowly and distinctly. His jaw was set grimly when he hung up the phone.

Ricky carried his fresh cup of coffee out

to the rear deck and sat down. He liked this section of the deck because he could look out over his gardens and not see buildings, the tennis court, or the pool, just natural greenery with bushels of vibrant flowers. He loved flowers. He leaned his head back on the chaise and closed his eyes. Once, he'd given his mother a marigold plant in a milk carton. She'd rushed outside and planted it right away at the edge of the front porch. He wished now he had looked last night to see if it was still there. Maybe it was one of those plants you had to plant every year. Annual or perennial? He had no clue.

He looked up when a shadow crossed his legs. He opened his eyes. "Gracie!"

"I thought you said you were leaving, Mr. Lam."

"I did. I was. My bags are by the front door. But I have to stay on a few more days. How are the dogs doing?"

"Just great. They trust me. They know they're going to be fed. My brother and sister are spoiling them shamelessly. They like us. Dogs know." She didn't explain what she meant by *dogs know,* and Ricky didn't ask because he understood.

"You look worried and troubled. Is there anything I can help you with? All you have to do is ask."

"Not right now. How's the article going?"

"Very well. I worked on it till long after midnight. Jonah is bringing up the photos this afternoon. He said they came out better than he expected. I just got a call from the *Times,* and if I can get this in to them by tomorrow, they're going to run it next week. Front page of the Entertainment section on Sunday. I hope you're as pleased with that news as I am."

"Are you going to let me read it before you send it off?"

"Absolutely. I'm going to finish it up by noon. Jonah is going to hand-deliver it to the *Times.* I'd like to ask permission to use your copy machine. I'll make a copy for you, and I need one for my files. Do you want to talk about anything, Mr. Lam? I'm a real good listener."

"The copy machine is on the second floor in my office. Use it anytime you want. It's a personal matter, Gracie, and something I have to handle myself."

"Well, I have to get going, so I'll leave you to whatever you were doing. I want to thank you again. You don't know what your generosity means to my family. Life certainly is strange sometimes. I won't bother you again. I'll try to stay out of your way."

"Gracie, you aren't bothering me. It's nice having you around. And you aren't in my way. I'm on overload right now, that's all."

"Been there, done that," Gracie quipped. "Bye."

"Bye, Gracie."

His little respite over, Ricky got up. He suddenly felt like an old man. Not even a wise old man, just an old man with an equally tired old brain. Inside, he turned off the coffeepot. He looked down at the manila folder. He hated to pick it up, but he didn't want it lying on the kitchen table. He carried it into what he called the TV room and slipped it under one of the cushions on the sofa. Just in case Gracie's journalistic instincts got the better of her.

Fifteen minutes later he was on the highway. His next stop, the bank where his mother had her safe-deposit box. He had to remember to ask who paid the rental every year. It would never have occurred to his mother to pay ahead on any kind of a bill. Philly then? He wondered if he would end up having a nervous breakdown over his brother.

Ricky drove steadily, the car stereo cranked to the max. He did his best to listen to the music. He'd never been very good about switching his mental gears. Philly always said he had a one-track mind plus tunnel vision. Philly had never really said anything nice to him. Never.

Ricky slowed the Porsche as he approached a red light. He looked in the rearview mirror and finger-combed his hair. He didn't look any better when he was done. He turned the stereo down as he pulled into the bank's small parking lot. He used the bank's back entrance and ended up at the little gate next to the vault. That was easy enough. He handed over his key to a matronly-looking woman with pink, tinted glasses. He knew the drill. He waited till she found the file card, asked him to sign his name, compared the signature before she opened her desk drawer for her key.

Together they walked into a room where the safe-deposit boxes lined three full walls. The number on his mother's box was

262. The woman fitted both keys into the locks, turned them, withdrew a long, narrow box, and handed it to Ricky.

"Room 3 is open if you want privacy," the woman said. Ricky nodded. The box felt light, like there was nothing in it. Maybe Philly had found a way to get to it and had taken the contents, whatever they were.

The room was small, no bigger than a broom closet. It held a shelf, a chair, and a wastebasket. After locking the door, he sat down and drummed his fingers on top of the box for a good five minutes as he played a game with himself called what's in the box? Maybe his first tooth. A lock of hair from his first haircut. His baby shoes. He flipped the latch that opened the cover. One lone white envelope.

Ricky marveled at how steady his hands were when he withdrew the envelope from the box. It wasn't sealed. Inside was a single sheet of paper with a man's name on it. Vincent Nolan? Underneath was an address in Los Angeles he didn't recognize. There was no phone number. A fat lot of good this was going to do him. *Who the hell is Vincent Nolan? What is so important about this man that my mother kept his name locked away in a bank? Could he be Philly's real father?*

Vincent Nolan. The name rang eerily in his mind as if he should know it. He folded the paper and placed it back in the envelope before stuffing the envelope in his hip pocket. He returned the box to the bank clerk and handed her his key. "I won't be needing the box any longer." He was going to ask the woman if she knew who paid the rental fee but changed his mind. Obviously the bill was sent to his mother's house and had gone into Philly's direct payment plan.

He was almost to his car when a thought struck him. *What happened to Philly's mail?* He supposed that after a certain period of time, with no forwarding address, the mail was simply returned to the sender. He didn't see any point to checking that out. He knew he was a poor excuse for a sleuth.

Vincent Nolan. He said the name over to himself, hoping it would resuscitate a long-forgotten memory. It didn't work. He could truthfully say he had never heard that particular name in his life. Yet, he knew the name from somewhere. Where?

As he tooled along the highway, his thoughts drifted to his past the way they always did when he was under stress. In the old days, he would simply have turned away and not looked back. That was the old days, when he didn't know what end was up. If he wasn't driving, he would have thrown his hands up in disgust. This was now. He was clean, dry, sober, and a responsible member of society, thanks to Philly. He couldn't discount the fact that he was a new father, too. He'd never followed through on anything in his entire life. This time he had to stay the course. For Philly, for himself, for his boys, and even for Roxy. Just the thought of Roxy lightened his mood.

Who in God's name is Vincent Nolan? Obviously, he was going to have to hire a private detective. Maybe Vincent Nolan, whoever he was, had nothing to do with Philly. Maybe he was a relative or a friend of his mother. Maybe he was her secret lover, and she kept his name safe so his father would never find out. The thought was so ludicrous, he burst out laughing.

"Who the hell are you, Vincent Nolan?"

Ricky shouted. He was glad no one could hear him because he felt so stupid.

It was past noon when Ricky returned home. All he could do was sit and think while he waited for Roxy to call him. The minute he entered the house, he started to pace. His head was so full of thoughts and memories, he thought he was going to explode. He knew he was approaching the situation all wrong. He felt *scattered*.

Philly would have a plan. He'd approach everything logically, then follow through on the steps he'd outlined. It wasn't that Ricky didn't trust his own judgment—he did. He knew in his gut he was afraid of what he was going to find out. Afraid he'd fail Philly, and in failing Philly, fail himself.

The phone rang. Roxy? His hello was exuberant. His tone stayed exuberant when he heard Max's voice coming over the wire. Max was almost as good as Roxy. "Is something wrong, Max?"

"No. I just had this crazy urge to talk to you. I'm up to my eyeballs with plans for Carnival, but all of a sudden, this weird feeling came over me . . . do you need me?"

Hell, yes, I need you. "You know what,

son, I do. Not in the physical sense at the moment. I'm wired, as you guys like to say." He related the morning's events and waited for his son's comments. He started to make coffee again, just to have something to do.

"Skip the private dick. If I were you, I'd sic Gracie on this. She's always talking about her sources. Let her put her money where her mouth is. Don't take that wrong now. I didn't mean it the way it sounds. How are the dogs and the article? Did she finish it?"

"The dogs are fine. She thinks the pups will be ready to start nursing maybe later today. She's got a handle on it. I like her, Max. A lot. By the way, Roxy is on her way here. Tyler's going to Camellia Island until we can sort through all of this.

"Gracie promised me a copy of her article this afternoon. It's going to get the front page of the Entertainment section next Sunday. When she brings it over, I'll fax it to you. Why don't you invite her for Carnival? I think the girl could use a bit of a break."

"Do you think so?"

Ricky grinned at his son's hopeful voice.

"If someone gave me an airline ticket and the promise of a week in Antigua for Carnival, I think I'd hop right on it."

"I'll think about it. What are you going to do, Ricky?"

"I'm going to sit here and stew on this till Roxy gets here. I think I might need a woman's perspective. I'm a piss-poor excuse for a detective, I can tell you that. I can almost guarantee I'm not going to like the outcome of this."

"Think in terms of a movie. Maybe that will make it easier for you to handle."

Ricky felt stunned at his son's words. They had like minds. "Maybe. Listen, I appreciate your calling. Gracie's coming across the lawn. I guess she saw my car and knew I got home. Hold on, Max, and I'll put her on the phone." Ricky laid the phone on the counter and walked outside.

Gracie handed him a thick brown envelope. "I really like the pictures."

"Max is on the phone. You can take it in the kitchen. I'll sit out here and read through everything. Be nice, Gracie. This is a humbling experience for Max."

"How nice is nice?" Gracie asked carefully.

Ricky laughed. "My mother always said you catch more flies with honey than you do with vinegar."

"My mother used to say the same thing. I want your honest opinion when you're finished," Gracie said, pointing to the envelope she'd handed Ricky. He nodded.

Stretching out on the chaise, Ricky read the article not once, not twice, but three times. In all of his years in Hollywood, no one had ever written such a glowing, honest article on him or his career. Gracie Lick had a way with words. She'd used every single one of his own quotes in regard to his colorful past. She didn't mince words anywhere. When he thought he could recite the article verbatim, and only then, did he reach for the pictures. Candid shots, yet professional, of Tyler and Max with the dogs and the pups. In one of them, Max had as much soap on him as the dogs. Their smiles were wide and genuine. The last picture brought a decided lump to his throat. It was the three of them looking into the sun, his sons' arms around his shoulders. The caption underneath read, "Father, and sons Max and Tyler." The boys

were going to love the article and the pictures. He could hardly wait to fax them off.

He looked at the printed words again,
homing in on a quote from both his sons.
Gracie had asked them their opinion of
their famous father and both of them said
the same thing, at the same moment, "He's
a hell of a guy."

Ricky savored the words. If he had one
wish at that moment, it would have been
that his sons said, "He's one hell of a father." He wondered if and when he would
ever earn that title.

He really liked his sons. He remembered
how he'd held his breath at the end of the
three-month trial period, wondering if
they'd stay on or head back home to their
mothers. He'd paced the floor that entire
day like a father-in-waiting. When midnight
approached, he couldn't stand it a minute
longer. He'd called then and asked. Max
asked if the three months were really up already. "Count me in," he'd said. When he
called Tyler he had asked, "Are you sure
I've been here three months already? I can
go for the long haul if you'll have me." He'd
walked on air for at least a week after that.

"See ya, Mr. Lam. When are you going to

read the article?" Gracie called over her shoulder.

"I read it, Gracie. You did good. I think you aced out Dickie Tee. You should send him a copy of this."

Gracie laughed. "I already did. The minute I finished it. I haven't heard back. His book will be a bomb. His publisher might even cancel his contract. If they do, the studio will cancel the movie. It pays to be front and center from the git-go. You really like it, huh? You aren't just saying that, are you?" Gracie said, fishing for a compliment.

"No, I wouldn't do that to you, Gracie. It was fair and unbiased. Like I said, you did real good. What I liked best was the line where my sons said I was quite a guy."

"Yeah, I liked that line myself. One of these days they're both going to call you Dad. You wait and see. I'm hardly ever wrong."

"Okay, Gracie. I'll go with your instincts." Ricky could feel himself beaming.

Gracie shuffled her feet. She looked nervous. "Max invited me to Antigua for Carnival."

"No kidding," Ricky said, trying to act surprised.

"Yeah. I'm going to think about it. I've never had a *real* vacation. The kind where you buy new clothes, get on an airplane, and stay in a hotel. I have to talk to my brother and sister to see if they can manage without me. Ah, did you . . . what I mean is . . . ?"

"Did I tell him to ask you? Come on, Gracie, my son has a mind of his own and doesn't need any coaching from me. Max has a crush on you, and I suspect you have a crush on him. If the two of you would stop squaring off against each other, you might find that you really are compatible. Then again, maybe you'll just become friends. Good friends."

"Oh. All right. Well, like I said, I'm going to think about it. I'll buy my own airline ticket, though. I will accept the hotel room because I know how hard it is to get one when Carnival is on."

"That sounds like a plan, Gracie."

"Did you just make coffee again? Do you ever drink it? That's wasteful, you know. How about if I pour us each a cup?"

"Okay."

A few minutes later, she set two cups of coffee down on the side table and took a seat in a deck chair.

"Tell me what's wrong. I'm very astute, you know. I know when things are bothering people. You tend to rub at your eyebrow when something is bothering you. My brother chews on his lower lip if something is troubling him. Your son Max tugs at his earlobe. I bet I can help you, and if I can't, I bet I know someone who can."

Ricky smiled. She reminded him of a bright, precocious squirrel. "Wait here a minute." He trotted into his TV room to retrieve the folder with the Mangarella file. He handed it to Gracie.

"Are you sure you want me to read this?"

Ricky nodded.

When Gracie finished reading, she replaced the papers and closed the file. "This is the information you were seeking on your brother, isn't it? Someone named Lorraine Woodworth is . . . was your brother's biological mother. She gave birth with a midwife in attendance. She was fourteen years old. She must have had some kind of job because her Social Security number is right here. Back in those days, you couldn't get a number unless you had a job. That alone is going to make it easier to trace her even if she married and has a new name. She refused to divulge the name of the father. It isn't all that unusual. That can mean one of two things. One, she doesn't know who the father is because she was involved with more than one boy. Two, the person is someone she's either afraid of or someone who didn't want his reputation tarnished. Which way are you leaning, Mr. Lam?"

"I don't know. I'd like to find her. She's sixty-two now. If she's still alive. I'm sure she's married and has a different name. I'm toying with the idea of hiring a private detective."

"Don't do that. That's just one more person who will know your business. You never know if you can trust them. Me, you can trust. I have the whole afternoon and evening free. Let me give it a shot. It's a good thing that guy's mother made copies of the files if the originals disappeared. Stuff like that only disappears when it's high-powered stuff. Get my drift?"

Ricky nodded as he pulled the envelope out of his hip pocket. "This was in my mother's safe-deposit box. I found it this morning. I don't know the guy but his name sounds kind of familiar. It must mean something for my mother to hide it in a safe-deposit box."

"Maybe he's your brother's father. Think about it. It makes sense. If we can find Lorraine Woodworth, we can ask her. This is the age of DNA. It's wonderful. In the meantime, I'll see what I can find out about him. If this turns out to be anything near interesting, can I have an exclusive?"

"Yes."

"Okay, Mr. Lam. Drink that coffee now and don't waste it."

"Yes, Mother." Ricky laughed.

Ricky woke with a start. He felt stiff and sore, disoriented, when he looked down at his watch. He yawned. He'd slept, curled up on the deck chair, for over six hours.

It was dusk, the end of a very long day. In the old days, he'd always liked the approach of nightfall because he could party up a storm. These days, he looked forward to sunrise and the beginning of a new day. He liked new beginnings. Actually, at this point in his life, he treasured them.

Sensing a presence behind him, Ricky half turned, then leaped off the chaise. "Roxy! I was going to pick you up. Why didn't you call me?" Jesus, he sounded like a fifteen-year-old. He almost reached out to her, to draw her close. He wanted to kiss her so bad he had to clamp his teeth together. He didn't want to scare her off.

Roxy smiled as she covered the distance between them and stepped into his waiting arms. "It was just easier to hire a car service. You know what the airport is like at this time of day. I missed you, Ricky. I . . ."

"No more than I missed you. Want some coffee? I've been making it all day and throwing it away."

"Coffee wasn't exactly what I had in mind." She leaned closer and whispered in his ear.

"No! You can really do that?"

"I came prepared," Roxy said with a little laugh. "Remember now, you said smoke, and I said fire."

"You offering up any kind of guarantee, Roxy?" He watched, fascinated, as she removed her powder blue jacket. She tossed it over her shoulder, her eyes never leaving his. One by one she kicked off her shoes. They flew across the deck.

"You're a little slow this evening, Ricky? Why is that?" Her skirt dropped to the floor. She stepped out of it. "You really need to move a little faster, honey," she purred.

Ricky's Docksiders slid across the deck at the same time he dropped his denim shorts. "Are we going for it right here, or do you prefer a nice soft bed?" he gasped as he pulled his tank top off. He whipped it across the deck. "How's this for speed?" he almost yelled as he yanked at his jockeys.

"Ahhh, I like that." Roxy continued to purr as she stepped out of her thong and twirled it by the edge. It was so wispy, it floated to the floor of the deck. Her bra, a skimpy affair whose straps were nothing more than lace and ribbons, dropped from her fingers to land on his upright penis. "Now, tell me again why you don't believe I can deliver on my promises." Her voice was so seductive, Ricky grew light-headed.

Ricky groaned as he reached for her. Together they fell to the deck. "I believe you, I believe you! You know our asses are going to be full of splinters, don't you? It might be exciting to pick them out of each other later." He couldn't believe he'd said what he'd just said. Talk about romantic fools. He could head the list.

"Your ass, not mine." Roxy laughed as she assumed the top position and proceeded to keep her promise.

The moon rode high in the sky when Ricky opened his eyes for the second time that night and asked if he was dead.

"You better not be dead, Ricky Lam. I have big plans for you tonight. This was just the appetizer. We haven't gotten to the main course. It's the dessert that's worth waiting for. Now, if you're telling me you need a little nap . . . well, that's something different."

"Nap? You must be kidding. No, I don't need a nap. Do you need a nap? I slept all afternoon. Do you want me to make you some coffee?" When had he started babbling like this? Jesus, he couldn't talk or think straight when he was around Roxy. He wondered if she noticed.

"Is that desperation I'm hearing in your voice, Ricky Lam? No, I don't want you to make me any coffee. What I want you to do is . . ."

"Okay. I can do that. Uh-huh, you bet. Absolutely. But not for a couple of hours." He guffawed. "C'mon, let's go upstairs to bed."

"God, that's the best offer I've had all day." Roxy giggled in relief as she trailed Ricky into the house and up the stairs to the second floor.

They sat together at Ricky's kitchen table, silly, satisfied expressions on their faces. It was six-thirty in the morning.

"Now, you can make some coffee!" Roxy said.

Ricky hopped off the chair to reach for the coffee canister. A wicked grin played around the corners of his mouth. He half turned, and said, "So what happened to the fire and smoke?"

Roxy reared back indignantly. "Are you complaining?"

"Hell no. I was just curious."

"Your smoke and fire are sitting in the Charleston airport. They wouldn't let me bring the firecrackers on the plane. Fireworks are legal in South Carolina. You can buy them anywhere. I had this grand . . ."

"Save it and surprise me when we get back. Hey, you wanna get married?"

Roxy sat up straighter in the chair. She clutched at Ricky's maroon robe, her eyes wary. "Are you serious?"

Was he? Hell, yes, he was. He liked her. No, he loved her. He really did. He said so. "It's not like we have to ask anyone's permission. I will tell my sons, and I guess you would want to tell your daughter. That's if you say yes. I guess you want to think about it, huh?"

"You really want to marry this old widow, your brother's wife?"

"Yeah, I do, Roxy. Hey, we've been working side by side for six months. I think I know you inside and out. You should know me the same way. Listen, though, there's something I have to tell you. I didn't want you to hear it over the phone."

Roxy propped her elbows on the table. "Are you going to tell me something that is going to upset me or make me mad?"

Ricky grimaced. "Probably a little of both. Here, drink this coffee."

"I don't want the damn coffee, Ricky. Tell

me whatever it is you didn't want to tell me on the phone."

"You aren't a widow. Philly was married to a woman named Lee Ann Oliver. He has . . . had . . . whatever . . . three daughters. I guess he was a bigamist. I suppose that's one of the reasons you couldn't claim half his estate. I don't know about all that legal stuff. Dammit, Roxy, I'm not making this up. Say something, for God's sake."

"I don't know what to say. What do you want me to say? How . . . why?"

"I don't know, Roxy. He provided for his family but not in any grand way. I'll take care of that. Did you have a clue, an inkling, anything?"

"No. This blows my mind. You must have been stunned. What . . . what is she like?"

"She's pleasant. Her daughters didn't have much to say. They live in a nice, quiet neighborhood. They're ordinary people. The house is nothing fancy or spectacular. Philly redid the kitchen himself to make it look like my mother's old kitchen. It's bizarre. You're taking this rather well. I thought you would be upset."

Roxy still clutched the collar of her robe.

"I think I'm in shock. Perhaps if you had told me this six months ago, I might have imploded. You're right, it's bizarre."

"They didn't know anything that would shed light on Philly. I left it at that. They didn't seem interested in me at all. They made lives for themselves and I don't fit into those lives and I'm thinking that's just as well."

"How are you coping with all these strange surprises about Philly?"

"Shit, I don't know. I've been trying to think like Philly. That was my first mistake, since we were like night and day. I'm having trouble trying to comprehend his double life. I thought you might be able to bring a female perspective to it. You lived with him for all those years."

Roxy shook her head sadly. "I'm sorry, Ricky. I just don't know what to say right now."

"This is what I think we should do," Ricky said, wanting to restore her good spirits. "Let's shower, get dressed, and go out to breakfast. I'll give you a half hour head start. I can be ready in ten minutes."

It was fifteen minutes past eight when Roxy entered the kitchen wearing a lime green sleeveless dress with matching espadrilles. It looked great with her tan. She hadn't bothered to blow-dry her strawberry blonde hair. Instead she combed it straight back. It was just long enough to lick the back of her neck. "You look great as usual. I'm so used to seeing you in dungarees and a hard hat that I'm always surprised at how good you look when you get dressed up."

Roxy eyed him from head to toe. He looked better than good, with his khaki walking shorts and cream-colored Polo shirt. His sandy blond hair was still damp from the shower. *He can still cut it in the looks department,* she thought. She wondered if her own eyes looked as worried as his.

Ricky was holding the door of the Porsche open when Gracie raced across the lawn. "Hold on, Mr. Lam. I have something for you."

"So quick? Roxy, this is Gracie. I told you all about her."

"It's so nice to meet you finally."

"Likewise." Gracie walked a little bit away from the car, where she could speak privately to Ricky. "Listen, Mr. Lam, it wasn't all that quick. I worked through the night. I haven't been to bed yet. My brother was working with me on his computer, so between us we logged a lot of hours. We came up with three Lorraine Woodworths. One of them lives right in L.A., and her married name is Farquar. One of the other women lives in San Diego, and the third one lives in Glen Burnie, Maryland. All three did live here in L.A. at one time. The Social Security number you gave me matches Lorraine Farquar's. Here, I printed everything out for you," she said handing him a file. "Do you want to run with it?"

"Damn, you're good. Thanks, Gracie. I owe you, big-time."

"No, you don't owe me anything. I was glad to do it. Your lady is real pretty. She looks nice, too."

"I'll tell her you said so. See ya later. Hey, did the pups start to nurse?"

Gracie laughed. "Yep, and they're piglets. Their bellies are so fat and pink. Everyone is comfortable and happy. Including me."

"Go to bed. That's an order," Ricky said over his shoulder as he climbed into the Porsche.

"So she's the one who has Max in a tizzy. Pretty girl. I hope it works out for the two of them. So what did she give you?"

"I believe she just found Philly's biological mother. Get the map out of the glove compartment. I think we'll pay her a little visit. After breakfast."

13

Ricky lowered the windows of the Porsche and opened the sun roof. He looked over at Roxy. "Do you mind if your hair blows around? It's too nice a day to sit in a closed-up car."

"I like the wind in my hair and on my face. I often wondered what it would be like to ride on the back of a motorcycle. I guess that's the young, adventuresome girl in me that never quite left."

"I still have a Harley from my wild young days. Say the word, and we can hit the road. I keep it in tip-top shape but haven't been on it in over twenty years. The studio threatened to cancel my contract if I didn't give it up."

"Is there anything you didn't do, Ricky?"

"That's rather doubtful. The sad part of it is, Philly said I did it all, but I really don't remember most of it. On second thought, let's forget the Harley. If you like to ride around with the wind in your hair and face, I can either buy a convertible or an open-air Jeep."

"You'd do that for me?" Roxy asked in awe.

"In an L.A. heartbeat."

"Why are we talking about such silly things when I know you want to talk about those papers Gracie gave you?"

"It's like making coffee and pouring it down the drain. It's something to do so I don't have to think or act on it because I'm afraid of what I'm going to find out about my brother. At the same time I'm wondering how it's going to affect me."

Roxy looked across at Ricky. She felt her heart flutter in her chest. She was falling in love with this man. Who was she kidding? She'd fallen in love with him the day he gave her back her old job.

"Oh, look, we're here. I always loved this place," Roxy said, pointing to a cozy little restaurant that looked like a Swiss chalet. "They have the best eggs Benedict. I always get those bananas they set on fire. That's what I'm having. I didn't eat a thing yesterday other than some chips on the plane. I'm starving."

"I don't think I ate either. We're a pair, aren't we?"

"Yes. Yes, I'll marry you, not yes, we're a pair."

Ricky swerved into a parking space and, in stunned surprise, forgot to step on the clutch. The Porsche bucked and stalled. "You're sure?" was all he could manage by way of words.

"I'm sure," Roxy said softly. "I'm really sure. But not till the Crown Jewel is up and running. How would you feel about getting married there?"

"In the desert, in a tent, in a tree house, I don't care. Do you want a big wedding, where you wear the white gown and I wear a white tux?"

"No, no, no. I think I'm a little too old to go tripping down the aisle in a white gown with a train. I want to wear a flowered dress and have flowers in my hair. Just simple, Ricky. A small wedding with your sons, my daughter, your housekeeper Ellie, Ted Lymen, Donna, a few close friends, that's it. We can honeymoon at the resort. We won't have to leave our suite for *days*. I can buy up a goodly supply of fireworks."

"Get the hell out of the car, Roxy, before I explode." Laughing, Roxy joined him. Their arms around each other's waists, they entered the restaurant, where they waited to be seated.

A young girl with a megawatt smile, bouncing hair, bouncing breasts, and bouncing feet bounced her way to a small secluded table in a sunny window. She waved her arms with a flourish. "This is my favorite table." Her smile showed a fortune in magnificent orthodonture.

"Take your time, Mr. Lam, we're running a little slow this morning." She bounced off to wait on another couple.

Roxy grimaced. "How can anyone be that cheerful, that bouncy, so early in the morning?"

"Youth, that's how." Ricky grinned. "Compared to her, we're *old!* There was a time when I came here every morning, and I always asked for this particular table. For some reason, I hated to leave, so I would slow down and dawdle over my food. It looks exactly the same as it did the last time I was here. Aren't things supposed to change? It has to be at least two years, and yet it still looks exactly the way I remember it. Different people, though."

Roxy looked around. Ricky was right. Not only was the restaurant cozy and comfortable, it was so clean it sparkled. The green-and-white-checkered curtains on the diamond-paned windows were crisply starched. The tablecloths were dark green cotton with green-checkered napkins. The captain's chairs were oak with checkered cushions. Luscious green plants that looked healthy and vibrant hung from the beams. The floor was wide, plank oak, and it, too, was clean and polished. A field-stone fireplace graced one wall. It burned, at times during the winter, whole cherry logs. The mantel held pictures of famous people with the owner, Mary Sue Duvane. The best thing about Mary Sue's was the smell of coffee and fresh-baked bread.

"That's your picture on the mantel, isn't it?" Roxy said.

"Yes. Me and Mary Sue on my Harley. She let me ride her around the parking lot. I don't think she trusted me on the highway. She passed away a few months before

Philly died. I think every movie star in town, myself included, showed up for the funeral. Mary Sue fed more out-of-work actors and actresses than you can imagine. I heard her son and daughter run the place now. They still help out-of-work actors and actresses."

"I never knew that. It's nice to know there are still some caring people out there. I'm glad you brought me here. This is charming. Just charming. I think I'd rather go out to breakfast than out to dinner. It just gives a good feeling for the start of the day."

Ricky gazed at Roxy in awe. "That's exactly how I feel."

The young waitress, whose name tag said she was Sophia, filled their coffee cups. "Would you like a menu, or do you know what you want?"

"Eggs Benedict and the flaming bananas," Roxy said.

"I'll have the same," Ricky said.

Two hours later, when the waiting line extended outside, Roxy and Ricky left the restaurant.

Roxy's face was clouded with worry when she wiggled around in her seat so she could see Ricky better. "Have you thought about how you're going to approach Lorraine Farquar? You can't just blurt it out. What if she's in frail health, or, worse yet, her husband doesn't know? Do you have a picture of Philly with you?"

"I thought I'd wing it, take my cue from her, that kind of thing. I have a picture of Philly and me the night I won my first Oscar. I keep it in my wallet. For some reason, that night, I really felt like we were brothers. Usually I felt like he was the warden, and I was the wayward prisoner. I need to get past all this shit, I really do."

"I understand that, but what if she denies knowing anything about Philly?"

Ricky pointed to the pocket on the driver's door. "The report from the adoption agency is right here, and it's all documented. The only thing we don't have is the name of the father, and I'm thinking it's the name on the paper in my mother's safe-deposit box. I'm not above issuing a threat at this stage. Like I said, I just want to put this behind me."

"I'm nervous, and I don't mind admitting it," Roxy said.

"You know what, Roxy, I've been nervous since the day Philly died, and I haven't been able to shake the feeling. We're coming up to Santa Monica now. Keep your eye on the map and tell me where to turn. I never liked this town, and I don't know why."

"The name Farquar is not a common name. I know I've heard it somewhere not too long ago. Maybe it was on the radio or television. Probably online since that's how I read the *L.A. Times*. Whoa, this is a pretty ritzy-looking neighborhood," Roxy said as she craned her neck to look at the high-end real estate. "Make a left, then another left, and that's the street where the woman lives. The house number is 22865. Not shabby," she said, when Ricky stopped the car in front of a house that was set back a considerable distance from the road. "At least fifteen thousand square feet. Bet there's a pool and a tennis court. Live-in help, gardener. As I said, not shabby. I don't have a good feeling about this, Ricky."

"I don't either, but we're going to do it anyway. We're here. What's the worst thing she can do? Tell us to leave? Deny everything? Threaten to call the police? I expect all of the above."

Together they walked up a flower-bordered walkway. Ricky rang the bell, sucking in his breath when he heard the melodious chimes inside. A maid with a gray dress, white apron, and perky little cap opened the door, her eyes full of questions. "My name is Ricky Lam, and this is Roxy Nelson. We'd like to speak with Mrs. Lorraine Farquar, please."

"Is Mrs. Farquar expecting you?"

"No, she isn't. Please tell her it's extremely urgent."

The maid looked doubtful. She weighed Ricky's words before she said, "Wait here." The door closed in their faces. Ricky stepped back when the maid opened the door. "Mrs. Farquar said she doesn't know either one of you and requested that I ask you what is the nature of your call?"

"Tell her it's personal and confidential. If you like, you can mention the name Vincent Nolan. If the name doesn't ring a bell with Mrs. Farquar, tell her it's about something that happened when she was fourteen years old."

When the door opened for the third time,

the maid stepped aside to usher them into a foyer that was as large as most people's living rooms. It was full of live trees, bamboo chests and chairs, and floor-to-ceiling windows. "Follow me, please."

The maid led them to a sunroom, or maybe the Farquars called it a solarium. Like the foyer, the room had wraparound windows allowing the warm sun to bathe the room in its golden glow, a perfect backdrop for the green plants and white wicker furniture with colorful cushions. Books and magazines filled the tables, along with a pitcher of frosty ice tea.

If Lorraine Farquar had been a little taller, and a little less thick, she might have been considered regal. She had high cheekbones, wide eyes, and a short neck adorned with a triple stand of pearls. She was fully dressed and coiffed. She raised a thin hand full of diamonds, an indication they were to sit on the love seat across from her. She tilted her head slightly, her eyes guileless and full of questions.

"I appreciate your taking the time to see us, Mrs. Farquar. I'm Ricky Lam, and this is Roxy Nelson. I need to ask you some questions."

Lorraine Farquar's harsh, raspy voice surprised Ricky. For some reason, he'd expected it to be soft and gentle-sounding. "Why is that, Mr. Lam? I don't believe we've ever met. I have, of course, seen some of your films, but I think I would remember if we had met in person."

"I'm not here about myself, Mrs. Farquar. I came about my brother, your son. The one you put up for adoption."

Lorraine Farquar looked around, a puzzled expression on her face as though she expected someone to shout, *Candid Camera!* "If this is a joke, Mr. Lam, it is in exceedingly bad taste. Whatever *are* you talking about?"

"I'm talking about my adopted brother. His adopted name was Philip Lam. I called him Philly. My parents adopted him when you placed him with the agency. I have all the records. Yes, the records were sealed, and yes, they were subsequently removed from the agency. However, Martina Mangarella had already copied the records and stored them in her home. She didn't try to sell them or offer them to anyone. But if someone managed to find her, she offered up the records. I got your records from her son, who is now the custodian of those files. I suppose what he and his mother did was illegal, but there are many people out there, like my brother, who needed to know they weren't throwaways. I think that's what Philly believed in his heart, that you threw him away."

The voice was just as harsh and raspy as before when Lorraine Farquar stared over at Ricky. "I think you must have me mixed up with someone else, Mr. Lam. I have no idea what you're talking about. I consider you shameless, and I deeply resent this intrusion into my privacy. I'd like you to leave now."

"Mrs. Farquar, did you hear what I just said? I said I have the complete file. That means your fingerprints, your picture, and a picture of Philly when he was brought into the agency. I also have his footprints. And your Social Security number. I'm not making this up. I realize forty-eight years ago it was a stain on a woman's reputation to bear a child out of wedlock, but it isn't like that today. My brother searched for you for years. For years, Mrs. Farquar. Personally, I think it was cruel to have the records removed. Do you have any idea what that must have been like for him, and I ask you that with all due respect?" When there was no response from the woman across from him, Ricky continued, "Well, do you?"

"How could I possibly know something like that? It's a ridiculous question to begin with."

"I wonder if I might have a sip of that ice tea, Mrs. Farquar," Roxy said. "I'm just getting over a terrible summer cold, and my throat is very dry."

"Of course. I'm sorry, I should have offered you tea earlier."

Roxy sucked in her breath when Lorraine Farquar picked up first a glass and then the pitcher. She handed the glass to Roxy, along with a small cocktail napkin. Roxy palmed the glass instead of holding it by the sides. "I feel a coughing spell coming on. Please excuse me. I'll wait outside if it's all right with you. I wouldn't want to spread my germs." She almost ran from the room, the glass still in the palm of her hand.

Quick on the uptake, Ricky stifled his grin. *Fingerprints.* How he loved that woman.

"My brother, your son, died six months ago in a tragic accident, Mrs. Farquar. He was also battling a terminal illness he hid from me. What harm can it do now to tell me the truth?"

"I'm sorry for your loss, Mr. Lam, but it has nothing to do with me. I'd like you to leave now. I find this whole conversation very upsetting."

"Will it be more upsetting if I go to the Associated Press or perhaps the Fox News Channel? How upsetting will that be to your husband and your family?"

"Are you threatening me, Mr. Lam? Or are you trying to extort me? Which is it?"

"It's neither, Mrs. Farquar. All I want is the truth. We live in a new world these days. DNA is a powerful tool. We have yours."

"That's . . . hogwash, and you know it. There's no way on this earth you could possibly have my DNA. No way at all." She was starting to bluster. Ricky almost felt sorry for her and his part in being such a bulldog.

Ricky leaned across the wicker, glass-topped table, where six issues of *Time* magazine lay scattered next to the latest copy of *Money* magazine. They looked like they had never been read. "Now, you see, that's where you're wrong, Mrs. Farquar. Don't you recall the letter you put in Philly's cardboard box? The carton you dropped him off in. You sealed the envelope. That means you had to use your own saliva to seal the envelope. *Voilà!* DNA. All these years later. Your DNA, your Social Security number, your fingerprints. That's pretty conclusive to my way of thinking."

Lorraine Farquar appeared to be visibly shaken. Still, she blustered. "I want you to leave, and I want you to leave *now!*"

"Please, just tell me the truth, Mrs. Farquar."

"If you don't leave, I'll call the police."

Ricky sighed. "I'll leave, Mrs. Farquar. Thank you for talking to me. Maybe I'll have more luck with Vincent Nolan." He fully expected his hostess to throw the pitcher of ice tea at him. Instead, she burrowed into the colorful cushions; her face was pasty white and fearful. "I can see myself out."

In the car, Ricky looked at Roxy, who was still holding the glass in the palm of her hand. She'd either emptied the contents or consumed them. He shook his head at her questioning gaze. "She's sticking with her story. But when I mentioned the name Vincent Nolan, she kind of shrank into herself. I thought she looked afraid. I'm not very good at this detective stuff. You, on the other hand, are the marvel in marvelous. In a million years I never would have thought of taking the glass. If I had a gold star, I'd give it to you." Ricky leaned over and hugged her. Roxy beamed.

"I feel sorry for her, Ricky. I remember what it was like to be pregnant at sixteen. I thought about giving Reba up for adoption, but when it came time to sign the final papers I couldn't do it. It wasn't easy those first years. Maybe Mrs. Farquar didn't have any other choice. It's possible her husband isn't the understanding type. I remembered who he is while I was sitting here waiting for you. He's that famous venture capitalist. He's incredibly wealthy.

"If she was nervous at the mention of Vincent Nolan," Roxy continued, "that might mean she's more afraid of him than her husband. Possibly both. What now?"

"I say we look for a private lab and see

what they can do for us by lifting the fingerprints off the glass. If the fingerprints match those on the letter, that's our proof.

"Before we go home, Roxy, I want to stop by our old house. There's a box in Philly's closet I want to pick up. With all the stuff I packed in the car last night there wasn't room for it. It won't take long."

An hour later, Ricky exited his old home, a blue cardboard box in his hands. He opened the passenger-side door and handed it to Roxy. She looked down at the black lettering and then up at Ricky.

It was midafternoon, and the sun was high in the sky when Ricky drove his Porsche through the gates of his Holmby Hills estate. As he and Roxy were getting out of the car, Gracie Lick, her red hair flying behind her, along with her shirttail, the mother and father dog running alongside her, shouted, "Mr. Lam! Mr. Lam! I think I found something! If I'm right, this is going to blow your socks off! I'll be right back. I have to go back to my office to get it." She was breathless with excitement. She called over her shoulder, "By the way, a letter from your attorney was hand-delivered earlier. It's on the kitchen table."

"Okay. Take your time. Want some coffee?"

"Are we going to drink it or look at it?" she called over her shoulder, a second time.

"Depends on what you have to show us."

"With what I think I found, we're all going to need some *hard* stuff in our coffee. I'll be right back."

"I like that girl, Ricky. You're right, she's perfect for Max. I'll make the coffee while you put *that box* somewhere."

"Since I can't have the *hard* stuff Gracie is talking about, you better make the coffee extra strong," Ricky said, his heartbeat accelerating.

14

Lorraine Farquar stared across the room at the French doors that had closed behind Ricky Lam. Her gaze was so intense, her eyes started to water. She looked down in horror when the triple strand of pearls around her neck broke, scattering across the floor. She needed to think. Really think. What a foolish old woman she was to believe this would never happen.

The maid in the gray uniform and prim apron opened the French doors, and said, "Luncheon is served, madam. Mr. Farquar called a short while ago to say he wouldn't be able to join you but suggested dinner at Estevan's this evening."

"I'm not hungry, Thelma. I would like some coffee, though. You can take away this ice tea. The ice melted, and it's too watery."

The maid entered the room, picked up the tray, and looked around. "I don't see the glass, madam. Oh, what a shame, your pearls broke. I'll pick them up."

Lorraine shook her head. "You can gather them up later." She suddenly realized what had happened to the glass. Not trusting herself to speak, she shrugged and waved the maid away. She knew they hadn't believed her. How sneaky and underhanded they were to steal a glass. For fingerprints, of course. How could she have been so stupid? Thank God Armand wasn't joining her for lunch. He would have picked up instantly that something was wrong. At least she would have the afternoon to compose herself before dinner.

Movie stars were such tacky people. They loved splashing their business in the media, thinking it made them more important. She hated the media because she knew they were capable of destroying her. She wished now that she had been more forthright with Ricky Lam. Perhaps if she'd thrown herself on his mercy, he would have left matters alone. Now he was going to dig and dig and dig. Eventually, he'd come up with all the right answers, and her life would come crashing down around her. No, no, that was wrong. He already had all the answers. Except one.

Did she dare make the phone call she had promised never to make? Did she have any other choice?

When the maid set the elegant silver service on the table and closed the French doors behind her, Lorraine poured the coffee she knew she wouldn't drink. Instead, she curled herself into the corner of the sofa she was sitting on. She started to cry. Not out of anger, not out of frustration with her situation, but out of grief. Her only child, a son, was dead, and she'd never known of his passing until just a few minutes ago. Life was so cruel sometimes.

She'd named her son Caleb in her mind because it was such a strong-sounding name. She knew he was going to need a strong name to survive in the world he was going to. The guilt and shame that she'd lived with all those years covered her like a shroud. Right then, right that second, she wanted to die so she could be with her son to tell him how sorry she was that she had listened to Vincent Nolan. She wanted to tell him how, during those first years, she'd driven around a fifty-mile radius, hoping for a glimpse of the son who was lost to her. She wanted to tell him how she'd gone back to the orphanage and pleaded with them to tell her where her son was. She'd been a runaway from Dubois, Pennsylvania, convinced she could make it in Hollywood. Convinced because at fourteen she looked like she was twenty. It was just a dream. If she'd had the money, she would have hired a lawyer to help her locate her son, but, unfortunately, she didn't earn much waiting tables, hoping some movie producer would spot her. That never happened either.

She cringed when she recalled the look of loathing she'd seen on the movie star's face. She understood that look because she'd looked at herself the same way during the nearly fifty years since she'd taken Caleb to the orphanage.

Her memory of that time in her life was crystal clear. So clear, she could see the memory shattering all about her. She'd read so many articles while she waited in doctors' offices with Armand, articles that said that, as one aged, memory faded. It was such a blatant lie, she'd been tempted to write to the magazine refuting the articles. Unfortunately, she had never mustered the courage to do it.

She hated Vincent Nolan with a passion that was unequaled. And, yet, back in her youth, when she wanted to fit in, to have fun and romance, she'd allowed him to seduce her. She knew better, and yet she had let it happen. Vincent was the rich college boy out looking for cheap thrills. That's what she was, a cheap thrill. All Vincent and his friends wanted were virgins, so they could notch their belts. Vincent had staked out his claim to the greasy restaurant where she worked and had his way with six of the other waitresses. He'd boasted later that she was number seven in his notched belt.

When she discovered she was pregnant, she'd contacted him. He'd said he would see her that evening after she got off work. She'd been so excited, dreaming about the handsome Vincent and living the academic life. She promised herself to take etiquette lessons, so she wouldn't shame him. She'd buy expensive creams and lotions, so her hands wouldn't be red and rough. She'd get manicures and pedicures and have her hair done once a week. She'd learn to play bridge and shop in the finest stores. The dreams of a young girl who thought she was in love. How incredibly stupid she had been.

That dream had crashed around her feet that night in the alley behind the restaurant. Vincent had looked at her in the dim, yellow light, disgust on his face. "Don't think you're pinning this on me! I'm not your free ride out of this hellhole. If you even think of accusing me, I'll have every single one of my friends say they had you for two bucks each. Who do you think the authorities are going to believe, me or you?"

All her virginity had been worth was two dollars. She'd cried for weeks. Maybe it was months, not knowing what she was going to do. The owners of the restaurant had helped her every way they could. A minister counseled her and managed to convince her adoption was the best thing for the baby. She'd agreed until she set her eyes on the pink-cheeked Caleb. She knew she would scrub bathrooms in dirty gas stations if she had to, just so she could keep him.

It hadn't worked out. She'd gotten sick, Caleb was sick, she had no money to care for him. She called Vincent again and threatened to go to the police if he didn't help her. Something in her voice must have convinced him she was serious. He'd showed up at the rooming house where she lived and snatched the sleeping child, who was rosy red with a fever. She followed him, sick and frightened out of her wits. She wanted to die when she saw him raise the lid of a Dumpster and drop the baby inside. What was more horrifying was that he *closed* the cover. She watched him look over his shoulder before he ran from the alley. Quicker than lightning, she opened the cover, climbed in, and rescued her baby. Somehow, she found her way to the minister who had counseled her and she told him her story. They stayed with him at the parish house until both of them were well enough to go to the orphanage to place Caleb for adoption.

And that was the end of her tawdry little tale as far as Vincent Nolan was concerned. These days, Vincent Nolan went by the name of Adam V. Nolan, vice president of the United States.

Lorraine looked down at the coffee in the bone china cup. She knew it was cold, but she drank it anyway. She probably had more in the way of luxurious surroundings and material things than Adam V. Nolan could ever hope to have. Her husband Armand, twenty-five years her senior, was a billionaire. He was a good man, a kind man, who lavished his wealth on her. The only thing he hadn't been able to give her were the children she coveted. Armand was old and frail and spent his days in a wheelchair. But he still managed, with the aid of a male nurse, to go to his offices three days a week.

Such a terrible secret.

Armand had an impressive Rolodex. He was also a heavy contributor to political campaigns. Wealthy philanthropist that he was, he knew everyone, and everyone knew Armand Farquar.

Lorraine left the sunroom and headed to her husband's in-house office, where she flipped through his Rolodex until she found the number she wanted. Armand was proud of the fact that the White House always returned his phone calls. Always. She wondered if they would return hers. Well, there was only one way to find out. She dialed the number from the little card in the Rolodex. She identified herself, clarifying that she was Armand Farquar's wife. "Please tell the vice president this is an urgent call and one that needs to be returned as soon as possible." She rattled off her phone number and spelled her last name slowly and distinctly.

The return phone call could come within minutes, hours, or possibly days. It *would* be returned, she just didn't know when.

Tears rolling down her wrinkled cheeks, Lorraine paced the confines of her husband's study. *Now what am I supposed to do,* she wondered. *How do I get through the minutes and the hours until he calls me back. God in heaven, what am I going to say to him?* She played different scenarios over and over in her mind. Nothing seemed right or even appropriate. The tears continued to cascade down her cheeks.

She tried to remember what she'd read about Adam V. Nolan over the years. When she was safely married to Armand and knew her future was secure, she'd allowed her obsession with Adam V. Nolan to come to the fore. She'd haunted the library and even kept a diary of sorts. Armand thought she was the best-read wife he'd ever had, and he'd had three before her. She didn't even know where that diary was now. That was all right; there was always the internet.

Lorraine was far from computer literate, but she did know how to check email for Armand, and she knew how to go to various websites that interested her. She looked for Keyword and typed in the vice president's name. She reared back when the man's whole life flashed in front of her. Well, *almost* his whole life. Her shoulders set grimly as she pressed PRINT again and again. When the printer grew silent, she got up, walked around to the machine, and withdrew a thick stack of paper.

Lorraine carried the papers with her to the sunroom, stopping only long enough to pick up her reading glasses from her bedroom.

The coffee service was gone, and her pearls had been gathered up and placed in a crystal candy dish. She knew she'd never have them restrung. In the scheme of things, a pearl necklace, triple strand or not, simply wasn't important. Her son could have attended college for two years for what the pearls cost.

Lorraine settled herself in the same corner of the sofa she'd sat in earlier. She perched her reading glasses on the tip of her nose and read through every single piece of paper she'd printed out. When she was finished, she looked at the telephone. For some reason, it looked ominous. She was surprised at how calm she felt.

Such an illustrious career. No hint of scandal anywhere in his life. One couldn't have scandals or skeletons when one had presidential aspirations. Lorraine flipped through the pages until she found the ones she wanted. She'd even taken the time to download the pictures of the vice president and his family. The caption underneath the family picture called the Nolans the All-American Family.

The all-American family consisted of a son who was a second-term congressman from Virginia. A second son was a cardiovascular surgeon who lived in San Francisco. A daughter, married to a senator from Illinois, was a psychiatrist with her own flourishing practice. There were nine grandchildren ranging in age from five years of age to seventeen. The oldest, a boy named Patrick, had an appointment to Annapolis.

Mrs. Nolan Senior worked diligently for the Red Cross, the United Way, and sat on five different charitable boards. She had silver-colored hair worn short with full bangs. Lorraine thought she looked like a female Buster Brown. Mrs. Meredith Nolan had graduated from Sarah Lawrence and never worked a day in her life for monetary remuneration.

Adam V. Nolan had been a two-term governor and a two-term senator before the president had tapped him to be his running mate.

All the Nolan money was tied up in blind trusts, according to their financial disclosure statements.

There was even a shaggy, lovable dog and a fat, white cat in the photograph.

The charming all-American Nolan family. She wanted to puke.

The phone rang. Lorraine snatched it the moment it rang. Her greeting was cautious.

It was Armand's nurse. "Is something wrong, Thomas?"

"I'm at the hospital. Mr. Farquar started to experience chest pains on the way home. I thought it best to bring him in and admit him. Your husband wanted me to tell you he's sorry, but dinner at Estevan's is out of the question. I think you should come to the hospital now, Mrs. Farquar."

"Of course I'll come. Thomas, tell me the truth, is it bad, or is this just a setback?"

"I'm afraid it's very serious, ma'am. I'll tell your husband you're on the way."

Lorraine ran through the house, out to the kitchen, then outside, where the chauffeur was vacuuming the interior of the Bentley.

"Stop what you're doing, Henry. You have to take me to the hospital right away. Thomas just called to say they had to admit my husband. We have to hurry, Henry."

"Yes, ma'am, we can go right now. Do you need to take anything with you?"

"No. No, I'm fine. Armand carries all his own medical cards."

For the second time that day, tears rolled down Lorraine Farquar's cheeks.

What would she do without Armand at

her side? For the past year the doctors had been warning her that this day was coming. They'd urged Armand to cut back, to become an invalid. He'd said no, he intended to live his days to the fullest for as long as he could. How she loved the man, admired him, doted on him. Why did this have to happen today of all days? Was it another omen of some kind?

"Can't you go any faster, Henry?"

"I'm already going ten miles over the speed limit, ma'am. You want to get there in one piece, don't you?"

"Yes, of course. I just don't want to be . . . *too late.*"

"Gracie, you look exhausted. You didn't sleep, did you?"

"No, I didn't sleep. I can sleep anytime. In my business when you're on a roll, you *roll*. Before I tell you what I found, let me tell you that Dicky Tee called me. He said my article was a piece of crap. He just said that because someone from the *Times* called his publisher, and he isn't going to be writing an exposé on you. He was so mad he was chewing nails and spitting rust. I could hear it in his voice. No one is going to write anything bad about you as long as I'm around." Her voice was so vehement, Ricky smiled.

"That's nice to know, Gracie. Thank you. I'm sure the boys will be relieved to hear the news, too. Maybe you should call them later and tell them the news."

"Maybe. I'm going to take a swim and a nap after I drink this coffee. If I can stay awake that long. See this," she said, pointing to a ten-inch stack of printouts. This is every person in the United States who has the last name of Nolan. My brother and sister helped me separate the V. Nolans to names like Vincent, Victoria, etc. Then we looked for the ones with a first name with a middle initial of V. Of course there were thousands of those. We stayed with it, though, concentrating on the ones we thought might be important. You know, with enough clout to make adoption records *disappear.*

"My sister, who is a high school junior is the one who homed in on the right name almost instantly. She's up on all that kind of stuff. Wally and I have been out of school a while. Adam V. Nolan," Gracie said triumphantly. She waited for a reaction.

"And that would be . . . who?"

"Mr. Lam, *think!*"

Ricky's eyebrows shot upward. "Do you mean . . . Gracie, are you sure?"

"Damn straight, I'm sure. The vice prez himself. He went to UCLA. All the dates are right. Well, what do you think?"

"I think I'm in shock is what I think. Philly's father is the vice president of the United States, and his mother is married to one of the richest men in the world! You were right, Gracie. If I were wearing socks, you would have blown them off. We can't be certain, though, can we?"

"I'm as sure as I can be. I'd stake my career on it, Mr. Lam. I downloaded the man's life. He is a paragon of virtue. And, he plans to run for the presidency in two years. He's already gearing up for the run. I guess if you want one hundred percent proof, you'll have to get it from Mrs. Farquar. I bet when you spring this on her, she'll buckle. Take this printout with you for your proof.

"Look, Mr. Lam, I finished my coffee. I'm going for a swim. If you need me, just call."

Ricky hugged the young woman. He hoped she would one day become his daughter-in-law. It would be nice to have a daughter. "I owe you, Gracie."

"Jeez, we aren't going through that again, are we? I owe you. Why don't we just say we're even, okay?' Night."

"I don't want to see you till tomorrow, Gracie!" Ricky called after her.

Ricky sat down at the table and stared across at Roxy. "What do you think?" His fingers played with the legal letter from Tim Andreadis, but he made no effort to open it. It was probably a bill.

"I think it's pretty scary. This is over and above anything I could have imagined. What are you going to do? You can't just call up the vice president and . . . and . . . tell him something like this. *If* you were able to get to him, he'd still deny it. Gracie's right. Mrs. Farquar is the only one who can help you. You need hard proof, Ricky? Think about who the man is."

"Okay. Since Mrs. Farquar has an unlisted phone number, we'll have to go back to her house in the morning. We can pick up the glass at the lab on the way and say we're returning it. For some reason, I don't think she's as coldhearted as she tried to make us believe. I think we frightened her.

It was natural for her to deny everything. Her nice life is going to be upset. I'm almost certain she didn't tell her husband. Would you have told, Roxy, if you were in her position?"

"No, I don't think I would have told my husband something like that. All of a sudden, I'm feeling motherly. I think I'll go upstairs and call Reba. After I call her, how about if I go to the store and pick up some salmon filets? I have this great recipe. I'd like to show off my culinary skills for you since we're going to get married. I hate eating out all the time."

"Good idea. I'll make the coffee. What about dessert?"

"How would you like a blueberry pie with vanilla ice cream?"

"I would love it. I'll be in the garage. I like to sit on the lawn mower and think. This is a sit-on-the-lawn-mower moment. Kind of like a Kodak moment. Did I ever tell you I used to mow lawns? So did Philly. He saved his money, and I spent mine."

Roxy nodded. "Big surprise." She gave him a half smile, then said, "You know, one of us should call Camellia Island and find out how things are going. I know Tyler is there, but I'd like to know how much progress they've made. We need to tell him to make sure the sprinkling system runs day and night, or the sod will turn brown."

"I'll do it. Go on, call your daughter. Don't be shy about telling her how much you love her either."

Roxy turned on her heel. "When did you get so . . . *parental?*"

Ricky shrugged. "If I had to pick an exact time and place, I guess I would have to say it was the moment I met Gracie Lick. I know that doesn't make sense, so let's just forget it. Maybe I'll figure it out one of these days."

Ricky stared off into space, his thoughts going every which way. Just to have something to do to take his mind off things, he reached for the envelope from Tim Andreadis and opened it. A short note from the attorney said the enclosure had been left with him by Philip, who'd told him he would know when to send it on. Ricky gasped. His brother had written him a letter? *A voice from the grave.* He started to shake and couldn't stop. He dreaded opening it, but he knew he had to do it. He offered up a prayer that he remembered from childhood that there would be nothing in the letter he should have taken care of in the last six months.

"I could burn this," he muttered as he made his way to the garage. He climbed up on the John Deere mower and sat. He stared down at the envelope. Maybe he needed to go back to the house and get a knife to slit the envelope. If he tried to open it, he might rip it apart. Maybe he could rip off the end, and the letter would slide out. He held it up to the light. The paper inside went all the way to both edges. If he opened it that way, he'd rip the letter. If he was lucky, the glue would have long since dried, and the envelope would just pop open. He tested his theory. The flap moved easily.

All he had to do was take out the letter and read it. "Damn, Philly, why did you write me a letter? Why couldn't you have just called me up the way you always did to chew my ass out? I hate letters from people who are dead."

Ricky removed the letter. His hands

trembled so badly, he had to use both hands to hold it. One sheet of paper. Small, cramped writing. He squeezed his eyes shut and took a great, gulping breath.

Dear Ricky,

If you're reading this letter it has to mean I've gone on to another place.

I suppose you have many questions. I guess I would, too, if I walked in your shoes. For so long, I wanted to be you because I didn't know who I was. I know you aren't going to understand that. Maybe, by some stroke of genius, you've ferreted out the truth. If not, let me give you the highlights. I was adopted. I didn't find out until I was around ten. I asked Mom, and she denied it, but I knew she was lying. To protect me, I'm sure. She admitted it before she passed away. It devastated me. There were no early pictures of Mom being pregnant like there were with you. There was no hospital picture of me. I didn't look like you or our parents. Sometimes I'd catch them whispering, a word here or there. They told me they didn't know who my par-

ents were. I don't know if that was the truth or not.

I went to the orphanage to try and find out. They told me the records were sealed and had been moved. I did everything I could, but I couldn't find out. I hired detectives, tried to bribe the personnel, all to no avail. That's part of my story.

The other part is, I married early on. I have three daughters. I really wanted a son to pass on my name, but then that wouldn't have been fair to the child since I don't know who I really am. I don't think it matters so much with girls as it does with boys. I think I did it just to father children so they would have a name. I was a terrible husband and a worse father. That's the main reason I didn't want you to take your own sons. My head isn't clear right now, Ricky, so this may or not make sense. I'm on some heavy-duty medications. I knew your boys would be better off without you in their lives, especially in their formative years because you were such a wild card and so damn unpredictable. I guess I was better off in the home I grew up in, too. But I didn't know that for a lot of years. I wasted so much of my life wishing and dreaming.

I know I was hard on you. Partly because I didn't want you to waste your life. The other part of me wanted to control you, to make you into what I would have liked to have been. I was so proud of you when you came out of rehab and didn't relapse. I know I screwed you up in other ways, and I'm sorry. Just know that I loved you the way a brother is supposed to love a brother.

By the way, I never really married Roxy. The minister was an out-of-work actor, so don't go thinking I'm a bigamist. I wanted to help her, but she turned on me, too, and I'm not blaming her. I gave her and her daughter a good life. They never wanted for anything.

I'm getting very tired right now. The main reason for this letter, Ricky, is this, I want you to find my parents and tell them I passed away. Tell them for me that had they kept me, I would have loved and honored them, just the way a son is supposed to love and honor his parents, until my dying day. Tell them how hard I tried to find them. If you find them, and you learn my father's and mother's names, please erect a gravestone with my real name on it. When I go to that place, I want to be able to introduce myself properly to the angels.

This is just a guess on my part, Ricky, but I think after my death, you contacted your sons. I hope you can be the father they deserve.

You were the one constant in my life, Ricky. For that, I thank you.

Be happy, Ricky, and enjoy your life.

I'll sign off now. I love you, kid.

Philly

Ricky knuckled his eyes, hoping to stop the waterfall running down his cheeks. Then hard, racking sobs tore at his shoulders. He hugged his arms to his chest as his grief overtook him. He rocked back and forth on the seat of the John Deere lawn mower.

Roxy watched from the patio. She wanted to run to him, but knew it wouldn't help. Instead, she sat down on one of the deck chairs and waited.

15

Roxy, wearing a wraparound apron, stood back from the grill and looked at Ricky, who was seated in a deck chair. He kept folding and refolding his brother's letter. Clearly, he was agitated. His eyes were wet and sad. She wanted to comfort him, but he was in his own little world. She checked the salmon and walked into the house to make a garden salad. She flipped the television set on with one hand, opening the refrigerator door with the other. Vegetables in her hand, she walked over to the chopping block, where she had a clear view of the fifteen-inch screen. While she skinned a stalk of celery, she heard the Fox announcer say, "And this breaking news just in." Breaking news usually meant something serious or momentous. Her eyes glued to the set, she peeled the outer leaves off a head of lettuce, and rinsed it.

"Wealthy venture capitalist and philanthropist Armand Farquar died late this afternoon. The eighty-seven-year-old Frenchman . . ."

"Rickyyyyy! Come in here right now!"

Ricky bounded off his chair, his heart pounding. He'd never heard that tone in Roxy's voice before. He blew into the kitchen like a whirlwind. "What's wrong? Did you hurt yourself? Did you burn yourself? What? Why are you shouting like that?"

"Ricky, look! Listen!" Roxy jabbed a stalk of celery in the direction of the television set.

Ricky turned in time to see the camera flash to the entrance of Cedars-Sinai Hospital and saw Lorraine Farquar leaning heavily on the arm of a tall man dressed in what looked like white scrubs. She appeared dazed as she was led away.

"Her husband just died. They interrupted to say it was breaking news. That poor woman! What she must be going through right now," Roxy said quietly.

Ricky's foot snaked out to draw one of the kitchen stools closer to the oversize chopping block. He propped his elbows on the block to stare at the screen. "Where does that leave us?" he said morosely. "I'm not being insensitive here. That guy," he said, pointing to the screen, "just said, eighty-seven-year-old Armand Farquar is survived by his wife Lorraine and a ninety-two-year-old brother who is in a nursing home in France. I'd go to her home in a heartbeat if I thought she needed us."

"I'm sure there must be attorneys, ministers, friends who will help her at this time. My advice is to stay away until after the funeral. Even then, it might be too soon. We can't impose on her grief. We waited this long, we can wait longer if we have to. I'm sure Philly would understand."

"You didn't ask me what was in the letter, Roxy."

"I figured if you wanted me to know, you'd tell me. Do you want to talk about it? Oh, my God! I forgot the salmon!" Roxy said, rushing outside to the grill. She looked down at the two charred filets. "How do you feel about bacon and eggs?"

"Sounds good to me. But not right now.

Let's go outside and sit on the deck. I want you to read Philly's letter. I want you to know from the git-go that Philly is just as important to me as Armand Farquar is to his wife. Right now, since reading the letter, he's even more important. So much for Tim Andreadis telling me my brother hated me."

Lorraine Farquar sighed with relief when the chauffeur stopped the car under the portico. She felt dizzy and light-headed. She wished she had eaten something earlier. She reached for Henry's arm and entered the house. Her housekeeper of many years held out her arms.

"There are some people waiting for you in the library, Miss Lorraine. Your attorney and Mr. Farquar's physician to name a few. I can send them home if you don't want to talk to them."

Lorraine shook her head. "Were there any calls?" The housekeeper pointed to a stack of message slips. She rifled through them. No call from the vice president. Sooner or later the White House would call. She patted the housekeeper's shoulder before she left the kitchen.

In the hallway leading to the library, Lorraine stopped, tilting her head to listen. The house was so quiet. Normally the house was quiet because there were no children, grandchildren, or pets romping about. It seemed to her, at that moment, to be unusually quiet, rather like a tomb. She shuddered at the thought.

Armand would never come here again. She was alone. And she was vulnerable. That would never do. Armand would expect her to carry on and grieve in private. Life, he'd always said, was for the living. With that thought in her mind, she squared her shoulders before she opened the door to the library. She allowed herself to be kissed on her cheeks, allowed those in the room to squeeze her hand in sympathy.

"We don't want you to worry about anything, Lorraine. We'll take care of all the arrangements. All you have to do is tell us what you want. A large funeral or a small private service," Dr. Blair Unger said quietly.

"Armand wanted to be cremated. A small private service. As you know, there is no other family. It will be just me, the servants, Armand's nurse, and any of you who care to attend. Tomorrow. I'd like the service to be at sunrise. Armand always loved watching the sun come up. The Tobias Mortuary will do nicely. I want my husband's ashes in an urn. I would appreciate it if you'd deal with the press. I appreciate your coming here, but right now I need to be alone. I don't need any medication. I'll be fine. Now, if you'll excuse me."

Upstairs in her room, Lorraine sat down on the edge of the bed. She cried for her loss. She felt so alone. The only other time in her life when she'd felt like this was the day she'd taken her son to the Oakhurst Orphanage.

What in the world was she going to do with herself. Armand had been her whole life. She couldn't see herself selling real estate or making pottery. She'd read once that women newly divorced or widowed had two choices, sell real estate or make pottery. She thought about her vast inheritance and what she was going to do with it. While she wasn't as old as her husband, she wasn't a youngster either. She had enough money to last her a hundred lifetimes.

Maybe Armand's passing was God's

way of giving her a second chance. She could do so much good with all his money. She could establish and fund organizations that dealt with children. And she could do it all in her son's name. She knew she could never make right what happened years ago, but maybe she could help make the system better somehow, the system that had failed both her son and herself.

Lorraine slid off the bed and walked over to her walk-in closet, which was just as big as her bedroom. She looked around before she pressed a button on the wall. A conveyer belt purred to life. Shoes, handbags, boxes with hats and scarves moved slowly for her inspection. She laughed then when she remembered how excited Armand had been when he'd surprised her with the conveyor belt. He'd always loved gadgets or things that made life easier. She plucked a pair of straw-colored sling-backs from the belt and set them on the floor. She waited till the belt made its second go-round, so she could select the bag that matched the shoes. The third go-round yielded a wide-brimmed straw hat with bright orange and lime green streamers. Armand loved that hat. She turned off the switch and walked over to the racks and racks of clothing she rarely wore. It took her thirty minutes to choose a fully lined pumpkin-colored dress with long sleeves.

Armand hated black. He'd made a point of telling her not to wear "widow's weeds" after he was gone. He loved vibrant colors. Once she'd bought him a pair of bright red, plaid golfing trousers. He'd worn them until they were threadbare. She smiled. She had her memories of their life together. All of them good. It was the other memories, the dark ones, that she had to make right.

Lorraine suddenly had the urge to putter around the kitchen, something she rarely, if ever, did. She knew how to cook. She'd had to learn early on. She was by no means a gourmet chef, but she could put together a meal. At the moment she felt like having French toast and bacon. Some fresh coffee would go nicely with the meal.

Maybe when her life was settled, if that ever happened, she'd take a trip back to Dubois, Pennsylvania. It would be nice to do something for the town. Possibly fund the library or set up a fund for a summer camp for underprivileged children. Something.

She wondered who lived in the big white house she'd grown up in, with the green shutters and the huge front porch. Her bedroom had been in the front of the house. She'd spent hours sitting on the window seat, staring out at the old sycamores that lined the sidewalk in front of the house. She'd had a decent life growing up, but she'd wanted more. She'd wanted excitement and to see her name on a marquee. She laughed.

The chime of the grandfather clock, the one Armand had gotten in Bavaria, startled her. How could it possibly be eleven o'clock? In a little less than six hours she had to be at the mortuary.

Her French toast slid onto a dinner plate. She added butter and syrup. She knew she wasn't going to eat it. She stared at it for a long time before her gaze shifted to the telephone on the wall behind her. Maybe this wasn't the time to make the call. Then again, maybe this was the *perfect* time to make the call. Before she could change her mind, she reached into her pocket for Ricky Lam's card. Without hesitation, she reached for the phone and dialed the number. She counted the rings.

It was late, maybe he was sleeping. He picked up on the sixth ring.

"Mr. Lam, this is Lorraine Farquar. I apologize for the lateness of the call. I was wondering if you and your partner would . . . Would you care to attend my husband's service tomorrow morning? In case you didn't hear the news, Armand passed away this afternoon. It's a private service at the Tobias Mortuary. At sunrise. We can . . . we can talk later. . . . Thank you for agreeing. I'll see you in the morning. Good night, Mr. Lam. Sleep well."

Lorraine wondered when she'd made the conscious decision to call Ricky Lam. True, she'd just made the call, but sometime during the past hours she knew she wasn't going to try and hide the truth any longer. A strange feeling of peace washed over her. A feeling she had never experienced in her entire life.

The bed beckoned. She was too tired to undress and brush her teeth. The world wouldn't come to an end if she slept in her clothes or didn't brush her teeth. She reached for a picture of herself and Armand taken in the south of France. They were both smiling into the camera. How happy they'd been. She clasped the picture to her chest before she curled into a ball on top of the comforter. She was asleep within minutes.

Ricky stared at the phone in his hand, then at Roxy. "You aren't going to believe who that was," he said, motioning to the phone.

"Mrs. Farquar?"

"Are you psychic?" Ricky asked in awe.

"No. I could tell by the look on your face. Did she invite you back to the house? How strange she would call you on the same day her husband died."

"She invited us both to her husband's sunrise service tomorrow morning. She said we would talk afterward. I'm thinking she feels safe talking now because her past won't hurt her husband. I doubt if it would have anyway. It was so long ago. When you're young, you do stupid things. I'm a prime example. People make bad decisions, decisions they later regret. Unfortunately, you can't unring the bell. Talking to us is one thing, but to invite us to her husband's service is something I don't understand."

"Maybe . . . this is just a thought, but maybe there really isn't any family. On either her husband's side or hers. Maybe she wants and needs a sense of family right now. It's a stretch by my way of thinking, but you could almost fit into the category of family. I guess she's going to own up to the truth. How did she sound, Ricky?"

Ricky thought about the question. His brow furrowed. "Is it possible to sound . . . peaceful under the present circumstances? She was matter-of-fact, but her voice was gentle. Sad, too. The day is almost over for us, and for her. Tomorrow is a new day. Maybe that's how she's thinking of it. In less than an hour, this day will be gone. None of us will be able to get it back. I don't know. Am I just talking to hear myself?"

"If you are, it doesn't matter. I'm kind of tired, Ricky. I think I'll go to bed since we have to get up early."

"I'm going to stay up for a while. It's a nice night. I might take a swim and just sit here and maybe smoke a cigarette. I'm thinking about taking up a pipe. What do you think, Roxy?"

"If that's what you want to do, then do it.

I'm for whatever makes you happy. If you tell me which suit you want for tomorrow, I'll get everything ready."

"Something conservative. It really doesn't matter."

"Yes, Ricky, it will matter to Mrs. Farquar."

"All right, the charcoal Armani. White shirt, the gray-and-black tie. It's probably hanging on the suit. I'll make some calls to find out where the mortuary is so we don't waste time getting lost in the morning. Sleep tight, Roxy. By the way, those eggs were delicious."

Roxy leaned over to kiss him lightly on the mouth. "What's wrong, Ricky?"

"Everything and nothing. I want my safe, boring life back. I want to get on with the business of trying to be a father, and I want to do my share on Camellia Island. The Crown Jewel was Philly's dream, and I want to be there to make sure it's everything he wanted it to be. It's where you and I will live when this is all over."

"I understand that. I think Mrs. Farquar is going to help you and help herself at the same time. Before you know it, we'll be back on the island. 'Night. Don't stay up too late."

Ricky smiled as he waved her away. He walked over to the pool, peeled off his shorts and tank top. Wearing just his boxers, he dived into the crystal-clear pool. He swam the length of the pool three times before he climbed out. He wrapped a towel around his shoulders before he padded into the kitchen to pop a bottle of Coca-Cola. He found some cigarettes in one of the drawers and carried them out to the deck. Finally, he was ready to *think*.

16

He jogged along the Tidal Basin, Secret Service agents in tow. He ran effortlessly, barely breaking a sweat. For a man his age, he was in excellent condition, so fit and trim, he knew he would put his opponent to shame in the primaries. Voters liked youth, and they liked healthy candidates. They also liked determination and fearlessness. He had all those attributes plus a score of others that would eventually allow him to claim the most coveted position in the land. He adjusted the blue bandanna that said ROADRUNNER on it, a gag gift from one of his agents. He really didn't need it since he kept his silvery hair in a brush cut. Even though he had never been in the military, he liked the look.

His thoughts whirled as he clipped along, his arms pumping to his heartbeat. He smirked at the sweat dripping off the agents running alongside him. So much for youth. He focused on what was ahead of him. That's what you had to do when you were involved in the political game. Fix a clear goal in your mind and don't deviate one iota. At times it had been a struggle, but he'd held firm, and at last his goal was almost within reach.

Adam Vincent Nolan thought about his family as he sprinted along. They were so perfect, the press had dubbed them the all-American family. A title he approved of. He was a shoo-in. Even the pundits had to agree.

The stopwatch hanging at his side beeped. He'd run his daily five miles. Now it was time to shower and start his day. He tried to remember what kind of schedule he had for the day. Other than to say it was full, he couldn't remember anything else. One way or another, he'd get his picture in the paper. He slapped at his forehead as his steps slowed to a slow jog. Armand Farquar. He had heard of his death on the eleven o'clock news last night. That meant a trip to sunny California. He liked Armand as much as he liked anyone. All that money. And Farquar had always been generous to his party.

He was walking now, faster than usual, in a hurry to get to his office. In his pile of messages there had been a call from Mrs. Farquar yesterday. Had she called before or after her husband's passing? He made a mental note to call her as soon as he reached the office. Sucking up to Armand's wife could only help him. Fund-raisers at their palatial estate, five-hundred-dollar-a-plate dinners. Oh, yes, major sucking up was called for. He wondered when the funeral would be. Probably tomorrow. Everything was going to get screwed up with a trip to California. His whole schedule would be shot to hell. Farquar's funeral would be an event. Everyone who was anyone would attend. He'd be in the front row, thanks to his position. Great photo op. Pictures with him placing a rose on the casket, pictures of him with the new widow, comforting and consoling her. He wondered if he would be asked to give the eulogy. He had a few tucked away that he could draw on. Short, meaningful, somber yet uplifting speeches. He tried not to think about how many funerals he'd attended as vice president during his five-plus years in office. He'd be glad when he was president and could pass that duty on to his successor.

Maybe he'd take his wife with him. Women liked to see another woman consoling and comforting the bereaved. It wouldn't hurt that his wife was incredibly photogenic either.

Adam V. Nolan waved to his agents as he entered the house. He was so golden, he positively *glowed*. He wondered if anyone else could see his aura.

Ricky was stunned the following morning when he and Roxy entered the mortuary to find so few mourners. For a man of Armand Farquar's stature, he'd expected half the world to turn out. He recognized the maid from the day before and the man who had been polishing a car when they'd first arrived. He would have bet his last dollar that the other mourners were lawyers and doctors. Private did indeed mean private.

A somber-looking man in a black suit

and slicked-back hair closed the doors. Ricky and Roxy sat down behind two gray-haired, distinguished-looking men. A minister wearing a white cassock with gold trim walked over to a small pulpit and opened a prayer book.

When the thirty-minute service was over, Ricky stood up with everyone else. He didn't know Armand Farquar any better now than when he had entered the mortuary. He knew what he did philanthropically and businesswise, but he didn't know who the *man* was. He wondered what Lorraine thought of the minister's words. She probably didn't even hear them.

Suddenly the other mourners were looking at him. He saw recognition in their faces. *They're wondering what an ex-movie star like me is doing here,* he thought. *Let them wonder.* He walked over to Lorraine and held out his hand.

"Thank you for coming. I appreciate it," Lorraine said. "I'll see you back at the house."

Today the maid wore a navy dress with a small white apron. She led them to the dining room, where a full breakfast was laid out on a sideboard. Lorraine was seated at the head of the table. She nodded. "Please, sit down. My husband would have liked this small, intimate breakfast. He hated ostentation of any kind. In many ways he was a very simple man. Much like me. We both loved seeing the sun rise in the morning. I told him once, during the early years of our marriage, how I always looked forward to getting out of bed and watching the sun creep over the horizon. From that day on, we both watched it every single day."

Ricky felt a chill race up his arms. "My brother's favorite time of day was sunrise. He felt the same way."

"Like mother, like son. Tell me about *my son,* Mr. Lam. Tell me every single thing you can remember even if you think it's insignificant."

Ricky talked until his voice gave out, at which point Roxy stepped in. "You do have family, Mrs. Farquar. You have three granddaughters and a daughter-in-law. I know they would love knowing they have a real grandmother. If you like, Ricky and I can take you to their house. Perhaps not today but when you're ready. Sometimes happiness comes out of tragedy."

Lorraine's voice was full of awe when she said, "Three granddaughters! Today. I'd like to see them today. Too much time has gone by. I don't want to waste my days. Can you see your way clear to taking me there today?"

"If that's what you want," Ricky said.

"It's what I want. Now, it's my turn to tell you my story." Like Ricky, Lorraine talked until her voice turned raspy.

The maid entered the room with fresh coffee. Ricky gulped at his, scalding his tongue. His hostess's words left him feeling dizzy and shaken.

Lorraine waited until the maid left the room before she said, "Yesterday, I placed a call to the White House, to the vice president's residence on the grounds of the Naval Observatory, and to the numbers my husband had listed in his Rolodex. So far no one has returned my call. I'm sure they will, though, as Armand contributed generously to both political parties. You can trust me to take care of this. It's my mission in life. Let's both be sure what it is we want from that man. I want an acknowledgment that Adam V. Nolan is my son's father. I want a birth certificate that states he is the father and I am the mother. I'm sure his DNA is on file somewhere. He is, after all, the vice president of the United States. Now, Mr. Lam, what is it you want on your brother's behalf?"

Roxy had to poke his arm to get him to respond. "I want a face-to-face meeting with him. I want him to resign from his office, and I want his promise that he will not run for the presidency. Then, ideally, I'd like to strip him naked and toss *him* in a Dumpster. Then when he pops out, I'd like a photographer from the *Washington Post* to conveniently appear to take his photograph. What part of all that don't you think I'll get?" His voice was so angry and fretful, Roxy placed a soothing hand on his arm to calm him.

Lorraine smiled wanly. "My husband always used to say, be careful what you wish for because you just might get it. Together, we'll work toward that end. I'd like to visit the cemetery where my son is buried. Will it be possible to stop there on the way to my daughter-in-law's home? On second thought, I want to visit my son's grave tomorrow. I want to go there alone. I need to . . . to . . . talk to my son."

"Of course. Also, today it might be more comfortable if you had your chauffeur drive you to Lee Ann's house. My car only has two seats, and you might want to stay longer. Roxy and I would just be in the way."

"Yes, you're right. That's how we'll do it."

"Roxy and I have to return to South Carolina, Mrs. Farquar. Do you have even a vague idea of how long it's going to take to make contact with the vice president?"

Lorraine's jaw set firmly. "Not one minute later than tomorrow morning. Armand's memorial service will be held tomorrow at eleven at Holy Trinity. I'd be very surprised if the vice president doesn't attend. By the way, I'm glad you didn't have my son cremated. I never understood why Armand wanted to be cremated. It's necessary, of course, if a person wants his ashes scattered somewhere, but then there's nothing left to show that the person ever existed. That sounds so cruel to me. People get such solace and comfort from visiting a deceased loved one. I'm sorry, I'm just rambling here. I'm ready to leave if you're ready."

The Longhorn Steak House was cool and dim, decorated in brass, dark oak, and burgundy wall hangings. It was comfortable, with well-padded booths, and the acoustics were actually good. Ricky waited for Roxy to slide into the booth before he sat down. The first thing he did was to remove his jacket and tie. "I feel like I've been on a weeklong drunk. Yesterday and today were mind-benders."

Roxy sighed as she tossed her straw hat onto the table. "I know what you mean." She looked up at the waitress. "I'd like a whole pitcher of sweet tea. With lots of ice. Ricky, would you prefer something else?"

"No, the tea is fine." The waitress left and returned a few minutes later with a frosty pitcher of ice tea and a basket of hush puppies. "I just wanted to sit here and *wilt.*"

Roxy leaned back in the booth. Her hand reached out for Ricky's. "You made Mrs. Farquar one happy lady today. She lost a husband but gained a family. That's pretty wonderful in my book, Ricky. I hope wherever Philip is, he knows what you're doing for him. Not many people would do what you've done. Most of them would have shrugged it off, and said, 'What the hell, he's dead, he'll never know.' I'm so glad you followed through. You know what else, Ricky, I could see Philip with Lee Ann Oliver. Her daughters are lovely. They look like Philip. So many tears were shed today. Sometimes things really do work out right in the end. I don't see the vice president granting you or Mrs. Farquar an interview, though. I have a feeling it's all going to turn ugly. You and Mrs. Farquar are going to be bucking the second highest office in the land, not to mention the Secret Service. All those agencies that are such watchdogs. Both of you are going to have to tread very lightly."

Ricky drained the tea in his glass and poured another. "I know. I think Mrs. Farquar has a plan. She didn't share it, though. No matter what, we're leaving the day after tomorrow. We'll have to carry through from South Carolina." He looked up when the waitress appeared to take their order. He looked at Roxy.

"I'll have the T-bone, medium rare, a

twice-baked potato, garden salad with blue cheese dressing."

"I'll have the same, but I'll take ranch dressing," Ricky said.

Ricky squeezed Roxy's hand. "Thanks for being here with me. I don't know if I could have muddled through on my own. I just want you to know that. And, yeah, I love you in the bargain. Do you think you might be interested in some *tomfoolery* later on?"

Roxy let a wry grin tug at the corner of her mouth. *"Tomfoolery,* is it? Is that the same as wild, passionate sex? An orgy of wet, slick bodies writhing on the bed amid groans and moans? Oh, my gosh, you're blushing! Yes. The answer is yes."

Ricky woke with a start, unsure what it was that had awakened him. Then he smelled the coffee and bacon. He bolted from the bed, pulled on his shorts, brushed his teeth, and ran down the steps to the kitchen. "And she's a good cook, too," he said, kissing Roxy lightly on the cheek. She had already showered, and she smelled as good as what she was cooking. He liked the long, cotton muumuu she was wearing.

Appliquéd on the back, and the front as well, were giant sunflowers. His girl had style. He grinned as he snatched a piece of crisp bacon. He poured coffee for both of them as he munched.

"Make yourself useful and do the toast. I like mine . . ."

"On the dark side. Gotcha. You all packed?"

"I'm packed and ready to go. I called the car service when I got up. They'll pick us up at three-thirty. Listen, Ricky, I can handle things. I know you want to see this through."

"Yes, of course, I do, but I can't get obsessed over it. That's what I was doing, Roxy. Mrs. Farquar is our best chance to reach the vice president. There's no way in hell I could get through to him. If Mrs. Farquar doesn't call soon, I'm going to call her after I finish this wonderful breakfast to find out if she's heard from Nolan and if he's going to attend the memorial service. Look, if all else fails, I'll sic Gracie on the VP. I bet he'll sit up and take notice if she gets on his case. Let her pester him. I can hire a good firm of private dicks if I have to. Whatever it takes."

"Okay, if you're sure. It will be a shame if we get all the way across the country only to have to turn back.

"Roxy," Ricky said, tapping his chin with his forefinger, "I wonder if when Mrs. Farquar called the vice president and left a message, she identified herself as Mrs. Armand Farquar, or as Lorraine Farquar. Lorraine is not a common name. In fact, I don't know a soul named Lorraine. Do you?"

Roxy shook her head.

"Well, don't you think the vice president might . . . remember the *real* name of Notch Number 7 on his belt?"

"He probably doesn't even know that Notch Number 7's name was Lorraine. I heard her say she was called Laney back then. Young girls always have nicknames. Look at me. They started calling me Roxy when I was five years old, and it stuck with me. You can't say that about the vice president, though. He told Mrs. Farquar his name was Vincent. He very deliberately left off the name he was known by, which was Adam.

"So, if what you're asking is, does he know Lorraine Farquar and Laney Wood-

worth are one and the same, I'd have to
say, no, he does not. I'm also sure the man
did not ever think about her again once he
walked away."

"But he left the baby there to die."

"Yes. If you had done such a terrible
thing, wouldn't you have blocked it out of
your mind? He had a political life to lead.
He came from a political family. Scandal
was the last thing he wanted. Back then, it
was boys will be boys. He said he'd get his
buddies to swear they all had her for two
bucks a pop. Now, whether those buddies
would have followed through is anybody's
guess."

"You know what, Roxy, I'm going to put
bloodhound Gracie on this. She can go
back to his college years, get his year-
book, see who he hung out with, that kind
of thing. I can make some phone calls and
put the wheels in motion just in case Mrs.
Farquar doesn't get to first base. College
buddies are college buddies forever. Presidents and vice presidents alike tend to
drag their old buddies out for pictures to
make themselves look good. I'll call them
all or, better yet, have Gracie call them. At
least one of them will still be in touch with

him. Hey, that's the way it happens in the movies. Forewarned is forearmed. Who better than Gracie to do this? What do you think?"

"I think it's one of the best ideas you've ever come up with. Go talk to Gracie. I'll stay here in case Mrs. Farquar calls. Plus, I have to clean all this up. I am so proud of you, Ricky. Philip would be proud of you, too," she said, kissing him full on the mouth. "Hmmm, you taste good."

Ricky backed off and wagged a finger under her nose. "None of that. We have work to do. When I get back, remind me to call Angie Garrison."

"And who might Angie Garrison be?" Roxy asked, glaring at him.

"Angie Garrison is a screenwriter. I called her a while back in the middle of the night. She actually took my call. She's a great lady. You're going to love her when you meet her. I told her Philly's story; she knows mine. I told her everything I knew but the outcome. I know it now. All she has to do is fill in the blanks. If I can't get a studio interested in the project, I'll produce it myself. I think Sandusky can pull it off. My tribute to my brother."

"See, that's why I love you," Roxy said. "People will get hurt, you know that, don't you?"

"Me, you, my boys, your daughter, we can handle it. Mrs. Farquar and her new family will handle it. I think she might fight me to put up the money if it comes down to my producing the movie. Maybe we can be partners. Mr. Adam V. Nolan is the one who will be hurt. He deserves whatever comes his way. Yes, his family will suffer for fifteen minutes, then they'll get on with their lives the way we all had to get on with ours. The way Mrs. Farquar had to get on with her life. I'm going to play the part of Philly. I know each and every member of the cast. I'm going to do it, Roxy. I swear to God, I'm going to do it!"

"I'll be right there with you, Ricky. Every step of the way."

"We make a good team, don't we?" Ricky said, his eyes sparkling.

"The best."

Ricky was halfway to the guesthouse in search of Gracie when she walked out of the garage. "Hey, Mr. Lam, what are you doing up so early?"

"I'm looking for you. I have another as-signment. Are you up for it?"

Gracie clapped her hands. "I'm up for it. By the way, Max called again. I'll be going to Carnival. I'm buying my own ticket, though."

"Gracie, I'm buying you a first-class ticket for this job you are about to under-take. Now, sit down and let me fill you in."

Gracie listened raptly. "Sure, I can find them if they're still alive. I even know how to get their phone numbers. There's more, right?"

"Oh yeah! A lot more. I want you to call every gossip columnist you know. I want you to tell them all I am coming out of re-tirement to produce a movie, starring my-self as my brother. You know what to say. I want you to call *Variety* and every other pa-per you can think of so it gets picked up and printed as soon as possible. I want things like, NEWS FLASH, THIS JUST IN! I know who I want in the film with me, and I'll be making my calls in a few minutes. You're going to be my press agent from here on in, so give everyone your phone number. The script is finished except for the names. I'll give you Angie Garrison's phone number before I leave. If it gets dicey, you know, those Washingtonians coming after you, have them call me. You really can handle this, can't you, Gracie?"

"You bet." Confidence rang in Gracie's voice.

"Okay, when I get to the airport, I'll buy your ticket and have them send it on to you. Unless you want one of those electronic ones."

"Nope. I like to hold something in my hand. Thanks, Mr. Lam. Gee, this is exciting. Can I go to the premiere of the movie?"

"Front-row seat, Gracie. Your brother and sister, too."

Gracie high-fived him before she sprinted off to the guesthouse to get to work.

Ricky looked upward. "I'm doing it, Philly. I'm going to make it right. It might not be the best plan in the world, but it's the only way I know how to do it. The end will justify the means."

It was after noon when Ricky made his last phone call. He leaned back in the kitchen chair and smiled at Roxy. "Okay, here's where we stand right now, this very minute. Mrs. Farquar is going to wing it. She realizes she won't have a chance for any kind of private conversation with the vice president. When his press secretary called her, she said that the vice president would have to return to Washington right after the service. Her new family is attending the service with her, which I think is very nice. She said that Philly and Lee Ann's youngest daughter looks exactly like the vice president's daughter.

"Angie promised to have the script faxed here no later than two o'clock. She's hand-delivering it to the studio for me. The studio said they would have a decision for me on it by the end of the week. They only agreed to my timetable because Sandusky told them I was prepared to produce it myself. I got a top-notch director who's willing to work on the project, got verbal okays on the actors, who will have to clear things with their agents. It's going to work. I can feel it. Gracie is putting the word out there. Everything is in place. All we need are the college buddies. If things go according to schedule, we should be able to start filming the first day of the new year. The Crown

Jewel will be up and running, and we'll be on easy street, timewise. I can't believe it's all falling into place.

"There is one thing bothering me, though."

Roxy pretended horror. "What could possibly be bothering you? Everything is working out perfectly. Whatever it is, you're probably imagining it," Roxy said soothingly.

"No, I'm not imagining this. I think we should suggest to Mrs. Farquar that she take her new family and go off somewhere for a vacation." Ricky looked down at his watch. "We have time, we can make the reservations, and they can be on their way by nightfall. I say we send them to Aruba or Antigua. For as long as it takes to get all of this under control. The stakes are really high, Roxy, and I think we both know how things work in Washington. Mrs. Farquar is no match for those people. Give me your honest opinion."

"Look!" Roxy said, pointing at the television. The one o'clock news was just beginning. The lead story was Armand Farquar's memorial service. "Look at his face! Oh my God! She must have said something. Did you see his expression, Ricky? Did you!" Roxy all but screamed.

The phone was in Ricky's hand before the scene switched to a five-car pileup on I-5. Lorraine Farquar answered the phone herself on the first ring. "Oh, Mr. Lam, I was just talking about you to my granddaughters. I said only nice things."

"Mrs. Farquar, I want you to listen to me very carefully. I'm assuming your whole family is there with you, am I right? Good. I just saw the film clip of your husband's memorial service this morning. What exactly did you say to the vice president, Mrs. Farquar?"

The voice on the other end of the phone suddenly turned jittery. "The vice president said my husband was a fine man and would be sorely missed. Then he said he regretted that we had never met over the years. I said, 'Oh, we met, Mr. Vice President, and I'm sorry you don't remember me.' I said, 'My name at the time was Laney Woodworth.' At that point one of his aides or his agents moved him forward. The line was very long. I guess I wasn't supposed to say that, is that what you're implying? It's too bad. I had to say it. I couldn't hold it in one more second."

"The people in Washington don't play by the rules most people play by, Mrs. Farquar. I'm going to make some plane reservations right now for you and your family. You're going to go to Antigua and stay at my resort. My son will take care of you and your family. Carnival will be starting soon. Don't pack anything. I want you simply to walk out of the house and have your driver take you to the airport. Don't tell him or your other servants where you're going. Simply say they'll see you when they see you, that kind of thing. The same goes for your family. I want you just to walk away. Can you do that?"

"I . . . I . . . yes, yes, I can do that. A man in his position wouldn't . . . would he . . . ?"

"The long and short answer is, yes. Now. I want you to leave *now.* Will your chauffeur keep quiet?"

"Of course. He's been with us since he was a young man. He was devoted to my husband. You're beginning to frighten me, Mr. Lam."

"I know, and I'm sorry. Leave now and

keep checking at the Continental counter for your tickets. I'll call you later."

Ricky repeated Lorraine Farquar's explanation of her meeting with the vice president.

"Oh, Lord, she really told him her name was Laney Woodworth? Tell me you're being an alarmist, Ricky."

"I am *not* being an alarmist. We have a bit of an edge at the moment. They don't know about *me*. Yet. There's a lot at stake here, and people tend to panic when the stakes are high. They go to extraordinary lengths to cover up things that could derail their ambitions. Accidents happen. Unexplained accidents. Grief-stricken widow isn't watching what she's doing and slips and falls to her death. Things like that happen all the time. Don't you read, Roxy?" Ricky asked sharply.

Roxy stared at the man she'd fallen in love with. Ricky wasn't one to panic or become melodramatic even though he was an actor. She forgave him his sharp tone. "It's just that this is like something out of a spy novel." The sunflower on the front of her muumuu heaved with the weight of her mighty sigh. "All right, all right, I believe you. I'll make the reservations. Coach versus first-class so as not to draw attention to them, right?"

Ricky nodded.

"Check on Gracie while I do it. I still have a credit card under Roxanne Nelson. I'll charge it on that."

Ricky nodded again as he ran across the yard to the guesthouse. He banged on the door. The dogs came running, barking shrilly as though to say invader, invader! "You got anything yet, Gracie?" he bellowed to be heard over the barking dogs.

"Give me twenty more minutes, and I'll be over. I just need to double-check a few things."

"Make it quick, Gracie. We're going to have to head out for the airport soon."

"Gotcha."

"Are you making *more* coffee?" Roxy asked, when Ricky entered the kitchen and went straight to the coffeepot. "Who's going to drink it? We have to leave soon."

"Gracie. That girl drinks more coffee than I do. How did you do?"

"I got all of them on a three o'clock flight. By the time they wait in all the lines, check in, buy a few things, have a drink, it will be time to board." Her voice turned shy when she said, "Ricky, do you think this dress is okay to travel in?"

"Absolutely. It's as pretty as you are. I scared you, didn't I?"

"A little. I go to the movies, and I read books and newspapers, but the movies and books are fiction. We're talking about . . ."

"The second highest office in the land. Think about the lengths you'd go to protect Reba. I know that I am capable of killing for my sons. That knowledge scares the goddamn hell out of me. We're the normal ones. People like us don't throw babies in Dumpsters and close the lid so they'll suffocate. People who do things like that wouldn't think twice about harming or scaring an old lady. When Mrs. Farquar gets to the resort, our people and the locals will take care of her. From that point on, we let it play out." Ricky looked up at the clock.

The screen door banged. "Are you making coffee *again?*" Gracie didn't bother waiting for a reply. "Here's what I got. I didn't have time to print stuff out. I can do that later and fax it to you at the Crown

Jewel. It'll be there before you. Can you read my writing?"

Ricky peered over her shoulder. He nodded.

"Good. There were three of them, four counting the VP. The VP met all of them in college. He roomed all four years with a guy named Buck Grisham. His real name is Thaddeus. They were thick as the proverbial thieves. Real hell-raisers. Name it and they did it. Buck is a nuclear engineer with NASA. They are still best friends to this day. Leon Franks is a lawyer, are you ready for this, in the Justice Department. Neil Carpenter owns a twenty-four-man accounting firm right here in L.A. Excellent reputation. We're talking really big bucks here. Once a year they all get together and party hearty. I got all this from the alumni newsletter. Every year they hold it in a different place. This year, in September, it's going to be held in Washington, D.C."

"Good going, Gracie. Listen, I need you to do something else for me. I want you to call Max and tell him Mrs. Farquar and a party of four will be arriving this evening. Roxy will fill you in on their ETA. Tell him to have hotel security guard them twenty-four/seven. You can give him all the details. Tell him no interviews and no comments to *anyone*. Tell him to hire more security if he needs to. Then I want you to call Tyler and tell him we're on our way, and he should head for Antigua to help his brother." He ripped the yellow sheet of paper from the legal pad. "I'm going to copy this. Roxy, fill her in on the times and what we accomplished this morning. I'll be right back. Damn, there's the car service."

Roxy talked as she pressed the code to the electronic gates. She was breathless when Ricky galloped into the kitchen.

"Drink the coffee, Gracie, and clean the pot. Pull out the plug. We have a ninety-minute layover in St. Louis. I'll call you from there." Ricky stopped long enough to hug her and whisper in her ear. "If I had a daughter, I'd want her to be just like you."

"I had one dad, but if I could have two, I'd pick you, too," Gracie said, her face pink with pleasure. "Hey, the pups are up and toddling around."

Ricky laughed all the way to the foyer where he grabbed his and Roxy's bags.

*   *   *

Gracie poured herself a cup of coffee and dutifully rinsed the pot. Now she could get down to business. First things first. She dialed the number of the resort in Antigua, announced herself, and asked for Max Lam, saying it was urgent. She all but swooned when she heard Max's voice.

"Max, this is Gracie. Your father asked me to call and give you a message. He and Roxy just left for the airport. Listen carefully, okay? Things are happening here that really aren't too good. This is what your dad wants you to do . . . ."

"Okay, I can handle that. I don't know where I'm going to find more security, though, with Carnival coming up. All the agencies are booked. Don't worry, I'll figure out something."

"Oh, I almost forgot to tell you. I have to call Tyler to tell him to head in your direction. I'll do that as soon as I hang up. Listen, I can send Wally if you need him. I know a couple of bouncers who work at clubs in town. You'll have to pay their expenses, but I guess you know that."

"I'll keep it in mind, Gracie. I'm glad Tyler's coming over. He's enough to scare anyone. What about you? You're the one making all the calls and stirring this all to a boil. What if they go after you?"

She was wondering the same thing but didn't say so. "I'm a journalist. I can't be forced to divulge my sources. This isn't some third world country. I can take care of myself. Are you worrying about me, Max?"

"Yeah. Yeah, I'm worrying. This whole thing is playing out like one of my father's movies. I'm . . . I'm looking forward to seeing you, Gracie."

"That's the nicest thing you ever said to me, Max. I'm actually looking forward to seeing you, too. Guess what? Your dad is getting me a first-class ticket for all the work I did for him. It's fair. Listen, if I marry you, can I stop working and live in the lap of luxury the way you do?" The silence on the other end of the phone caused a frown to build on Gracie's face.

"Yeah. I plan to keep you barefoot and pregnant." Gracie slammed down the phone so hard it bounced off the counter. Instead of picking it up, she stuck her head under the cold water faucet. When she came up for air, she muttered, "Wiseass!"

17

Gracie paced Ricky's kitchen, his words ringing in her ears. She could feel her insides start to crumble. She'd been hard as nails for so long. It was almost a relief to let her guard down and just be Gracie Lick. Who was Gracie Lick? Did she even know?

She was an overachiever. Brash and ballsy. An in-your-face reporter. Petite in stature, she used her mouth to get what she needed. Sometimes it worked; sometimes it didn't. When it didn't, she fell back to regroup and plan strategy. Most times, strategy worked.

Gracie Lick, family matriarch. She knew how to cook hamburger and weenies a hundred different ways to stretch the family budget. She knew how to shop at thrift

stores for her little family. She was protective of all those she held dear. She knew
how to be humble and grateful at the same
time. Someday, she was going to make
some man a wonderful wife. But first she
was going to finish school and maybe think
about going for her master's. Education
was important, and if she had to scrub
floors or wait tables, she would do it to
make sure her sister got a college education.

More than anything she wanted a real
family, her own children, babies to nurture
and love. She wanted a husband who
loved her above all else, one who would
bring her soup when she was sick, even if
it was the canned kind that he just heated
up. A husband who would take time out of
his own busy day to call and say hello and
ask how her day was going. A husband
who would hold her hand when they took a
walk after dinner. A husband who would
clean up after their dog and not make a big
deal over it.

Would Max Lam make a good husband?
She thought so. They were like oil and water, and that was her fault. Well, mostly her
fault. Maybe he felt as insecure in relation-

ships as she did. Or maybe she felt inferior, and he felt superior. Or, maybe he thought of her as superior, and he felt inferior.

Gracie realized she was still pacing. She always paced when she was agitated. She sat down and looked around. She was there for a reason. She had a job to do. Why was she thinking about Max Lam? *Because I'm wondering how I measure up where he's concerned.* She looked down at her cutoff shorts and Keds sneakers. She wasn't a fashion model, that was for sure.

Sighing, Gracie sat back down and focused on the task at hand. How best to do this? Her brow furrowed in thought. Should she go straight for the jugular or beat around the bush? The jugular, she decided. She scribbled frantically, little squiggles that only she could decipher. She read what she'd written over and over until the words slid from her lips without sounding rehearsed.

Whom to call first? The VP's best friend or the lesser friends. Who would be the easiest to reach? The rocket jockey at NASA might be twiddling his thumbs. Hell, why mess around. Why not make the first call to the VP himself? Why not indeed.

There was no way the VP's press secretary or his personal secretary, if she managed to get that far, would take her call. That meant she would have to state her case to some faceless person, which would mean one more person besides the original four would know what was going on. Too bad.

Gracie picked up the phone, homed in on the telephone number she wanted from the yellow paper, and dialed. Her breathing quickened when she was passed from one operator to another and finally was talking to the vice president's private secretary.

"This is Grace Lick, ma'am. I'm a freelance reporter with the *Los Angeles Times.*" It was true, her article would be in Sunday's edition. "I'm writing an article on a movie that Ricky Lam, the movie star, is going to produce. It will be going into production the first of next year. Just recently I did an article on Mr. Lam that will appear in this Sunday's edition of the *L.A. Times.* While doing my research, I came across some rather odd events that date back to the time the vice president was in college at UCLA. I was wondering if you could have the vice president call me to discuss those findings. I can, of course, talk to all his college friends, but I would like his own personal version. If he's too busy, I understand. It just makes it so much easier for us reporters when we can actually speak to the person in question. I'd like to leave my phone number for the vice president. No, ma'am, that's all I care to say at the moment. Thank you for your time, ma'am." Gracie rattled off her phone number and quickly hung up the phone.

She dialed the second number and asked for Neil Carpenter. The operator put her on hold. Seconds later a voice identified himself as Neil Carpenter. Gracie went into her spiel with gusto. She finished up with, "Would you care to comment, Mr. Carpenter?"

"No, Miss Lick, I wouldn't care to comment. I think you're mistaken in your facts. You might want to recheck them."

"Well, actually, Mr. Carpenter, Laney Woodworth is the main fact. Mr. Ricky Lam is the second fact. Oh, did I forget to tell you that Laney Woodworth is Mrs. Armand Farquar. Mrs. Lorraine Farquar. Her nickname back then when you guys were notching your belts was Laney. Does that ring a bell?"

"I'm sorry I can't help you, Miss Lick. Now, if you'll excuse me, I have a business to run." A second later the connection was broken. A smile on her face, Gracie drew a line through Neil Carpenter's name. She finished the coffee in her cup and poured a second one.

Whom should she call next, Buck Grisham or Leon Franks? Maybe she should wait a few minutes to give Carpenter time to call the others. She had plenty of time. Ricky wouldn't be calling for a while. Maybe she should be more blatant with Buck Grisham. And extremely careful with Franks, the lawyer at Justice. She doodled on the pad in front of her while she sipped at the coffee, which was strong enough to grow hair on her chest.

In the end, she had to leave a message for Franks, who was out of the office. She left a detailed message saying it was imperative she speak with him on an extremely personal, confidential matter. She left her phone number and her cell phone number to be sure she didn't miss his call.

Gracie flexed her fingers as she prepared to dial the main number at NASA.
She wondered if Carpenter had called Grisham to warn him.

Best friend, Buck Grisham. Best friends
were known to lie for each other. The big
question was, would Buck hang tough
thinking the VP could beat the scandal.
Being invited to the White House as the
president's best friend would look damn
good in the media. Or would he run for
cover so as not to be tainted? She didn't
know. She tapped her fingers on the table-
top. Well, she would never know if she
didn't make the call.

Gracie drew a deep breath before she
dialed. She listened to the automated list
of options, finally opting to press zero for
the operator. "I'd like to speak to Buck Grisham, please. This is Grace Lick. I write
for the *Los Angeles Times*."

He had a barking kind of voice. Or
maybe it was an intimidating kind of voice.
Gracie's back went ramrod straight. No
one intimidated Gracie Lick. "Mr. Grisham,
this is Grace Lick. I write for the *Los Angeles Times.* I'd like a minute of your time."

"That's about all the time I can give you, so talk fast."

"Mr. Grisham, I just did an in-depth article on Ricky Lam, the movie star. While I was doing my research I came across some things that led me to other things. I was wondering if you would care to give me a quote about your relationship with Adam Vincent Nolan in regard to that game you and your chums played back in college. The one where you all notched your belts. Wasn't it something like ten virgins, and you won the prize or something like that?"

"What *are* you talking about, Miss Slick? Are you sure you don't have me mixed up with someone else?"

"Lick. L-i-c-k. No, you're the one I want. I already called your other friends, Carpenter and Franks. I have a call in to the vice president."

"That's all well and good, Miss Lick, but what does that have to do with me?"

Gracie smiled at the uneasiness she was hearing on the other end of the phone. "It has a lot to do with you, Mr. Grisham. Laney Woodworth told me that Adam Nolan told her if she accused him of anything, he would have his three buddies swear they had her for two dollars each. Are you denying that?"

"This is the first I'm hearing about it. Who the hell is Laney Woodworth?"

"She was a young girl in Los Angeles who worked waiting tables. Her story is Adam Nolan, your friend, notched his belt with six other waitresses before he got around to Laney Woodworth. That in itself wouldn't be worthy of newspaper coverage, but then Laney found herself pregnant by Adam Nolan. He told her if she tried to blame him, he would have the three of you say you all had her for two dollars each. The child in question was Ricky Lam's adopted brother. Now do you see why Hollywood finds it interesting enough to make a movie of the story? By the way, that little waitress I just told you about is Mrs. Armand Farquar. Lorraine Farquar. She's ready to go public. Think DNA, Mr. Grisham."

"This is preposterous! You're talking about the vice president of the United States. Are you some kind of shakedown artist? It isn't going to work, Miss Slick."

"Lick. L-i-c-k. I guess you *can* go up

against Hollywood *and* Lorraine Farquar if you want to. I commend your loyalty. Our bottom line here is, by your best recollection you don't remember anything, there was never a notch-your-belt game, and you never heard of Laney Woodworth. I can quote you on that, can't I?"

"No, you cannot quote me on anything!"

"Does that mean you're going to hang up on me? When I'm on a story and people hang up on me, my nose starts to twitch. That tells me I caught you off guard, and you need time to come up with a story you hope will pass muster."

She'd hit a nerve, she could tell.

"I don't know anything about a pregnancy or a child. I'm being paged. I'm not hanging up on you, but I really have to cut this off."

"Will you take my call if I call you again?" Gracie asked.

"Not without a lawyer present. Good-bye, Miss Lick."

Gracie scribbled furiously so she could accurately report to Ricky when he called from St. Louis. She was more than satisfied with the calls she'd made. The switchboard at the Naval Observatory was going to be mighty busy.

Gracie spent the next two hours collecting phone numbers and calling every gossip columnist in Hollywood. Her old boss was at the top of the list. When she was finished, she'd netted herself four hundred dollars for hot tips.

Tomorrow morning and all week long the buzz would be that Ricky Lam was coming out of retirement to star in and produce a film having to do with his brother's life and a scandal in the White House.

Sometimes, like now, when she'd done something she was proud of, she longed to have a pat on the back or a kind word. To that end, she picked up the phone again, dialed the resort in Antigua, and asked to be put through to Max. When she heard his voice she relaxed. "Hi. I just wanted to tell you what I accomplished this afternoon. You know, just in case, that kind of thing." She rattled off from her notes, stopping only to take a deep breath.

"Oh, God, Gracie, I don't know what to say. What if . . ."

Gracie was so pleased with the concern in Max's voice, she literally purred. "Hey, it's out there now, and there's no stopping it. If anyone tries, it will just make it worse. You mention scandal in the White House, and red flags go up all over the place. I can sit back now and wait for them to come to me. Every tabloid reporter worth his salt is on it as we speak. Trust me. By tomorrow morning all the Woodward and Bernstein wannabes will be on it."

"Gracie, come here now! You said Ricky was going to get you a ticket. You can come now."

"Yes, but I told him to have the airline mail the ticket. It won't get here for a few days. Don't go spooking me. I can get paranoid on my own. I'm okay. I have those two dogs now, and they are devoted. Wally's better than a cop. No one is going to come after me. They don't even know where I am, for heaven's sake."

"Will you come as soon as you get the ticket?"

"You know what, Max, I think I will. Not because I'm afraid or anything like that. I want to see you. Probably three days, and I'll be landing on your doorstep. I'll call you again when I know something, okay?"

"Okay, Gracie. Thanks for calling."

All of a sudden she felt jittery. It had to be all that damn coffee she'd been drinking. She rinsed the pot twice.

It was time to do something for Gracie Lick. She was going on-line to order new clothes to take to Antigua. She had $400 coming to her for her hot tips, so she could afford to have whatever she bought sent by overnight mail. The $400 plus the $500 she'd saved on rent would be more than enough to get some decent island wear.

Gracie picked up her laptop, set it on the table, and plugged it in.

An hour later she knew she had an impressive ten-day wardrobe. She had sexy underwear, colorful sandals, shorts in every color of the rainbow, with matching halter tops and tees. Four linen dresses, one long white one with a slit up the side, three short ones in mint green, tulip pink, and daffodil yellow. All had matching straw hats. Her most extravagant expenditure was a clingy, sexy, champagne-colored silk dress with matching strappy shoes that looked positively sinful. The last thing she did was click on Barnes & Noble, where she ordered two books, overnight express, by her favorite author, Stella Cameron, to read on the plane.

Drunk with happiness and self-satisfaction, Gracie turned off the computer, checked the coffeepot one last time, then headed for the guesthouse. Mr. Lam would be calling soon from St. Louis for an update. She couldn't wait to tell him that it was time to kick back and watch the stuff hit the fan!

18

The long, winding driveway leading to the Crown Jewel was bordered by the lush, green grass and exotic palms the island was known for. Ricky stopped the golf cart and hopped out. He held out his hand to Roxy. "Seeing it on a blueprint, seeing it in a color drawing just doesn't do it justice. It looks . . ."

" . . . royal. It looks like it goes or ends . . . someplace beautiful and mysterious. Oh, Ricky, it's beautiful, and it's just a road." Excitement rang in Roxy's voice. She squeezed Ricky's hand so tightly he winced.

"It's amazing what a crew can accomplish in just a few days. I can't wait to see the building."

"Me too! Hurry up, Ricky. This is so exciting! Our baby is about to come to life."

Ricky grinned from ear to ear. *Our baby.*

They traveled the last quarter mile with Roxy sitting on the edge of her seat as she tried to take in everything at once. Ricky parked the golf cart next to the construction trailer. Together, they ran around the far end to stare at the structure they had created.

The Carolina sun beamed down on the sprawling building, with its mix of marble, slate, and old brick bathing it in an iridescent glow. Philly was right, it was a crown jewel.

"Rubies, emeralds, sapphires, which one does it look like?" Roxy demanded breathlessly.

"Like all of them sprinkled together. How did you ever come up with the idea to mix the marble, the slate, and the brick? It changes color with the sun. It's magnificent," Ricky said, his voice ringing in awe. "Jeez, look, isn't that Ted Lymen?"

"Yo, boss! What do you think?" the retired stuntman asked as he waved his arms about. "Before you ask, your son sent me here. He said he didn't like the looks of the plantings. He said they didn't 'talk' to him."

"Well, they're jabbering now. Jesus, how'd you do it?"

"I moved stuff, bought more stuff. By the way, you have excellent credit. Those palm trees cost eighty grand. The object was to make everything look like it's been here forever. Just like the resort. When you drive up, it doesn't look new. That's because of your choice of building materials. It's almost untouchable if you know what I mean. I think your guests will consider themselves privileged to be able to come here. That was your objective, wasn't it? I'm heading out in a few hours. I was summoned, I came, I conquered, and now I'm leaving. Max called and said he needed me. It's all done, Ricky. Keep the sprinklers going night and day. This heat is wicked for new plantings."

Ricky clapped his old friend on the back. "You did good, Ted. Listen, did you hear the news?"

"Yeah, Tyler filled me in. Never thought you'd go back, Ricky."

"Just this one time. It's for Philly. I gotta

do it. How about coming back after Carnival? We have a lot of catching up to do."

"You got it. Nice seeing you again, Roxy. Keep this guy on the straight and narrow now, you hear?"

"I'll do my best." Ted threw his arms around Ricky for a bone-crushing hug. "Listen, buddy, I'm thinking of tying the knot. Maybe around Thanksgiving. I want you to be my best man."

"You son of a gun! Anyone I know?"

"She's a third-grade schoolteacher from Memphis. She was watching me work one day. She said I was doing it all wrong and proceeded to show me how to do it."

Ricky laughed. No one told Ted Lymen he did things wrong. "Was she right?"

Ted's burly chest puffed out. "In theory, but she didn't take into account the sandy soil." He pushed his baseball cap farther back on his head. His spiky gray hair was matted to his head with sweat. He brought his arm up to wipe his forehead with the sleeve of his shirt. He grinned. "I can't believe I'm gonna get married."

"Hell, I can't believe it either," Ricky said, clapping him on the back again. "I can top

that, though. Roxy and I are getting married over Christmas."

"No kidding! Congratulations!" He
kissed Roxy on the cheek, and whispered,
"Good choice, girl."

"I know." Roxy laughed. "Boy, do I
know."

"See you around. Remember what I said
about those sprinklers," he called over his
shoulder as he sprinted off to oversee a
load of pine straw that was to be used as
mulch around the plantings.

"Let's take a deep breath and check out
the inside. The painting should be done
and the wall hangings up. They said the
lobby would be finished yesterday." Roxy
crossed her fingers as she skipped forward.

"Oooh, oooh, oooh!" was all she could
say. Ricky gawked.

"I said elegant and royal with a warm
fuzzy, touchy-feely feeling. They got it! My
God, they actually got it!" Ricky watched
as Roxy ran around the lobby checking
this, touching that, peering at something
else, craning her neck to be sure she didn't
miss anything.

Ricky was saved from a reply when his

cell phone rang. He walked away so he could better hear the caller. He felt a grin stretch his facial muscles as he listened to the excitement ringing in the studio head's voice. His grin stretched even wider when his old boss said, "I'm fielding calls right and left. Everyone wants details! You might want to think about making a statement."

"One of these days!" He watched as Roxy moved from chair to chair and sofa to sofa, testing the softness and comfort.

He laughed out loud! They were on a roll!

Buck Grisham looked like a chopped-off tree stump. People referred to him as squat. He stomped around his office, coming down hard on his heels with each step. He was not a patient man, and he hated conference calls because invariably one of the parties was unable to hear the other two. He kept mopping at his bald head as he paced. He reached into the drawer of his desk to grab a handful of chocolate-covered raisins, which he popped into his mouth. Just as he chomped down on the sticky mess, he heard the operator say, "I have both your parties on the line now, Mr. Grisham. You can start when you're ready."

Buck swallowed hard. "Leon, Neil, you there?"

"We're here," both men said in unison.

"What the hell is going on, Buck?" Neil said. "Some woman called yesterday, and I ended up hanging up on her. Look, I don't intend to get involved in any of Nolan's shenanigans. I personally don't give a shit if he is the vice president."

"The man's going to be president! Of these United States! Friends are supposed to help friends. We've always stuck by one another. This is no different," Buck said.

"I beg to differ, Buck. I'm not talking to anyone without a lawyer present. No one is hanging me out to dry because of something Adam did almost fifty years ago. That little waitress gal is Armand Farquar's widow. Think about the kind of clout she has. Since you were always tight with Adam, I suggest you get on the horn and tell him this isn't something he's going to be able to blow off. Two bucks a pop. That's the most disgusting thing I ever heard of. Even if he had asked me, and even if I was dumb as dirt back then, I wouldn't have agreed. How about you, Leon?"

"No way. I'd never lie under oath. If he said it to that little girl, he wasn't counting on me. I want to make sure I have this all straight. That reporter called all of us. She left a pretty detailed message, I can tell you that. I'm not getting involved in some political scandal. I'm a senior attorney at the Justice Department, for God's sake! I have a family and grandchildren who look up to me. I'm seriously thinking of packing them all up and heading off to Europe for an impromptu family vacation."

"Listen, Buck, while I was shaving this morning, I had the TV on. That movie star's studio issued a statement saying Ricky Lam was coming out of retirement to star in a movie about his brother. Then they threw in a teaser about a scandal that would rock the White House. I'm taking my family on a vacation, too. None of us got a call from Adam. What's he going to do, ignore this?" Neil demanded.

"How the hell should I know what he's doing or what he's going to do? I put in a call to him last night, but he hasn't returned it. Remind me not to call either one of you if I ever find myself in a jam," Buck snarled.

"Cancel my reservation for that good old boy reunion in September," Neil said.

"Cancel mine, too," Leon said. "If Adam fathered the waitress's child, that has nothing to do with me. Hell, I never knew any of this until yesterday. The way I see it is this is between Adam and the woman. You might be on the hook, Buck; you were Adam's roommate for four years. No one is going to believe you didn't have anything to do with this. You're on your own, buddy, so don't try dragging me into it. I'm hanging up now. Don't call me again, either."

"I'm with Leon on this all the way. I'm hanging up, too, Buck," Neil said.

"Son of a bitch!" Buck Grisham seethed as he glared at the phone receiver in his stubby hand. He replaced it in the console on his desk. It rang almost immediately. He picked it up, his eyes wary, his voice cautious. It was the operator saying his second conference call was ready to be put through. "I'm sorry, operator, I need another fifteen minutes."

Buck broke the connection and immediately dialed Adam Nolan's private number, wondering if he was making a mistake. He canceled the call before it had a chance to ring. Leon and Neil were right.

He sat down in his chair, which fitted him like a glove. He wasn't guilty of anything. Yes, he'd known about the girl's pregnancy. Yes, Adam had told him what he'd said about the two bucks each. At the time, he'd laughed. What the hell was the big deal? The girl had gone away quietly. Obviously she'd had the baby at some point. More than likely she placed it out for adoption.

Buck racked his brain as he tried to recall anything else Adam might have told him about the waitress. Other than the two-dollar business he could only recall one other conversation, when Adam had gone to meet the girl after she had called him dozens of times. When he got back, he'd opened a bottle of beer, looked at him, and said, "I took care of it. I don't ever want to talk about this again." And they never had.

Buck felt a chill race up his spine. He picked up the phone, pressed nine for an outside line and punched in his home phone number. "Judith, how would you like to go to South America for a few weeks?"

* * *

Just as Gracie was about to leave to start her vacation in Antigua, the phone started to ring. She'd been fielding questions over the phone for two solid days, saying whatever popped into her head. The only person who hadn't called her was Adam Nolan, and she'd bet her last piece of bikini underwear that it was not he. Still, hope springing eternal, she finally picked up the phone. "This is Grace Lick," she said in her most professional voice.

"Please hold for the vice president of the United States, Miss Lick." Gracie almost strangled herself on the telephone cord as she gyrated and wiggled so she could get out her tape recorder and press the RECORD button. She was illegally taping the vice president. Bile rose in her throat at the mere thought. She'd placed her call to him three days ago. He was just now returning it. She struggled to take a deep breath.

"Miss Lick, this is Adam Nolan. I understand you called me the other day. I apologize for not getting back to you sooner, but the nation's business has to come first. I hope you understand."

"Oh, I do, Mr. Vice President."

"What can I do for you, Miss Lick?"

"As I said in my message, I just wanted to know if you would care to comment on the movie Hollywood is going to film after the first of the year. Ricky Lam is coming out of retirement to star in the movie. He's going to be playing the part of his brother. As I said in my message, when I was doing in-depth research on Mr. Lam for an article I was writing, which by the way will appear on Sunday in the *Los Angeles Times,* I came across some very odd information. It all led me to dig a little deeper, and in the process I came across Lorraine Woodworth. Her nickname was Laney when she was a teenager. An *underage* teenager at the time she met you and your friends. Let's see, they were Buck Grisham, Neil Carpenter, and Leon Franks. She said you got her pregnant and refused to take responsibility and that you went so far as to say your friends would swear they had her for two bucks each if she had any thoughts of naming you as the father. That baby, Mr. Vice President, was Ricky Lam's adopted brother. The same baby Laney Woodworth said you snatched from her, put in a Dumpster, and left to die. Fortunately for you, and for the child, Laney had followed you and rescued the child. Is there anything you would like to say?" Gracie's breath escaped her lips in one long *swoosh* of sound.

The laughter, even though it sounded forced, was the last thing she expected to hear. "Miss . . . Lick, was it? I'm always amazed by Hollywood and what they come up with. I sincerely hope you're jesting. If you're serious, I'll have to put you in touch with our attorneys."

Gracie's back stiffened. Did the man live in a bubble? Or was he bluffing? Well, she knew how to play that game. When she'd worked for the tabloids, the publisher got sued on just about every issue of the slimy rag. "I have a pencil, Mr. Vice President. Give me the name of your attorney, or is it just the general White House counsel? You know, sir, you could call those three friends of yours. I spoke to them personally. You can also call the studio to verify what I said. The script has been written and turned in. You do know, don't you, that Laney Woodworth is now Lorraine Farquar, the widow of recently deceased Armand Farquar? She told me she called you but that you hadn't returned her call. I guess you have no comment. Or can I quote you on the Hollywood business and putting me in touch with your attorneys?"

"No, you may not quote me, young woman. Why are you doing this? All you reporters are muckrakers. Tell me right now how I can get in touch with that movie star. I'm going to put a stop to this immediately."

"I resent that, Mr. Vice President. Facts are facts. I don't care if you are the vice president, *SIR*. What you allegedly did is far worse than anything I could ever *think* about doing. Mr. Lam is at Camellia Island in South Carolina." She rattled off his phone number.

Gracie thought she heard him say, "My attorney will be in touch with you."

And this was the guy who might someday run the country. He'd never get her vote, that's for sure. She shrugged. She'd done her part. The rest was now up to Ricky Lam and Lorraine Farquar.

Now it's vacation time! All the new clothes! Well, minus one piece of underwear. An exotic island! Ten whole days!

Max Lam! Woweeee. "Here I come, Antigua!"

Gracie sashayed out of the house and out to the waiting car. She'd splurged on a car service because it was something she'd always wanted to do. She felt like Cinderella going to the ball.

"Anna, cancel the rest of my appointments. I think I'm coming down with a bug of some kind. You can reach me at home if it's an emergency." Was it his imagination, or was his secretary looking at him strangely? His heart pounding in his chest, Adam Nolan left his office.

He entered the vice presidential quarters twenty minutes later, shouting his wife's name. Where the hell was the other half of the all-American family? Then he remembered what day it was. His wife's late day. That meant he had the house to himself. Behind these walls, he could think and plan his strategy. He could call his friends, seek their advice. He could turn on the news and watch it for the rest of the day to see if he could work some damage control. In his life, he'd never felt such fear. Well, maybe one other time. The night Laney Woodworth told him she was pregnant.

Who in the hell would have ever thought that skinny little waitress with the big boobs would eventually become Armand Farquar's wife? Certainly not I.

Nolan poured himself a triple shot of cognac and gulped at it. He paced up and down the library, his favorite room, back and forth, up and down. When the amber fluid was gone from his glass, he poured more. When that was gone, he thought about the faceless son he'd never known. Did he look like him or did he favor the greasy-haired waitress? Now he had to deal with Hollywood trash.

He visualized a gurgling drain and saw all his hopes and dreams swirling away. All because of some trashy waitress and some dickweed movie star. Maybe he could appeal to Armand's widow. Or the kid. Where was the kid? Probably looking for acknowledgment so he could brag that his father was the vice president on his way to being president of the United States. Yeah. Yeah, the kid was his best bet. Only he wasn't a kid anymore. He must be forty-seven or forty-eight. A man. You couldn't reason with a kid, but you could reason with a man. All he had to do was find the kid. How hard could that be? He'd use the internet.

The computer came to life with the Great Seal of the United States on the screen saver. He stared at it and felt like crying. He reached out to touch the screen. It was almost his.

Nolan flexed his fingers before he typed in the name, Ricky Lam. He reared back when the screen exploded to life with flashing pictures of the famous star. He was incredibly photogenic. Hollywood and the fans loved him. He read tributes, testimonials. Twenty minutes later he realized his own life story compared to Lam's was extremely boring. He scrolled down the site map until he saw the word, *Biography*. He clicked on it and read about the star's life. He found it interesting, found that a fifty-thousand-member fan club was current and equaled only by Elvis Presley's. His parents were deceased, and he had a brother named Philip, who was his business manager. The last time the site was updated was a year before Lam's Holly-wood retirement.

Nolan continued to read but eventually gave it up. All he had discovered thus far was his son's name.

He turned to his Rolodex and dialed Buck Grisham's number, only to be told he was in South America for six weeks and no, they didn't have a number where he could be reached.

Next he tried to reach Leon Franks, who, it turned out, was out of the country, and Neil Carpenter, who happened to be away on business. Pure bullshit! What kind of friends were they if they didn't stand by him? They could all just kiss his ass. They weren't going to be on the VIP list for the Inaugural Ball or the swearing-in cere-mony.

The last name on his list was Mrs. Ar-mand Farquar. He probably should have called her first. He shuddered when he re-membered how startled he had been at her words the day of her husband's service. He'd actually stumbled, he'd been so stunned. That same night, his wife had commented on his strange look, asking him what Mrs. Farquar had said to him.

He'd made up some story, but for the life of him couldn't remember what it was. It was a lie, so what did it matter.

His hands were shaking so badly he needed both to hold the glass. He drained it before he set it down on the edge of his desk. He punched in the number from the card in the Rolodex and waited. A cool, aloof voice informed him Mrs. Farquar was out of town. She had no idea when the madam would return and she didn't offer to take a message.

Like that was really true. Did she think he just fell off the turnip truck? "Tell Mrs. Farquar the vice president of the United States called. I'd like her to return my call as soon as possible."

Nolan sat down in his chair. He stared at a family picture sitting on the corner of his desk. The same picture the media had dubbed the All-American Family. What a crock. If they only knew he had another son someplace. Where? Where was his flesh and blood? Suddenly he wanted to know. He *needed* to know.

He looked over at the piece of paper where he'd jotted down Ricky Lam's phone number. He knew he wasn't sober enough to make such an important phone call. He'd catch a few winks and make the call later. Movie stars never went to sleep.

19

Roxy watched from a distance as the golf cart Ricky was in swerved off the road and around to the back of the resort. He appeared either to be looking for something or at something. She used her hand to shield her eyes from the glare of the sun. With the agility of a cat, Ricky leaped out of the cart and onto the hood and continued his intent scrutiny. She called out to him twice, but he was too far away to hear her. What *was* he looking at? She sighed. One of the plants or one of the trees must be crooked.

Ricky liked to eyeball everything, at times actually getting down on the ground to peruse something from a snail's vantage point. Invariably, he was right. She found herself chuckling at that and some of his other antics.

At present, he looked like a bronze Adonis in his shorts, work boots, bare chest, and hard hat. She knew how that bare chest felt against her own bare chest. She shivered in the ninety-degree temperature. Sweat dripped down between her breasts. She wished she could go braless, but her ample bosom prevented such a luxury. She waved frantically when she saw that Ricky was looking in her direction. She motioned for him to join her. She watched in fascination as he made a half turn off the hood of the golf cart, somehow hooked one of his legs around the side of the bar holding up the canopy, and landed smoothly in the driver's seat. A lean, muscled, sensuous cat. She shivered again. This time with anticipated pleasure.

"Whassup?" He grinned, stepping out of the golf cart to wrap her in his arms a few minutes later. He felt so good.

"You had a call. Actually, you had two calls. Gracie called; she arrived in Antigua safe and sound and is probably sunning herself or sleeping as we speak. I can never keep the time differences straight in my head. All is well on her end. Your other call was from the vice president. There was no secretary involved. He found it very hard to believe I did not know where you were or that I was unable to reach you. There was no charm in the man's voice at all."

Ricky laughed. He removed the dark blue bandanna he had tied around his neck. He wiped at his face and neck before he stuffed it in his pocket. "Did he say he was going to call back?"

"No. He said you were to call him the minute you got his message." Roxy held out his cell phone.

Ricky waved it away. "That will be the day! See that fourth palm from the end. It's off by six inches. It throws the whole row out of whack. Get that guy from the nursery and have him fix it. Today. Did Max or Lorraine call?"

"I thought you wanted to talk to the vice president. No, neither one called."

"I do. Look, my one goal from the beginning was to try and figure out what made my brother the person he was. I found that all out. I'm satisfied, and I can handle it. Philly asked one thing of me, and that was to tell his parents, if I found them, that he had died. I'm going to do what Philly wanted, but I'll be damned if I'm going to do it on the phone. Hell, I don't even know if the man knows his son is dead. I want to see that bastard's face when I tell him. If the veep wants to talk, he's going to have to come to me. The way I look at it, we owe him squat. We could make it easy on him and go to Antigua. That way we'll all be there. Let's do that, Roxy. I can be ready to go in a heartbeat. Charter a plane and make all the arrangements. Call Max and clue him in." Ricky looked at his watch. "I have to meet with the pilot and take him to the hangar so he can check out our brand-new helicopter.

"Roxy, think about this. We'll get there just as Carnival gets underway. For the first time you can be a spectator instead of working behind the scenes. Call your daughter and ask her if she wants to join us."

"I called her earlier this morning, and she's snowed under. Maybe next year. Did you check out the progress on the clinic?"

Ricky sighed. "Roxy, I couldn't even find the damn place. When you said secluded, you meant secluded. I took one of the golf carts and started out but got sidetracked. Guests who come to use the facility will love the privacy you arranged. I'm kidding," he said, at Roxy's stricken look. "Of course I looked at it. It's magnificent. Patients can get their face-lifts, nose jobs, implants, whatever, without fear of anyone seeing them. I think the reflecting pool was a particularly nice touch. I don't know when I've ever seen so much *vegetation*. It smells heavenly. Those tea olive trees were a stroke of genius. Look, I gotta run. I'll be back in an hour. Ninety minutes tops. I can be ready to go anytime after that."

The cell phone in Roxy's pocket rang. Ricky waved his hands as he sprinted off. He couldn't wait to see the brand-new helicopter.

Roxy clicked on the phone. "Roxy Nelson," she said coolly.

"Miss Nelson, this is Adam Nolan, the vice president. Has Mr. Lam returned?"

"Yes, Mr. Vice President, but he had to leave again. However, he did leave a message for you. He said to tell you he does not discuss personal, private matters on the phone. Mr. Lam is leaving in a short while for Antigua. I can give you a number where you can reach him once he arrives there to set up your own appointment. Or, *I* can schedule you for a personal appointment, which is probably the only way you're going to be able to talk to him."

The voice on the other end of the line started to sputter. "I don't believe this. Did you tell him who I am?"

"Yes, Mr. Vice President, I told Mr. Lam exactly who you are. Right now Mr. Lam is taking possession of a new helicopter, he's also in the middle of building a new resort and overseeing a million details, while at the same time negotiating with Hollywood and actors' agents for a new movie he's agreed to star in the first of the year. On top of that, he flies back and forth to the other two resorts his corporation owns on a regular basis. He is rather busy. As I said, I might be able to tentatively pencil you in for the day after tomorrow. What would you like me to tell Mr. Lam, Mr. Vice President?"

Roxy doubled over laughing when she heard the phone disconnect in her ear. How politically incorrect!

*   *   *

His head pounded. He wasn't sure if it was from all the cognac he'd consumed the night before or if it was from fear. Fear, he decided. Fear that he was going to see his hopes and dreams going to hell. All because of one mistake.

He cringed when he remembered what he'd heard on the twenty-four-hour news channel earlier. So far the press were parsing their words rather carefully. The innuendos, the sly digs were there with only a thin veneer covering the hard words. The tabloids were going hunting, the legitimate press, along with his political enemies, would join the fray shortly. That was a given.

Buck Grisham had warned him once that his cocky attitude would be his undoing. The phone rang. He stopped his frantic pacing to stare at it. "Adam Nolan," he said.

"This is Ricky Lam, Mr. Vice President. I'm returning your call."

The vice president didn't think about his words, he just blurted out what came into his head. "What in the damn hell did I ever do to you to warrant this attack on me and the office I hold? What's all this claptrap

I'm hearing on every news channel? You can tell all your pretty studio people I'm going to be suing them as well as you. How dare you tarnish the office I hold and my reputation!" He banged his fist on the table to drive home his point before he realized Lam couldn't see what he was doing.

"Everybody in this life has to do what they have to do, Mr. Vice President. I returned your phone call as a courtesy, and to tell you I never discuss personal business on the phone. I'm leaving for Antigua in an hour. If you want to talk to me, that's where I'll be, Mr. Vice President."

"Don't you hang up on me you . . . you . . . you *movie star*. You're talking to the vice president of the United States!" Too late. The phone *pinged* in his ear. Frustrated, he slammed his cell phone down on his desk.

Nolan beeped the head of his Secret Service detail, who came on the run. "I want to go to Antigua today. Do what you have to do, and I don't want to hear scheduling excuses either. I'm the vice president. I can do what I damn well please."

After speaking to his press secretary, informing her he was taking a short two-day vacation in Antigua, he called the head of his private security staff. He cleared his throat, trying to sound like the forceful vice president he was supposed to be. "Carmody, I'm going to Antigua, Ellen has the details. I want you to take care of something for me, and I want it taken care of ASAP. There's a reporter named Grace Lick who writes for the *L.A. Times*. She's stirring up trouble. All those trashy Hollywood people crawl out from under rocks. I want you to keep her away from the media for a few days, and I don't want to read about it in the papers. I will not tolerate any excuses in this matter. Just so we're clear. Take care of it, Carmody."

He bellowed for the housekeeper. "Do you go to the movies, Melba?" he asked, when she appeared in the dining room doorway.

"On occasion, sir."

"Do you like that movie star, Ricky Lam?"

"Yes, sir, I do. My husband and I have seen all his films. My favorite was, *Noon Magic*. He doesn't make movies anymore. He retired at the height of his career. I guess that was a good career move on his part. Going out while you're still on top, that kind of thing."

"Why would he do something like that? Movie stars are addicted to seeing themselves on the big screen and television as well."

"I think Mr. Lam's situation was a little different. His brother was killed during a freak accident when they were filming the last scene of the movie he was working on."

Adam Nolan sat down on the closest chair with a loud thump. "Killed! His brother died! You mean he's *dead?*"

"Yes, sir. It was in all the papers and on the news at the time. Mr. Lam just walked away from Hollywood. Is there anything else, sir?"

"No. On second thought, yes, I'd like some more coffee." Coffee was the last thing he wanted.

The brother is dead! Then what the hell is this all about? Suddenly his shoulders felt lighter. Dead was dead. All along he'd been thinking his illegitimate son was going to appear, and say, "Hi, Pop, remember me?" He did some fast calculations in his head. That meant the brother, *never my son,* had been dead for six months. What the hell was all the fuss about? He could feel his shoulders straighten. He could make this all go away. He was almost positive he could do that. The absence of a living, breathing body to stare him in the face bolstered his confidence. All he had to do was get a bead on it, and intimidation would do the rest.

"Carnival never ceases to amaze me," Roxy said as she eyed the colorful dress the island visitors were wearing. "Where do these vendors come from? It's like they spring up out of nowhere. In your life you will never see so much food. Your brother hated Carnival and always made sure he left before it started."

"It's so . . . *frantic,*" Ricky said, as his eyes searched for his son.

"This is nothing. Wait until the last few days. No one sleeps. It's nonstop partying for four days. For some reason, I thought you'd been here for Carnival. Our guests love it. The steel bands are really worth seeing and hearing. The Calypsonians and the Deejays start it off with the opening at

Carnival City at the Antigua Recreation Ground in St. John's. Almost all of the special events are scheduled there. We had to run a jitney on the half hour to accommodate our guests. Around the clock. It's just a smaller version of Mardi Gras. Oooh, there's Max! Yoo-hoo, sweetie! We're over here!"

He looks happy, Ricky thought. He said so to Roxy.

She laughed. "He's in love." She squeezed his hand. He squeezed back.

"It's a zoo!" Max shouted. "It's like this everywhere. Follow me."

In the car, headed for the resort, Max turned to face his father. "I heard on the news that the vice president is arriving late today. I lost all security that I had. Local law enforcement commandeered everyone working privately in security on the island. We're okay, we got it covered. There's a big push for the American flag, though. I guess you got the veep on the run, Ricky. The news said the vice president hasn't taken a vacation in six years, and this is his first. He wanted to experience Carnival. We all know it's bullshit, but it *is* what they're saying."

"How are your special guests?" Ricky asked.

"They are having the time of their lives. Lorraine, she told me to call her that, and her daughter-in-law are great friends. The girls met some young people, and they're palling around. Ted is watching over them. They understand what's at stake here, so they're being cooperative. Like I said, I got it covered. Tyler runs interference. I'm just sorry I can't be spending more time with Gracie."

"Well, we're here now. Spend some time with her. Roxy and I can fill in for you. Don't you get a headache from all of this?"

Max laughed. "I have a headache from day one till the last day. Do we have a game plan or what?"

"I have to work on that. Did the news say where the vice president was staying?" Ricky asked.

"In a private home as someone's guest. They didn't elaborate. The locals are pretty pissed that he chose this time to visit. It's all they can do to handle the revelers. The arrival of the vice president only adds to their troubles. They're being decent about

it, though. Good PR for Antigua." Max
looked into the rearview mirror. "You're
lookin' good, Roxy."

"Well, thank you. How's Gracie looking?"

Ricky and Roxy watched Max's neck
turn pink. "Real good."

Fifteen minutes later, Max swerved up
along the winding road that led to the resort. "Whew, I'm glad I don't have to fight
that zoo on a regular basis. Why don't you
two freshen up. I'll collect everyone and
meet you on the Calypso Deck. How does
an hour sound? Just for the record, we're
at one hundred percent occupancy. Tyler is
bunking in with me."

"Sounds good to me," Ricky said, helping Roxy out of the car. He watched with
pride when the staff rushed up to her to either hug her, shake her hand, or kiss her
cheek. She took time for all of them, asking
about their well-being, their families, and
whatever else she could think of. "We're
just guests this time around. I expect you
all to wait on us hand and foot. No slack-
ing, now," she joked.

"All right. Let's hit those showers. We'll
see you in a bit," Ricky said as he clapped

his hand on his son's back. "Monitor any calls that come in for me, Max."

"Gotcha."

They could have posed as mother, daughter, and family, Ricky thought as he walked out onto the Calypso Deck, where Lorraine Farquar, her daughter-in-law, and granddaughters sat waiting for him.

"You go ahead, Ricky," Roxy said. "I'll join you later. I want to walk around and talk to people. I don't want them to think I'm ignoring them. I made a lot of friends in the years I worked here."

"Take your time." Ricky kissed her lightly on the cheek, not caring who saw him. He watched her as she walked away, her hips wiggling provocatively. She looked back over her shoulder and winked. He grinned, then laughed out loud, again not caring who saw or heard him.

On the Calypso Deck, Ricky impulsively leaned down and kissed Lorraine Farquar's cheek before he shook hands with Lee Ann. He eyed the three sisters and grinned. "You don't want to be here, do you?" They blushed as one. "Go on, have some fun. Us old folks will sit here and discuss your sunburns." He smiled as they scrambled from their chairs and ran off to do whatever it was his appearance had interrupted.

"It's nice to see you again, Ricky. There are no words to thank you. One moment my life was turned upside down, and, before I knew it, it turned right-side up again. I called my housekeeper to see if there were any messages. Adam Nolan called twice and wants me to call him. Of course I didn't. I didn't tell the housekeeper where I was either."

Ricky nodded. "My son told me he heard on the news that the vice president is arriving sometime this evening. He called me several times. I returned his call but wouldn't discuss matters with him. The fact that he's coming here tells me he is very worried."

"What . . . what are we going to say when we meet with him?"

Ricky smiled. "I know exactly what I'm going to say. I think you should say whatever you want. All the things you've always wanted to say that you bottled up. My press agent," he said, referring to Gracie Lick, "put the spin out before she left to come here. It's not going to go away.

There's no way he can defend himself. My thinking, and I could be wrong, is that he's going to try to get us to issue some kind of statement saying this is just Hollywood hype to ratchet up interest in a movie I'm making. That is not going to happen. We're on our own turf here and not inside the Beltway."

Ricky looked up when he heard the sound of running feet and heard his name being called. He turned around, curious. "Max! What's wrong?"

"Dad, I need you right now! Hurry up! Tyler will stay with the ladies."

Did he hear correctly? *Dad, I need you right now! Dad!*

"Go, go," Lorraine Farquar said. "Do what your son wants."

"Can't you go any faster?" Max said, running down the hall, calling over his shoulder. "Pick up your feet!"

"What's wrong? Don't tell me the vice president arrived and you slugged him!"

"It's worse than that," he said, throwing the door open to his suite of rooms. Ricky gawked, his eyes almost popping out of his head.

"Gracie!"

"She fell asleep in the sun. She's frozen in that position. I called a doctor, but with Carnival, who the hell knows when he'll get here. We have to do something!"

"Go find Roxy. Bring Mrs. Farquar and Lee Ann up here. Now, Max!"

"Ah, Gracie, this was supposed to be a fun vacation for you. We'll . . . we'll do something. Didn't anyone warn you about the sun here? It's all right, don't talk."

"I feel like my skin is stretched too tight," Gracie said through clenched teeth. "I had on a thirty-five sunblock. I feel like I'm on fire." She started to cry.

Roxy raced through the door. She gaped at Gracie before she turned to Max and Ricky. "Leave us alone. I know what to do. Go find a damn doctor," she hissed to Max.

Lorraine Farquar and Lee Ann Oliver entered the room just as Ricky and Max were leaving.

"It's bad, isn't it?" Gracie whimpered.

"There, there, dear, nothing is as bad as it seems," Lorraine said soothingly. "Tea bags, lots and lots of tea bags in tepid water. It's the same principle as biting down on a tea bag after you have a tooth pulled.

It's the tannin in the tea. I think it has medicinal properties."

"I always used vinegar on my girls when they got bad sunburns. It takes the heat out of the burn," Lee Ann said.

"I always used Noxzema because it felt cool," Roxy said. "Aloe first, though, for the healing properties.

"Gracie, hold tight, okay? I'm going down to the kitchen to get everything. We'll stand her up in the tub and . . . and drizzle the tea bag water over her. Then we'll drizzle the vinegar and then pat her down with the aloe. How does that sound?"

"Like a plan," Lee Ann said. Lorraine nodded.

Roxy kicked off her high-heeled sandals and ran out of the room.

Max and Ricky dogged her every step, demanding to know what she was doing and why she was doing it. "Will one of you just find a damn doctor! I can't believe one isn't staying here. We always have doctors staying here. Move! Both of you! Do I have to do everything?"

"No, ma'am," Max said smartly. "Is she going to be all right?"

"Of course she's going to be all right. I

just don't know when that will be. You're still standing here. When I give you an order, you hop to it, mister. That goes for you, too, Ricky!"

If they'd had tails, they would have been between their legs when they retreated from the kitchen. "She's going to be okay, isn't she, Dad?"

Dad. There it was, the magic word he never thought he would hear. And he'd heard it twice. "Roxy wouldn't lie about something like that, Max. Let's check the computer to see if there's a doctor staying here."

Five minutes later, Max whooped with pleasure. "Dr. Carlyle Byrd from Marietta, Georgia, is staying on the fourth floor with his wife and his wife's sister. I have no idea what kind of doctor he is. He might be a Ph.D. for all I know. I can almost guarantee they aren't in their rooms. I'll ring both and leave a message on the voice mail. We can also have him paged in case they're at the pool, gym, or one of the bars."

Ricky looked at his son's shaking hands. "Let me do it, Max. Go ahead, but they aren't going to let you in the room. I'll be up as soon as I finish here."

"This must be like having a baby where the father can't do anything but pace the floor," Max said morosely. "I want to do something."

Ricky left instructions for the desk clerk if Dr. Byrd called in from the page or returned to the hotel. He sighed. Life certainly was strange. He wrapped his arm around his son's shoulder and walked him down the hall. He could feel Max leaning against him. It was a nice feeling. A real nice feeling.

20

It was after ten o'clock when Gracie Lick fell asleep. Dr. Carlyle Byrd, a pudgy, balding man with shell-rimmed glasses, looked around at the worried faces staring at him. "She's going to be fine. Uncomfortable, but fine. You acted quickly, and that helped a lot. I'll check on her first thing in the morning. She should sleep through the night with the shot I gave her."

Dr. Byrd looked at Ricky. "Do you think you could find me some transportation into St. John's? I'm a steel band aficionado. I had to do months of sweet-talking to get my wife to come here. I don't want her to start harping on me. She wanted to go to Hawaii."

"Absolutely, Dr. Byrd, I'll take you myself. Your stay is on the house."

The doctor beamed his pleasure.

When the door closed behind Ricky and the doctor, Roxy took charge. "We're going to take turns staying with Gracie. Two-hour shifts each. I'll take the first shift. Lorraine gets the second, Lee Ann the third, and you, Max, get the early-morning shift. She's going to be all right, Max, so wipe that look off your face. You have a resort to run, so do what you're paid to do. Gracie is in good hands."

"All right, Roxy."

"Max."

"Yes."

"I know your history with Gracie. When guests come to the islands for the first time, especially those who have never had a *real* vacation, like Gracie, they do things like fall asleep in the sun. She did put on a thirty-five sunblock. Someone should have warned her about the sun here. I'm thinking that was your responsibility, and you screwed up. I mention this so you won't say or do anything that will embarrass or hurt Gracie. Just so you know, your father loves that girl."

Max's head bobbed up and down. He remembered the day his father had said he admired Gracie and went on to say he did not admire him or his brother. "I hear you, Roxy."

"Okay. Take care of business now."

Lorraine Farquar patted Gracie's head. "I feel, Roxy, like I stepped into another world. All of a sudden, I have this wonderful family, and an extended family as well. This mothering business is wonderful. I always knew it would be. I cheated myself all those years because I was such a coward. I am so glad you and Ricky found me. With Armand's passing, and don't think I'm not grieving, because I am, I don't know what I would have done."

Roxy smiled as she kissed Lorraine's cheek. "Try to get a few hours' sleep."

It was a difficult thing to do, but Roxy walked over to Lee Ann Oliver. "I'm sorry for both of us. In his own way, Philip brought us all to this place in time. You have three wonderful daughters and an equally wonderful mother-in-law. I found my soul mate in Ricky. Even though the circumstances were . . . less than we would have liked, we still have to be grateful to

Philip. I hope we can be friends when we finally lay all this to rest."

"I hope so, too," Lee Ann said. "No, no, let's not hope. Let's make it happen. Now, if you need us, call."

"I will. Thanks for all your help this evening."

"There's nothing I wouldn't do for that little girl," Lorraine said, pointing to Gracie. "She made it happen. I wish Armand was here so he could meet everyone." Her voice was so sad, it brought tears to Roxy's eyes.

"I think he's watching. I wouldn't be a bit surprised to find out Philip is orchestrating everything from . . . *up there*. I know he's smiling down on all of us."

Lorraine patted Roxy's hand as Lee Ann ushered her out of the room.

"It's just you and me, kid," Roxy said, sitting down on a chair close to the bed. She stared at Gracie, wondering if she'd ever been that young. She smiled when she remembered the panic on Max's face. And the love. "I think, my dear, you're going to get the brass ring," she whispered.

*   *   *

The lobby of the resort was as busy at eleven o'clock at night as it was at eleven o'clock in the morning. Sleep was something that came with a question mark. Or an exclamation point. Still, it wasn't rowdy, but it was noisy as little groups tried to figure out the best way to get to St. John's, where all the action was.

Tyler sensed his brother's approach. It was uncanny the way he was so tuned to a brother he never knew existed until a few months ago. He turned and grinned.

"Yo, Bro. There's miserable, and then there's *miserable*. You fall into the latter category. I heard about Gracie. Is she okay?"

"Yeah, the doctor said she'd be okay, but her vacation is spoiled. I don't know who was looking forward to it more, she or I. I swear to God, Ty, I told her not to stay out in the sun. I told her to ease into it and to use a good sunblock. She listened, but she fell asleep under a palm tree in the shade, then the sun moved on. The rest is history. Roxy and the ladies took care of her until the doctor showed up. They kicked me out. They're taking turns sitting with her."

Tyler clapped his brother on the back. He looked around, his gaze sweeping the lobby for any sign of trouble. Seeing none, he said, "The place doesn't look like it's going to implode anytime soon. Let's catch a beer. I'm buying. Besides, I want to talk to you about something."

"I want to talk to you about something, too," Max said, following his brother. As always, both young men were totally oblivious of the admiring glances being sent their way.

Max perched himself on one of the barstools close to the door. In the holiday atmosphere, you had to be alert for any sign of trouble.

Tyler handed Max a bottle of Corona. They clinked their bottles, grinning at each other. "What did you want to talk to me about, Ty?"

"This," Tyler said, setting his beer bottle down on the high bar table. He fished in his pocket to withdraw a small jeweler's box. He opened it.

Max gaped. He looked at the sappy look on his brother's face. "So, who are you giving this to?"

"What do you mean who am I giving this to? Donna, of course."

"What happened to Rosalie, Corinda, Miriam, and Stephanie?" Max needled.

"Nothing happened to them. They're all nice girls. They helped me see that Donna is the one for me."

Max continued to needle. "Does Donna know? Did you tell Roxy or Ricky?"

"No. Should I have told them? I don't have to ask permission, you know."

Max shrugged. "When are you going to give it to her?"

"Tomorrow. Okay, that's my news. What did you want to talk about?"

"I called Ricky 'Dad.' Twice. I called him 'Dad' twice, Tyler. It seemed like the most natural thing in the world. I was panicking over Gracie."

"How'd he take it?" Curiosity rang in Tyler's voice.

"He didn't. I think he heard me. Hell, I was yelling at the top of my lungs. I guess he rolled with it."

"So, are you going to be calling him Dad from now on or what?"

"I don't know. I guess if it feels right, I will. He feels like my father. He really does.

How about you? Have you called him 'Dad' yet?"

"No. I think of him that way, though. I bet he marries Roxy before the end of the year. Ten bucks, Bro."

Max snorted. "That's a sucker bet. I feel like we're a family. Do you feel that way, Tyler?"

"Yeah, I do. Want another beer?"

"Sure. Uh-oh, scratch that beer, Bro. Do you see what I'm seeing?"

"Oh, shit! Where's *Pop?*"

"*Dad* drove the doctor to St. John's. He'll be lucky if he gets back here by three in the morning. Hop to it, Bro."

"It's true, they do all look alike. I see eight of them," Tyler said. "They wear these microphones inside their sleeves. Then they bring their wrists up to their faces and talk into them. I saw that in a movie."

"I saw the same movie. Let's head them off at the pass. They look pretty fit to me."

"It's an illusion. We're the ones who are fit." Tyler grimaced.

The brothers watched as the Secret Service agents fanned out across the lobby.

"They have no jurisdiction here," Tyler hissed in his brother's ear.

"I don't think it matters. Remember this, they're *packing*. Don't even think about starting anything. Like our father says, courtesy goes a long way. C'mon, let's beard this lion."

Long-legged, purposeful, synchronized strides brought them right up to the courtesy desk and into the face of the agent who had just identified himself as Special Agent Zirconie.

"I'm Max Lam. This is my brother, Tyler Lam. What is it you want, Agent Zirconie?"

"I'd like to speak with Ricky Lam. Can you tell me where he is?"

"He isn't here. He's in St. John's. I'm not sure when he'll be back with everything going on. I can give him a message."

"We'll wait."

Max looked at his brother. "How about waiting someplace other than the lobby. People are already staring at you. You guys need to *dress down* when you come to a place like this. In case you haven't noticed, you reek Secret Service. Sit in the bar. You can see everyone coming or going through the lobby. My father will enter through the lobby."

"We'll stay in the lobby," Agent Zirconie said.

"No, Agent Zirconie, you won't stay in the lobby," Max said. "I run this resort. What I say goes. You have no jurisdiction here. This is not the good old USA, in case you had forgotten. Before you bring it to a firestorm, you might want to call the vice president to make sure he's okay with your hanging out in my lobby. *Retreating* is not a dirty word. I'll clear the bar for you."

Agent Zirconie eyed the two brothers for a full minute before allowing his gaze to sweep across the milling crowds in the lobby. Whatever he saw in the brothers' faces convinced him to move off. A cell phone materialized in his hand.

"We can take him," Max whispered.

"What's with that *we* stuff? Remember the last time we ended up in jail? In case you forgot, I haven't. There are *eight* of them. Eight. We number two."

Agent Zirconie returned. "We'll wait in the bar. There's no need to clear it. Notify us the minute Mr. Lam returns. No funny stuff, boys. And, no, you couldn't take me, even on your best day."

"That's a matter of opinion," Max said coldly.

The agent murmured something into his sleeve. He looked up at Max, and said, "No, it's a fact."

The brothers watched as the agent made his way to the bar to sit down on the same stool Max had vacated.

"What now?" Tyler hissed.

"Now you go upstairs and tell Roxy to call Ricky. I don't know if he took his cell phone with him or not. I'll stay down here and keep my eyes open. Those guys aren't stupid. They probably have agents covering all the entrances and exits, and one of them is probably out at the end of the driveway. Just because we only saw eight doesn't mean there aren't more outside. Look nonchalant, Bro."

Tyler sauntered off, his destination the kitchen and the outside entrance that would take him up to the Calypso Bar. From there he took the elevator that would carry him to the fourth floor, where he let himself into Max's suite.

"How is she?"

"She's sleeping." Roxy said. "She really hasn't moved. It's a restful sleep. What's going on?"

Tyler filled her in.

"Your father had his cell phone. Let's see if he has it turned on." She dialed the number and waited. Ricky picked up almost immediately. Roxy handed the phone to Tyler.

"It's going down, Dad. What do you want us to do? They're waiting for you in the lobby. Hell, they're all over the place."

Ricky thought he was going to bust wide open. *Dad*. His son just called him "Dad."

"Don't do anything, and don't antagonize them either. I heard on the radio that the vice president arrived a little while ago. The locals have recommended he stay in his quarters for security reasons. That has to mean his agents are here to take me to him. I don't want to do that in the middle of the night. Morning will be time enough. I want Lorraine to be with me when we meet. I'm going to go to one of the casinos and hang out till morning. I doubt they have much authority over here, but I don't want to cause any problems at this stage.

"Show them some hospitality, and don't

let Max piss them off. Don't tell me he already did that!"

"Sort of, kind of, but not really. They act like they're programmed. The word *robot* comes to mind," Tyler said grimly. "I guess I'll see you in the morning then."

"Yes, around seven or so. Tell Lorraine to be ready to leave as soon as I get there."

"Will do."

After Tyler relayed his father's plan to Roxy, she sighed. "I can't wait for all this to be over." She stood up, rolling her shoulders back and forth. The door opened, and Lorraine Farquar stepped into the room.

She walked over to the bed and stared down at Gracie. "I think she looks a lot better, don't you?" she whispered. Roxy nodded.

"Get some sleep, dear. I brought a book with me. The time will pass quickly."

"Ma'am, I was just speaking with my father. The vice president is on the island. Dad wants you to be ready to go with him at seven o'clock in the morning. There are Secret Service agents all over the place. As far as I know, no one knows you're here but us. My father wants to keep it that way."

Lorraine nodded before she shooed them out of the room.

"I'm going to bed unless you need me, Tyler."

"We got it covered, Roxy. Hey, wait a minute. I want to show you something."

Roxy stared down at the diamond winking at her in its velvet nest. "It's beautiful. I'm assuming it's for Donna. I'm so happy for you, Tyler. When are you going to give it to her?"

"Tomorrow. Today, actually," he said, looking down at his watch. "Sleep tight, Roxy."

"You, too, Tyler," Roxy said as she headed for the elevator.

It was a beautiful house, with beautifully landscaped grounds. It was a pity he couldn't appreciate the beauty at such a late hour. His host or hostess was absent, thanks to whoever made the last-minute arrangements. There was a live-in housekeeper to see to his needs and, of course, the agents guarding him.

He'd tried to cloak the whole trip in secrecy but knew word had leaked out. Possibly by either his host or his hostess because they were American. In the end it probably wasn't going to matter.

It was one minute to midnight according to his watch. Somewhere in the house, a clock chimed the hour. Any hope of meeting with Ricky Lam so late was just wishful thinking. Still, he wasn't going to call off his agents. That movie star needed to know exactly who he was dealing with. The morning would be soon enough.

He had finally relaxed. In just a few hours he would be able to lay all this nonsense to rest. Hollywood would have to find someone else to torture because it sure as hell wasn't going to be him.

They converged on him like a swarm of locusts when he walked through the lobby at six forty-five the following morning. Agent Zirconie identified himself before he drew him aside, and said quietly, "The vice president of the United States would like you to accompany me to where he's staying. You can drive your own car if you like. He said the two of you had a phone conversation in which you said you would agree to meet with him. The vice president is on a very tight schedule, Mr. Lam."

"This might surprise you, Agent Zirconie, but I'm on a pretty tight schedule myself. I need time to shower and shave. I can be ready in half an hour, not one minute sooner. I also need a cup of coffee."

"I find that satisfactory, Mr. Lam. I'll be waiting right here for you."

Ricky nodded as he made his way to the elevator. The minute the door closed behind him, his clenched fist shot in the air.

Roxy was brushing her teeth when Ricky entered their suite. He kissed her lightly on the cheek before reaching across her to turn on the shower. "I have half an hour to shave and get dressed. Call Lorraine for me and have her come to this room. We'll meet the agents together. Did you order coffee? How's Gracie?"

"It's on the way, and Gracie is doing okay. Max is with her now. She's going to be doing a lot of sleeping. That's a good thing, Ricky. Are you nervous?"

"Hell yes, I'm nervous. I imagine Lorraine is a physical wreck. It doesn't matter because we're going to do what we have to do so Philly can rest in peace. I could really use some coffee, Roxy. By the way, I won sixty-six dollars at the casino last night. How would you like to go to lunch?"

"I'd love it if you're buying! Coffee's here," she called as she opened the door. While the waiter poured the coffee, Roxy rang Lorraine Farquar's room.

"It's Roxy, Lorraine. She's doing fine, she's sleeping. Ricky wants you to come down to our room by seven. Secret Service agents have been in the lobby all evening. They don't know about you, yet. I'll talk to you later."

Roxy carried the cup of coffee into the bathroom, along with Ricky's one cigarette.

She returned to the sitting room and turned on the television. It was too early for the talk shows and gossip, so she was forced to settle for local news, which bored her to tears.

She closed her eyes and thought about Philip Lam. She hoped he was in a better place. A place where he was finally at peace. Her eyes snapped open when Ricky snapped his fingers.

She smiled. "What is it, Oh Mighty Sir? Ooh, you look good, and you smell good, too." And he did, in his creased khakis and

white button-down shirt, whose sleeves
were rolled to the middle of his arms. She
did love his deep tan and the whitish crin-
kles around his eyes. Her heartbeat quickened.

"What were you thinking just now?"
Ricky asked.

"Before or after I opened my eyes and
saw how delectable you looked?"

"Before."

"I was thinking about your brother, hoping he's in a better place and finally at
peace."

Ricky sat down opposite her. He
propped his elbows on his knees and
stared at her. "That's so strange, Roxy. I
was thinking almost the same thing. Actually, I was talking to him in my mind. I was
telling him we were in the home stretch.
Where's the file?"

Roxy pointed to the table. "It's all there. I
guess the agents will have to look through
it."

"It doesn't matter to me if they see it.
They can't repeat or talk about it. The vice
president might have some objections, but
I don't much care." He got up when a

knock sounded at the door. He opened it to admit Lorraine Farquar.

She looks scared out of her wits, was Roxy's first thought. In the time it took her heart to beat twice, she was across the room. "You can do this, Lorraine. You're the big player in this game. Don't let the man or his office intimidate you. Think about that wonderful new family you have now. Think in terms of all the years that man robbed from you. Ricky will be right there beside you."

"Bless your heart, Roxy, for everything. Yes, I'm very nervous. I know I can do it because I have to do it. For Caleb. That's my son's name."

Roxy and Ricky watched in awe as the older woman's shoulders stiffened and her gaze grew determined and defiant. "I'm ready now, Ricky, to rip out that son of a bitch's guts."

"Attagirl, Lorraine. Kick ass and take names later. That was always your son's motto." Roxy grinned.

"I'm so glad you told me that, dear. Thank you. I just love hearing things about him."

*   *   *

He was dressed in a charcoal gray suit.
His shirt was pristine white, his tie conservative. Every hair was in place. He didn't
think he would be nervous, but he was.

He hadn't slept a wink. Instead, he'd
paced, rehearsing what he was going to
say to the movie star. When he felt he had
it down pat, he practiced in front of the
vanity mirror to make sure every facial expression, every nuance was letter-perfect.
He'd always been a quick study as well as
a quick starter.

The first rule in intimidation was to have
your adversaries sitting while you remained
standing, so you could tower above them.
And if the tide turned in the adversaries' direction, you never let them see you sweat.
You smiled like you knew a secret you
weren't ready to divulge.

Everyone had a price. What was Ricky
Lam's? He had to admit he didn't know. It
couldn't be money, the man was a million-
aire many times over. He owned vast
amounts of real estate and these resorts.
He already had all the fame he could handle. Power. One could never have enough
power. Power was the most powerful
aphrodisiac in the world. Power was the

one thing the man didn't have. A man, any man, would be a fool not to covet power. When he was president, he would appoint him ambassador to some godforsaken place. If that didn't work, possibly a more important role in his new administration.

That's exactly what he would do.

The knock on the front door was so loud, Nolan almost jumped out of his skin. Not bothering to wait for the housekeeper, he opened it himself. He felt his insides start to crumble when he looked into Lorraine Farquar's eyes. She shouldered her way past him as though he were a homeless vagrant. Ricky Lam followed.

Nolan closed the door, knowing the perimeter was well guarded. He knew he had to seize the moment. He turned, his face schooled to blankness. "It's nice to see you again, Mrs. Farquar." He held out his hand to Ricky, who merely stared at him, his hands clenched into fists inside his pockets. The manila envelope was tucked under his arm.

"Let's get to it, Mr. Vice President. Time is money, and I'm a busy man. By the way, that was my brother's favorite saying."

"Your brother is dead. Why are you doing this? What can you possibly hope to gain?"

"I'm trying to do the only thing my brother ever asked of me. He wrote me a letter before he died. He searched all his life for his real parents. It was important for him to know what his name was. His real name. He died not knowing. He asked me to tell his parents he died and had they kept him, he would have honored and loved them till the day he died, because that's what a child is supposed to do in regard to his parents. Now, I've told you. That's all I came here today to tell you."

"What is it *you* want, then? Are you going to stop that stupid movie business?"

"No. What *I* want is for you to resign your office and leave Washington. That's what I personally want."

"Well, that isn't going to happen, Mr. Lam. I'm running for the presidency."

"No, *Vincent,* you will not be running for the presidency," Lorraine said. "I want you to sit down, and I want you to read every single piece of paper in this envelope. Then I want you to tell me what you're going to do." She tossed the envelope to him. He had no recourse but to reach for it. He refused to sit down, though.

Nolan's insides churned as he read through the contents of the envelope. "This is blackmail!"

"No, *Vincent,* it is not blackmail. What you have in your hands are statements of fact. Because of you I never got to know my son. You threw him away, and I rescued him. You can lie and say you didn't do what you did, but I don't think your adoring public will believe you. I'm going to do the talk-show circuit as soon as I go back home."

"For Christ's sake, Lorraine, he's *dead.* What good is this going to do for anyone?"

"Just looking at you makes me sick. Hearing you say those things makes me want to vomit. He wasn't some piece of garbage. He was a human being. He was my son. He was your son, too. Personally speaking, I'm glad he wasn't part of that phony all-American family of yours. I think he would have been very disappointed in you. You weren't fit to lick his boots."

"And I suppose you were fit. You were out there peddling your ass when you were fourteen years old. What does that make you, *Mrs. Farquar?*"

"It makes me underage, Mr. Vice President. Notch Number 7. You do remember that, don't you?"

"He's dead, let him rest in peace." His voice sounded so desperate, he thought he was going to be sick.

Ricky bounded out of his chair when Lorraine started to cry. "My brother didn't matter in life, and he doesn't matter in death. Is that what you're saying?" His voice sounded so threatening, the vice president backed up several steps.

"That's not what I said." He was going to get sick any second.

Ricky reached into his pocket for his wallet. He stared at the picture of himself and Philly before he handed it over. "I want you to look at your son. I want you to commit his face to memory because his face is going to haunt you for the rest of your days, Mr. Vice President. One last thing, my brother wouldn't have been impressed with you one little bit."

Ricky looked at Lorraine, who was dabbing at her eyes. She stood up and walked to Ricky's side. "My son kept the box I took him to the orphanage in. It said, Baby Doe #7. I wanted you to know that, *Vincent*. I also want you to know I'm going to get a new birth certificate for my son. And we'll be changing his death certificate, too. I guess I don't have anything else to say. Ricky, what would my son say if he were here now?"

Ricky smiled as he reached for Lorraine's arm. "He'd say, Mr. Vice President, you are a piss-poor excuse for a man."

He didn't want to beg or grovel, but he was doing it. "Please, Lorraine, Mr. Lam, don't do this. I have a family. I'll appoint both of you to prestigious positions in my administration. I'll do whatever you want. Please . . ." He reached for Lorraine's arm.

She shook him off. "I think what my son would have said to you is what I myself think right this moment. You are a piss-poor excuse for a man."

Outside, in the early-morning sunlight, Lorraine, her eyes full of tears, hugged Ricky, while the Secret Service agents looked on, their expressions stoic. "I feel . . . I feel, not good but close to it. Can I take my family and go home now?"

"I think so. I might have panicked when I

told you to come here. I didn't know what to expect."

"You were right. I think he's evil. When do you think he'll resign?"

"Not one minute before he has to. But he will. He's not our problem anymore, Lorraine."

Ricky turned to Agent Zirconie. "You better start looking for someone else to protect." Not expecting an answer, Ricky was stunned to see the agent give him a thumbs-up.

"What are you going to do now, Ricky?" Lorraine asked as she settled herself in the car.

"I'm going to get on with my life. How about you?"

"I think I'm going to do the same thing. I have a lot of things to take care of first, though. I'm so glad you agreed to let me move Caleb's body. He'll be good company for Armand. I'm going to erect a new stone. I know just what I want it to say. I'm going to bury his new birth certificate with him. That will make him . . . you know . . . *official.*"

Hot tears pricked Ricky's eyes. "I think Philly would like knowing that. I'm sorry,

Lorraine, he's always going to be Philly to me."

"I understand. We make a pretty good team, don't we?"

"I think we did okay. Philly would have loved you."

"Thank you for saying that." Lorraine leaned back in the seat and closed her eyes.

Her life was just beginning.

Gracie feigned sleep when Max entered the room. This was probably the end of whatever chance they had at a relationship. Roxy had reluctantly given her a mirror so she could see her face. It was as red as her hair. And blistered. *What is he doing?*

She felt like a greased pig that itched. The nice doctor had said she could get up and go outside. "You're going to start itching soon," he'd said. Another nightmare to look forward to. *Damn, how could I have been so stupid? Why is Max tiptoeing around?*

Gracie felt rather than saw Max sit down on the chair next to the bed. That had to mean he was staring at her. *Oh, God!* She wanted to cry. *Damn, I really like him*. Now she had to bolster her defenses and get smart-mouthed again. She strained to hear what he was saying without letting him know she wasn't sleeping.

"God, Gracie, I feel so bad for you. I wish . . . I wish so many things. When you wake up, we're gonna have a picnic. I brought some sand up from the beach and spread a blanket. It's a poor excuse for a beach picnic, but it will have to do for now.

"I had the chef make up all this food. You know, food the island is known for. We have pawpaws, bananas, and the Antiguan sweet, black pineapple, some mangoes and sapodillas. Crisp red snapper filets we can eat with our fingers. I had him make us a conch. We eat it raw, with a real fine mix- ture of chopped hot and sweet peppers, cucumber, and lemon juice. The chef said he'd make you some cockles and whelks, which you eat with a buttery garlic sauce. Some curries and my favorite, wonderful ducana, which is a solid hunk of grated sweet potato mixed with coconut and spices and steamed in a banana leaf. You can eat that with your fingers, too. I'm try- ing here, Gracie. I don't want you to go back home only remembering this miserable experience with the sun.

"Listen, I'm sorry about all that crap I pulled on you. You triggered a button in me, and I didn't know how to react. Like Tyler says, I tend to bluster and say things I wouldn't normally say. I liked you from the git-go. I really did. My grandmother would say you're full of spit and vinegar. I like that in a girl. You didn't let me get away with anything. I liked that business with the dogs, too. That showed me who you really were that day, and I liked what I saw.

"I want to get to know you better, Gracie. I'm going to ask my dad if I can transfer to the Crown Jewel when it's up and running. At least for a while. That way I can fly to California on weekends to see you, or you can come to see me. You have to finish college, that's a must. I know your family has to come first, and that's the way it should be. I'm not really an oaf, Gracie. I think what I am is a guy who is falling in love with you.

"I'll just sit here now and wait for you to wake up. Tyler's taking my shift this morning, so I can stay here with you."

Lordy, Lordy, Lordy. How can I remain

quiet after a confession like that? She couldn't. She turned her head slightly. "I fell in love with you that night at Whispers. You pushed my buttons, too. When this is behind me, and I don't look like a lobster, let's start over and just be Gracie and Max."

"You were awake the whole time I was spilling my guts," Max sputtered.

"I don't know. At first I thought I was dreaming, and I didn't want the dream to end. Are you sure I'm still not dreaming?"

There were more ways than one to skin a cat, and she knew them all.

"No, you're not dreaming. I made us a picnic."

"Really?"

"Yeah. You wanna be my girl?"

"Some guy said that to me when I was sixteen."

"It's a universal expression. I heard my dad refer to Roxy that way. She's his girl. Donna is Tyler's girl. Ted's girl is named Inez. They're getting married over Thanksgiving. My dad is getting married at Christmas. Tyler's going to tie the knot next summer. Marriage must be a pretty wonderful thing if they're all doing it."

"Hmmm. I think marriage is whatever two people make of it. I'm my own person, Max. I'll never take crap from any man. Either we're equals, or I'm gone."

"Yeah, yeah, that's how I feel."

"I'm keeping my own name, too. That's if we ever . . . you know. How do you feel about that?"

"Hey, I'm okay with it. Max Lick-Lam. Max Lam-Lick. It doesn't have much of a ring to it."

Gracie burst out laughing. "Mine is going to sound just like yours." She continued to laugh when the door opened.

"We can come back later," Ricky said.

"No. Come on in. There's enough food for everyone. What better way to end a crisis than a picnic? Did everything go okay?"

"Yes, everything went just fine. I'll be taking my family home tomorrow," Lorraine said. "I'm sure we'll see one another at your father's wedding. He very kindly invited all of us."

"So, Nolan's going to resign?" Gracie said.

"I don't see that he has any other choice. He might fool himself for a week or so, but his party will put pressure on him. Two weeks tops."

Lorraine Farquar looked from one to the other. "This is just like a movie where everyone ends up happily ever after. I want to thank you all from the bottom of my heart for all you've done for me and for . . . my son."

Ricky reached for Roxy's hand and squeezed it tightly. "You can rest easy, now, Philly, your mom has it under control."

"Thanks, little brother."

Later, when they talked about it, everyone in the room had a different take on what happened.

Roxy had just finished helping Gracie slip into an oversize muumuu for her picnic with Max when the door opened, and a tall man entered after a brief knock on the door. He identified himself as Agent Carmody and said, "Everyone, stand down. Clear the room except for Miss Grace Lick."

The occupants froze in place as they stared at the man in front of them, except for Ricky, who moved forward. "What's this all about? I just came from the vice president's house. Everything has been settled. Perhaps you should call him before we call our own security."

"I gave you an order, mister. Stand down and clear the room except for Miss Lick. I won't tell you a second time."

"It's okay, Mr. Lam, I'll talk to him. Do what he says," Gracie said.

"Like hell!" Max blustered.

"Yeah, like hell," Tyler chimed in.

And then everyone moved in different directions. Ricky saw Gracie totter forward on her sunburned legs, watched as Max moved to her side and Tyler leaped over a hassock. He saw the man pull out a gun and move it to chest level, saw the stance agents always assumed when they were prepared to fire. Closest to Gracie, Ricky raised his arm, an instinctive move, the kind of move his mother used to make when he was in the front seat of the car, and she stopped short. A protective gesture, nothing more. Lorraine Farquar stumbled, bumping into Roxy, who then collided with Agent Carmody. The gunshot sounded like thunder in the small room as they watched

Ricky Lam fall to the floor, the front of his white shirt stained with blood.

It was Lorraine Farquar who called for the ambulance while Tyler and Max wrestled with the agent. Roxy and Gracie were on their knees screaming at the top of their lungs as they both tried to cradle Ricky against them.

The agent subdued, his ankles and wrists bound with belts, Max slammed him into a chair with Tyler behind him, a tie wrapped around the agent's neck.

"Is Dad okay, Roxy? He isn't going to die, is he?" Max demanded, his voice choked.

"Oh, God, I don't know, I don't know. Where's the damn ambulance? Where's that doctor who is staying here? Somebody do something! Oh, God, oh, God!"

The door burst open, and the paramedics rushed through. Everyone stood aside, allowing the medics to do what had to be done. Everyone babbled at once, but they were all asking the same thing, is he going to be all right? The medics' response was low and hushed. "We're doing our best. Move aside now."

Max wiped at his eyes, as did Tyler,

when the gurney was wheeled out of the room. The three women huddled together, crying uncontrollably.

"We need someone to stay here with this guy till the locals get here. They'll know what to do with him."

"I'll stay till they get here. The rest of you go to the hospital," Lorraine said.

"Do you know how to shoot a gun, Lorraine?" Tyler asked.

"Actually, Tyler, I do. Hand it over. Ah, a Sig Sauer. My husband had one of these. Go on now, he's safe with me. I'll join you as soon as I can."

"If the bastard so much as twitches, shoot him," Tyler snarled.

"I can do that, too. Run along, son, your father needs you now," Lorraine said, waving the heavy gun in every direction.

An hour later, in the small, island hospital waiting room, Gracie wailed that it was her fault. No amount of comforting helped her; even Max couldn't comfort her.

Roxy cried into a wad of tissues, oblivious to the others.

Max walked outside into the balmy air. Even there at the hospital he could hear the sounds of revelry. It sounded obscene.

He felt a hand on his shoulder. "Do you think he'll make it, Ty?"

Tyler didn't trust himself to speak. He shrugged. He finally found his tongue. "It was an accident, Max."

"Yeah, I know. That doesn't make it any better. He was trying to save Gracie. You have to ask yourself what kind of man would do something like that. Do you think he thought the agent was going to shoot her? What? I need some goddamn answers here, Tyler."

"We can worry about all that later. Our only concern right now is our father. I wish . . . I wish . . . so many things."

"Yeah, me too. Isn't it funny how you just take life for granted. We should have been a little nicer, less hard-nosed. The guy has done everything humanly possible for both of us. Did you ever thank him? I didn't. I wish I had now. I wish I had said it every day. I wish I had called him every day just to say, hey, Dad, how's it going?"

"Yeah," Tyler said, sitting down on a low wall. "Would have, could have, should have. I was praying before."

"Me too. What the hell is taking so long?"

"I don't think there's a time limit when you're trying to save someone's life, Max."

Both young men looked up when a shadow crossed their path. "Any news on your dad?" Lorraine asked.

Both Max and Tyler shook their heads.

"For whatever this is worth, the locals took Mr. Carmody away. They called the vice president's residence from the hotel. The Secret Service descended en masse just as I was leaving. They said Carmody wasn't one of them. He's a private security guard Nolan employs." She patted both of them on the shoulder. "I hope you both know what a very special person your father is."

"We know. We were just talking about that before you arrived."

Lorraine patted them on the shoulder again before she entered the hospital.

The three women all huddled then, sitting as close to one another as they could, hoping to draw strength from one another. No words were spoken.

It was four o'clock when the surgeon strode out into the waiting room. "I can't make any promises," he said, "but I feel confident when I tell you I think Mr. Lam will fully recover. The next twenty-four hours will tell the tale. He's in recovery now. He'll be moved to Intensive Care in about an hour. You can each see him for a few minutes. I'm sure seeing you all will aid in his recovery. We'll talk tomorrow."

All five babbled as one, their tears mingling as they hugged and kissed one another. Then they sat down and waited for the minutes to crawl by, silent, as each said a prayer of thanks.

The hour passed slowly, but no one minded.

They were on their feet the moment a nurse motioned them to follow her. They lined up like a family because they were a family, outside the large glass window. Roxy did her best to stifle the sob that erupted from her throat. Gracie cried quietly into the sleeve of her muumuu. Max and Tyler pressed their faces against the glass willing their father to open his eyes. Lorraine Farquar stepped back so that Ricky's family could crowd next to the window, her eyes wet.

"If we all close our eyes and concentrate, maybe we can will Mr. Lam to open his eyes," Gracie said, her voice a bare whisper. They all looked at her, then did as she suggested.

When Ricky's eyes remained closed, Roxy sighed. "I want him to know we're here."

"I'm sure he knows, dear," Lorraine said. "Armand always knew."

"Look how still, how white he is. What happened to his sun tan?" Max asked. He looks . . ."

"Say it out loud, and I'll deck you right here," Tyler hissed.

Gracie moved to the side when the charge nurse walked over to the door. "You get one minute each," she said, opening the door. The little group looked at one another as both young men deferred to Roxy. She shook her head. "He's your father, you two go first." They needed no second urging as they rushed into the room.

Max walked to the side of the bed, his eyes glued to the still form in the high hospital bed. "Hey, Dad, it's me, Max. The doctor said you're gonna be okay. You know, really okay." He looked across to the other side of the bed at his brother, his eyes defiant.

"Dad, it's me, Tyler. Listen, we only have

a minute, and Roxy wants to come in. I . . . I'm sorry I gave you such a hard time. I don't understand why you didn't boot my ass all the way home. I guess dads don't do things like that. We'll be back. It's Roxy's turn now."

Ricky tried to open his eyes, but they were too heavy. He wanted to signal to his sons that he'd heard them. Or was he dreaming? Did he just hear the magical word he'd dreamed of for so long?

He felt her hand in his, felt her warm tears as they dropped on his hand. He did his best to squeeze her hand. And then he slipped back into a deep, natural sleep knowing his family was looking after him.

His family.

21

It was an unseasonably cold December on Camellia Island. Perfect weather for the grand opening of the Crown Jewel on Christmas Eve. Roxy was jittery, Ricky even more jittery. If he inspected the staff once, he inspected them a dozen times. Everyone, including Roxy, told him he was worse than an expectant father as he picked up pieces of lint no one else could see.

His family, and it was a rather large one these days, scurried to and fro, making sure everything was in readiness for the four o'clock arrival of the first guests.

The thirty-foot Christmas tree, decked out with fresh camellias by Roxy, twinkled to life when Max threw the switch. The base of the tree was surrounded by a red velvet skirt that held magnificently wrapped gifts. The sight and scent of the tree were so heady, Roxy felt faint. Garlands and wreaths, all done with camellias, hung everywhere. Bayberry candles in the shape of Christmas trees were on all the tables and on the registration desk. The gifts under the tree, wrapped by Gracie and Donna, were for the staff, compliments of Ricky and Roxy. Their bonus checks had been given out earlier, the gifts "a little something personal" for all their hard work and devotion.

Holiday music could be heard throughout the hotel, even in the elevators, where decorative balsam wreaths carried out the holiday decorating scheme.

An elegant buffet with a sculpture of Santa and his eight reindeer graced the middle of the table. Every food known to man would be served, along with the finest wine money could buy. The elegant Lenox china had a colorful poinsettia in the center of each plate. The napkins matched perfectly. The silver was sterling, and it sparkled on the red velvet cloth.

Everywhere the eye could see there

were touches of Christmas, giant red velvet bows, beautiful holly, one-of-a-kind
glass-blown ornaments, and pinecones
crackling in all the fireplaces. Whole cher-
rywood logs burned brightly.

"Okay, boss, you can come outside
now," Ted Lymen said. "I'm getting ready
to turn on all the outside lights. You better
tell me you love it because it took me five
whole days to string the lights. How many
poinsettias did it take to make up that wire
concoction for that forty-foot tree? You
told me, but I forgot."

Ricky grinned. "Two thousand. It was
Roxy's idea to fashion all that wire into a
tree with circles to hold the pots of poinsettias. They just placed the last one about
twenty minutes ago. Talk about taking it
down to the wire. It's magnificent, there's
no doubt about it. I'm ready. Throw the
switch, Ted!"

Lorraine Farquar clutched at her heart.
Lee Ann Oliver gasped, as did her children.
Roxy's jaw dropped. Ricky grinned from
ear to ear as he pounded his friend on the
back. "It's a wonderland! How many
lights?"

"I want you to be surprised when you

get the light bill." Ted guffawed. "You did say go all out. This is all out," he said, waving his arms about.

"Is the sleigh with the wheels at the dock?" Roxy queried.

"Yep, with eight prancing reindeer just waiting to bring your guests to your doorstep. Listen, I gotta run. My new wife is waiting for me, and so is my new tux. I'll see you at six. If you need anything else, call."

"I think we pulled it off, Roxy," Ricky whispered in her ear. "I think we should get dressed, too. We have to be in the lobby when the first guests arrive. Please tell me no one canceled."

"Are you kidding! People have been confirming for days now. Some wanted to bring extra guests, some wanted to extend their stays, but no one canceled. The reservation list is three times longer than it was last week."

"Oh, oh, let's get out of here. The first load of press is arriving, and we aren't dressed. Max and Tyler can handle it. I'm sorry Reba couldn't make it, Roxy."

"Me too. Another time."

Roxy ran her fingers through her hair, her

eyes miserable as she stared at Ricky. She crooked her finger. "Walk with me, Ricky, I have something I have to tell you. I wish now I had told you before but . . . I wanted to . . . but the mother in me wouldn't allow it. It's been eating at me for months now."

Ricky placed his hands on Roxy's shoulders as he looked down into her eyes. "Whatever came before is not important. I don't want you to feel you have to tell me everything about your life. All I want, Roxy, is for both of us to be happy. When this is all over, after the movie, after the kids are settled, I want us to come here to live and be together for the rest of our days. That's *all* I want, Roxy."

"It's what I want, too, Ricky. I don't want secrets between us. I've had enough of that to last me a lifetime. Just let me say what I have to say, okay?"

Ricky shrugged. "Okay, Roxy."

"It concerns Reba. Sometimes that girl can be loving and kind, and sometimes she can be hateful. I regret that we were never close. I don't even know if it's possible at this stage of our lives. Reba marches to a different drummer. She . . . liked Philly. She wanted him to act like a father, but that wasn't Philly's style. He was always polite and formal with her. She hated that. She cherished the memory of Philly's hugging her when she told him she was going into reconstructive plastic surgery. One hug, Ricky. One stinking, lousy hug. It was what she craved.

"When Philly died, she was livid that he hadn't left her anything. Not because she wanted his money it turns out, but because she thought it meant that she wasn't important to him. She was convinced that if he hadn't died, she could have persuaded him to love her, to be a real father to her." Roxy shook her head. "She's the one who went to the studio, to that tabloid reporter, and told them everything she knew. To hurt you, Ricky. She did it to hurt you. I think her emotions twisted her thinking and she blames you for Philip's death because he was killed on your movie set. There are no words to tell you how sorry I am. I had to tell you because . . . I love you and don't want to have to choose my words, look over my shoulder, or lie to you about why Reba does or doesn't call.

"Reba will not be working with us at the surgery clinic. I've made it clear to her that she has to straighten herself out, put her vindictive streak behind her and apologize to you before she's welcome here. I will not allow her to destroy what you and I have.

"The sad thing is, at first I blamed Philly for the way she was. That was so unfair of me. I kept telling myself she was just another one of Philly's casualties. All I know is, I did the best I could. That's it."

Ricky smiled. "And you think that all matters to me. It doesn't matter to me, Roxy, not one little bit. What bothers me is you seem to think you lost your daughter. Time will take care of everything. Look at me, I'm the living proof. Took me twenty years. Oh, Roxy, you have all the time in the world. Together, maybe we can make something happen, but only when the time is right. You okay with that?"

"Very okay. God, Ricky, what did I ever do to deserve you and all this happiness?"

"It was meant to be, I guess." He kissed her lightly and gave her his famous Ricky Lam smile, the smile that thrilled women the world over. This time it was strictly for Roxy, the love of his life.

"And to think I almost lost you," she said, her smile fading.

"Don't think about that now. It's all in the past." Once again he dazzled her with a smile.

Roxy returned it, her eyes bright with tears. "What'd you buy me for Christmas, big guy?"

"I'm not telling. What'd you buy me?" Ricky nudged as he pulled her toward the elevator. The moment the door closed, he kissed her long and hard. "Merry Christmas, Roxy."

In the lobby, Gracie looked up at Max. "By this time tomorrow, they'll be man and wife. Are you happy about your dad's getting married?"

"I love Roxy. She's the best thing that ever happened to my dad. He knows it, too. Unless someone uses the chapel tonight, they'll be the first ones to use it tomorrow."

"Would you look at your brother, Max! That's disgusting!" Gracie chirped.

"He's kissing Donna under the mistletoe. That's why we hung it up. What's disgusting about it?"

"Sometimes you are *thick,* Max. When I say I don't like something, you take up the opposite view. I thought if I said that, you'd want to kiss me, too."

"Oh."

"That's it, oh."

"No, that's not it. If you wanted me to kiss you, why didn't you say so? You sure aren't bashful, Gracie."

"Girls shouldn't have to ask guys to kiss them. You're supposed to want to do that. What good is it if I have to ask? No good, that's what."

"Gracie, shut that mouth of yours and pucker up. The reason I didn't kiss you was there's a guy over there with a camera. You want to see yourself on the front page in the morning?"

"Make sure they spell my name right!" She sashayed away. "Your loss," she flung over her shoulder. "You aren't any fun either!"

Max caught up with her at the waiting elevator. He shoved her inside. The minute the door closed, he pressed the HOLD button. "You want to be kissed, huh? Okay, girl, I'm gonna suck your tonsils right out of your throat. What do you think of *that!*"

Gracie backed herself into the corner.

"You can't do that! There's no way you can do that!"

"Oh yeah?"

"Yeah."

He advanced on her, one step at a time. "We'll just see about that! What are you looking so smug about?"

"You know why you can't do it, Max? You can't do it because I don't have any tonsils."

Max stared at her for a full minute before he doubled over laughing. "Are you ever going to let me win?"

"Nope. You said something about kissing me. I'm waiting," she singsonged.

"Do you love me, Gracie?"

"Yes, I do. Very much. Do you love me?" This was serious stuff. She hoped she didn't burst out laughing.

"Yeah. More than I ever thought I could. I bought this for you yesterday," Max said, fishing in his pocket. "The box is upstairs. He reached for her hand and slipped the diamond on her finger. I picked it out myself. If you don't like it or if you want a bigger one, we can exchange it."

"Oh, Max, it's beautiful." Tears welled in Gracie's eyes and rolled down her cheeks.

"No, I don't want to exchange it. It's perfect. I got you . . . us, four days in Vail, Colorado, the day after New Year's. It kind of pales in comparison."

"No, it doesn't. Just the fact that you remembered I love to ski and particularly love Vail is enough. Merry Christmas, Gracie."

"I lied, Max. I still have my tonsils!"

"Awk."

At three-thirty in the afternoon on Christmas Day, the minister looked at the beaming couple standing in front of him, and said, "I now pronounce you man and wife. You may now kiss the bride."

The assembled guests clapped and whistled as Ricky kissed his new bride. "I love you," he whispered.

"Not as much as I love you," Roxy whispered in return.

"Is this our first fight?"

"It will never happen.

"Merry Christmas, everyone! I'm going to throw my bouquet! Get ready!"

Every female in the lobby gathered around. Roxy took two steps forward and tossed her bouquet high in the air. The guests watched as the bouquet fell apart in two sections. Half of it fell into Gracie's outstretched hands; the other half fell into Donna's hands.

"Did you do that on purpose?" Ricky whispered. "Or do we have a dud for a florist?"

Roxy smiled.

Epilogue

Twenty-seven Months Later

Roxy watched her husband out of the corner of her eye. What she was seeing was the happiest man in the world. And that happiness had nothing to do with his nomination for an Academy Award. It had everything to do with his two sons, their wives, and the two toddlers crawling around on the floor. Five dogs circled them protectively as they gurgled and cooed.

Everywhere you looked there was baby gear, dog toys, suitcases. Baby food and baby bottles lined the kitchen counter. Diaper bags hung over the backs of chairs, with cuddly blankets and stuffed toys.

Grandpa's house.

"Six more hours till we tread down that red carpet," Roxy said, coming up behind him. "Are you nervous, honey?"

"Not one little bit. I told you the minute I heard about the nomination that I didn't care if we won or not. Just the fact that *The Brothers* was considered good enough to win a nomination told me all I needed to know. I don't miss this place at all. I don't mean the house, I mean Hollywood and the film industry."

"I knew what you meant, Ricky. *The Brothers* is the odds-on favorite. It's almost a given that you're going to win Best Actor. I bet Philip's wings are fluttering at ninety miles an hour."

Ricky laughed as he visualized a scene with Philip sitting on a cloud, his feathered wings rustling with impatience. "I have something I have to do, Roxy. I won't be long."

"John Deere is waiting for you. I wiped him off a while ago. Go on. I want to check with Gracie and Donna. They are so excited about going to the Academy Awards. I think Gracie is going to explode. We're doing each other's hair, so take all the time you want."

Roxy sighed with happiness. In the whole of her life she'd never expected to be this happy, this contented. She stepped over baby toys and dog chews, stopping only long enough to clean up a pee puddle. She laughed. This family business was something else.

In the garage, perched on the John Deere, Ricky leaned back, his thoughts ricocheting all over the place. Through the open garage door he could see a fluffy white cloud moving across the sky. He stared, blinked, then burst out laughing. The formation of the cloud looked just like a human form with wings. Wings that were fluttering wildly. The cloud moved. He blinked again. The formation looked like it was bowing. *Bowing.*

Ricky hopped off the John Deere and ran to the house. Before he opened the door, he looked upward, but the cloud had disintegrated. He waved. He didn't feel silly at all.

They were a family as they exited the stretch limousine. The minute they stepped on the apple-red carpet, hordes of reporters descended on them. Always gracious, Ricky held up his hand. "I'll talk to all of you, but one at a time. First, though, this is my family." He introduced each member, one at a time.

"Do I expect to win? I have no idea. What I do know is I'm in some sterling company with the other nominees. No, I don't think I have the edge because the vice president resigned. That was a long time ago. I'm so proud of the movie I'm bursting with pride. You'll have to ask these lovely ladies what they're wearing. Other than to say they look beautiful, I know nothing. Roxy?"

"Escada," Roxy said.

"Valentino," Donna and Gracie said in unison.

"We're all wearing Chanel," Lorraine Farquar, said pointing to her family.

"Look, Max, there's that weasel Dicky Tee," Gracie whispered. She inched closer to her husband when she saw the venom in the tabloid reporter's face.

"Don't you dare give him the finger, Gracie! There are cameramen everywhere. We both know you could take the little slimeball with one hand, but wait until the awards ceremony is over, and I'll help you."

Gracie looked up at her husband. "For you, honey, anything." Max groaned.

And then they were all inside and seated front row center.

Ricky leaned back and shifted mental gears to neutral. He clapped, half listened, laughed when everyone else laughed. He just wanted the whole thing to be over. If they paid him his weight in gold, he wouldn't come back to Hollywood.

He heard his name from some far-off place before he felt the pain in his shoulder. "Ricky, you won! You won for Best Actor!"

He was back in the present, a stunned look on his face. He stood up, looked around at his family, and grinned. He was halfway up to the stage when his sons made Academy Award history by standing on their chairs, their fists raised in the air. "Hey, Hollywood, that's our *DAD!*" The stunned silence was followed by loud applause and laughter.

Ricky stopped on the second step from the top, turned, and retraced his steps to where his sons waited. He gathered them close, and only those seated nearby heard the words, "Hearing you say that is better than winning an Oscar."

It was a standing ovation when he finally made his way to the stage to accept his Oscar. His speech was probably the shortest in Academy history. "I just want to thank everyone in the world." He raised the statue high above his head, his vision blurry. But not so blurry that he didn't see the feather that floated down to alight on the head of the statue he was holding in his hands. He looked at the feather, then at a young actress sitting in the third row, directly in his line of vision. She was wearing a feathered boa. A *pink* feathered boa. The feather he plucked from the statue was white. He stuck it in his pocket, his heart lighter than air. And then, for the second time that night, history was made when he returned to his seat to hand the Oscar to Lorraine Farquar. "This really belongs to Philly. Since he isn't here, it goes to his mother. I'm going to keep the feather," he whispered.

Lorraine Farquar nodded, seeming to understand as she wept openly, along with half the audience, the half that didn't care about smearing their mascara.

An hour later it was over. *The Brothers* took home four Oscars: Best Picture, Best Female in a Supporting Role, Best Actor, and Best Director.

"Let's go home, family. Ellie is probably ready for a nervous breakdown with those two toddlers and the five dogs."

Ricky reached for Roxy's hand. "You know what, this is Hollywood," he said, stamping his foot, "and it's just a red carpet!" He laughed. "They're going to roll it up in a few hours. That means it isn't real. What's real are all of you!

"Thank you all for enriching my life and showing me what real love and family are all about!"

"And he's a ham, too!" Max shouted.

"Takes one to know one!" Ricky laughed as he hugged Roxy to his side.